'... series emerging as a modern classic'
Stephen Baxter

'... SF thriller that opens a portal on a
new and exciting series'
Alastair Reynolds

'No one offers action-packed, meticulous,
suspenseful and consistent hi-tech futures better
than Peter Hamilton, and *Salvation* cranks
all of that up five notches'
David Brin

'Beyond epic . . . Accept no substitutes, this is the
real deal. You need *Salvation*'
Ian McDonald

'Savage, brilliant and compelling. A masterclass
in tension and spectacle'
Gareth L. Powell

'The classic Hamilton cocktail of techno-thriller,
far-future vision and action adventure shaken into
an intoxicating combination'
Justina Robson

'I devoured it right to the scintillating end . . .
A dazzling tale of humanity face-to-face and
toe-to-toe with the ultimate enemy!'
Michael Cobley

'A thoroughly enjoyable read'
Neal Asher

'Action-oriented hardcore science fiction at its page-turning best'
Guardian

'A vast, intricate sci-fi showstopper . . . the journey grips as hard as the reveal'
Daily Mail

'Exciting, wildly imaginative and quite possibly Hamilton's best book to date'
SFX Magazine, **5 stars**

'Peter F. Hamilton just keeps getting better and better with each book . . . a virtuoso treat'
Locus

SALVATION LOST

Peter F. Hamilton was born in Rutland in 1960 and now lives in Somerset. He began writing in 1987, and sold his first short story to *Fear* magazine in 1988. He has written many bestselling novels, including the Greg Mandel series, the Night's Dawn trilogy, the Commonwealth Saga, the Void trilogy, Chronicle of the Fallers, short-story collections and several standalone novels, including *Fallen Dragon* and *Great North Road*.

Find out more about Peter F. Hamilton at

www.facebook.com/PeterFHamilton

By Peter F. Hamilton

Peter F. Hamilton

SALVATION LOST

BOOK TWO OF THE SALVATION SEQUENCE

PAN BOOKS

First published 2019 by Macmillan

This paperback edition first published 2020 by Pan Books
an imprint of Pan Macmillan
The Smithson, 6 Briset Street, London EC1M 5NR
Associated companies throughout the world
www.panmacmillan.com

ISBN 978-1-4472-8138-2

9 8 7 6 5 4 3 2 1

A CIP catalogue record for this book is available from the British Library.

Typeset by Palimpsest Book Production Limited, Falkirk, Stirlingshire
Printed and bound by CPI Group (UK) Ltd, Croydon, CR0 4YY

List of Major Characters

2204

Yuri Alster *Connexion Security chief*

Crina *Connexion Security bodyguard*

Eldlund *Callum's aide*

Anne Groell *Connexion Security, New York chief*

Callum Hepburn *Utopial senior troubleshooter*

David Johnston *Supreme Commander Alpha Defence*

Emilja Jurich *Utopial leader*

Kohei *Connexion Security, London chief*

Loi *Yuri's aide*

Kandara Martinez *Dark-ops mercenary*

Alik Monday *FBI senior special detective*

Jessika Mye *Neána metahuman*

Gwendoline Seymore-Qing-Zangari *Connexion finance director*

Horatio Seymore *Social services agency adviser*

Lucius Soćko *Neána metahuman*

Ainsley Baldunio Zangari *Connexion founder & CEO*

Ainsley Zangari III *CEO of Connexion TranSol division*

Southwark Legion

Adnan *Tech-head*

Piotr Ramin *Leader*

Tronde Aucoin *Printer*

Gareth Brabin *Nethead*

Ollie Heslop *Planner*

Lars Wallin *Muscle*

Claudette Beaumant *Legion scam target*

Lolo Maude *Ollie's lover*

Jade Urchall *Lieutenant in London crime family*

Vayan

Crew of the Morgan

Dellian *Squad leader*

Ellici *Tactician*

Falar *Squad member*

Janc *Squad member*

Kenelm *Captain of the* Morgan

Mallot *Squad member*

Ovan *Squad leader*
Rello *Squad member*
Tilliana *Tactician*
Tomar *Squad member*
Uret *Squad member*
Wim *Bridge officer*
Xante *Squad member*
Yirella *Designer of Vayan*

Fintox *Neána metavayan*
Motaxan *Neána metavayan*

See the end of the novel for the Salvation timeline.

Vayan Calling

The dark, cold bulk of the Neána insertion ship had been travelling through interstellar space for twenty-two years before it flew across the faint twinkling specks of the star's cometary belt. Half a light-year ahead, its G9 target star shone with a strong silver-white glare, casting its intense rays over a family of twelve planets. The fourth planet, a small, solid world, was emitting a bright babble of radio signals – a source which a Neána abode cluster had picked up when the Vayans began their tentative first broadcasts fifty-three years earlier.

A trio of moons orbited the warm, life-rich fourth planet in eccentric million-kilometre loops above its white clouds, lush continents and deep blue oceans. Two of them were now also emitting electromagnetic signals; the radio waves were coming from the pioneering research bases which the native Vayans had recently constructed. Forty-seven different Vayan clans were operating space programmes, putting aside their conflict-heavy history to collaborate on the great adventure out across the gulf of space.

The insertion ship flew in north of the solar ecliptic, shedding cold mass in irregular bursts like a black comet – a deceleration manoeuvre which took nineteen months. This was always the riskiest part of the voyage. The Vayans had thirty-two robot space probes currently traversing their solar system, sending back a great deal of crude science sensor data to their homeworld, as well as to high-powered observatories on the larger moon. The chance of one spotting the insertion ship was slim, but the controlling sentience took no chances. By the time it passed the innermost gas giant, it was down to twenty-five metres in diameter. It had no magnetic field, and the outer shell was fully radiation-absorbent in every spectrum, making it invisible to any telescope.

As it closed on Vayan, it detected a spaceship departing one of the three stations in low orbit, a nuclear fission rocket sending it on a ten-month flight to the fifth planet. A crew of eleven Vayans were crammed into its small life-support cabin – emissaries of their species' exuberant spirit, boldly outbound on their first interplanetary flight. Given the Vayans had only launched their first chemical propellant rocket into orbit seventeen years earlier, the insertion ship's controlling sentience was impressed by the speed of their technological progress.

During its long, lonely voyage between the stars, it had monitored the plethora of signals broadcast from Vayan, building up an extensive knowledge base of the species' history and culture. Socially, they were organized along clan lines: a protective imperative bestowed by their distinct reproductive biology. Each female had up to ten mates, who all fertilized her egg cluster over the course of her fifteen-year adult life stage. When she was ready to gestate, she became immobile, feeding on the pre-digested pulp provided by her mates as her wombs began to swell. Giving birth to up to fifty infant Vayans was her last living act – though the insertion ship had recently picked up broadcasts speculating that modern medical techniques might be able to prolong female life after birth. From what the controlling sentience could understand, the concept was regarded as far-fetched and almost heretical – though, so far, the Vayans seemed to have avoided the whole concept of deities and religion.

Physically, the Vayans had four legs supporting a rounded double-section body with eight upper arm-limbs. There was a long prehensile neck on the top, lifting up an ovoid cranium containing eight eyes and a combination ear/echo sonar organ, providing all-around perception. Their particular sensorium neurology meant

2

they'd evolved past the concept of front and back and now had the capacity for free-ranging motion. That specific analytic ability gave the controlling sentience some difficulty when it came to developing equivalent thought routines for the six Vayan body biologics which it was now growing in its onboard molecular initiators. Fortunately, Vayan biochemistry was relatively easy to replicate.

As it closed to within a million kilometres of Vayan, the insertion ship discarded the last of its reaction mass as it performed a final deceleration manoeuvre. Now it was basically just falling towards the southernmost tip of the Farava continent. The lights of night-time urban citadels sparkled across the continent, linked by the slender blue-green threads of bioluminescent transport rails. Tiny course-correction ejecta refined the ship's descent vector, steering it towards the coast, which was still thirty minutes from greeting the dawn. Even if some Vayan telescope chanced to find it now, it would simply appear to be a small chunk of natural space debris.

It hit the upper atmosphere and began to peel apart into six pear-shaped segments. The remaining matter broke away in fizzing sparks that produced a short-lived but beautiful starburst display streaking through the mesosphere. Below it, sheltered under their blanket of thick winter cloud, the clan packs of Gomarbab – the southernmost urban citadel on Vayan – remained oblivious to their interstellar visitor.

Each segment continued down, aerobraking with increasing severity as the atmosphere thickened around them. They slowed to subsonic velocity three kilometres above the surface, plunging through the clouds.

The segments were aimed at a small cove a few kilometres east of the urban citadel, where the gentle undulating frost meadows ended in high cliffs above pebble beaches. A hundred metres from the shore, six large splash plumes shot up into the air like thick geysers, crowning and splattering down on the slushy ice that bobbed about in the sub-zero saltwater.

The Neána metavayans floated to the surface. All that now remained of the insertion ship's landing segments were thick layers of active molecule blocks which covered their mottled blue-green hide like a blanket of translucent gel, insulating them from the cold. They began to swim to shore – an action which the native Vayans avoided as much as possible.

The narrow strip of pebble beach was interrupted by brown bracken fronds shooting up from the wider cracks. A tall cliff loomed above it, with a narrow V-shaped gorge that offered a slippery pathway up to the frost meadows. The metavayans scrambled a short way up the incline as the pale dawn light began to seep through the murky clouds. Their last protective layer liquidized, draining down into the stones, where it would be flushed away by the next high tide.

'We made it,' one emitted in a stream of fast whistles: the local clan dialect.

'I was concerned about the landing impact,' said another, the female of the group. 'Fortunately, I am undamaged. These bodies are sturdy.'

'My skin is puckering,' a third said. 'This locale's temperature is below optimum.'

The first one reached into a bag that had been strapped to his upper body and pulled out clothing modelled on commercial imagery which the Vayans had broadcast six months earlier. 'I believe we should cover ourselves as quickly as—' He stopped in alarm.

A creature emerged from behind a large boulder at the base of the cliff. In all the years the insertion ship had monitored broadcasts from Vayan, no mention had been made of anything like it on the planet. The alien had a bipedal symmetry, with double-segment legs emerging from the base of a flat torso section. A pair of arms with limited articulation protruded from the top, on either side of a squat neck that supported a bulbous head covered in tight, thin-looking ebony skin. Twin eyes gazed down at the metavayans. The creature was more than twice their height and walked towards them in an alarming motion that was mostly lurches.

It was clad in a thick green garment. An arm was extended, with the five small manipulator digits at the end curling around a metallic cylinder. An orifice on the creature's head opened and it produced a low, slow hooting noise.

The cylinder began to talk in Vayan. 'Pleased don't be alarmed,' it said. 'We have been monitoring your flight for several months. We didn't try to contact the insertion ship directly, for fear it would self-destruct. We know how determined you are to protect your abode clusters.'

'What are you?' the first metavayan asked. 'Do you share this world with the Vayan?'

The creature's head twisted from side to side, and it began its ponderous hooting again. 'My species is human, and my name is Yirella,' the translator told them. 'I'm afraid there's no such species as the Vayan. We invented them and their entire civilization in order to lure the Olyix here. We never expected a Neána ship to arrive as well. However, I welcome you to this star system and invite you to join us in the fight against our common enemy.'

London

25th June 2204

The warm twilight sky roofing London was a gentle stratum of pastel colours: a rose-gold horizon washing up to deeper cerise which swiftly drained down to star-clad darkness at the apex. Ollie Heslop had to squint into the fading sunlight as his boardez carried him west along Plough Lane, leaving the old Wimbledon Stadium behind. Big hologram hordings were shining from the stadium walls, their consumer products twisting and turning to display many stylish elements. The last one featured Sumiko, advertising her new drama game. She wore a plunge-necked scarlet silk dress, her divine three-metre-high face smiling down in slow-mo as he slid past. PAK virals spilled out of the hazy glow, pinging Tye, his altme, with the game's trailers. Ollie had to grin back at that bedtime come-and-get-it look she bestowed on anyone passing below. It was an omen, he decided; he'd had a crush on the Hong Kong actress for years. At fourteen he'd covered his bedroom walls in mov-i posters of her. And now here she was, the goddess of photons, blessing him as he made his way to the raid.

A happy smile lit his face as the hologram slipped away behind him, and he focused on the darkening pavement ahead as Tye blocked the PAKs. Shadows were growing deceptively deep amid the big plane trees, whose century of growth had turned the road into a major urban greenway. Tye had to trigger a visual-enhancement routine, feeding Ollie's tarsus lenses with an amplified image so he could sashay the boardez around paving slabs shifted and elevated by the tree roots. Nothing he could do about the boardez's powerful little wheels fantailing damp pavement algae across his boots, though. He'd chosen those boots specifically for this raid: shin-high black leather, laced tight with sunglo orange straps – pumping the cool factor hard. They were paired with glossed leather crotch-gripper trousers, a snow-white T-shirt – tight to show off toned abs – and a scuffed green jacket that came down to his knees. Sleeves with purple sparkle piping were crumpled back to his elbows. Reproduction antique smartCuffs rode both wrists, containing his darkware. A Leninist worker's cap in dusky grey felt with a prominent enamelled red star completed his image: poised, youthful good looks, riding the boardez with a strut, radar gaze scanning around, always challenging, telling the world to stand back for the hot street playa. The only thing he wasn't showing was his own face. A fleshmask adhered to his skin, darkening his pigmentation and rounding out his cheeks.

Ollie was taking point for his crew, his mates, his blood brothers, who called themselves the Southwark Legion. It was a name known to weary social workers and community police from back in the day, when Ollie was at the borough's state academy trying to pass his National Digital Industry exams. They'd stuck with the handle after they left and the changes began. Some of the original crew had drifted away into jobs and even careers; others had started to hang when their own crews were broken up. Now there were the six of them remaining – hard core on multiple levels and still in their twenties . . . though Piotr was pushing twenty-eight.

Tye splashed a scan on Ollie's lens and he checked the Legion's positions. Not too close to each other, but tight enough to pull off the timing which the raid demanded. He'd spent a week planning this out, determining everyone's positions and timing down to the last decimal. Every action interlocked, and for every possible glitch a counter-move. It was his thing, designing and refining, coming

7

at the problem from every angle to try and find the flaws before they happened.

So now orchestrating their deployment was down to him, too.

Piotr was twenty metres back, hands clasped urbanely behind his back as he rode his boardez in an impeccably straight line. His chosen fleshmask gave him a vampire pallor, but even so he looked polished in clubbing threads: red shirt, gloss-black lace tie, slick snakeskin grey waistcoat and navy trousers. He hadn't gone over-board muscling up, but the civilians on Plough Lane that evening instinctively knew what a total hardarse he was and parted obedi-ently for his humming boardez. Piotr was the Legion's sort-of leader. He knew people in London's underworld who pulled in contracts and favours, earning the Legion some decent respect among the major families and gangs – the ones they were so desperate to be accepted by.

Piotr's bagez wasn't tagged to his altme – at least not if anyone ran a forensic audit – and it trailed him by a good hundred and fifty metres. Like most London streets, Plough Lane had a perpetual swarm of bugez and trollez trundling after their owners, and more of the little vehicles chasing down the central clear path on delivery routes, both legitimate and otherwise. Nobody kept track of them, or cared. Why would you? Traffic management was the job of the G8Turings.

The bagez slowed as it wound around a particularly tall plane tree, immersing itself in the deep shadows underneath. Piotr trig-gered the release. A small hatch opened on the base and three creeperdrones scampered out. They looked like pigmy possums, measuring nine centimetres long and weighing in at forty grams, with an agility equal to the rodents they mimicked. Tronde Aucoin, the Legion's lord of printing, had spent a couple of days assembling them, extruding components from phials of exotic, expensive crudes. Works of art, Ollie acknowledged, even though it was his own customized code which animated their artificial muscles, giving their sleek bodies a fluid motion indistinguishable from living crea-tures. And all for the few seconds of exposure before they went underground.

The tiny creeperdrones dived down a pavement grille and wriggled their way through cracks in the ancient drain walls to reach the utility ducts that ran under the street. If any person or any program did notice them in those precious moments, they must have passed as real. Tye reported zero alerts in the local civic nodes.

Piotr's bagez traced a slow curve across the road and trundled off to the Julan Finance office, further back along Plough Lane.

'Two minutes,' Ollie announced. He saw Lars Wallin grin in anticipation, teeth bared like a jungle predator cat snarling as it approached its prey. Lars was ten metres away, on Ollie's left – a hulking twenty-two-year-old who always wore a gym singlet to show off his physique. Some of the muscles which were straining the fabric were genuine, pumped by weights and steroids; the rest were Kcell grafts. His nose was mashed flat against his face, and both hands had heavily scarred knuckles from more fights than even Ollie could remember. Even now, after a couple of years in the Legion, Lars made Ollie nervous. If you gave the IQ tree a good shake, it wouldn't be Lars who fell out of the topmost branches, and he took a couple of nark capsules most days to keep his aggression in check. But he'd been cold turkey for thirty-six hours now.

The tactical scan showed Ollie their taxez approaching from the opposite direction. He was proud of that taxez. It was darkware he'd tailored which had pirated the vehicle from the Heürber Corp, a business which had captured the majority of London's private passenger vehicle franchises. Further tailoring made the taxez the Legion's bitch. Tonight it carried Tronde and Adnan; the interior cameras revealed them sitting next to each other on the curving faux-leather bench, looking absurdly relaxed, as if they were heading out on a double date. Ollie disapproved of that stance, worried they might have taken a nark to beat back the nerves that were jabbing up his own spine. Except Tronde never took nark; he even refused to eat printed food, despite or perhaps because of working with printers all day long. Ever since a nasty outbreak of pustulant hives – a bad reaction to the enhancement he'd made to his dick – he'd rejected modern medicine to become a true vegan health freak, and now had homeopathic remedies for every ailment. Tonight he

9

was dressed in jeans and a black T-shirt under a jacket that looked two sizes too big, and wore a fleshmask that had African-black pigmentation. As Tronde's family roots were pure Nordic, Ollie wondered if that mask could be considered racist – a particularly stupid thought given what they were about to do. *Nerves.*

Sitting beside Tronde, and immune to his friend's new politically incorrect features, was Adnan. The Legion's tech-head was dressed in a plain white thobe with a long chequered keffiyeh headdress to compliment his minimal fleshmask, which had given him sunken cheeks and a sharp pointed beard for the evening. A wide silvered shade band covered a third of his fake face; he wore it to hide his eyes. Adnan had gone for a complete refit and now had metallic orbs that offered wide-spectrum reception. They allowed him to see node signals, and even tagged the emissions, so he could read the digital code directly, via his altme: Ramoos. Ollie thought that was extremely cool, although he held back from committing himself. There was something about having his eyes taken out that chilled him at a primal level.

'Get ready,' Piotr warned them.

Ollie watched a green and grey light amplification visual from the creeperdrones as they wriggled their way along the utility duct. It was jammed with dozens of cables, all encrusted with decades of dirt and rodent droppings which rubbed off on the creeperdrones' fur as they pushed forwards.

'Load the packages,' Ollie ordered Tye. The altme splashed a yellow and purple data grid, showing his darkware packages loading into the solnet nodes along Plough Lane.

Gareth had coded most of them; the Legion's nethead nerd, who knew more about software than Ollie, Tronde and Adnan combined – appropriately enough, given Ollie thought his personality must have been written by a Turing. Right now Tye was showing Gareth sitting cross-legged on a low wall close to their target office, which was not where Ollie's plan had positioned him. Gareth had serious issues with following basic instructions. Ollie just hoped he hadn't been sitting there for too long; the police Turings would pick up on that. Which Gareth would know better than anyone . . .

Ah, fuck it.

Ollie closed in on the rendezvous point. The way he swerved around people with micro shifts of his weight was second nature. He'd been riding boardez since he could walk, and it was all he could do to hold back on powercurves up the wall and angled skid-brake twists to kerb-hop. But the Legion was on a raid: serious shit. The majors wouldn't appreciate someone still living his youthful moves in the middle of a job.

The creeperdrones were crawling over the power junction relay that supplied the commercial buildings he was sailing past. Piotr and Lars were closing in on him as he neared the Klausen Nutrition offices just before the junction. The taxez was visible up ahead, trundling carefully along Plough Lane's central clear path.

'Another house has been placed on the market,' Tye announced.

'Now?' Ollie asked – not that he was surprised a house had come up, but he clearly hadn't organized Tye's priority ratings properly. This wasn't the time to be splashing results from the search patterns he'd loaded. Even so, images zipped across his tarsus lens: a wonderful old French house in lush gardens, atop a rock cliff, the Mediterranean sun sparkling on the waves below. Steps carved into the rock switch-backed down to a small private cove. The asking price was seven point two million wattdollars.

'The deal has been closed,' Tye said. 'Bidder paid eight point three.'

Ollie checked the elapsed time. Twenty-seven seconds. 'Way too much anyway,' he muttered. *But it looked perfect. One day . . .*

He made an effort to focus on the job, replacing the dream house with a splash of the schedule. Everything was running smoothly.

'Ten seconds on my mark,' Ollie announced. He could feel his heart rate bumping up. Excitement was fizzing around his veins, better than any nark hit. This was what he lived for. The money was only a small part of the deal – okay, essential for him, but still small. The feeling he got from this kind of raid was like nothing on earth.

The creeperdrones spread themselves wide on the relay casing, tiny claws holding fast. Tye triggered the first darkware package: a

11

basic sensor hijack. The civic surveillance sensors along Plough Lane either started relaying a mix of adverts or powered down. It meant the borough's cybercop G8Turing would be focusing on the area, running diagnostics and using killswitch blockers on Ollie's darkware. 'Go for the diversion,' he told Tye.

Another batch of darkware went active inside the nodes. These were coded to infiltrate Julan Finance with ransomware. It started to spread through the company's office network.

The creeperdrones exploded, ripping apart cable and relays. All the streetlights went out, along with most of the hologram hoardings – including Sumiko. Green emergency lights started to come on in the commercial buildings, as if Plough Lane was suddenly dressing up for Halloween.

The taxez braked sharply outside their actual target, the Klausen Nutrition office. Its doors sprang open. Ollie, Piotr and Lars rode their boardez right up to the vehicle and jumped off. The boardez folded themselves up. Ollie picked his off the ground and slipped it into his belt pouch. Tye showed him a flock of police drones closing on the Julan Finance offices four hundred metres away. Underneath the drones, the pedestrians and boardez riders along Plough Lane had stopped to look around in confusion as power and digital connectivity were taken from them – basic human rights since before they were born. Sickly green luminescence revealed the unease manifesting on their faces.

'Lars,' Piotr snapped. 'Door.'

A grinning Lars stepped up to the Klausen office's sliding glass door and quickly rolled the flat purple charge tape across the glass.

They all turned their backs and hunched down.

'Ollie,' Piotr said. 'Entry.'

Ollie gave Tye the go-ahead. Darkware overloaded the Klausen Nutrition office network, while in the distance Piotr's bagez fired eight micro missiles at the Julan Finance office. Their solid rocket exhausts made a high-pitched thunderclap of noise as they accelerated hard, producing dazzling plumes that streaked out across Plough Lane, cutting straight through the leafy plane trees. Too late, the police drones started to scatter. Lost amid the terrific noise, the charge tape detonated. The door's glass shattered, showering the steps with sharp crystalline gravel. An alarm block high on the wall started shrieking, its red strobe blazing. Piotr raised an arm and there was a small blue flash from inside his cuff. The alarm fell silent, its fragments raining down.

'In,' Piotr commanded, scanning the street to see if anyone was paying attention. As they hurried through the broken door, the Legion's taxez drove away.

It was dark inside. Tye increased the resolution on Ollie's visual enhancement routine, allowing him to see the blank, bland corridors with their identical doors leading to identical offices. The buzz had started for real now. The thrill of being in the office building, of making the play, was overwhelming, magnifying every sight and sound ten times above normal. Ollie never wanted the thrill to end.

Piotr led them towards the back. The storeroom's thick carbon door filled the end of the corridor. Ollie scanned it with the sensors in his smartCuffs. 'Deadlocked,' he said. 'The alarm system has backup power, but my darkware is blocking it. You'll have to reset the system after the power is restored before you can get the bolts to withdraw. Their electromagnets are dead.'

Piotr nodded and crooked a finger. 'Lars.'

Lars grinned and eyed the door as he would a late-night challenger in the pub. The rest of the Southwark Legion flattened themselves against the corridor walls. Lars ran at the door, lowering his shoulder.

Ollie raised his eyes in dismay as Lars ran past, yelling wildly. The door could have been opened with ten minutes of delicate instruments, fibre-optic cable grafts, power-line splices . . .

Lars hit the door, shoulder flesh thudding into carbon.

'Not bad,' Adnan admitted grudgingly as his cyborg vision measured the door quiver in its frame.

Lars backed up the corridor. Then he charged again.

The third charge saw the bolts tear free of the frame, and the door burst open. The carbon facia was undented. Lars would be wearing his shoulder bruise medals for a week, but he grinned his champ grin as he led the Legion into the storeroom.

Ollie had to admit, sometimes you just needed to go basic.

The storeroom was full of metal racks, floor to ceiling. Aisles were barely wide enough to walk down. Loadez had stalled at the end: sad plastic cylinders with three robot arms hanging limply. Tiny red LEDs glowed forlornly on their upper casing – a paltry glow that shimmered off the tall designer bottles of nutrient crude and vitamin pastes destined for exclusive food printers.

Piotr stared around in approval. 'Tronde, Adnan, take 'em out.'

Tronde and Adnan stood at the end of the storeroom. Both of them struck the same pose: arms down, held away from the hips. Bomb drones modelled on spiders emerged from folds in their baggy clothes. In the storeroom's gloaming, it looked as if the pair of them were dripping big globs of fluid. The little machines had a dark composite casing, with no attempt to make them appear authentic.

The bomb drones scuttled along the aisles and started to climb the racks, clinging to the shelf supports. Piotr watched until he was satisfied they were positioning themselves correctly.

'Let's go.'

They hurried down the length of the storeroom to the one-metre cargo portal, used to transport products from the main Klausen factory. The portal door itself was dark, the entanglement still active but not open. Beside it was a physical door to the narrow road behind the building, with an emergency fire-exit bar across it. Piotr shoved the bar and the door opened easily.

They piled out into the dark road. Their taxez was there, waiting for them. It was a tight squeeze with all six of them squashed onto the circular bench, but they were giddy with the adrenalin rush. As the taxez began to drive away, Piotr said: 'Blow it.'

Ollie nodded and Tye sent the signal to the bomb drones. Everybody squinted through the taxez's curving transparent body-work as the bomb drones detonated in a single synchronized blast, as unspectacular as he'd hoped they'd be. There was a brief, gloomy flare of yellow light from inside the storeroom, and the fire door flapped about from the pressure wave, but that was it. Inside, the racks would be crumpling as their support legs were severed by the tiny, precise charges, collapsing like giant dominoes to send the precious bottles smashing into each other and the floor, their contents ruined.

'Oh, yeah,' Tronde grunted. 'Champion, us.'

Ollie could see how happy Tronde was that his devices had done their job and grinned, giving his friend a big thumbs-up. 'Nice work.'

'My man,' Tronde said appreciatively.

The taxez turned out of the road and began to pick up speed.

'I don't get it,' Lars said. 'Don't get me wrong, I enjoyed it, like. But what's the point of just smashing stuff up? Why's Jade paying us to do that?'

'It was a protection job, Lars,' Ollie said. 'Klausen didn't pay what they owed to Jade and Nikolaj, and whatever the hell they're part of—'

'One of the major North London families,' Adnan said quickly. 'It has to be. They got so many contacts.'

'Whatever. The raid was the point, see. We cost Klausen big tonight. Not going-out-of-business big, but enough to make them sit up and take notice. Next time Jade or someone turns up asking for a little insurance payment, they know she's not all piss and farts and they cough up the readies.'

'It's more than that,' Piotr responded smoothly. 'We showed Jade we can deliver on a contract, that we're reliable people. That's the real point.'

Lars stuck out his lower lip. 'Yeah, okay, got it.'

'We came together tight, tonight,' Piotr said. 'There aren't many crews who could pull this off. We just made the majors sit up and take notice.'

Ollie grinned at his friends, seeing plenty of happiness in the taxez. *This is why Piotr is in charge; he knows how to pull us together.*

'You think after this Jade is gonna give us the gig for the power relay station?' Adnan asked, unwinding his keffiyeh headdress. Sweat glinted in his slicked-back ebony hair.

'Could be,' Piotr said.

'Come on, we showed her we can pull off a decent gig. She's

got no reason to keep it from us any more,' Ollie grunted, only half-bitter. The *big deal* of the relay station had been dangled in front of the Legion for over a year now. Jade and Nikolaj always said there would be bigger jobs once the Legion showed what they were capable of – jobs that never quite materialized. In his mind, Ollie had these scenarios of old-time blags playing out: breaking into bullion vaults, or diamond merchants. The kind of thing that used to happen a hundred years ago, before asteroid mining and starflight turned rare materials into just plain old materials.

'Not up to me,' Piotr said. 'But I'll make it clear to her how much we want it.'

'Not too much,' Gareth said. 'Don't make us sound desperate.'

'Like I don't know how to handle a contract,' Piotr shot back.

Ollie smiled and settled back on the taxez's curving bench, glad to be out clean, and sad that the buzz was starting to fade. But this was them, the Legion, his friends: the banter, hot nightlife, boys, girls, being playas. Everything life could give, he was taking it.

*

The taxez took just under ten minutes to get them back to Southwark, going through the big portal in the Government and Commercial Services hub to emerge out into its twin on Chadwick Road. From there it was a two-minute drive parallel to the old raised railway.

The Legion occupied one of the old brick archways under the railway line, just off Consort Road – a disused commercial yard that stretched for a few hundred metres between dilapidated housing stock and the railway viaduct. The way in was past a pair of metal gates smothered in a jumble of overlaid graffiti, with only the newest symbols glowing in weak phosphorescent greens and purples. Local kids rode cranky old boardez along the weed-clogged pavements or grouped-up in doorways, exchanging nark formula files or immersive porn, or gossiped about game celebs. They wore what they could afford to print: poor replicas of the major style houses, with cheap dull tints and pixelated patterns.

The same kids whose alienation and resentment took out the

civic sensors every time a council contracting team came along to reinstall them; the same kids who acted as scouts for the Legion, with a bit of hero-worship thrown in. It was useful; nobody unknown could walk these streets without being clocked. They were the layer of protection no police office G8Turing could predict or subvert.

Thumbs-up and smiles greeted the Legion's taxez as it slowed and nudged past the gates. Wheels trundled silently across the long dirty puddles that swamped the undulating concrete.

Their archway was halfway along the crumbling cliff of dark brick, protected by big wooden doors that hadn't opened in decades. The taxez pulled up outside and the Legion went in through a small door set into the larger pair. Above them, dark curving brickwork was slimed with algae, while somewhere deeper in the darkness water dripped onto a dank floor. A long metal freight container took up most of the space inside.

Tronde had printed the locks for it, with Ollie supplying the customized security software. Bolts snicked back as Tye sent the codes. Ollie stepped inside, smelling the too-familiar stale air and weird vapours from the fluids feeding Tronde's printers. Once upon a time, the interior had been an office that could be hauled onto construction sites. It wasn't exactly a supervillain headquarters like you'd find in a Hong Kong drama game, but six expensive (stolen) printers were stacked up together against the rear wall, where Tronde produced all kinds of items. Galley kitchen cupboards and tall metal cabinets stored weapons and bottles of crude. The central table held a state-of-the-art game matrix player, with enough processing power to handle six sensesuits and vision-immersion helmets simultaneously. Reaction couches were crammed next to each other, ready for when the Legion went gaming together – something they hadn't done so much lately. A couple of paper-thin screens stuck over one wall came alive as they swaggered in, the filters pulling reports of the raid on the Klausen offices. It was still too early for an official police statement, but officers were already outside the building, drones unrolling *do not cross* tape. A Metropolitan Forensics Corp truckez pulled up outside and the techs got out, looking like astronauts in their sealed white clean suits. Various carrez rolled along after them, like baby animals following their mothers. A small crowd hung back around the tape. Ollie noted that the streetlights were all back on.

An exhilarated Lars clamped his hands on Ollie's shoulders. 'What do you reckon? Are we out clear?'

Ollie did his best not to flinch. 'Yeah, we're clear.'

'Way to go, us!'

They started dumping the kit they'd used on the raid. Ollie handed his fleshmask to Tronde, who dropped it and the others into a Clemson vat. A sickly-yellow sludge of eight-letter DNA yeast oozed over the flaccid masks. It would take several days, but the yeast would break them down into fresh monomers that could be printed into something new. The facial patterns the police G8Turings had collected from the raid would be utterly useless.

It killed him to do it, but Ollie stripped off his trousers and jacket. They went into a different Clemson vat, along with the boots. He kept the worker's cap, though. That was hardly unique in London's outlying boroughs.

His trousers for the rest of the night were flared purple, with gold-snakeskin boots. Jade Urchall arrived when he was threading his belt on, the one with the slim dark-gloss dragon buckle. There was something about Jade that always disturbed him. The woman was probably mid-thirties, but Ollie could never tell if she'd had telomere treatments. She had badly styled sandy hair, a rounded jaw and light brown eyes that always seemed slightly unfocused, as if she was coming down off a high. She wasn't big, though certainly not petite, either; her clothes were always cheap prints from a fashion file that'd missed a decade of upgrades. Everything about Jade made her utterly unremarkable – not what you'd expect from a member of a major crime family. Which was probably what disturbed him the most. When she was in the room, all he could think about was what kind of peripherals she had.

Piotr gave her a guarded welcome.

'Good job, boys,' she said, and held up a small bag. The Southwark Legion grinned at the sight of it. When they ran a job for Jade, she always paid half in nark – and normally it was zero-nark, the strongest possible. Ordinary chem-extruders could never get the composition quite right; it took specialist equipment and a topgun chemist. The effort was worth it, however. Zero-nark could be cut over ninety per cent, which made for a huge profit.

Tronde claimed the bag with a victorious smile and took it over to his bench.

'And the rest?' Piotr asked pleasantly.

'Don't you trust us?' Jade said, with a hint of a challenge.

'Do you trust *us*?'

She shook her head chidingly. 'Boys, boys. Check your account, Piotr.'

Piotr's eyes closed for a long blink as he read the finance display splashing across his tarsus lenses. He smiled. 'We got it.'

Gareth high-fived Ollie, and the rest of them relaxed – properly now.

Lars and Gareth wandered over to watch Tronde cutting the zero-nark. Adnan hadn't stopped staring at Jade. 'So when are we going to get it?'

'Get what?'

'Fuck's sake! Come on. You've been prick-teasing us about the relay station for months.'

If Jade was annoyed, it didn't register on her bland face. 'People have been watching your progress. Tonight was impressive, and that was noticed by the right people.'

'Yeah, so?'

'So you'll hear from me when we need something . . . larger.'

'Oh for fuck's—'

Piotr's hand closed on Adnan's shoulder, squeezing. Not hard, but enough to warn him. Personally, Ollie would have been interested to see how Jade would react to an outright threat.

'Some news on that soon,' Piotr said pointedly.

'Damn right,' Jade replied.

Ollie didn't really believe her, but at least she hadn't said no.

*

Tronde had already started cutting the zero-nark when Jade moved over to his desk. She handed him a small packet containing a dozen plain white hemispherical pads, a centimetre across, fatter than the ones he was preparing.

'For you,' she said.

'Thanks,' he muttered, keeping an eye on the small stainless steel mixing crucible, with its tiny robot arms blending the product to an even consistency.

'Be careful with this stuff,' she told him. 'Hifli doesn't normally include benzo and a dopamine lifter as well. This is a dangerous formula.'

Tronde shifted his glance to her as he put the hifli pads in his pocket. 'I know, that's the point. We need an unbreakable dependency.'

'Oh well . . . as long as you know what you're doing.'

Tronde scowled at the sarcasm in her voice and turned back to the sensitive mix in the crucible. It took another thirty minutes to complete and load the new substance into one-shot medic pads, by which time, thankfully, Jade had departed. Each of the Southwark Legion took their share of the pads. They were mostly going their separate ways tonight, thank crap. Lars, Tronde knew, was going to the Danish Warehouse, where the unlicensed cage fights would carry on until dawn. He'd sell his pads to the other muscle-overloaded spectators, making decent money, but gamble it after on the fights, yelling praise and insults at his chosen contenders. His skin would be flushed demon-red, veins bulging obscenely, pupils tiny as the stupid prick pumped some of the pads for himself. If he got lucky – in his terms – he'd have a fight with some of the crowd.

Piotr and Adnan were due at a student party over the river at Archway, where university freshers were busy celebrating their new freedoms away from home for the first time. Easy marks for pads, and lacking the courage to argue price or how low the cut was.

Gareth was off to a different party, some secure crypt with his tech friends, where they'd cruise the lownet – a virtuality closed to the G8Turings, where the darkheads ran their trades.

Just as Tronde stood up, Lolo Maude arrived. Sie was Ollie's friend, and in Tronde's opinion serious bad news. Like every omnia, sie was tall, even taller than Lars – but unlike him, slim and elegant with it. Tronde always reckoned the Utopials were trying to modify themselves into elves, which was pretty dumb.

Lolo embraced Ollie swiftly, kissed him, then looked nervously around the room, hir shoulders hunched almost fearfully. That, Tronde could understand; if the kids outside didn't know sie was with Ollie, sie would have been beaten up as soon as sie entered the district.

Southwark was a strange place for a Utopial to wind up; it was even more obvious how exotic sie was in such a place. Lolo had come to Earth from Akitha on a student exchange programme. And in that respect, sie was unremarkable. As with so many before hir, the temptations of a strange decadent old world had proved too alluring. Sie was beautiful to look at – most of the Legion had noticed a strong resemblance to Sumiko. And with hir mysteriously sensual body, too much for Ollie to resist – not that he'd tried. Tronde was certain sie only chose Ollie for the zero-nark he could supply, because that was the kind of calculating whore sie was. For all hir manners and smarts, sie was brittle and needy, which was a dangerous combination. Tronde worried Ollie would say too much to hir when they were fucking – because sure as whale shit fell deep, sie wouldn't keep hir mouth shut if the police ever questioned hir.

'I've had a word with Ollie,' Piotr had said when Tronde mentioned his misgivings to him. Which ordinarily would be enough, but in this case . . .

'We're out of here,' Ollie announced happily.

'Where to?' Tronde asked, and there was just enough edge in his voice to make Ollie hesitate, his smile dimming a couple of watts.

'Clubbing.'

'I know a great place just off Regent Street,' Lolo said. 'Diole.'

Nyin, Tronde's altme, immediately splashed details of the club across his tarsus lenses. It was the kind of place which boasted an A-list clientele, but in reality only had the youthful rich and wannabes.

'Have fun, kids,' Piotr laughed.

Tronde watched the two of them leave the ageing metal container, unable to help the scowl creasing his face.

'He'll be fine,' Adnan said.

'I don't give a shit about him, but *it* bothers me. *It*'s weird. I don't trust it.'

'Don't fret,' Piotr said. 'How long has Ollie ever held on to anyone?'

Tronde didn't bother answering, Piotr was right; Ollie was as pan as you could get, craving every experience possible, quickly and often. It meant he went through sex partners like he was upgrading corporate-issue software. None of them ever lasted more than a couple of weeks before he was back hunting fresh meat. It was the main reason Piotr had chosen Tronde out of all of them to take the lead on their most ambitious (and expensive) scam. It had to be played perfectly. Tronde prided himself that he *got* people: the way they behaved, they way they thought and reacted. Some had a menu of flaws that made them hugely complicated and unpredictable to the point of instability, while others with similar flaws were ridiculously simple. Claudette Beaumant, for one.

The others all wished Tronde good luck as they left, heading off to celebrate Saturday night the way it should be done: amid heat and hologram light and nark-tweaked senses. Tronde walked away from the old railway arches by himself, heading up Copeland Road to the junction with Rye Lane where the Connexion hub stood. Four minutes later, he was twelve hubs around the loop and in Richmond.

Claudette Beaumant lived in one of the big houses halfway along Lichfield Road, its painted stone-mullioned windows almost obscured by the leafy horse chestnut trees bordering the central clear path, branches knotted together overhead to form a dark green living tunnel.

Tronde sent his code to the lock pillar. Sensors scanned him, and the gate swung back. Claudette was waiting in the hall as the door opened, smiling in welcome. Forty-five years old (she claimed), with a face that'd been doused in way too many conflicting treatments during the last two decades in a frantic attempt to retain the fresh, beguiling features she'd possessed when she was twenty-two. As far as Tronde was concerned, she'd wasted a lot of money. Her skin looked like something that'd been sprayed over a plastic framework, then dusted in too much make-up.

She didn't even say anything, just kissed him, pressing up tight in anticipation of an eager physical response. Claudette had paid as much attention to her body as she had her looks. Gyms, personal trainers, anti-cellulites, Pilates, diet, all combined to give her an athletic frame that really *could* have belonged to her twenty-something self. That and implants – expensive printed stem cells, not Kcells – which gave her a great pair of tits. Most of which were on show beneath a lustrous flapper dress with a short skirt. What straight male wouldn't respond?

'Where've you been?' she complained.

'Busy with the lads. You know.'

'No, I don't. Come on. The table is booked for like ten minutes ago.' She grabbed his hand and pulled him back out of the front door and into the street. A Class One taxez trundled along the clear path and stopped outside the gate. It was a short ride to the restaurant, the whole of which she spent kissing him and fussing about his jacket. It was the one she'd bought for him last week, along with a silk shirt that was hand-tailored – and even Tronde had to admit it looked as good as it felt against his skin. The clothes weren't cheap, but Claudette wanted to show him off to her friends. Her toyboy. Her hot bit of street rough. The savage she'd tamed, who gave her great sex all night long. *Hell, you should see him with his clothes off. But hands off, bitches, he's mine.*

As the luxury taxez started to slow, she flashed him an anxious glance. 'Did you bring it?'

'Sure,' he replied reassuringly and patted his jacket pocket.

'Good. We'll leave early. I want you.'

'You want me because I'm a bad boy. Everybody knows that.'

'Yes.' A flicker of greed unsettled her cherry-red glossed lips, then she was herself again. The bright dazzling gal about town, the Richmond superstar, the friend you always had a great time with.

And there they were, all those equally glitzy friends, waiting for her when the taxez pulled up outside the restaurant.

We could have walked, Tronde thought. *It wouldn't have taken much longer, and it was warm enough.* But no, Claudette didn't walk like some common person; a Class One cab was her minimal requirement when she was out to meet people – and always the *right* people. That was one of the many things he hated about her, the way everything she wanted she could afford. She never asked or thought what anything cost.

Her friends swooped with shrill greetings that set his teeth on edge, tossing admiring – and calculating – looks his way. False jollity – *so very glad to finally meet you.* Air kisses. How he despised those. Big hair like works of art. Short, low-cut dresses, plenty of thigh and cleavage exhibited – almost as prominent as the glittering bling draped around necks and weighing down fingers. No cheap printed repro here; these women wore jewellery crafted by London's exclusive artisans.

Their men were indifferent to him. Husbands, partners, even a couple of lads who'd lucked out: male candy with game-star looks and toned muscle, enjoying the pampered ride. Whores. No doubt they thought the same of him.

The group had a big table in the centre of the restaurant. Their voices were loud all night. Names were gossiped: celebs he'd never heard of and couldn't be arsed to check with Nyin. Holidays bragged about. It was non-stop. They didn't just talk; sentences were shrieked out with vocal cords turned up to eleven. A penetrating sonic barrage that threatened a headache.

Claudette's hand kept sneaking under the table, playing with his crotch, trying to tweak a reaction from him. He kept his expression deadpan, talking banalities to the woman on his other side. Her leg was pressed up against his, too, rubbing gently. He kept his cool about that and the thousand other small verbal abuses he was subjected to, proving to himself that out of all the Southwark Legion crew, he really was the right one for this.

Copious wine was poured from two-hundred-and-fifty-wattdollar bottles into large cut-crystal glasses and drunk without any appreciation. Tronde ordered a beer to start with, then kept to sparkling water. The food was delicious, he admitted, artistically presented and cooked to perfection. In his head he was calculating the cost; this one meal was more than the price the Southwark Legion had paid the matcher for Claudette's name. And it had taken plenty of hard graft to pull so much cash together.

Finally, it was time to go. Claudette, who was now giggly-drunk on a heady combination of white wine, lust and egotism, swayed against him as she urged him towards the door, their arms entwined. Spirited innuendoes sliced through the air behind them like claws grasping for fleeing prey.

Claudette managed to keep her persona intact until they got back to the house. Then the cracks began to show.

'You have got it, haven't you?' she asked urgently.

Tronde hardened his voice, becoming stern – the way that enlivened her. 'I told you I have it.'

'Yes, yes, of course.'

Tronde realized she wasn't as drunk as she'd made out at the restaurant. Her eyes flicked about, as if expecting someone else to be in the house – someone who mattered. The police (to catch them and incarcerate them). A journalist (exposing her crimes). Because now she was about to do Bad Things. Excitement and anticipation made her breathless. She kissed him again, desperate to pull him into the intrigue, because this was a stairway down to the thrilling underworld where upper-middle-class women like her never went.

'It's not cheap,' he said smoothly. 'This stuff is so rare my usual bloke didn't have any left. I had to go to someone new, which is risky. This dealer, he's got connections that go right to the top.'

'Oh god, you were careful, weren't you? I don't want you hurt.'

He grinned. 'I'm a bad boy. He knows that. We respect each other.'

Her gaze was worshipful.

'The money,' he prompted.

'Yes, yes. How much?'

Nyin sent her altme a finance transfer package for three thousand wattdollars. The tiniest hesitation crinkled the mascara around her eyes.

'I want this again,' he said. 'I want us together when we use.'

'Right. Absolutely.'

Claudette's money swirled down a digital sink into the lownet, vanishing.

'Good girl. Now what have *you* got for *me*?'

'The best,' she promised. She took his hand and pulled him directly up the stairs.

Her bedroom was hideous: pink and purple and black, frilly cushions everywhere. Large, salacious charcoal drawings hung on the walls.

'I'll get ready for you,' she said as she hurried into her en suite bathroom. 'Don't go away.' A flash of concern, insecurities showing.

He laughed, casual and arrogant. 'I'm not going anywhere. You know how hot your body is. I've been getting hard for days thinking what I'm going to do to you tonight.' He gave the decorous art porn a meaningful glance.

Claudette simpered, claiming the role of the boudoir seductress in her lair: feminine wiles irresistible to the unsophisticated boy from the wrong side of the metroloop.

The smile fell from Tronde's lips as soon as she shut the door. He had to concede the matcher was worth the money. Outwardly, Claudette was poised and knowing, her social status making her invulnerable. She had breeding – both parents' families did, stretching back generations. With it came the sure knowledge that she was where she deserved to be in the world.

Then one day, chance had sent her walking across the matcher's field of view. He'd seen the flaws, the loneliness her trust-fund money brought, the hidden loss of self-esteem inflicted by both husbands leaving her, compounded by a string of indifferent lovers. An absent uncaring family. Chinks in the glossy armour that Tronde could prise open to worm his way in, before allowing the specially mixed hifli to do the rest. Claudette Gizelle d'Voy Beaumant was vulnerable, a life empty of goals and filled by sameness had left her yearning for something new, something different, something with edge. A young stud worshipful of the body she'd devoted herself to keeping supreme – because that's what the *right people* did with their endless golden days. A kid whose poverty allowed her to be completely in charge this time around. And a kid who also had the secret codes to a darker, more exciting, level of pleasure.

How lucky she'd been that the agency sent him around to repair one of her home printers when it unexpectedly flatlined. He knew his job well, so he wasn't stupid. A tight T-shirt showed off firm pecs as he gave her some cheeky banter. His stories of a rough childhood and running with the wrong crowd were fascinating to someone of her background. But he was turning things around now, with a job he was good at – so not a danger, every instinct told her. And that torso . . . Appearance was everything to Claudette, to her world.

Tronde had stripped off by the time she emerged from the bathroom. The stuff she was wearing now . . . He hadn't got a clue if it was supposed to be lingerie or a bikini. It was made of black wet-look leather strips, stretched taut over what little flesh they did cover. All very nice pretend slave girl. He guessed one of her husbands must have got off on it.

She gazed down eagerly at his groin. Two years ago, Tronde had spent a couple of days in a clinic getting Kcell implants in his dick. Not just to increase size, but to give him complete control through Nyin. He could stay erect for as long as he wanted, when he wanted. Like now.

'Come here,' he told her.

Claudette moved like a hostage following orders, quick and awkward so she didn't disappoint her captor. He enjoyed the display of urgency; it was a sweet preview of what was to come, providing he played this perfectly. It wasn't a new scam, but it was one her artless rich-girl brain would never think to watch out for. This simply didn't happen to her. Nobody would do such a thing, not in real life. Some people were bad, but not to this degree, not outside a Hong Kong gangster virtual, because everyone she met was fundamentally decent.

The hook was in already. The interesting man, naughty but nice. She'd try him out and brag about it amid wild giggles with her girlfriends. Once she got him into bed, he'd sheepishly conjure up a couple of pads. 'I've got some hifli; let's try it together.' And who hadn't heard of hifli, one of the few restricted narks the authorities still took very seriously, on account of the human wreckage it left behind? The nark that scrambled nerve impulses, so the brain interpreted every sensation as pure pleasure: heat, cold, touch, pain, taste, some even said sound . . . Because he wanted them to take it 'together', the risk was obviously negligible.

She found that sex with a hifli-befuddled brain was good. *Really* good. And that first time he only gave her a weak load.

But he'd confessed it was the best ever for him, too, even though his pad was blank.

Can we do it again?

A couple of times later, with the dose slowly increased, he couldn't get any. I'm out of money, sorry. That was okay, because she had plenty. So can you bring some? I'll pay . . .

Claudette sat on the bed with breathless anticipation, smirking at his tireless erection. Tronde held up the two pads, careful to place his blank tenderly in her eager hand. 'Look what the bad boy brought you.'

'Lucky me.' She moved to apply it on her neck, above the carotid, so the hifli would be carried quickly into her brain.

'Wait,' he commanded.

There was a pout, but he leant forwards and kissed her. Trust; it was all about trust. He was her lusty young rogue who wanted her for the hot dirty sex her fantastic body could perform and nothing else. Certainly not her money. He was validation that she remained a highly desirable sexual animal, justly yearned for on those terms alone. Proof she had got this so very right.

'We're doing this together,' he'd say, so full of reassurance. And put his pad on her neck. She'd press the identical little white hemisphere to his skin, and they'd squeeze in unison.

Most times, the scam would last a few weeks, until the girl's credit was gone and she was a broken husk. But it could be played harder if you were brutal enough and the reward was worth it. If you could find the right victim, one who would give you *everything*.

Tronde watched the face he found so abhorrent grow slack,

pupils dilating as the hifli sluiced into her synapses. He was pretty sure they didn't need to use Jade's special version. The mild doses he'd given her so far had rendered her pliable and hungry for more – but it never hurt to be sure. So the benzo-mix it was.

It worked, too; she took off her saucy black straps without a qualm when he ordered her to. Breath juddered out of her mouth in jubilant gasps as the fabric slithered over her skin, conjuring up delectable sparkles of bliss.

If hifli made that feather-light stroke euphoric, sex was devastating.

He observed her helpless squirming with detached interest as he refined the sinful indignities which proved the most physically stimulating for her.

Again and again she wept and convulsed as she climaxed on his machine cock, each time leaving her craving more. She was so delirious she never realized the joy wasn't shared, that they weren't together after all. It was the implacable Kcells providing him with all the time he needed to overload her nervous system until, at the end, she simply collapsed into a fugue state.

Tronde walked calmly around the bedroom, opening boxes and drawers so Nyin could catalogue the contents and produce a valuation. Tonight he simply helped himself to a couple of diamond rings; he knew a fence who could get him a decent price and there was no need to be greedy. She would wake in the morning and, without the nark charging her bloodstream, the world would be dry and bland and numb. She'd clamour for more, pester him to bring her the glory that only came from him and the nark.

Twinned with the dopamine boost, she should start descending rapidly into full-blown addiction, with a strong side effect of mounting neurosis. Paranoia would creep in, to bond with the dependency. And he would supply an eternal quantity of himself and the nark, quenching her all-consuming needs. It would cost her. Satisfaction and relief wasn't cheap, but there were millions in her trust fund. Played right, he could drain most of that out before her inexorable total breakdown. By then he'd be gone, a name known only to impotent therapists from her tearful screams.

Tronde stood over her inert body with its unnervingly open empty eyes, watching the twitches that still afflicted her limbs, and for the first time that night managed a genuine smile. The future was going to be a grand place to live.

The Assessment Team

Kruse Station, 26th June 2204

Callum Hepburn walked through the newly threaded portal from the Nkya research base with no idea what was on the other side. A smug Yuri hadn't volunteered that detail.

Straight away he found himself face to face with a five-person security team. All of them were tall and dressed in dark energy-absorbing armour, their contoured helmets like outsize silver skulls. Small stub nozzles had risen out of their forearms and shoulders, making them bristle like nervous porcupines. Several small delta-planform drones hovered silently in the air above them, black glass lenses aligned on everyone coming through the portal.

The security team waited until Jessika crossed the threshold, then formed up around her – a development she treated with complete equanimity. Kandara, who walked beside her, gave the team a significant look.

'Treat her with extreme caution,' she told them. 'We have no idea what she's capable of.' Then she paused and tipped her head to regard Jessika quizzically. 'Are you a she? An it?'

'She,' Jessika replied. 'That's how I was created.'

'Did you Neána steal humans, too?' There was an edge to

Kandara's voice, something that told Callum she was itching for an excuse to unleash violence.

'Good grief, no! I was developed inside a biologic initiator during our voyage to Earth. We all were.'

Kandara shook her head in disapproval. 'Whatever.'

Callum looked around curiously at his new surroundings. It was a large cylindrical airlock chamber, he decided, not much different from the set-up he'd just left behind: the same basic metal tube with a composite grid floor, every surface gloss-clean, with no expense spared on the ancillary equipment ribbing the curving walls. A sleek portal-threading mechanism sat at one end, while the opposite end had blanked-out windows on either side of a circular hatchway. So although it looked like an airlock, it could as easily be a high-security reception cell, and his inner ears could sense the tiny but definite aberration of spin-induced gravity. They were in space somewhere, on a station or habitat. His altme, Apollo, informed him that the local network was restricted, and he wasn't on the access list.

'The node interfaces are very sophisticated,' Apollo said. 'It's a high-level G8Turing in charge. But –'

'Yes?'

'I have encountered this key structure before, when accessing Level One Utopials' networks.'

Callum took another look at the tall security team, then glanced at Yuri, who had just stepped through the portal. The Connexion Security chief had been carrying the initial micro-portal through which the others had threaded, allowing them to leave Nkya; so Callum had assumed they were going to a Connexion facility.

'Where are we?' he asked.

The answer came from the last person he was expecting.

'Kruse Station,' Jessika said. 'In the Delta Pavonis system.'

Callum stared at her in surprise. All he could see was her swinging the fire axe, its blade shattering Feriton's skull to cut into his brain. Except it wasn't his brain; there'd been an Olyix brain nestling in his cranium instead, one that was quantum entangled with the other four in its quint. The aliens had seen and heard everything that'd happened on Nkya; they knew they'd been exposed. In fact, Callum reasoned – given the Olyix had that ability – their spies probably knew every dirty little secret the human race possessed.

'Kruse?' Kandara queried. The corporate mercenary sounded both startled and pleased.

'Yes,' Jessika said. 'It seemed . . . appropriate.'

'And you know this how?' Alik Monday asked.

Jessika gave the FBI agent a sad smile. 'I'm the deputy director of the Utopials' Olyix Threat Assessment Bureau.'

'You're fucking kidding me!'

Her smile turned wicked. 'Who better? Once you get over the irony.'

The hatch opened at the far end of the chamber and three more omnia entered. They all wore pale grey uniforms with purple piping along the jacket and down the trouser seams, while slimline over-skirts came down to the knee. Also shared was a hairstyle: they'd chosen corn-braiding, arranged in complex curves. Despite living in the Delta Pavonis system for the last ninety-two years, Callum still felt slightly perturbed by the level of conformity running through the Utopials' culture, and it was becoming more prevalent among the younger generations. As if to emphasize it, the trio shared the same uneasy expression, none of them able to meet Jessika's gaze.

'I'm Captain Tral,' the oldest said. 'Welcome to Kruse Station. I'm afraid we will have to run some basic scans before anyone can progress further.'

'Basic?' Alik said.

'The Captain is being polite,' Jessika said. 'Sie means as thorough as our technology can provide.'

'Oh yeah?' Alik folded his arms and stared at Tral.

'Just go with it,' Yuri said in a tired voice. 'We need to get through procedures and start deciding what to do next.'

'They don't care about your weapon peripherals,' Jessika said. 'They just have to make sure you're not Olyix, or have any Kcell implants. The scanners are good enough to detect a single Kcell in your body. I know; I helped draw up the specifications.'

Alik's strangely rigid features remained impassive, yet Callum suspected that he was badly tempted to use one of those peripherals to shut her up. The tableau was broken by Lankin and three of his medical staff coming through the portal, escorting a gurnez which carried the unconscious body of Lucius Soćko. The Neána looked so perfectly human that Callum still couldn't quite believe Jessika's claim that they were both aliens. Behind that came another gurnez that held Feriton Kayne's dead body in a transparent biohazard container.

Lankin looked around, slightly confused by the antagonism tainting the chamber. 'What now?'

'Now,' Alik said with forced cheerfulness, 'we follow procedure.'

*

The scan was nothing, of course. On the other side of the hatch was a short corridor with pearlescent walls. You walked down it unencumbered while a multitude of ultra-sophisticated scanners analysed the thirty-trillion-plus cells which made up your body, alert for a very specific anomaly. Kcells had a similar biochemistry to human cells – good enough to function symbiotically with human organs and immune systems – but not identical.

Callum knew he didn't have any Kcells, but for some reason he couldn't help the feeling of apprehension as the hatch shut behind him and he began his solo walk down the short corridor. A whole file of *what if* scenarios kept playing out in his mind. And if the Olyix had set him up, innocence would be hard to prove.

A door opened at the far end of the corridor and Callum stepped through into Kruse Station, letting out a shaky breath as he did so. The surroundings continued to remind him of the research base he'd just left behind on Nkya. Less pioneering outpost here, perhaps, but it shared the same efficient utilitarian appearance.

A couple of Utopials in the station's grey uniform were waiting and deferred respectfully as they escorted him along more corridors. Apollo was still locked out of the local network. Callum wound up in a conference room that could have belonged to any part of his life. There was a big table down the centre made from some claret-red rock and polished to a shine, comfortable leather execu-tive chairs around it, and even a crystal vase of white lilies giving off a sweet scent. The only thing missing was a window. Conference rooms, in his experience, always had a view – across cities or nature (gorgeous panoramas of jungles, mountains and oceans) or even the astonishing vistas of space, from gas giant rings to alien planet-scapes.

The only reason you wouldn't have a window was security. Heavy security. Callum's shoulders quivered as if an Arctic spectre was slipping along his spine.

'I got this, chief.'

'Huh?' Callum turned around then to see that Eldlund had followed him into the conference room. The young omnia was giving him a concerned look, and for a moment Callum felt insuf-ferably old.

Eldlund held out hir hand, opening hir fingers. A small snow-white pad rested in hir palm.

'What the hell . . .?'

'It's the same for me,' Eldlund said in sympathy. 'Look.'

Callum realized his assistant's hand was shaking. He looked down at his own hands to see even more pronounced tremors. 'Oh, bloody hell.' He didn't want to admit it; that was the problem. Didn't want to acknowledge the terrible violence Jessika had unleashed – and, worse, the shock that the Olyix were implacably hostile. That the human race was being manipulated, the helpless, hapless victim of a superior species.

'Here,' Eldlund urged. 'The nark's mild, I swear. It'll blunt the edge, but you'll still be able to think okay.'

Callum just took the pad and pressed it to his neck. Didn't bother asking for details, impressed – in a strange way – that Eldlund would even be prepared for such an eventuality. Sie was the perfect assistant, supportive and concerned, with plenty of compassion thrown in. Just like every Utopial omnia.

'It's not just the shock,' Callum confessed. 'I've known Jessika for getting on twelve years now, and I never suspected a thing. She's a fucking alien! And . . . nothing. No hint of anything odd, no giveaways. For Christ's sake, she knows more about popular culture than I do! Smart, good sense of humour . . . How can she not be human? And how could I not see it? Twelve fucking years. Holy shit.'

Eldlund gave him a moderately sympathetic grin. 'If it makes you feel any better, Yuri's known her for a lot longer, and he's security. Better: security that was supposed to be watching for alien spies.'

Callum smiled weakly. 'Yeah, he is, isn't he?'

'Absolutely. So stop beating yourself up over this. Now – take a moment, and I'll get you a coffee.' Sie went over to the drinks dispenser and fussed around.

Watching hir busying hirself with the coffee, Callum felt obscurely grateful that his grandkids were all omnia. *We did the right thing coming to Delta Pavonis.*

He felt the nark starting to soothe his hot nerves, allowing him to relax, and returning a comforting level of lucidity to his mind. The way he liked to think, the way an engineer observed and analysed the universe.

Alik Monday walked into the conference room and gave the two of them a curious glance. Callum was quite envious of how calm the FBI special detective appeared, but then he guessed Alik must deal with violent scenes on a regular basis. Whereas he hadn't encountered physical conflict since Zagreus, and that was over a century ago now.

'I guess you and I are both in the clear, then,' Callum said cheerfully and took a seat at the table.

Alik simply scowled.

Yuri and his assistant Loi came next, conversing with Captain Tral. They were quickly followed by Kandara and Jessika, along with the Neána's armoured escort and five drones.

'I'm going to ask again,' Alik said as he sat next to Callum. 'Where are we? What is this place?'

'Kruse Station is basically the Delta Pavonis equivalent of Sol's Alpha Defence,' Jessika said. 'This is where the fight against any alien invasion of this star system will be coordinated.'

'Ironic, considering you're already inside,' Emilja Jurich said.

Callum sat up straight as she walked into the room. The joint founder of the Utopial movement brought an imperial presence greater than any hereditary monarch could ever manage. Today she was wearing another of her customary high-collared dresses, made from turquoise and scarlet Indian silk over which gold Aztec-style symbols slithered like reef fish. Emilja acknowledged him with a sardonic smile, her light grey eyes twinkling.

'Thanks for this,' he said with as much irony as he could project. He'd never wanted to be part of the assessment team, but she had been unusually insistent.

'No problem,' she replied.

Throughout the years he'd spent as her chief technology adviser, he'd come to respect then admire Emilja's drive and ambition for the new society she'd helped found. Her political ability, in terms of building consensus amid the stubborn self-righteous grade one citizens of Delta Pavonis, was remarkable, too. And yet for all that time some deep-seated instinct had niggled away that she was holding something back from their working relationship. *Now I know.* A distrust of the Olyix, just as intense as Ainsley Zangari's.

So he wasn't in the least bit surprised when Ainsley arrived right behind her, escorted by three aides. For someone over a hundred and seventy years old, the CEO of Connexion was in fantastic shape. Callum acknowledged this even while telling himself he wasn't envious. He couldn't even begin to guess how much money Ainsley had spent on various genetic treatments – certainly orders of magnitude greater than Callum ever had. Ainsley's hair was as thick and dark as any thirty-year-old's, while his skin had none of the motionless sheen afflicting Alik's face, leaving him with features rugged enough to star in a Hong Kong interactive. Since the single time they'd met in the flesh, a hundred and twelve years ago, Ainsley had grown more youthful. The personality, though, the urbane self-assurance that surrounded him like an old-time saint's aura . . . That belonged to something ancient, and not particularly benign.

The self-styled richest man in history gave Callum a wry look. 'Hello, Callum,' he said gruffly. 'Been a while.'

Callum matched his ex-employer's indifference. *Two can play that game.* 'Aye, it has.'

His composure was only slightly thrown by Alik's bass chuckle. Ainsley sat next to Emilja on the other side of the table from the assessment team, with a couple of the sharp-suited aides standing attentively behind him, and another sitting at the table. Now that limited access to Kruse Station's network had been granted, Apollo ran identity checks. Inevitably, the trio were all family. Tobias and Danuta Zangari – Ainsley's grandchildren, who were in their forties – flanked their grandfather as they surveyed the assessment team with judgemental expressions. And claiming the prestigious chair beside his grandfather was Ainsley III; at eighty-two, he was the oldest of all the grandchildren. He had devoted his life to the company, rising steadily until he was now CEO of Connexion's TranSol division. Callum wondered if his eerily similar features had been subtly altered over the decades to emphasize the Zangari family bond; they certainly looked like brothers if not almost identical twins. Solnet gossip whispered that Ainsley III was the favoured successor over his own father, Ainsley II.

Callum was amused by the way Tobias and Danuta both exchanged a fleeting acknowledgement with Yuri's assistant, Loi. Checking up on a junior family member always came first for a Zangari.

'We'll take it from here,' Captain Tral told the squad as the Zangaris established that one of their own had come through safe and sound.

The armed figures left, leaving the drones floating discreetly in the air behind Tral, who took the seat to Emilja's left.

'So exactly who the fuck are you?' Ainsley snapped at Jessika.

'I am a member of a mission sent to Earth by the Neána to warn you about the true nature of the Olyix, and to help you resist them.'

'So you're not a Neána yourself?' Ainsley III queried.

'Physically, no – and I have no memory of, or information about, what a Neána looks like. My body is a biologic unit, grown by the insertion ship that brought us to Sol. However, I do have certain abilities that humans lack, all of which we are prepared to give you to aid your fight.'

Kandara leant in closer, her black tank-top revealing tense biceps. 'You're an android?'

'I'm not really sure worrying about definitions is going to be useful at this point,' Jessika said. 'But my body is very human.'

'I want to know how much free will you have, or if you're just following a program.'

'I believe I can be classed as fully self-aware. My thoughts run in a human neural structure. The insertion ship generated my personality around the imperative to help humans survive the Olyix. If I have any hidden commands, they have not yet become apparent.'

'But then you would say that,' Emilja said.

'I certainly would. Our exposure to you was always going to generate deep suspicion. All I can say is that I believe you will come to trust me and my colleagues as the Olyix reveal their true intent.'

Ainsley gave Yuri a worried glance, a slow flush creeping up his face. 'Which is to kidnap us? All of humanity?'

'Essentially, yes. They will send their Deliverance fleet through the wormhole terminus inside the *Salvation of Life*. Humans will be collected and cocooned.'

'Like those poor bastards we found in the Olyix transport ship your colleague hijacked,' Alik muttered. 'Jezus H Christ.'

'When will the Olyix crusade start?' Emilja asked.

'It will have begun the second I put that axe through the quint agent's head,' Jessika said. 'The *Salvation*'s onemind will work out pretty damned fast that I'm a Neána, so it'll know that right now you're either warned, or being warned.'

'Go back,' Yuri said. 'The onemind?'

'The *Salvation of Life*'s controlling intelligence,' Jessika said. 'The transport ship on Nkya had a single controlling brain, remember? Well, the same goes for the *Salvation of Life*. And it's to scale, too.'

'And where does the *Salvation*'s wormhole lead to?' Yuri asked.

'Back to a gateway that connects directly into their enclave.'

'Their homeworld?'

'I don't know. My information is that the enclave is a section of spacetime that has a much slower timeflow than outside, so the effect is one of flying through time – like a relativistic spaceship which doesn't move. The timeflow can be manipulated, of course – reverting to a normal flow to allow the Olyix's ships to emerge, and for their network of monitor stations to report the detection of new sentient species emerging in the galaxy. Such a construct would by necessity be large – and presumably big enough to encompass the Olyix homeworld.'

'But you don't know,' Alik said. 'Not really.'

'I have the information I was given, and that's what I'm here to deliver to you. I don't see why the Neána would lie, or why they would create me to warn you, if it wasn't real.'

'You need to give us some kind of proof,' Ainsley said sharply. 'Fuck, the decisions you're expecting us to make on your word – the word of a species we've never heard of, and who supposedly hides somewhere between stars . . . If you truly know us, you'll know that's an impossible ask.'

Jessika gave him a direct stare. 'Was Feriton Kayne not evidence enough?'

'That revelation was persuasive,' Emilja admitted. 'And we'll know more when the xenobiology department has examined his remains.'

'Its remains,' Eldlund said. '*It*. Not human.'

Callum thought about reprimanding his assistant; this was the grown-ups' table, after all. But he held back. The kid did have a valid point.

'Yeah,' a discomforted Ainsley said.

'Look,' Jessika said. 'In order to speed this along and get where we need to, I suggest that you accept what I'm saying with a healthy dose of scepticism – which will fade as you see the Olyix mission begin in precisely the fashion I've told you. At the very least, you have to acknowledge that some of your concerns have been borne out by Feriton Kayne. They have infiltrated your senior security organizations and engaged in some serious covert acts, subverting your ability to defend yourselves. That alone should warrant taking my warning seriously. The very least you can do is prepare yourselves.'

'Wait,' Alik snapped. 'You're talking about Cancer, aren't you? Was she an Olyix?'

'Most likely,' Jessika said. 'They'll have hundreds of cored-out human bodies walking around Sol and the terraformed worlds, gathering information.'

'Fuck,' Yuri grunted. 'How compromised are we?'

'It could be worse,' Jessika said. 'I initiated the procedures to deep bioscan everyone entering any of the critical facilities in the Delta Pavonis system, and most of Sol's Alpha Defence command centres have similar protocols.'

'Connexion was starting to initiate an equivalent policy,' Yuri said, and sighed. 'Hindsight is a fucking wonderful thing.'

'Look closely, and you'll probably find Feriton or some other Olyix agents were the ones slowing it down,' Jessika said.

'Sonofabitch,' Ainsley growled, his fists clenching so tight his knuckles whitened. 'I fucking knew it!'

Ainsley III's hand came down over his grandfather's – a re-assurance that was also trying to restrain the anger. Callum was nonplussed by the old man's raw rage; he'd always assumed the larger-than-life persona was part of the act, of being The Ainsley Zangari on the solnet streams. In private, he must be more accom-modating and political, surely?

'We have one person's word for it,' Emilja chided. 'A person who also claims to be an alien. I'd urge some caution about accepting everything she says at face value.'

'All right,' the richest man who'd ever been said grudgingly. 'But what happened to Feriton proves the Olyix have been spying on us, and it can't be for any good reason. You've gotta give me that.'

'I'm not denying what's happened,' Emilja said. 'I'm just saying our response cannot be to lash out blindly. We need to think this through.'

'Okay,' Ainsley III said in a reasonable tone. 'Suppose Jessika here is right and the Olyix are worse than we ever figured. What sort of protective measures are we talking about?'

'All of them!' Ainsley shouted.

Callum knew the nark he'd taken was working. He should have

been in a state of complete panic at the idea of the Olyix invading, but he faced Jessika with curiosity rather than alarm. 'Earth's shields,' he said. 'How secure are the cities?'

'I can't make any guarantees,' she replied. 'My colleagues and I did our best to expose the vulnerabilities in your defences. You responded quite well. But you're going to have to declare a full level-one global emergency.'

'Now we're talking!' Ainsley said.

Jessika nodded. 'The city and habitat shields have to go active now. That way we'll see which ones actually function. Even if the *Salvation of Life* launches a Deliverance fleet in the next six hours, it will take them days to reach Earth. That gives us a small window to re-establish control of any shields they've disabled.'

'Six hours?' Yuri asked, aghast. 'You're fucking joking, right?'

'No. Now that the Olyix know you have been informed of their true purpose, they will move swiftly. Any hesitation on their part just allows you more time to prepare, so they will want to prevent that.'

'And apart from raising the city shields, what else would you advise?' Emilja asked.

'You need to be on guard for acts of sabotage. What the Olyix need is for governments and security agencies to be incapacitated. They'll try to cut solarwell power to Earth's grid, then shut down solnet and most of the Connexion hubs. Without those basics, your society will be unable to function, let alone defend itself. But their biggest problem is the terraformed worlds. The way your portals have allowed you to spread out from Sol in a relatively short time is unusual in our experience. They'll have to make a huge effort to secure the transtellar portals, which will allow them to take their invasion out to the planets you've settled.'

'Won't they just send more arkships to the stars we've reached?' Loi asked.

'They might have to,' Jessika said, 'especially if you can prevent them from capturing the portals. But that will take time and add an order of magnitude to the complexity of their invasion.'

'All right,' Kandara said in a sceptical voice. 'We alert the security agencies, defend the transtellar portals and switch on the shields. But that's just passive defence. That doesn't stop anything; it just buys us time. So how do we defeat them?'

Jessika gave her a puzzled look. 'Defeat them?'

'Yeah. Defeat them. Shoot their Deliverance fleet out of the sky. Blow up the *Salvation of Life*. Nuke this enclave of theirs back into whatever stone age they had.'

'You can't.'

'What the *actual fuck*?' Ainsley exclaimed.

'They cannot be defeated,' Jessika said, looking around the table, hunting understanding. 'They are too well established, too powerful.'

'Then, for Christ's sake, what—?'

Emilja held a hand up. By some miracle Ainsley halted his tirade, but his face was a mask of rage.

'So what do you expect us to do?' Emilja demanded. 'You clearly have some idea. Whatever sent you here had a reason.'

'To warn you,' Jessika said. 'To stall the invasion long enough that some of you can flee out into the depths of space. Your habitat construction ability is impressive. You will be able to build your refuges in the emptiness between stars. This way your species will survive.'

'No,' Emilja said simply. 'That is not survival. To even say such a thing shows that you do not understand us at all. We cannot live on, hiding in fear. That would give the Olyix an absolute victory. No. We need to resist this. We need to defeat them, to prevent them from ever doing this to us or any other species ever again.'

'You don't understand,' Jessika said. 'We don't even know how long they have been persecuting this insane campaign. Millions of years, most likely. Their enclave accelerates through time, lifting them out of life in real spacetime. There is no way in, and no way to reach them. They only emerge to conquer, and to steal your minds for their so-called god. You cannot fight them, for you can never find them. Even if those who survive the invasion go on to develop the most advanced weapons imaginable, what can they do? Remain vigilant for a million years waiting for the Olyix to emerge on another invasion? No society can last that long and retain its purpose. Decadence will set in. You will decay or forget. You will fall from whatever peak you reach. And then they will come again and scoop up whatever remains.'

'Is that what happened to your species?' Alik snarled.

'I don't know what we've done. I don't know what we became or where we went. All I know is I am here to help however I can.'

'A biological civilization may well fall eventually,' Eldlund said, 'but a digital-mechanical one would not.'

'And the relevance of that is?' Alik asked sourly.

'Those who survive this invasion and fly to safety in interstellar space could build an army, an armada that would never die. Our von Neumann ships would visit every star system in the galaxy over that million years and turn them all into armed fortresses. I'd like to see the Olyix survive that.'

Emilja directed a humourless smile at Eldlund. 'Let's just put the eternal death robot navy in the bank for now.'

'Why?' Ainsley asked. 'Sounds like a fucking good idea to me.'

'Because we have twenty billion people who are about to have their bodies taken away from them,' Emilja retorted. 'That is our immediate problem. Once we've prevented that from happening, we can focus on what to do next.'

Ainsley shrugged extravagantly. 'Whatever. But I still go with not being defensive the whole goddamn time. These sons of bitches need to be shown there's a price to be paid for what they've done.'

'We will hit them,' Yuri said, 'and hit them hard. But from what we've seen and know, Jessika may well be right about them launching an insurgency offensive. That cannot be allowed. We have to go to alert status. Right, Alik?'

Alik Monday flinched, but went on to give Yuri a grudging nod. 'Yeah. That's going to be my immediate recommendation. Putting agencies on alert costs practically nothing. If this turns out to be bullshit we lose nothing and everyone had a good drill.'

'It is *not* bullshit,' Jessika said forcefully.

'I dig that. But you've gotta see the politics behind this, right? You want a Sol-wide alert, you got to play the game. Something this big, people up at the top of the chain will be scared shitless of making a false call. They gotta be eased into it.'

'But you don't think it's bullshit, do you?' she persisted.

Alik took a long breath, his stiff facial muscles shifting towards an expression of concern. 'No. This is some serious shit going down right now, that's beyond question. And until we establish exactly what the Olyix's intensions are, I say, take precautions.'

'Thanks, mom,' Ainsley growled.

'Best you're going to get,' Alik said stubbornly.

'I need to run Connexion's response,' Yuri said. 'Make sure we're protected correctly. Specifically, protecting the transtellar hubs.'

'Agreed,' Ainsley III said.

Callum glanced at the little clump of Zangaris in mild surprise, but Ainsley himself didn't seem bothered that his grandson was making decisions independently.

'Take Loi with you,' Ainsley said. 'Make fucking sure those transtellar hubs are safe. You have total authority to protect them, any resource you need. Keep those bastards out of my company.'

'Yes, sir.'

'I need to get to D.C., right now,' Alik said. 'Something this big, you gotta do it in person.'

'Of course,' Emilja said. 'Keep me and Ainsley in the loop; we'll coordinate our response with Earth's global Political Action Committee contacts. That should give us the political clout to have Sol's Alpha Defence also brought up to critical alert status within the hour. Callum?'

'Yes?' He so nearly added: ma'am.

'I'd like you to represent the Senior Council at Alpha Defence, please. Make sure they understand just how serious this is for everyone. We can't afford reticence.'

'Of course.' As Callum said it, Apollo was splashing a message from Eldlund across his tarsus lens. **I want to help**. He looked over at his assistant, seeing the silent desperation behind the young omnia's handsome face. 'I'll take Eldlund with me.'

That didn't even merit an answer from Emilja; she just nodded in a distracted fashion.

'Danuta,' Ainsley said. 'You go with Callum. Help apply some family weight on Alpha Defence.'

She nodded crisply. 'Yes, Grandfather.'

Callum refrained from comment. With Loi accompanying Yuri, and now Danuta assigned to him, the old man was using family to oversee everything. *Politics or paranoia?*

'And me?' Jessika asked. 'What about me?'

'What about you?' Ainsley said.

'At the very least I can advise.'

'Once – *if* – this happens, then your continued contribution to our assessment will be welcomed,' Emilja said.

'I understand. I'd like to remain here and wait for Soćko to recover.'

'You think he will?'

Jessika smiled slyly. 'We're quite resilient; he'll recover. I hope in the next couple of hours.'

'Very well.' Emilja stared at Tral. 'Escort her to the medical facility, but be ready to bring her back up here.'

'Yes, ma'am.'

'I'll go with her as well,' Kandara said. 'Just in case.'

'If that makes you happy and relaxed,' Jessika said.

'My dear, no one is ever going to be relaxed around you again.'

Callum stood up and exchanged a glance with Alik, who was also getting to his feet. Weirdly, he felt a surge of optimism, which he didn't think was entirely down to the nark. 'I hope you're persuasive when you put the case to Earth.'

'You believe her, then?' Alik jerked an accusing thumb at Jessika, who was staring at him with interest.

'Until something better comes along, sure thing.'

London

26th June 2204

A night of exuberant clubbing followed by plenty of sex he'd fuelled with doses of zero-nark left Ollie's drained body sleeping well past midday. He would have carried on sleeping longer but for the insistent piccolo tone Tye started firing into his audio peripheral. It woke him with a sharpness that was high on the bitter resentment scale.

'What?' He kept his eyes screwed shut, preventing the tarsus lens from activating. The last thing he needed right now was bright neon graphics shining directly into his optic nerves.

'There's a problem in the kitchen. A pan of callaloo is boiling over. Your grandmother is in her room and she is not responding to any alerts from the house network.'

'Oh, crap.' He groaned, and blinked, which switched on the lens. 'Show me.'

The image Tye splashed came from a servez drone in the tiny kitchen downstairs. Callaloo was one of his grandmother's favourite dishes, though Ollie couldn't stand it. She'd been boiling the leaves in coconut milk before adding the printed lobster meat waiting on the oak chopping block. The gooey mess in the pot had boiled up like a primary school's snazzy volcano science experiment gone wrong, foaming over the rim and flowing across the induction hob's glossy black surface, where it was solidifying rapidly. Thin vapour layered the air above.

'Bollocks!'

The hob should have shut down immediately, but its ancient sensors were shot. And the even older household Turing was only a G5, not up to real decision-making, especially when a human had put the pan on in the first place.

'Switch the hob off, and clean up all spillage,' he ordered.

'What about the food that was being cooked?' Tye asked.

'It's no good now. Dump it.'

The image juddered as the servez rolled forwards. It was an old Yanasi model, for which Tronde had printed new components while Ollie himself had tweaked the software, improving the feedback sensitivity of its manipulator arms. He watched as the pan was taken to the sink. Tye got the household Turing to switch on the waste disposal, and the blades started chewing down the ruined meal. A second servez began to clean the sticky mess off the hob.

'Is Grandma all right?' Ollie asked.

'Her medical feeds indicate she is awake and retains full physical capacity,' Tye told him. 'She is accessing the *Brisbane Bay* soap drama.'

'Right.'

Brisbane Bay was one of several soaps that Grandma followed with religious devotion. Ollie relaxed his muscles as gloom closed in on him like a winter fog. He knew the exact conversation that waited for him when he got up – again.

When he turned his head he was looking directly into Lolo's sleeping face. Sie was gorgeous. He'd never admit it to anyone in the Legion, but yes, sie did look a lot like Sumiko. At night, hitting the clubs and bars together, everyone would look at hir with secret envy and Ollie relished their longing. Seeing him with Lolo, they knew he was a playa. Sie was also randy the whole time, almost as much as him, and when it came to fucking, that agile omnia body offered a great many erotic permutations. It would all be perfect if sie would just bloody stop talking about romance and where their relationship was going. Actually, if sie just stopped talking . . .

Lolo woke, smiling as sie saw Ollie studying hir. The happiness faded. 'What's wrong?'

That voice, sultry and concerned, was like a vocal caress along his thighs. Sure enough, when Ollie glanced down – smug that he didn't need artificial help the way Tronde did – his morning erection was straining away urgently. 'Nothing.'

'There is. I can tell. You're upset.'

'Maybe.' Ollie wormed his hand between their bodies, groping a pair of Sol-class tits before sliding fingers down those long flat abs to find the stiff shaft.

'Is this your answer to everything?' Lolo's protest sounded very half-hearted.

'You know it is.' He tightened his grip. 'And *this* means you're the same. What was it you called it? Body-honesty?'

'You're lucky I'm male-cycling.'

'Huh?'

'I can't get hard if I'm in my female cycle.'

'Really?' That surprised Ollie; he'd assumed sie was in hir female cycle, what with all the endless talk about feelings and crap like that. His fingers probed eagerly below hir balls, slipping into the folds of skin concealing hir clitoris. He laughed at the abrupt shudder of joy his brashness kindled in hir. 'Turned on is turned on.'

'Ollie, please, you can't just . . .'

His other hand stroked hir face, shushing hir as he marvelled at the silky-smooth skin. No girl he'd ever been with had skin that smooth. Tronde had once viciously claimed Utopials were trying to become elves. *He may have had a point.* The faerie were reputed to have a prodigious sensual appetite.

'I need this,' he said, and started kissing hir. It was manipulative, but he didn't care. Sex was a great way to ignore problems, and no way was he going to confide in Lolo. The last thing he wanted was earnest questions and sincere sympathy for his family situation. 'Hey, I think I have a pad left.'

Lolo hesitated, hanging in the emptiness between shame and craving. 'That isn't why I'm with you.'

'I know.' Ollie fumbled around on the floor, pulling at the puddle of creases below the bed that were his precious purple trousers. He held up the remaining white hemisphere, enjoying the now sombre expression before him – so very like Sumiko going into combat. Laughing, he pushed the pad down onto Lolo's dick.

'You beast,' Lolo exclaimed as Ollie triggered it. But hir eyes were already watering as the zero-nark invaded hir erectile tissue. 'That's not fair.'

Smirking, Ollie told Tye to restart his sex playlist they'd been listening to last night. Sumiko's husky voice oozed out of the bedroom's pillar speakers, singing a power ballad from a couple of years back. 'I love this one.'

Lolo giggled, a long dirty admission of capitulation. Sie let Ollie's hand steer hir head down his torso, skilful mouth nibbling and licking lovingly as sie went. Ollie lay back as the oral foreplay began, all thoughts of his demanding family scattering from the bright pleasure heating his blood.

*

At least the shower worked properly. So many things in the ancient little house on Copeland Road rattled along on the edge of functionality. Ollie let the hot jets sluice over him and rubbed a handful of lavender-scented shampoo into his hair. Then conditioner. Always two conditioner applications. He never understood why so many of his friends didn't bother with conditioner. It was the key to making hair look great.

He spent nearly twenty minutes in front of the mirror, first using a blow-dryer on his hair then carefully teasing in the oil and shaping the buoyant quiff into curving wings that came down over his ears. The red tint in his tips was still vivid, enhancing the look. Playa!

Peering closely at his own image, he checked the forehead. Everything all right there for sure. He was way too young to have a receding hairline. That was just silly paranoia triggered by Bik's taunts.

Clean, wearing a fresh T-shirt and expensive real-cotton jeans, hair flawless, he was ready to face the world, Lolo, his family –

Lolo was skulking in the bedroom, always on edge at the possibility of having to interact with an old-Earth-style family – especially this one. Utopial group families were so much easier, sie'd explained at boring length one night. Less expectation and criticism, more belief and encouragement. That constant stream of implied superiority always irritated Ollie.

'I'll see you tonight,' Ollie said by way of greeting.

Lolo's grouch deepened. 'You just want me to go away now that you've fucked me.'

Yes. 'No. I've got stuff to do, that's all. Boring stuff.'

'I can help.'

'Lolo, seriously, you don't belong in that part of my world, okay?'

'Are you going to steal something?'

'Oh, bollocks.' Hands on hips. Angry at himself for the stereotype posture, but mostly angry at hir. 'Why are you always so difficult?'

Lolo came over to him, arms going around his shoulders in a needy hug. 'I'm not being difficult, I just don't want to see you hurt or arrested . . . or worse. You mean everything to me, you know that. Those Legion people you hang out with are dangerous.'

Ollie looked up at the not-Sumiko face above his head. 'They're not dangerous to me. I grew up with them; they're my friends.'

'You need new friends.'

'Not now I don't. We're about to make us some serious money.'

Lolo hugged him tighter. 'You've been saying that for two months now. Just . . . be careful.'

'Sure. I'll call you when I'm ready. We can go out clubbing again.'

'You only want to go clubbing so you can check out the hot flesh.'

'For fuck's sake, listen to yourself some time!'

'It's true,' Lolo wailed.

How can sie possibly be in a male cycle? 'No, it's not. Look, just go, will you? I'm on the clock, here.'

Lolo hung hir head. Eyes watered again: nothing to do with zero-nark this time. 'You're angry. And I know you're upset about something. I won't ask you what's wrong, I swear, but promise me you'll call.'

'Sure.' *The next blue moon in a month that has a Z in it.*

'Okay then.' A tentative smile. A last hug. And sie was making hir way downstairs, hunched over so sie didn't bang hir head on the ceiling.

'Holy shit,' Ollie muttered as the front door shut behind hir. It really was tempting to end it right there and then, be done with the constant drama. But for all hir neuroses and neediness, Lolo was impressively hot and dirty in bed.

He sighed, checked that his munificent hair hadn't been ruffled by those stupid hugs, and went into his grandma's room.

Centuries ago, back when the house was built, there were no hologram screens bigger than the internal walls, let alone fully interactive stages. The house needed to adapt to belong in the modern world. Ollie had installed the projectors and sensors as best he could, turning half of the room into an interactive suite. But the stage area still looked like a ghost cube was squatting on the threadbare carpet, with the window shining through it.

Sure enough, Gran was sitting in the big armchair he'd got her a year back, just on the edge of the sparkling laserlight. She never used the interaction function, but did set the stage projectors at high resolution so the soaps played out before her, banishing the real world. Ollie scrutinized her for a moment. She'd put on weight this year – not that she was eating more, but she hardly ever ventured out of the house now. That lack of exercise was starting to trouble him.

Eighteen months ago, his grandma's spinal osteoarthritis had progressed so far that she could barely move for the constant pain. It'd taken all the money Ollie had and then some, but he paid for Kcell treatments to the facet joints in her lower back where the cartilage had worn away. The operation was performed in a decent clinic, too, one over in Richmond. The alien replacement cells had worked perfectly, and the painful inflammations had subsided. But now she was becoming forgetful, and she was a lot quieter, too – nothing like the outgoing ever-cheery woman who had brought him and Bik up by herself after their mother had walked out.

'Hi, Gran. How you doin'?'

She happily presented her cheek for a kiss. 'My boy, are you all right?'

'Sure.'

'I thought I heard you arguing with your new girlfriend, the tall one.'

'No. We're fine.' Trying to correct Gran about Lolo's gender was a universe of complications he wasn't yet ready to venture into.

'Good. I like her. She's very pretty.'

Ollie prayed he wasn't blushing. 'Yeah. She's great.'

'But never marry someone that nags and complains the whole time. It wrecks everything.'

'Yes, Gran.'

She chuckled. 'Oh, I know you don't listen to me, my boy, but I'm right about that.'

'I know you are.'

'And don't wait too long before you settle down, either. I've told you that before, haven't I? I should have had children much earlier, and so should your mother.'

He squatted down beside the chair, studying her tired eyes. 'Gran, did you start cooking some callaloo for lunch?'

She frowned. 'Goodness, is it lunchtime already?'

'It's three o'clock.'

'I must stop watching all these soaps. They're fun, but they do steal so much time away.'

'Yeah, but you like them really, so go for it.' Ollie smiled up at her, trying to bridge the gap between the passive old woman before him and that tough, determined person who had taught him how to code when he was barely a teenager, showing him routes onto the lownet. Maybe the change had come during his brief time at university – before he was thrown out for using the campus network to probe the defences around finance houses.

'I'll go and put some callaloo on right now,' she said. 'You must be starving, poor thing.'

Ollie checked with Tye. The servez had finished clearing up the mess in the kitchen, and the utensils were all in the dishwasher, which was vibrating through its heavy-soil cycle. Inventory check:

they didn't even have printed food left in the fridge, never mind any of the natural vegetables Gran preferred. She'd forgotten to buy anything fresh. 'I'll get us a deliverez from Bembé's. You like their chicken roti.'

'Oh, no, dear. They're so expensive. Don't waste your money.'

'S'okay. I'm flush right now, Gran.' More lies. He'd taken a loan from Jade (which the rest of the Legion didn't know about) to help pay for her osteoarthritis treatments, which he was still paying off. Money which cut deep into every take from the jobs which Jade bestowed – and how bitter was that irony? But that was not a debt on which you ever missed a payment, not ever. Jade had been very clear about that. She'd even played at being reluctant to arrange it for him, which gave him a scary notion of the kind of people whom he now owed. It meant he could barely afford to go clubbing any more. But all it would take was that one big job Jade kept promising, then his dreams would be back on track. The new house, somewhere nice, which meant a long way away from Copeland Road. Somewhere good for his grandma and Bik.

He knew exactly what that would be; its image glowed like a jewel at the centre of his brain, and Tye had permanent monitors scanning the estate agents for it. A place next to the sea, maybe some rugged Mediterranean coast (but always with a beach), a slick clean white cubist house which was mostly glass, with marble floors and staircases, and one of those swimming pools with the edge that meshed with the horizon. It would be in a town which didn't have sink estates and gang kids hanging on streets. Grandma could sit out in the sun, which would be good for her, then in the afternoon she'd walk into town to meet up with a bunch of nice friends. Bik would go to the local college, a decent one – one where pupils wore a smart uniform with a blazer – maybe get himself on a sports team. A real sport, not bloody parkour. Then, when his little brother got motivated and grew the right attitude, university. It didn't have to be Ivy League, but one where graduates could walk into any corporate job, or even be welcomed by a habitat or on a terraformed world. Then with family sorted, Ollie would open a club overlooking the beach – a fantastic club, where all the hot people came to party at night.

It would happen. He just needed to buy them out of Copeland Road. One big job . . .

He left Gran in her room and stood on the top of the stairs, trying to breathe against the rising anger. He hadn't done it. *Again*. The test was simple enough. One drop of blood, a pinprick Gran wouldn't even feel. The nanopore chip would read her ApoE structure. He'd know within a couple of minutes if she really did have early-onset Alzheimer's.

It was treatable, that was the good news. Everything was treatable these days. But the London Civic Health Agency only covered residents for emergency accidents and basic medicine. Anything serious and you had to have insurance. Gran didn't have any. Her coverage had ended ten years ago when her employer, a council finance agency, made her whole department redundant. The G8Turings that were coming on line turned out to be cheaper and more efficient than an office of humans.

And the new generation of customized biotech glands which secreted anti-Alzheimer's drugs into the patient were ball-bustingly expensive. Enough so that Ollie couldn't raise it – at least, not while he was still running his current debt. Jade had made that very clear when he'd asked her. So confirming his suspicions about Gran would be utterly pointless. There was nothing he could do to help her at the moment, other than make her as cosy as possible.

He told Tye to order up the food. Bembé's promised it would be there within twenty minutes.

Bik was in the cramped downstairs lounge, his back to Ollie, stuffing something into a small backpack.

'What's up?' Ollie asked.

Bik was good, Ollie had to admit that. Didn't give a guilty flinch or stop what he was doing, just finished tightening the pack's straps. Then straightened up and turned around to smile at his big brother. 'Goin' out with the équipe, man.'

Ollie stared down at the kid, trying to keep it together. Sure they were half-brothers, but there were times when even he didn't think that was possible, they were so opposite. Bik was small: twelve years old and only about one-thirty centimetres tall – and skinny with it. His skin was so much darker than Ollie's paler North African tone. There was a vague memory in Ollie's head of Bik's father, who had the same deep ebony shade – a man who'd only featured in their lives for about six months. But where that man had a bald head with glowing magenta tattoos, Bik had a huge aurora of wild black hair that flopped about with every motion. People said it made him the cutest kid on the street. All that meant was he could get away with a whole load of crap others couldn't.

'Where?' Ollie asked, but he knew. With Bik, he always knew.

'Dulwich Park.'

'Just—'

'Yeah, yeah. I'll be *careful*. Cos that's how you really practise the art.'

'Fuck's sake,' Ollie hissed in exasperation. Bik lived for parkour. He was solid with a whole équipe of local kids who swarmed the area's dilapidated buildings, performing extreme tumbles, flips, rolls and somersaults as they careered around walls and rooftops. Now they'd added parkour in the trees to their catalogue of crazy. Humanutang, the équipe called it. Their heroes were orang-utans, and some of the serious stars of the variant were body modifying towards that simian ideal.

Two months ago, when Bik was zipping between branches, he'd missed his hold and fallen five metres. At least his fractured arm had qualified for immediate London Civic Health Agency treatment, and the sheath of Kcells they wrapped around his humerus had knitted the bone back together quickly, leaving it at least as strong as before.

The Health Agency hadn't cured his dumbarse brain, though. To Ollie's dismay, nothing could stop Bik re-joining his équipe and leaping through the huge old London plane trees which now dominated the city's roads. It was the reason the area's older kids had started to use the équipe for deliveries. Never anything major yet, just small packets of nark travelling down a route no drone could follow.

'Only the park,' Ollie insisted.

'Yeah, *Mum*. It's practice, innit?'

Then what do you need the backpack for? But Ollie didn't ask. He wanted to believe – very badly – that Bik really was just heading out for fun and thrills with the équipe, that the humanutang kids would spend the evening swooping around the park in a glorious gymnastic exhibition that made everyone else smile and point in delight. Same as he wanted to know Gran's ApoE composition. *Why am I so scared the whole time? I run with the Legion, for fuck's sake.*

'You done your schoolwork?'

'Piss off.'

'Hey! I'm serious, okay? You need to do that crap. It's the only way out of here.'

'That's bollocks. You did it. You went to university. You're still here, though, int'cha?'

'Because I screwed up, okay? Happy?'

Bik's expression went blank; he hadn't been expecting raw honesty. 'No way, you ain't a screw-up. You run with the Legion.'

'That's not how you measure it, Bik. Come on, you're smart. You've got to be ready for when we get out of here. You've got to have decent coursework scores.'

'I don't want to leave. That's all you, innit?'

'You think this is a good place for Gran? Wake up and take a good look at her.'

'That ain't fair. I don't want to split from me équipe is what. You can take Gran out. I'll be okay here; there's so many trees. They're taking back the streets, ain't they? Did you know, this whole area used to be a forest before it was a city? It's true history, see.'

'We're a family. We watch out for each other, and we go together.'

'This is your house-by-the-sea kick, innit?'

'You seriously want to stay in this hovel all your life?'

'What's an 'ovel?'

'Hovel. H! Access a dictionary for once. Fuck!'

'Oh fuck off!'

'Bik, it's coming, okay? I'm going to get us out of here. We're going somewhere decent where you haven't got to make drops for bad boys. Be ready for that, you grab? There'll be trees where we're going, I promise. Better than any growing here.'

Bik did a perfect teenage shrug of indifference. 'Whatever.'

Piotr's icon flashed up in Ollie's tarsus lens. He let the call through.

'You need to get your arse down here,' Piotr said.

'What?'

'Jade's here. This is it.'

'What is?'

'The *one*, dumbarse!'

Ollie shook his head as he realized what Piotr was talking about. 'You're fucking kidding me!'

'No. And Ollie, it's a short timetable.'

'Crap. Okay, I'm on my way.'

'Ten minutes, max.'

'Got it.' He cancelled the connection.

'What's up?' Bik asked.

'I've got to go out. There's a deliverez coming in fifteen minutes. Make sure Gran eats the meal, okay? That's important.'

'Sure. Is it pizza?'

'No. Chicken roti.'

'Oh, Ollie! I hate that stuff, man. Why didn't you order pizza like a real person?'

'Yeah? Real sorry about that, princess. Think on this: after we leave, you'll be able to eat whatever you like.'

Bik tipped his head to one side, hair shifting in a galactic swirl. 'Yeah, right.'

*

Ollie used his boardez to slice over to Consort Road, the quickest way from his house. He arrived at the crumbling railway viaduct at the same time as Gareth, who turned up in a two-seat cabez. Ollie pushed the gate open as the cabez trundled away down the road, eyed belligerently by a group of kids. Younger than Bik, Ollie thought. At least they weren't hanging from the overgrown trees.

'That is some weird shit going down,' Gareth said.

'Huh?'

'On solnet. All the news streams are carrying it. The allcomments are going apeshit.'

'What?'

'Haven't you accessed?'

'I've been busy.'

Gareth smirked. 'Sure.' He did a mock glance behind Ollie. 'How's Lolo?'

'Fuck you. What's happening?'

'Twenty-four cities have powered up their shields,' Tye answered.

Ollie paused on the threshold of the muddy yard, regarding the news stream images Tye was now splashing. Daytime cities saw blocks of skyscrapers immersed in an umbra from an invisible eclipse, the sky dimmed to a pallid gentian blue. Across Earth's night-time, the stars had vanished from the sky, leaving city grids glimmering brightly underneath an eerie emptiness. 'What the fuck?' He couldn't help but glance up. The azure sky above London was starting to drift into twilight. It all looked perfectly normal.

'Dunno,' Gareth said cheerfully. 'The government say it's a global exercise, nothing to worry about. So that's fucking scary. Allcomments are saying it's either a dinosaur-killer rock that no one saw—'

'We know all the asteroid orbits,' Ollie said in immediate exasperation.

'So? This one could be interstellar, coming in at ninety degrees to the ecliptic.'

'Really? Is that possible?'

'Anything's possible. Other thing allcomments is banging on about is an invasion.'

'A what?'

'The Olyix are invading.'

'Bollocks.'

Gareth laughed. 'Right.'

'It'll be a scam,' Ollie decided. 'A Wall Street scam. That many shields use a shitload of power. The solarwell companies can jack up prices. Boards and bankers walk away with a billion-wattdollar bonus.'

'Makes sense.'

The rest of the Legion were already in the old metal container, all smiling tightly, nerves visible in tics and taut muscles. Their excitement hit Ollie like a slap of pheromones, heightening his expectation.

'What's going down?' he asked.

Piotr gestured at Jade Urchall. Ollie hadn't seen her when they came in. Now she was suddenly a dominant figure, commanding attention.

'Your trip to Klausen really impressed my friends,' she said. 'We'd like you to visit the Croydon power grid relay station and disable it for us. Cut off all the power; shut down the whole district it supplies.'

'Yes!' Ollie hissed, hands clenching into hot fists. This was it, the big job Jade had been dangling before them for months. And the money she'd talked about would clear his debt. His clifftop home was so close now he could smell the saltwater.

'I want you to hit it in two hours.'

Ollie blinked. 'What? You've gotta be shitting—'

'We can do that,' Piotr said, giving Ollie a warning look. 'But it will cost extra.'

'Piotr,' Jade mocked, 'are you trying to negotiate? With me? Are you sure that's the right thing to be doing?'

'You have to admit, this is sudden. And unexpected.'

'Unexpected? So you aren't prepared?'

'Oh, we're prepared,' Ollie blurted. 'Are we ever!' He'd been studying the plans of the relay station ever since Jade had mentioned the place, doing his thing; running through angles of attack, coming up with a bunch of ideas, dismissing some, refining others. Tye didn't even need to splash the layout, he was so familiar with it.

'No, actually, we're not,' Tronde said.

'Hey!' Ollie shot back. 'We can do this. I got it all worked out.'

'Sure we *can* do it,' Tronde admitted, 'when we have all the systems we need for Ollie's plan. I haven't printed everything yet. And we don't have any explosives; storing them here is way too risky.'

'Anything extra you require will be delivered,' Jade said. 'Give me a list.'

'That sounds like desperation,' Piotr said.

'It's all down to timing,' Jade said. 'Unfortunately, some factors came together earlier than we expected, but this job never had a fixed moment. That's why I've had you working out how to handle it.'

'What factors?' Adnan asked.

'Someone has been preparing to use the Commercial and Government Services hub on Purley Way in Croydon,' she said. 'Every non-portal function in the hub is supplied with power by the relay station. If that power goes off, the hub will essentially be unusable for a while. The goods which are going to be routed through the hub tonight are vital to several companies. Delays make them vulnerable to certain market forces. That's all I can say.'

'That can't be right,' Gareth said. 'There's a dozen C&G hubs around Croydon that companies can use.'

Jade shrugged and smiled slyly. 'That depends on the value of the items you're transporting, and the pre-approved security route.'

'But—'

Piotr's hand rose up, shushing him. 'It's still going to be expensive.'

'We have a small contingency fund,' Jade said, 'but I'd urge you not to be greedy. We'd like to continue this relationship after tonight.'

'Fifteen per cent.'

'Four.'

'We'll argue for a while so no one loses face, and agree on ten.'

'Nine,' Jade said.

'Deal.'

It was all Ollie could do not to punch the air in victory.

Vayan

Year 54 AB (After Bioforming)

I watch.

I process therefore I am.

I have no designation. I may name myself if the correct events occur and I upgrade.

For now I am the watcher.

My current form is my eighth level.

The first six levels of my activation facilitated my interstellar flight: acceleration, astrogation, deceleration.

I arrived at this G9 star one thousand, five hundred and sixty seven (Earth) years ago.

Upon arrival I went into a high polar orbit around the star's main gas giant planet.

I activated level seven, disbursing a shower of perception fronds which then ride the solar wind, out towards the stars. Their infinitesimal omnipresence allows me to observe local space far beyond the cometary belt.

Fifty-seven years ago I detected a ship decelerating out of interstellar space.

The starship contained no sentient biological entities.

I determined the starship was of human origin.

The starship contained von Neumann systems which multiplied exponentially, then bioformed the planet.

I determined it was a human trap to attract the Olyix.

Five years ago another starship arrived.

It is called: *Morgan*.

There are binary and omnia humans on board.

I now detect a small mass decelerating towards the bioformed world.

The mass has sophisticated shielding. I did not detect it approaching the star system.

I activate level eight.

A new type of perception fronds are released.

They are still minute, a chain of molecules. But longer than before. My risk of detection is correspondingly higher.

I determine the new arrival is a Neána insertion ship.

It is not hostile.

I watch six Neána metavayans land on the bioformed world.

A human greets them.

I watch.

I wait.

It is what I do – until *they* come.

They will.

*

The urban citadel was called Igsabul, nestling on the confluence ridge where two wide rivers flowed into one. In a history that never existed it was born a port and trading centre, swelling over the centuries as the trader clans expanded their reach. Territorial wars were fought with neighbouring citadel-states, with Igsabul always victorious, until its domain became an empire which dominated half a continent. Increasing wealth and technological progress saw skyscrapers rising above the elegant buildings of earlier times. Cool blue-green strands of light wove out of the citadel to web the rugged countryside as the transport rails linked up with other citadels. While down on the coast, rocketships rose on intense spears of chemical flame.

Dellian directed the small plane to fly a tight curve around Igsabul's central buildings so their passenger had a clear view of the towers. Outwardly, the plane was the same technology level as late twentieth-century Earth, with afterburning turbojets and a lean delta planform allowing it to reach Mach three point five. Authenticity was the mantra of the lure. However, no twentieth-century plane ever had a fuselage that was half-transparent, made from a crystal that could only be produced in a molecular extruder. Nor was any autopilot ever as sophisticated as the genten which controlled the flight systems. There weren't even any manual controls, which put Dellian in mind of the flyers back on his home-world, Juloss.

'Quite something, isn't it?' he said. The translator wand produced a flurry of high-pitched pulses, like speeded-up birdsong.

Fintox, one of the male metavayan Neána, was sitting on a mushroom-shaped chair halfway along the fuselage, next to Yirella. He whistled out a fast response. 'It looks substantial.'

'It is,' Yirella assured him. 'But the buildings have no internal structure; there are no rooms or corridors. They're hollow shells with a heated structure to fool thermal scanners, and the windows all have lights shining out. It appears completely real from a distance.'

'Our insertion ship certainly believed it to be.'

'All the world's a stage,' Dellian said.

Yirella smiled at him, and sent: **Nice quote**, to his optik.

These days he didn't put up any resistance when it was her turn to choose a drama for them to access together in the evening. And in return she didn't push high culture on him every time – just as he didn't insist on only pulling historical action adventures out of the *Morgan*'s archives. He'd surprised himself by the way he actually quite enjoyed Earth-set rom-coms. False nostalgia, she called it, the warm soothing glow of an unreal past.

'I can see vehicles moving down there,' Fintox said.

'Yeah. They just drive around and around on long circuits. That way, any Olyix sensor satellite will see purpose. Same as the Vayans walking around down there on the ground – though we don't think a flyby probe will have the resolution to make out individuals. But we don't want to take the chance. After all the effort we've put in to Vayan, it would be a killer for it to fall down because we couldn't be arsed to make that final detail.'

Fintox's long neck twisted his head around so all eight eyes were focused on Yirella. 'You have initiated a population of biologic Vayans, like us?'

'No. These are androids. Biomechanical bodies, whose technology is several levels below Neána biologics. They walk around in large numbers during the day, and smaller numbers at night.'

'How many urban citadels have you built on Vayan?' Fintox returned his gaze to the sprawl beyond the curving fuselage.

'Twenty-three thousand. But they're not all the same size as Igsabul. There are also vast areas under cultivation in the countryside. Then we have thousands of ships at sea, and aircraft flying about.'

'All spewing out hydrocarbon combustion pollution like this one,' Dellian added.

'We even discharge "waste" into the seas,' Yirella said. 'There are toxic blooms around the coast that sensors could pick up if they look for them.'

'This is an effort beyond anything I have a memory of,' Fintox said. 'And the data our insertion ship provided us with are considerable.'

'That's the whole idea. Who would ever fake an entire civilization? It has to be real. Right?'

'It would appear to be as you say.'

Dellian suppressed a second smile. Diplomacy was clearly another trait the metavayan had been given by the insertion ship. He told the plane to change course, turning so they headed for one of the largest buildings. It was a fluted pentagonal skyscraper with flat concrete landing pads extending from the top quarter, as if it was sprouting chubby leaves. The plane produced metallic clunking sounds as it deployed its VTOL jet nozzles and their auxiliary turbines spun up loudly. *You could take some details too far*, he thought.

They landed in the centre of a pad, and a 'crew' of Vayans came scurrying out to refuel the plane. The door swung open and Yirella had to bend almost double to get through it. Fintox followed her out. When Dellian emerged, he was startled by how strong the wind was – a sensation not helped by the lack of any safety railing around the pad. The noise of traffic from the streets below was a constant background thrum, and the air smelt weird, as if there'd been a big chemical spillage nearby.

'There are significant amounts of combustion pollutants in the air,' Fintox said.

'Mainly yes,' Yirella said. 'But the bioforming was necessarily rushed. Our algeox pushed oxygen into the atmosphere so it would support carbon-based biology, but scrubbing out the trace chemicals is proving more difficult. We decided just to leave those elements in. In any case, we didn't want to resemble Earth too closely.'

Fintox was moving his head from side to side, viewing the jagged citadel skyline. 'Did you design the planet's vegetation as well as the Vayans?'

'Not so much. The plants are all terrestrial. We tweaked them slightly, so the leaf shapes are different. But it was considered that actually growing Vayan plants with a distinctive genetic structure was finally taking things too far. Our hope is that Vayan will be convincing enough to draw the Olyix here. They won't actually land and take plant samples before their arkship appears.'

'I understand.'

Dellian thought he did well not to roll his eyes.

'What?' Yirella challenged quietly, as Fintox continued to study the chaotic sprawl of buildings around them.

'Nothing.'

'Don't give me that.'

He sighed. 'Fifty years of radio broadcasts, and still no sign of the Olyix.'

'You're so impatient.'

'There must be some kind of Olyix sensor station within fifty lightyears.'

She quickly glanced at Fintox, then bent down and kissed Dellian on the top of his head. 'They're on their way. Okay?'

'They'd better be. We don't want another false hope like the Neána.'

'Saints, Del, I'd hardly call the Neána arrival a false hope. Is that what the squads are saying?'

'Detecting the insertion ship got people excited. You know that.'

Her lips compressed into disapproval.

The three of them made their way into the skyscraper through an archway and onto a narrow walkway that Dellian could see ringing the hollow interior. The slim metal grid he stood on brought a sensation of vertigo greater than on the pad outside. Fortunately, as it was designed for humans, it had a handrail, which he gripped tightly. The space inside wasn't entirely empty; a surprisingly sparse honeycomb skeleton of bonded carbon struts supported the entire structure. It meshed with three gantry towers running up the length of the skyscraper, each with a couple of magtracks to carry cage lifts. He eyed them with distaste. Lifts were ancient history, and the only reason he even recognized them was their constant appearance in combat-training simulations. The instructors assumed Olyix structures would be filled with them. Yirella had told him once it was because the *Salvation of Life* had used them extensively.

'Are these things safe?' he muttered as the cage door rattled open. His databud was unfurling statistics graphics across his optik, all reassuring figures and graphs of the lift's safety margins. But it still didn't *feel* safe.

Yirella gave him a puzzled glance as she politely gestured for Fintox to enter. The lift descended quickly and they went out onto the streets of Igsabul.

Instinct stirred Dellian's blood as the *otherness* of this place crowded in on him. Nonhuman creatures ambling along, their four legs rocking the rounded body, while eight arms mostly dangled like thick ropes. The skyscraper architecture was chunky – primal-level wrong. His eyes were irritated by a glow on the edge of ultraviolet emitted by the rails cutting down the centre of the road. Crude ground vehicles belched out thick streamers of diesel fumes as they sped past.

'Damn, it's good,' he said. It was utterly convincing. And alien was what he lived to fight.

Fintox focused on him. 'Have you not seen this before?'

'I've seen recordings of the citadels, sure. But I've never been here in the flesh. We try and keep human activity on Vayan to an absolute minimum.' Now he thought about it, he hadn't set foot on a planet since they left Juloss. His gaze shifted to the open sky above. It made him feel vulnerable – anything could fall out of it.

'In my opinion, taking authenticity to this degree is an unwelcome aspect of our paranoia,' Yirella said. 'Frankly, if some stealthed Olyix spy satellite can see me and Dellian walking around down here, then we've lost anyway. But that level of mistrust is what being chased across the galaxy will do to a species.'

'It does appear to me that this citadel is a forgery,' Fintox said. 'Do you mind if we walk for a while?'

'Not at all,' Dellian said. 'This trip is all about proving our purpose to you. Take as long as you like. Go where you want.' His databud was running a fringe display in his optik, showing the other metavayans being escorted around different citadels. The six of them had been impressively calm since they arrived, but certainly wouldn't commit themselves to helping the *Morgan* and its mission without verifying the lure. He could hardly blame them for that. Just looking around at Igsabul in all its enormous solidity made it difficult to accept it was all fake, the galaxy's greatest drama show. And he knew it was phoney; he'd seen the project's early design concepts back on Juloss, listened for hours to Yirella happily explaining away some quirky aspect of Vayan culture she'd dreamed up. But to actually go ahead and manufacture a whole fake civilization . . . Since the Neána had turned up, he'd started to wonder if perhaps humans weren't coming across just as fanatical as the Olyix. *What else could we build if we were free?*

They came to a junction of seven roads and waited for Fintox to choose one. The metavayan set off down the third street, pausing for the traffic to stop at a crossing point. Dellian grinned privately at that; the autodrives would have braked the vehicles even if they'd run out right in front of one. So maybe Fintox was subconsciously adapting to the charade. *Do metavayans have a subconscious?*

Yirella was in full tour-guide mode, chattering away about aspects of the citadel, its social composition and architecture. 'Each building has its own radio station,' she was saying. 'We skewed their clan society to demonstrate a partisan pride. That way, each clan broadcasts its own news and information constantly, because only it speaks the real truth.'

'She's being modest,' Dellian said. 'Every clan having its own radio station was her idea.'

'I was being practical. It supplies a valid cultural reason for so many radio stations, which make Vayan easier to detect across interstellar distance. This world shines in the electromagnetic spectrum.'

'Indeed it does,' Fintox said. 'I listened to many clan broadcasts while I was being created.'

'If you don't mind me asking, did you like Vayan music?'

'Some of it, yes. Why do you ask this question? Is it important?'

'Not important. But interesting – especially to me, from an anthropological point of view.'

'How so?'

'Because it's not real. The "music" – along with all Vayan art – is an artificial construct, a fiction. It was extrapolated by gentens once we fed the original parameters in. Then after the basics were established – the guidelines for what our Vayans would like and dislike – the gentens kept composing new tunes. But you see, the only people who would enjoy such a thing are Vayans, yet they don't exist. Rather, they didn't until you were created. Your mind was formatted by the insertion ship to appreciate the music, because that's what the ship truly believed a Vayan mind would enjoy. While, in actual fact, it has no realistic basis, because there is no Vayan culture – nor are there any real Vayans.' She gestured at the android bodies walking past.

'There are now,' Fintox said. 'We six are real Vayans.'

'Just as the metahuman Neána were real humans,' Dellian said.

'But you won't reproduce,' Yirella said. 'I mean, will you?'

'No.'

'So you're the first and last of your species. I don't know if that makes me sad or not.'

'If you wish there to be Vayans, you can create them yourself, for real. Molecular initiators can create biologically perfect Vayan bodies. We are proof they function. Humans are good concept designers.'

Yirella gave the alien a troubled look. 'We can't. Not with the threat of the Olyix hanging over the galaxy.'

'We're not gods,' Dellian chided. 'Even without the Olyix, we wouldn't do things like that.'

'Wouldn't we?' she asked.

He held her gaze. Sometimes their conversations were little more than good-natured arguments. It was one of the great things about being with Yirella, that she had different views on so many things. There were times when he thought it was like looking into his own future; so much of what she said he eventually came around to agreeing with – even her fury at being born for war, at having no choice. He still wanted the fight, but these days he could certainly appreciate the immorality which arose from that lack of choice. It just didn't bother him as much as it did her. He supposed that was because he believed in the coming war, and that afterwards they'd either be dead or free to live however they wanted. She called that fatalism – when she was being kind.

*

The supersonic jet took them back to Timsal, a small citadel in the mountains on the edge of Igstabul's domain, which in reality was the continent's operations centre for the lure, its gentens coordinating the activities of every citadel and farm.

It was raining as they landed on the flattened apex of a hemispherical building: a heavy downpour that produced wide grubby rivulets sliding over the structure's curving sides, enriching the algae slicks. The pad retracted down to the hangar level where they disembarked.

'Would you like to see more citadels?' Yirella asked. 'Or some farm estates? We'd have to take ground transport to them, I'm afraid. In terms of Vayan economics, they don't really qualify for visits from passenger jets.'

Dellian silently shook his head at that. Before today he hadn't really appreciated the exhaustive level of detail involved in maintaining the fiction of Vayan civilization.

'I do not believe that will be required,' Fintox replied. 'Igsabul was compelling. Are my colleagues returning?'

'They will all finish their first assessment visits within the next ninety minutes,' Yirella said. 'We are scheduled to regroup on Bennu.'

'I am interested to see your advanced facilities.'

They walked over to the building's hub. It had three circular portals, two metres wide, their edges a complex braid of silver cords, with indigo sparks visible slithering along inside. The aperture was a blank pseudosurface; it was impossible to tell if it was solid or not. Dellian sent it his code and the entanglement expanded.

'We keep the interplanetary portals closed unless we need to use them,' Yirella said as she walked through, 'so the quantum signature is even fainter to detect.'

'I am again impressed by your adherence to security procedures,' Fintox said.

Dellian followed them out into Bennu's hub.

*

Bennu's habitat was a torus ten kilometres in diameter, and two wide, rotating slowly to provide Juloss-standard gravity around the rim – apparently equivalent to one point one Earth gravity. The oval cross section interior housed a single swathe of subtropical parkland, with a roof composed of crystal that had a slim sunstrip running along the apex. Dellian never quite understood the point of having a transparent roof here. It wasn't as if there was anything interesting outside. If you squinted against the glare, all you could ever see was attitude thrusters and navigation strobes winking away on the extremities of machinery.

'Welcome to lurker central,' he said to Fintox.

But the alien wasn't listening. He'd curved his neck back, allowing all eight eyes to stare upwards. His voice was so high it was virtually inaudible, a bat squeak. The translator wand took what seemed an age to turn it into human speech. 'Those are not stars. Where is this place?'

'We're inside a small cryoplanet,' Yirella said. 'Eleven AUs out from Vayan's star. It had a rock core enveloped by eighty kilometres of ice. We hollowed out its centre to make Bennu; this cavity is a hundred and fifty kilometres wide. So it's secure; our thermal emissions won't leak through to the surface for a thousand years.'

Dellian pointed. 'That group of lights: that's the *Morgan*. Those over there, that's one of three shipyards; they're assembling more assault cruisers for our attack fleet. The components are all made in initiator blocks – the big truncated icosahedrons you can see floating around near the cavity wall.'

'You have accomplished so much,' Fintox said. 'How long have you been here?'

'The seedship arrived fifty-seven years ago,' Yirella said. 'It started broadcasting Vayan clan radio signals, and its von Neumann systems began bioforming the planet. We arrived five years ago.'

'Relativity time arrears,' Dellian explained. 'We started out at the same time, but the *Morgan* travelled slightly slower than the seedship.'

'You built this redoubt in only *five years*?' Fintox asked.

'Our von Neumann systems go exponential themselves first, then when there's enough of them, we crash-build what we need,' Yirella said.

'You are a very advanced species. I do not understand what we can do to aid you.'

'Part of our technology, like the initiators, is derived from Neána scientific advances, given to us by your emissaries to Sol. They were on a mission like you were. We are hoping you might have fresh or different knowledge that might help us. The truth is, we know nothing of the Olyix outside of their assault on Earth.'

'What were you going to do for the Vayans?' Dellian asked. 'The Neána who came to Earth gave us the knowledge to fight the Olyix and weapons that would help.'

'That is also our mission,' Fintox said. 'That is always what the Neána do. But I am not sure we can add anything to your resources. They appear to surpass what we have.' There was a long pause as he continued to watch the sprinkling of lights drifting through the vast cavern. 'May I ask why you did not follow the suggestions of our emissaries?'

'What do you mean?'

'Our advice is always that a species retreats into the space between stars. It is in that emptiness you can live for millennia in peace.'

'That's not us,' Dellian said firmly. 'What would be the point? So ten generations live a peaceful life in a habitat. So what? They can't go anywhere, they can't do anything. Then decadence or entropy claims them and they die out. It would've been better to be captured and taken on the Olyix pilgrimage to the end of time.'

'I do not think you mean that.'

'Oh, Saints, but I really do! Just waiting here is frustrating enough. Think how we'd feel after a hundred years of doing nothing, a thousand, ten thousand . . .'

'Living safely provides you the opportunity to evolve. Especially with your scientific abilities.'

'Evolve into what? We want to be free!'

Yirella held up a hand, giving Dellian a cautioning look. 'This is what you can explain to us. How do you see that evolution? Is it one that will end with us having a technology so powerful we can face the Olyix and end their tyranny? That is difficult for us to comprehend; our technology essentially plateaued in the centuries after we left Earth. Or are you talking about spiritual evolution?'

Dellian tried not to groan at that, but his lips betrayed him. Yirella of course picked up on the sound that escaped and scowled a warning. He just hoped the metavayan didn't know enough about human psychology to notice.

'I believe we may need stronger or more nuanced interpretations to answer fully,' Fintox said. 'However, I question your belief that a society that has evolved into maturity will decay. We have not.'

'That's something Jessika and the others never told us,' Yirella said. 'How old is Neána civilization?'

'I do not have that information.'

'In case the Olyix capture you?'

'Correct. We determine that there is more than one abode

cluster in this galaxy, therefore the Neána must have dispersed widely from our home star.'

'You mean you didn't know for sure there were other Neána abode clusters in the galaxy?'

'No. As I do not know the location of the one which dispatched our insertion ship. Nor do I have any knowledge of what it is like. Myself and my colleagues were only issued with basic facts.'

'Well, there has to be more than one,' Dellian said. 'We're over six and a half thousand lightyears from Earth, so there's no way your abode cluster is the same one that sent Jessika and the other metahuman Neána to Earth.'

Fintox straightened his neck and looked directly at Dellian, who found the eight-eye stare somewhat unnerving. 'How long has your *Morgan* ship been travelling?'

'I told you: five years. That's internal ship time.'

'I don't understand. Are humans capable of travelling faster than light?'

'Only through portals. We also have the technology to generate negative energy for wormholes, which your colleagues helped us extract from the Olyix.'

'But we don't use wormholes,' Yirella said. 'We're not sure how well we understand the science, which may make us vulnerable to Olyix detection.'

'Negative energy has some good weapons capabilities, though,' Dellian said cheerfully. 'As the Olyix will find out.'

'How long have humans been travelling?' Fintox asked.

'We abandoned Earth ten thousand years ago,' Yirella said.

'You travelled in the *Morgan* for ten thousand years?'

Dellian let out a short laugh. 'Saints, no. A generation starship arrives at a star system with a planet we can bioform to Earth-norm, then we stay there for four or five hundred years. It's all the time we can risk exposing ourselves. It's enough to allow a society to grow and enjoy life as it should be lived. But for that whole time, hundreds of portal-carrying ships are flying onwards at a fraction under lightspeed. Then, when five centuries are up, the entire population leaves on a fresh fleet of generation ships, each one going in a different direction. They'll each settle in a new star system, and the cycle repeats.'

'Then once they're clear, it's us that leave,' Yirella said.

'You?'

'A squadron of warships. Every settled planet produces a generation of fighters at the end. It's *our* job to engage the Olyix in battle and with luck defeat them.'

'How many humans are there in the galaxy?'

'Impossible to know. But if we've been successful, there should be trillions of us, riding outwards along a wavefront twenty thousand lightyears from edge to edge.'

Fintox said nothing for a long moment. 'That is a fifth of the galaxy.'

'Roughly, yes. And we'll keep on expanding at close to lightspeed. The planets in the galactic core are uninhabitable, of course; there's too much radiation to allow bioforming in there. So the wavefront will sweep around it and merge again on the other side. But there's a historical faction, call them coreists, who believe that the core is the safest location for human civilization. It won't be a planetbound society; we'll live in orbital habitats that don't move on every few hundred years. That way we can finally build something substantial. Coreists believe that society will develop into something capable of challenging the Olyix threat directly.'

Fintox emitted a long stream of whistles. Dellian waited, but the translator said nothing. 'Convert,' he told his databud.

'Not possible. It is not a language I have a translation routine for.'

'That's not right. We invented every Vayan language.'

'Fintox did not speak in any of them. His call might not be a language. Just an emotional emission.'

'What kind? Is he happy? Sad? Impressed?'

'Unknown.'

'Well, fuck.' Dellian exchanged a nonplussed look with Yirella. He guessed her databud was giving her the same replies.

'If you ask me, I don't think sheltering in the core is any different from a habitat skulking in interstellar space out here,' Dellian said briskly. 'However you look at it, we'd still be hiding in fear. And if we were going to have superweapons that could smash the Olyix enclave in one shot, we'd have built them by now. Face it, we've had ten thousand years.'

Fintox finally spoke again. 'What happens to a bioformed planet after you have left it?'

'The Olyix destroy it if they find it,' Yirella told him. 'We have copies of data files a generation ship picked up over three thousand years ago, which we think came from high-energy broadcast stations left to watch our abandoned worlds. Broadcasts powerful enough to span half the galaxy, so generation ships and new-settled worlds can detect them. They show planets with terrestrial-style biospheres being struck repeatedly by large asteroids. Extinction events.'

'They're frightened of us,' Dellian said. 'As they should be. Our generation ships have spread so wide now that our species will always remain outside their grasp. There are simply too many of us.'

'We hope,' Yirella said. 'Ironically, we've become so good at staying silent as we flee, we don't have any contact with other humans. Statistically, there are so many generation ships that some will meet at new star systems, especially on the other side of the galactic core. But how would we ever know?'

'If I understand correctly,' Fintox said, 'your generation ships seed every star system they encounter with terrestrial life, then dispatch more ships onwards to do the same.'

'We don't seed every star system we reach,' Yirella said. 'It's selective. Those that have proto-biospheres, or planets with indigenous life, we leave alone. To do anything else would be unethical, obviously.'

'I am relieved to hear that.'

'Well . . . *we* wouldn't,' Dellian said. 'Who knows what *some* strands of humanity do these days?' He grinned, only to receive an angry glare from Yirella. 'What? We've got to be the most diverse species there's ever been by now.'

'I'm sure,' she said stiffly. 'But any starfaring species will have a basic level of decency. All human societies need that to maintain cohesion. They wouldn't be able to function effectively, otherwise.'

'The Nazis functioned pretty efficiently.'

'That concept came before our current civilization took shape,' she said. 'And it died out quickly.'

Her icon bloomed in Dellian's optik, unfurling text. **Stop talking about our flaws. We have to get them on side.**

Sorry, he sent back.

She smiled effusively at Fintox. 'Would you like to go to the meeting room now? Your colleagues should be transferring up here soon. Captain Kenelm will be eager to know your opinion of what we are doing.'

'That would be welcome. Is it possible to have refreshments?'

'Of course. I'd appreciate knowing what you think of the food we've synthesized for you.'

'Ah. This will be like the music. It was never truly real until we arrived.'

'Indeed, yes.'

Dellian gave the metavayan a half-bow, which brought his head down level with those unnerving eight eyes. In such a context it seemed mocking to him, rather than a show of respect. 'I'm going to go now, but I hope it all goes well for you.'

'Are you not attending the meeting?'

'No. I'm scheduled for a training session.'

'I hope it succeeds,' Fintox said.

Yirella came over and touched his arm. 'I'll see you tonight.'

'Sure. Have fun in the meeting.' He stood on tiptoes and kissed her, enjoying the mischievous glint she flashed him.

*

Dellian went through three hubs to reach the habitat's gym. 'Disconnect from the network,' he told his databud, and used his squad leader code to authorize it. Being constantly connected to the network was the norm in Bennu for everyone, all the way up to the Captain hirself.

'Confirmed.'

He paused while his optik graphics furled up, giving him a perfectly clear vision, then made his way down several flights of stairs, into the sub-levels. This part of the habitat was a redundant underworld of unused rooms and interminable corridors. All of it was completely empty, waiting to be assigned a purpose that would never come. Its endless repetition geometry was designed by a genten, one to which nobody had ever explained that Bennu's human population would never grow.

The room he arrived at was no different from the countless others, its door distinguished only by an irrelevant serial number. There wasn't even a lock to keep out the uninvited; its anonymity was its security. In any case, they used a different one each time.

Over thirty people were already there when Dellian entered. He didn't have the exact numbers without network tracking pings, and not knowing gave him a curiously edgy sensation. *Welcome to Earth's barbarian age, where nobody knows anything for sure.* Those who had come to watch the fight were mainly men from the squads, though he wasn't entirely surprised to see six or seven omnia from the crew had turned up. They towered over everyone else, but their faces held the same anticipation and excitement. Boredom affected omnia just as much as binaries.

Xante and Janc greeted him warmly.

'I brought a med-kit,' Janc said.

Xante laughed, his arm around Dellian's shoulder to shake him. 'It won't be our boy that needs it.'

Janc's face registered a degree of concern. 'You sure you want to do this?'

'Oh, yeah,' Dellian said. He thought it best not to tell his friends just how long he'd been waiting for this moment. *I'm not really a vigilante stalker – but hey, if the opportunity's there . . .*

'Just . . . keep it together, okay?' Janc said.

'Don't worry.' Dellian grinned, projecting reassurance. Privately he hoped he wasn't being too confident.

He started to strip off and ran a quick check through his nerve induction sleeves, gauging the feedback from the slender threads woven into his musculature. He could feel his combat core cohort at a reflexive level; since the boosting operations back on Juloss, they had become a truly flawless extension of his own body. The six ex-muncs were somnolent now, a state he beefed up with a status lock. The last thing he needed was for them to come hurtling to his rescue halfway through the fight.

When he was down to his shorts, Xante started wrapping tough cloth strips around Dellian's left hand. 'Okay, go in fast and hard. Understand?'

'You'll need to,' Janc said. 'That is one tough-looking fucker.'

'Oh, encouraging,' Xante growled.

Dellian looked across the room, where Tomar was getting ready in the middle of his friends. The man's hands were already bound and seemed to be bigger than Dellian's. He threw a few mock punches, generating whoops of approval from his own bunch of supporters.

'Watch your balls,' Janc said stoically. 'He's the kind who'll go for them.'

Xante winked. 'Don't we all?' He bound up the right hand, and gave Dellian a quick kiss. 'This isn't to the death, remember.'

'Got it.'

'Oh, Saints.' Janc groaned. 'Go for a knee slam. If you crunch his mobility, you'll have a better chance.'

'What do you mean, chance?'

Ovan, another squad leader, walked into the middle of the room. 'All right,' he called out. 'Everyone, back against the walls. No help to either of these two dickheads except for medical. Clear? We don't want to replay the Uret–Balart war. The Captain will have to notice if we all wind up in the clinic.'

Dellian smacked Xante on the shoulder. 'That means you.'

'You're just lucky Yirella isn't here,' Xante countered. 'Now shut up and open your mouth.'

'That's what you always say.'

Xante's expression hardened, part worry, part exasperation. 'This isn't a fucking training sim! Get serious. Now!'

Dellian did as he'd been told and opened his mouth wide. Xante shoved a mouthguard in. Imagination provided Dellian the sensation of his glands pumping away inside his skull like rogue hearts, squirting out neurochemicals. They bumped up his focus, his speed. Banished fear.

'Okay, you two dickheads,' Ovan yelled. 'It's over when you know it's over. Begin!' He scurried back to the wall.

Dellian dropped into a crouch, fists ready, and padded forwards in a big-cat hunting stance. Tomar was doing the same thing. Guttural, testosterone-fuelled cheers from the spectators rang out. The room and racket vanished, and all Dellian saw was the Juloss orbital arena, with the two teams of thirteen-year-old boys from Immerle and Ansaru bouncing around the hurdles in fluctuating gravity as they chased the flagballs. Boys and one girl. And the Ansaru's number eight deliberately going for a bone-breaking tackle on Yirella.

He yelled the old Immerle game call and pivoted fast, leg shooting out, going for a strike on number eight. But Tomar was bigger and quicker now. He spun in counter, arm slicing down. Pain shot through Dellian's elbow as the man's fist connected. He whirled away out of range, but Tomar used his own momentum to follow. Another blow, to the ribs this time. Dellian lashed out with his right foot. Knee kick, but not accurate enough. His heel slammed into Tomar's upper thigh.

'Loser then and loser now,' Tomar taunted.

So he does remember! Dellian lunged forwards. A fist crunched into his nose and blood spurted, but he got in a dangerous blow to Tomar's left ear, sending the man staggering back, momentarily disorientated by the pain. The spectators howled approval.

Two minutes later Dellian was limping badly on what he suspected was a fractured ankle. His chest was slick with blood and he couldn't see out of his right eye. Tomar, with at least two broken ribs, was struggling to draw down a full breath, and there was blood coming out of his mouth where his cheek was torn and swelling. More blood from cuts and impact wounds trickled down his body. They shared them almost equally.

Dellian went for a zero-style caveman tackle, head down, arms wide to vice crush. A knee slammed into his chest, but he managed to ram his head into Tomar's damaged ribs. A third one cracked, forcing the last air in the man's lungs to come out in a mangled scream. Dellian went over backwards, trying to roll smoothly.

Somehow the coordination was lacking, making it more of a sprawl and scramble for balance. Tomar was coming for him again. Respond with a kick to the vulnerable knee. Precision off, but hard heel contact on upper thigh anyway. *Saints, so nearly a balls kick. That would have won it.* Impact knocked Tomar sideways, not before his fist punched cleanly into Dellian's unguarded stomach.

Dellian was aware of being on the floor, not sure how he got there, bitter vomit splattering out of his mouth and taking the mouthguard with it. Instinctive rush to get to his feet – so vulnerable on the ground. Up and ready – difficult to balance on the bad ankle. And seeing Ellici in front of him, struggling as Xante held her back, shouting loudly, face furious, tears – *Ellici? How does she know about this—*

Tomar's spin kick caught him perfectly. Pain vanished behind darkness.

*

'Idiot.' Spoken by Xante.

Dellian managed to open one eye. That small action brought a wholly unreasonable amount of pain with it. 'Aww, fuck.'

Janc's worried grin filled his blurry vision. 'You're alive. Does it hurt?'

'Fucking fuck!'

'I think that's a yes.'

He tried to lift himself up. Far too painful. 'What . . .?'

'Just don't move. Your nerve shunts will block the worst pain.' *Liar!*

'This'll help clear the rest,' Xante said.

Small, hard circles were pressed against his flesh. Some of them stuck. A damp cloth wiped at his swollen right eye as cold sharp tendrils wormed their way progressively through his veins, sucking out the pain. 'What happened?' This time when he tried to lift himself he succeeded in getting his head off the ground. He saw Ellici standing behind Xante and Janc, tear streaks still fresh on her face.

'Hey, don't worry, I'm okay,' he mumbled at her through a rapidly numbing mouth. Xante winced, his face expressing the kind of pain Dellian was feeling.

'What?'

'It's Rello,' Ellici snivelled.

'Shit, what about him?' Instinctively, Dellian looked to check his optik display, the little fringe cluster of icons that represented each of his squadmates: those wondrous brothers, lovers, lifefriends. The icon cluster was always there, enabling them to watch out for each other, no matter what, when or where. Except when he'd cancelled his link to the habitat network to keep the fight off official records. Right now there was nothing.

'He's dead, Dellian. He killed himself.'

Kruse Station

26th June 2204

The medical department took up an unexpectedly large slice of the station's toroid, an open section long enough that Kandara could actually see the floor's gentle upward curve as she followed Captain Tral and Jessika. It was like walking through a newly built cyber-factory that hadn't yet been fitted out with its systems. Walls, floor and ceiling were all glossy white, bisected with dark structural girders so the space resembled a modern art installation.

Something to do with the bleakness of the soul.

The depressing layout wasn't helped by the big treatment bays created by circular glass walls; their distant spacing amplified the section's nascent theme of separation. Her footsteps echoed relentlessly between them, louder than the soft buzz of the security drone escort sliding through the air above, their weapon muzzles discreetly retracted.

Only two of the fifty bays were being used. One contained Feriton Kayne's corpse lying on an operating table. A five-strong xenobiology team was clustered around, wearing full-body hazard suits the same colour as the station's uniforms, their faces peering down behind helmet visors as the tangle of surgical arms hanging from the ceiling began to probe the alien brain tissue. To Kandara, the instruments looked like something left over from the Spanish Inquisition. But then hospitals always unnerved her, ever since those last two hopeless hours of her mother's life in the emergency trauma room.

The other occupied bay had twin stacks of intensive-care modules standing beside Soćko's gurnez. Lankin and a couple of the station's medical technicians were in attendance, but didn't appear particularly concerned. They had Soćko covered in sensor discs to monitor his vitals. A couple of the security drones hovered near the ceiling, also watching.

As soon as the three of them entered the bay, additional security shields slid up out of the floor, sealing them inside. All Kandara could think of was a large-scale lab cage, the type they trialled dangerous toxins in. 'How's he doing?' she asked.

Lankin indicated one of the screens on top of a stack, where coloured graphics danced a slow regular tempo. 'Brain activity is picking up. And his blood chemistry has almost normalized.' He glanced at Jessika. 'Is there anything else we should be doing?'

'No. He'll recover, I'm sure.'

Kandara watched her closely, trying to work out if the concern was genuine. It seemed to be; but then, human emotional reactions were probably just a routine handled by alien algorithms inside that nonhuman shell. *But I'd grown to like her. How?*

She normally prided herself on her instinct, but Jessika had crept in under the radar. Just like Feriton Kayne. And that put every reflex on a hair trigger, powered by suspicion. The demons inside her head were rattling the cage her glands' neurochemicals used to contain them.

'Is there anything about you that's real?' she asked abruptly.

Lankin and Captain Tral gave her a surprised look. Jessika merely affected a weary sadness.

'What you see is what you get,' Jessika said.

'Okay, so tell me: how many of you are there?'

'The Neána? Four of us were grown in the insertion ship.'

'That's like a politician's answer. How many ships?'

'I genuinely don't know. It may have been just us, or there may have been more. Personally, I think there must have been other missions. Among senior government figures and globalPACs, the level of mistrust directed towards the Olyix is higher than I'd expect to occur naturally. It makes me believe other Neána are out there, kindling suspicion. I have no proof of that, because I was never given that information. Emissaries work on a need-to-know basis. The abode cluster the insertion ship came from is very security conscious.'

'So Neána live in abode clusters?'

'Between the stars, yes.'

'Are they similar to our habitats?'

'Again, I don't know. Abode cluster is simply the most meaningful translation.'

'Or not,' Tral said.

'Misinformation?' Kandara asked.

Sie shrugged. 'It's what I'd do.'

'We discussed that between ourselves,' Jessika admitted. 'Our origin might be nothing more than an abandoned Neána equivalent to a von Neumann machine. Given how powerful the Olyix are, it would make sense to leave this galaxy altogether if you can.'

'So why not "advise" us to do that?' Kandara asked. 'Why tell us to hide?'

'The Andromeda galaxy is over two and a half million lightyears away. Your technology is not advanced enough to build a habitat capable of flying that distance. Nor is ours – at least not with the knowledge I have. The distance is simply too great.'

'We've been running project studies on trans-galactic travel for a couple of centuries,' Lankin said. 'The resources are far beyond even Utopial society. For any chance of success when travelling sublight, you'd essentially have to take an entire solar system with you. And even then, given the timescale, whatever species began the trip would have evolved into something completely different – or died out – by the time you arrived. If it's the second scenario, that leaves the mother of all impact problems if the solar system's star didn't decelerate.'

'Accelerate a whole star system,' Tral said with amusement.

'Theoretically, that's within the ability of a Kardashev level three society,' Lankin told hir.

'A what?'

'Kardashev level three is as far up the evolutionary and technology scale as a species can get. Essentially: god. Though some postulate that level four is also possible, we just can't really envisage what it might be like.'

'A Kardashev level three would be able to squash the Olyix like a bug,' Jessika said. 'The problem is, the Olyix arrive long before anyone even reaches Kardashev level one.'

'You just said the Neána escaped the Olyix,' Kandara said. 'If your people are hiding between the stars, won't they be evolving to that level?'

'Possibly. But I'm what they sent you. And the Olyix are still around. So it doesn't look as if they're there yet. Sorry.'

'Or your abode cluster didn't want us to have Kardashev-level technology, particularly weapons,' Kandara mused. 'I get that; humans running around the galaxy with planet-killer guns wouldn't be my idea of a fun era to live in.'

'If we had the weapons that could eliminate the Olyix,' Jessika said, 'then we would have used them ourselves.'

'Okay, so let's build some trust here, you and me. Like we used to have. Who are the other two that came with you and Soćko?'

'Lim Tianyu and Dutee Gowda. A month ago, Dutee was in South Africa, while Lim was on Tnjin in the Trappist system. Happy now?'

'A month ago?'

'We're not in constant contact, Kandara. G8Turing pattern recognition might pick that up.'

'Fair enough. Will they be getting in contact now?'

'I expect so, as soon as the invasion begins.'

Kandara got Zapata to splash mainline news streamers across her tarsus lens. There was nothing about the Olyix yet, so she told the altme to watch for any new mention of them. 'When did you all arrive?'

Jessika smiled at the question. '2162. We splashed down in the

Beagle Channel. Crap, but that water is cold! It's enough to put a girl off swimming for life.'

'So where's the ship that brought you here?'

'Gone. Each function it performed, every manoeuvre, was achieved by consuming and converting its own mass. Launching us down through the atmosphere was its last task. There was nothing left after that.'

'Convenient,' Tral muttered.

'Integrating into human society was relatively easy for us. You stream a lot of dramas about criminals and undercover agents. Documentaries, too. Inventing a valid history for myself was simple.'

Kandara laughed. 'You learned tradecraft from solnet fiction shows?'

'Some of it. Yes.'

'So switching between Utopial and Universal societies was all bullshit?'

'Pretty much. Being an immigrant excuses a lot of ignorance, and it means no one in your new location is ever going to meet the family and old friends you reminisce about. Your personal past is what you tell people it is – backed up by official files, which were all forgeries.'

'Mother Mary! Well, we both know you fooled me – each time.'

'I'm sorry you feel that way. For the record, my friendship towards you is genuine. I like you, Kandara.'

'You have real emotions, then?'

'Of course. They're integral to self-determination. Emotion governs the majority of human responses.'

'Interesting. But, for instance, if you had a choice between rescuing a child from certain death, or accessing critical data from an Olyix . . .'

Jessika chuckled. 'Have you ever considered becoming a solnet talking-heads show host? I don't think even they would ask something so ridiculously hypothetical. And for the record, I would save the child. That's not even emotion, that's simple logic. The child situation would only happen once, and every life is precious. If the

Olyix information exists, there will be many opportunities to retrieve it.'

'She got you there,' Lankin said cheerfully.

'Okay.' Kandara gestured at Soćko. 'Do you love him?'

'Like a brother. Which is as close to a true definition of our relationship as language and circumstance allow. And on the logic front, having him conscious will help enormously in the fight against the Olyix.'

'So having him sabotage the Olyix transport ship was all part of your plan?'

'Not specifically. Soćko and I knew the Olyix would be snatching humans for various experimental trials so they could prepare their cocooning strategy. Our goal when Yuri was assigned to investigate Horatio's disappearance was to insert Soćko into their operation; that way he'd be able to see what they were doing and how far into the human underworld their influence extended. We succeeded in a way we didn't quite anticipate.'

'So Soćko let himself get captured?'

Jessika sighed. 'Yes. The advantage of that is that it's helped us expose them to you. But the waiting was tough like you'll never know.'

'And in the meantime you've been busy feeding Ainsley's paranoia?'

'Come on, it didn't need much feeding. Suspicion is practically self-propagating in Universal culture, so I moved out here to Delta Pavonis to work on level-one Utopials. I have to say, Emilja is far more rational and sceptical than Ainsley.'

'But you made it happen,' Kandara said. 'You convinced her.'

Jessika waved an arm expansively. 'Yeah. Mind you, she was always a little doubtful about the Olyix anyway, and she's smart with it. The Utopials' existing Security Bureau wasn't anything near effective enough – you saw that first-hand when we worked together. It was collecting too much contradictory information about the Olyix: the disinformation my colleagues and I were creating, and the Olyix countering that with their own disinformation. None of it rang true, but there was too much noise for it to be nothing.'

'No smoke without fire,' Kandara said.

'Exactly. And once I was embedded in the Bureau, I could point our investigations in the right direction, at the people disappearing, even the sabotage missions being launched against Delta Pavonis. It took a few years, but the Senior Council was persuaded. Once that happened, the Home Security Bureau got a huge resource allocation, which I helped guide.'

'And you suggested me for the assessment mission to Nkya?'

'In a roundabout kind of way. Feriton drew up a list of possibles. I concluded it was people he was suspicious about. You were on it because of your showdown with Cancer on Verby. Naturally, the Bureau supported your inclusion because of that earlier mission.'

'Uh-huh. And the others?'

'Yuri I'd worked with before. Ainsley trusted him implicitly, and Feriton must have suspected him because Yuri always seemed mistrustful when it came to the Olyix, so he was coaxed onto the team. Alik was another of Feriton's suspects.'

'What about Feriton himself?'

'My number one suspect. That spy mission they sent him on to *Salvation of Life* was seriously bad news. Ainsley's people simply had no idea what they were dealing with.'

Kandara squinted through the security screens at the other bay, where Feriton's corpse was being analysed. 'Is his brain still alive, do you think?'

'Oh, undoubtedly. The Olyix will have cocooned it. Hell, it's probably back in their enclave by now, along with all the other early test subjects.'

'Mother Mary!'

There was a certain glint in Jessika's eye. 'So you *do* believe me.'

'We'll see.'

The Moon

26th June 2204

Callum wasn't entirely surprised to find the Alpha Defence reception chamber was very similar to the one he'd walked into at Kruse Station; there were just more human troopers on guard this time. Their armour was heavy-duty and matt black, with shoulder-mounted weapons already being aimed at everyone coming through the portal. The lieutenant in charge, Amahle, was so tall that at first he thought she was omnia. Her helmet was off, though she clutched it tightly to her side as she regarded him suspiciously.

'Callum Hepburn?'

'You got me.' Apollo sent his personal code to the base's network, which she seemed completely uninterested in.

Eldlund followed him through the portal, with Danuta Zangari right behind hir. Having Ainsley's granddaughter along was like owning a personalized badge of authority.

'This way, please,' Amahle said.

Callum started walking. He wasn't used to low gravity. Terraformed worlds were all chosen for their approximation to Earth in size and mass, giving them a similar gravity, while every habitat rotated to provide Earth-standard gravity at the rim. But Alpha Defence was on the moon, buried nearly eight kilometres deep below the regolith. He concentrated on making slow careful movements, trying never to make sharp turns. That way the momentum he built up would keep him moving in the same direction. Even so, he could feel his toes lifting off the floor, leaving him gliding him forwards in a gentle loping movement. The last thing he wanted now was to stumble and fall in slow-mo, because as sure as Aberdeen was cold in winter, there Eldlund would be, considerately assisting him to his feet again like a care assistant in a retirement home.

Sure enough, the tall omnia seemed to be having no trouble walking in the one-sixth gravity field. Callum didn't understand how that could be, not with those gangling limbs. But then Amahle moved with even more grace. Cursing youth under his breath, Callum made it to the portal door without losing too much of his dignity.

They went through into a plain metal-walled anteroom. There was a physical door at the other end, standing open so he could see it was as thick as any bank vault. A transparent secondary door was closed just inside, with two armoured figures standing guard. When he looked up, he could make out the outline of hatches in the curving ceiling; he declined to think of the weapons waiting behind them.

The transparent door slid open and Amahle escorted them through into the Command Centre. Alpha Defence had been set up in response to the *Salvation of Life*'s arrival, with all the corresponding concern about an alien spaceship containing prodigious quantities of antimatter. Following a time-honoured tradition of government bureaucracy, committees and sub-committees formed, had expense-account lunches and agreed to combine various existing agencies – mainly counter-insurgency services, and space-debris monitoring offices – then produce a single budget passed by the Sol Senate. The aim was to provide a network of early-warning sensors extending two lightyears out from Sol so that no alien spaceship could ever get close without being detected the way *Salvation of Life* had. In addition there was going to be a comprehensive array of high-orbit weapons platforms above Earth to engage any hostile ship that did get close. Alpha Defence also – theoretically – had override authority to order city shields to be switched on.

A grand project with a noble aim: defending humans against whatever threat might be lurking out there in the galaxy. It was officially inaugurated in 2150.

By 2204 the sensor network extended just past the Kuiper belt, with funding for its second tier the ongoing subject of a partisan battle in the Sol Senate finance and resources committee that had so far lasted eight years. Of the projected eighty giant weapons platforms needed to provide triple-layer protection around Earth, fifteen had been built and nine were in service, with a further eight under construction, and plagued with redesign problems, massive cost overruns, along with numerous contractor financial malfeasance cases under investigation from the Senate procurement office.

Callum knew the basic history. But the Command Centre didn't reflect the malaise that beset the agency. It was a circular room with a concave floor, mirroring the Theophilus crater, which it sat eight kilometres directly below. Taking up the entire centre was a holographic bubble display depicting the solar system. The habitats in their myriad orbits sparkled within their designator tabs: a rainbow orrery that was itself englobed by thousands of white course vectors of all the rocks and comets that crossed Earth's orbit. Winding sinuously through them were purple vectors of ships under power, mainly carrying new solarwells in towards the sun, where they'd be dropped into the corona to siphon out power which would supply the whole Sol system with electricity. There were also vectors of ships heading out to virgin asteroids, where rock-squatting Turings could declare themselves independent and offer zero-tax registry for corporations. Directly opposite Earth, in the planet's Lagrange Three point, the *Salvation of Life* gleamed a malignant scarlet.

The officer in charge stood in front of the spectral orb, hands on hips as he stared intently at the display. He was a thickset man whose straight-backed posture made him look impressively authoritative in the force's blue and black uniform. Callum narrowed his eyes as the officer turned to greet them. There was something about the man's bald head and thin wire-rimmed glasses that he found irritatingly familiar. The memory was elusive, which he hated; it was an experience which was growing more frequent these days. He gave up and asked Apollo to run a match.

'Adjutant-General David Johnston, Supreme Commander Alpha Defence, on a five-year secondment from the British military General Staff office.'

'The Gylgen emergency clean-up,' Callum exclaimed.

'Oh, well done. I was wondering if you'd remember.' Johnston gave Danuta a shrewd glance before smiling at Callum. 'I was sorry to hear you died shortly after that. Still, nice to see you're recovered.'

Callum grinned and put his hand out. 'Modern medicine. It's a fucking miracle.'

'Quite.' Johnston's grip was proof he didn't spend all his time deep underground behind a desk. 'And on the subject of miracles, I think we might be needing another about now. If you could oblige . . .'

'Sorry, miracles aren't my department.' Callum looked around the Command Centre. There were three chairs spaced equidistantly around the display bubble, an empty one next to Johnston, and two others with Alpha Defence captains sitting in them. Both of them had hologram cubes of data floating in attendance like geometric halos, holding a great deal more information than could be splashed across a tarsus lens. He frowned, peering through the sparklehaze of the bubble, trying to see the rest of the operatives. 'Where is everyone?'

Johnston gave him a sly smile. 'We *are* everyone, my boy, us precious few.'

Dread spread down Callum's spine like a creeping frost. 'Three people? To defend the whole Sol system?'

'Three humans, and one of the largest G8Turing cube arrays ever built. Basically, we're here to provide overall strategy; the Turings take care of everything else. It's actually the perfectly simplified command structure that every general has dreamed of since the Tumu Crisis.'

'Okay. As an engineer I always approve of simplified systems. But what systems do we actually have?'

Johnston gave Danuta another pointed glance. 'If the intelligence I've just been given is correct and the Olyix are about to invade, we can probably slow them down by a few hours.'

'Fuck! What about the weapons platforms?'

'All nine of them?' Johnston asked quietly. 'We might manage to get a few hits in if hostile alien ships do approach Earth, but they're not highly manoeuvreable.'

'Then what's the bloody point in having them?'

'The weapons platform strategy was to have eighty of them, in three distinct cis-lunar orbits. An onion-layer defence, if you like. That way it would be extremely tough for anything to approach Earth from space. But the thing is, we do have reliable sensor coverage out beyond Pluto. And if another arkship, or armada, is flying towards Sol, we'll be able to see its exhaust emission from a lightyear away as it decelerates. Nothing can creep up on us. On top of that, governments and companies have explored nearly every star system within eighty lightyears. There's nothing intrinsically hostile out there. As a military man, I appreciate the huge political support Alpha Defence receives from Connexion. Unfortunately, what we've learned about this region of the galaxy has shown us the most dangerous thing out there is fourteen exoplanets with primordial soup atmospheres, which might – or might not – produce multicellular life in a billion years' time. It's difficult to gather political determination in those circumstances. We've never faced any threat.'

'Until today,' Danuta said.

'Yes. Until today.'

'So what can you do?' Callum asked.

'Based on what I've been told about the potential size of the Olyix invasion, I believe we can buy Earth's countryside and ribbon-town populations a little extra time to get under the city shields.'

'That's it?'

It might have been the telomere treatments Johnston had received, thickening and stiffening his skin against the onset of age, but there was no expression of remorse showing on his face. 'Yes.'

'I might be able to help,' Danuta said.

Both Callum and Johnston gave her a curious look.

'What sort of help?' Callum asked.

'The Connexion Olyix Monitoring Office has a contingency planning team,' Danuta said. 'Given Ainsley's level of mistrust, it was only prudent to have a viable response in the event of a worst-case scenario.'

'Oh, hell, you went more than theoretical on this, didn't you?' Callum asked.

'Yes.'

'What have you got?' Johnston asked.

'If the *Salvation of Life* initiated a hostile act, we would be able to strike at it with WMDs.'

'Weapons of mass destruction? You mean nukes?' Callum exclaimed. 'Fuck! Ainsley Zangari has his own personal stash of nuclear weapons?'

'Contingency only,' Danuta said. 'And it's not Grandfather alone who authorizes their use. There is a commission that has to approve their activation.'

'A commission of Zangaris?'

'Yes.'

'Let me guess, you're on the commission?'

'I have that privilege.'

'How many nukes?' Johnston asked.

'We have thirty warheads, with a yield of seventy megatons each. They can be deployed through the portals we have surrounding L3, either on high-acceleration missiles, or stealthed low-velocity astrodrones.'

'Seventy megatons? Bloody hell, that's big!'

Danuta's lips twitched a knowing smile. 'Big enough to crack open an asteroid.'

'So much for the '68 disarmament treaty,' a piqued Callum said, 'and everything that was done to preserve it.'

'They're laser-triggered fusion warheads,' Danuta said. 'We don't use fissionable material. And they were only built for one purpose: defending us. I think we all now agree that was justified.'

Callum wanted to snap a smartarse reply at her, but held his tongue.

'Okay,' Johnston said. 'So what do you even need Alpha Defence for?'

'Your sensor network,' Danuta told him. 'We have L3 under total surveillance through our portals, but if what Jessika said is true, then we could be facing a fleet of warships.'

'Deliverance ships, she called them,' Eldlund said. 'She said they'd come out of the *Salvation of Life*'s wormhole.'

'Whatever they're called, we need to track them,' Danuta said.

'That we can do,' Johnston said.

The image in the bubble display shifted, with Earth expanding until it filled the whole sphere. Continents were etched in neon purple, with cities glowing vivid orange. But as Callum watched, some of the orange patches began flicking over to a vivid blue. Johnston gave the planetary globe a satisfied nod as the transformation spread.

'Are those the shields?' Callum asked.

'Yes. We issued the Code One activation order just as you arrived. We're early, of course, playing it very safe, so they won't all go on. There are plenty of defence agencies that like to assert their independence for political reasons, especially with no physical evidence of an emergency. But this many responding, initially, is promising; it means we don't have to waste time chasing after everyone. You and your allies can apply political pressure through the Sol Senate on any recalcitrant governments.'

Danuta shook her head disparagingly at the predominantly orange-shaded cities on the North American continent. 'Oh, typical.'

There might have been a smile on Johnston's lips, but Callum found it hard to tell. 'Don't worry, Alik will knock 'em into shape.'

'South of the border not too great at taking orders, either,' Eldlund commented.

As Callum watched, a few cities in South America were turning from orange to blue. The process was achingly slow. He couldn't help himself, and checked Aberdeen, finding it glowing a reassuring sapphire. Not that he'd been back there for a century, and any family was so distant now they were just names Apollo maintained in low-priority contact files. But still . . . the old hometown. Edinburgh, he was pleased to notice, was also secure under its thick wall of bonded air.

Yuri's face splashed up on the wall behind Johnston's chair. 'We think it's starting,' he announced.

'No change to the *Salvation of Life* status,' Johnston said.

'Maybe not, but my department is reporting a significant rise in incidents down here. The interstellar hubs are being subjected to digital attack. The G8s are stopping most of it, but auxiliary systems are getting badly chewed up.'

'Any physical sabotage?' Callum asked.

'Possibly. Communication with several hubs is either confused or out, even with our secure backup channels. We're sending tactical teams now to find out what's actually happening. I've ordered isolation protocols for all interstellar portals – at both ends.'

'Ah, crap,' Callum muttered.

Alik's face appeared next to Yuri's. 'No sign of this invasion fleet then, huh?'

'Not yet,' Callum said.

'Okay, well, the good news is that D.C. is now a believer. Some important people around here were deeply disturbed by what I explained to them. The Pentagon will be complying with the Alpha Defence request for the city shields to be switched on.'

'Order,' Johnston said. 'Our *order* to activate city shields.'

'Whatever. And guess what? The first one up is going to be Washington itself.'

Callum grinned. 'No self-interest there, then.'

'Absolutely not. Just leading by example, is all. Yuri, NYC will also be up in the next ten minutes.'

'Thank you.'

Johnston suddenly stiffened and turned to the display bubble. 'Christ almighty!'

'What?' Callum asked – not that he needed to. He knew. He'd known from the moment he'd looked into the fractured skull of Feriton Kayne and seen the alien flesh squatting there. *It's real. Sweet shit, it's actually happening.*

'All communications with the Lobby just dropped out.'

'Dropped out?'

'Cut. Hit by darkware. Powered down. Sabotaged . . . Whatever, they've gone. We're getting nothing.'

'How many people on board?'

'It's the main commercial transfer station for the *Salvation of Life*. There's a lot of traffic through there.'

'How many?'

'Probably two thousand permanent technicians. The service shuttles need plenty of maintenance.'

'Yuri!' Callum said.

'Way ahead of you. My first order was closing all the portals to the Lobby. *Salvation of Life* has no portal link to the rest of the Sol system.'

'There's a change-of-status alert coming in,' Johnston said. 'Getting a visual.'

The bubble display instantly switched to the alien arkship. Callum was captivated by the sight. The vast cylindrical mass was venting mountain-high jets of white gas from fissures in its smooth rock surface. Curving plumes that glimmered in the raw sunlight, forming a beautiful, ephemeral wheel slashing vigorously across the stars.

'Did you do that?' Callum asked.

'No,' Danuta replied. 'We haven't launched anything.'

'Then what the hell's happening?'

New York

Yuri's day-to-day office was on the eighty-second floor of Connexion's global headquarters, a one-hundred-and-twenty-storey tower on West Fifty-Ninth Street. It gave him an unsurpassed vista of Central Park and the city beyond, as well as putting him on top of his fiefdom: the Security Division, which occupied the eight storeys below. The floors above were taken up by the executive and board offices, which gave him an insight into Ainsley Zangari's priorities back when he was founding Connexion. The CEO had always been very protective of his corporate child, as confirmed by the location of the Security Division's operations centre, buried at huge expense nine floors below ground level in an ultra-secure basement. It was a flower-shaped chamber with a petal segment covering each of Earth's continents, then one for the Sol system habitats and another for the industrial asteroids, with the last petal dedicated to the interstellar hubs. Each segment had a display bubble in the centre, with four or five operatives sitting around it on couches, from which they could direct paramilitary firepower, G8 Turings and intelligence operatives that rivalled – and, in plenty of cases, surpassed – the armed forces of small nations. The strategy centre in the middle of the flower, its stamen, was formed by open archways into each segment, allowing the duty officer to oversee events in each sector.

It was Anne Groell's luck – or misfortune – to be sitting in the central couch when Yuri and Loi arrived from Kruse Station. Yuri told her to keep her place and run operations for him; she'd been with Connexion Security for forty-three years, and before that served eight years in the Devil's Brigade, Canada's elite special forces. He respected her professionalism and grace under pressure.

Though even she muttered 'Motherfucker' when he briefed her on what might be about to hit them.

Reports of odd malfunctions and hub breakdowns began almost as soon as he and Loi arrived. Within minutes, it was clear an organized sabotage operation was being run against Connexion. The scale of it began to worry Yuri; it was a lot worse than he'd been expecting.

He told Boris, his altme, to open an ultra-secure link to the Olyix Monitoring Office. They'd built it inside an asteroid called Teucer, out in the Jupiter Trailing Trojan cluster, a vast swarm of asteroids following the gas giant's orbit around the sun. The clandestine stash of nuclear weapons which Connexion physicists had built there was the one thing that gave him hope that they might just manage to strike the Olyix hard before any real threat emerged.

Boris splashed the Teucer armoury icon on his tarsus lens, and he saw that Danuta was also accessing the secret station out in the Trailing Trojan asteroid cluster. Ainsley III had issued the code to five people, providing redundancy in case the Olyix sabotage was better than anyone was predicting. The responsibility was awesome – especially if they were wrong about the Olyix. But Yuri couldn't shake the image of that alien brain nesting parasitically in Feriton's shattered skull. He'd wanted Ainsley and Ainsley III to launch their nukes at *Salvation of Life* the instant he regained secure communication with the Zangari family executive, but they'd overruled him, saying they needed final proof. 'If we're wrong, we'll be committing genocide,' Ainsley III had pronounced.

The Teucer armoury needed authorization from two code holders. What surprised Yuri was Ainsley himself not immediately loading his override code in. But these days things were different; the old man no longer had supreme authority over everything. The family had started reining him in over a decade ago.

'Let's have Alpha Defence on line,' Yuri said. 'We'll coordinate with them.'

Anne nodded curtly. The Luna Command Centre appeared on a screen between a couple of the archways, showing Callum standing next to Johnston. 'We think it's starting,' Yuri told them.

'No change to the *Salvation of Life* status,' Johnston replied.

Which made Yuri doubt Jessika. He hated that – especially as she'd saved his life thirty-two years ago, which admittedly coloured his feelings. Back then he'd been so much more decisive; age wasn't turning out to be wisdom, just uncertainty.

As he explained the outbreak of sabotage to Alpha Defence, Boris gave him an ultra-secure link to Danuta. 'I think we need to arm the warheads,' he told her. 'This sabotage isn't just coincidence. Jessika predicted this.'

'I don't know,' she replied. 'What if Jessika's Neána are the hostiles and we fell for the disinformation?'

'Shit. Okay.' He'd half-expected Danuta to agree unconditionally and provide an iron-clad confirmation bias. But now . . . *She's as paranoid as me, for fuck's sake. There's just so much at stake.*

Alik joined the session, and Yuri had to admit he was reassured that New York's shield would be switched on. Even deep below Connexion's tower, he'd felt vulnerable to the open sky. His relief didn't last long. Groell splashed the sensor images of *Salvation of Life* inside a big hologram cube. He frowned at the huge fountains of vapour jetting out from cracks that were appearing in the arkship's surface. Cracks which he saw were slowly growing wider and wider.

'All communications with the Lobby just dropped out,' Johnston said.

Yuri held his breath as a change-of-status alert began. He kept watching the image of the arkship with its giant plumes of bright vapour seething outwards.

'Did you do that?' a subdued Callum asked.

'No,' Danuta said. 'We haven't launched anything.'

'Then what the hell's happening?'

'You told them about our strike capability?' Yuri asked Danuta in surprise.

'Yes. It's important Alpha Defence understand every option.'

Yuri wanted to disapprove. He knew it was stupid, but trusting Callum was still difficult. Which was a poor reflection on himself, he acknowledged grimly. 'Good call.'

'Those cracks are forming up into an exact radial,' Loi said. 'They're opening around the entire circumference near the rear end.'

'Call Jessika,' Callum said. 'She might be able to tell us what's happening.'

Loi gave Yuri a desperate look. 'She already has.'

'Just do it!' Yuri snapped. 'Map the internal chambers on the image for me,' he told Boris.

The hologram schematic changed, becoming translucent to show the ghostly ovoid biochambers within the arkship. Everyone could see the cracks were opening around the middle of the secret fourth chamber at the rear.

'Bloody hell,' Callum spat. 'That's the chamber Jessika said housed the wormhole.'

'Looks like they're jettisoning the whole rear section,' Yuri said. 'The part which houses the antimatter drive.'

'Because they don't need it any more,' Callum said. 'And this action will open the wormhole to space.'

'Fuck! The Deliverance fleet is going to come out. It's really happening.'

'Yuri, I'm giving my authorization for the strike,' Danuta said.

'I'm adding my code,' Yuri said hurriedly. He almost smiled when he saw all five authority codes were loading into the Teucer armoury. *Unanimous!*

A text from Ainsley III splashed across Yuri's tarsus lens. **You're on the ground, Yuri, take command of the strike.**

'Move to activation stage,' he told Boris as the command icon gleamed indigo in his lens. 'Do we use the missiles or go for a stealth delivery?' he asked Danuta.

'I'd say missiles,' she said. 'Olyix defence capability is an unknown, so speed may be our one advantage. And we have to prevent those Deliverance ships from coming through.'

Too late for that, Yuri thought. The hologram cube was showing the arkship's radial crack was now over a hundred metres wide on the surface. He told Boris to send the launch codes.

Deep inside the Teucer asteroid, the first five nuclear-armed missiles slipped out of their storage silos. The asteroid's G8Turing splashed the sequence across Yuri's tarsus lens. It gave him the multispectrum image from the five stealth satellites orbiting two million kilometres out from the *Salvation of Life*, each of which had a portal back to Teucer. Analysis showed the massive gas plumes gushing from the arkship's expanding fissure were an oxygen/ nitrogen mix: its atmosphere, from the fourth chamber. And the density was dropping off fast. The chamber must be almost empty. Sensors also started to pick up gravity waves emanating from the arkship. The huge forward section began to accelerate slowly, increasing the separation distance from the discarded antimatter drive.

'A gravity drive?' he said in amazement.

'Jessika wasn't lying,' Callum said quietly. 'It's all true.'

'Our sensor satellites are detecting negative energy signatures,' Loi said. 'Wow, they're powerful. Off-the-scale powerful.'

'That's got to be a wormhole,' Yuri said bitterly. 'They're not shielding it any more.' He ran through the G8Turing's tactical projections. The Teucer missiles were only minutes away from launch. They'd be sent through the portals to the satellites, along with five hundred electronic warfare missiles to blind and confuse the arkship's sensors during their approach. At full acceleration, it would take them ninety-seven minutes to cover the distance to their target. 'That gravity drive is going to complete the arkship separation before our missiles get anywhere near. The wormhole will be open to space.'

'Then some Deliverance ships get through,' Danuta declared. 'We can live with that. But we need to finish this. Speed is our advantage here. We must be able to kill that wormhole before their entire fleet arrives.'

Instinct told Yuri it was never going to be that easy. He held his tongue.

'Launch in ten seconds,' Boris said.

'We're using our nukes,' Danuta announced to Alpha Defence.

'What fucking nukes?' Alik shouted.

'Connexion developed a fallback option,' Yuri said, and any other day he would have laughed out loud at the agent's reaction – exactly the same as Callum's. 'A last resort. Just in case.'

'Goddamn Ainsley! That paranoid son of a bitch. Do you have any idea how much crap D.C. would pour over your heads if that news ever got out?'

'They'll pin a medal on Grandfather now,' Loi snapped back.

Yuri's ultra-secure link to Teucer dropped out. 'Oh shit! What—?'

'I've got nothing,' Danuta said in alarm.

'That link *cannot* fail,' Yuri said numbly. 'Nothing can interrupt . . . oh. No. No. No!'

'Commander, what sensors do Alpha Defence have in Jupiter's Trailing Trojans?' Danuta asked.

'Same coverage as the rest of the Sol system,' Johnston told her. 'We have everything out to the Kuiper belt under observation.'

The Trailing Trojan point appeared in a cube in front of Yuri. In reality, the Jovian Lagrange point was an elongated zone over five AU wide, spread out along the gas giant's orbit. It contained more than half a million asteroids over a kilometre wide. Seventeen of the larger ones hosted industrial complexes with their attendant corporate nation habitats, and a further hundred and twenty had rock-squatter Turings. Even though it was over a hundred kilometres in diameter, Teucer was one of them.

Alpha Defence had thirty-seven sensor satellites in the region, so even at the speed of light visual coverage across the entire zone had a time lag of several minutes. Yuri stared intently at the green digits that tagged Teucer – waiting. Waiting . . . Fifty seconds later, Teucer flared, a solar-bright cataract like the tail on the devil's own comet.

'Motherfucker!' he spat. The rage and dismay triggered by the sight immobilized him for a long moment. When he finally felt his hands clenching into fists, it was inordinately difficult to resist not punching something – the archway, Loi . . . He hadn't been so close to completely losing it since his conscript days in the Russian Army. In the end he let out a snarl of fury. 'Feriton! It must have been that shitfucker Feriton. He knew about Teucer and our stockpile of nukes. Motherfucker, we even took one to Nkya in case we needed to shut down the site in a hurry!'

'It wasn't him,' Callum said sadly. 'Not really. Hell, man, they have his brain in a pickle jar. They extracted every memory, that's how they knew how to fool all of us into thinking his body was still human.'

'Yes. Thank you, captain fucking obvious!' Yuri retorted. He couldn't tear his gaze from the lonely asteroid that he'd invested so much faith in. The irradiated vapour cloud was now dwindling, sublimating away into the solar wind.

'Just saying . . .' Callum grumbled.

'Yes.' Yuri got a grip, still straight-backed as he turned to the faces on the screens. 'So . . . I'm guessing when his body became an Olyix quint, it – they, whatever – would have checked out our secret observation base. Fuck, that's what I would have done. Standard procedure. They discovered our warheads and sabotaged them.'

'They know what they're doing,' Callum said. 'Jessika told us they've done this before. Many times.'

'We can still beat them,' Alik said. 'Jessika and the rest of the Neána came here to help us. They know how to counter all this. And now . . . Now we know she's been telling the truth. We'll listen to her. Properly, this time.'

'Admirable confidence,' Johnston said. 'But unless anyone else has a secret stash of nuclear weapons, and a working delivery system, we're going to have to fight them on the ground.'

'Callum?' Yuri asked.

'No.' Callum shook his head. 'The Utopials don't have secret nukes.'

Yuri almost said: *That you know of.* But he knew how pointless that was. 'All right, then. On the ground it is.' He took a breath and focused on what needed doing in an ideal situation, and what was practical. 'Okay. Anne, lock down all company facilities – and I mean *all*. Everyone inside a Connexion facility is to have their skull deep scanned, and no one gets in without a deep scan either. If the scan team find someone walking around with a quint brain in their head, eliminate them.'

'Eliminate . . .?'

'Exterminate. Those alien fuckers are to be killed immediately. Are we clear on that?'

'Yes, sir.'

'Good. Call in all our off-duty security personnel immediately. I don't care what they're doing, they're to be armoured up and ready to deploy as soon as they've passed that deep scan exam. So, initial priority is our own internal hub network. As of now, it is only for use by security personnel – no exceptions; make sure executives and top management understand that. They can be arrogant bastards, but today they join the sheep. Second, the national centre hubs. They're the core of our global network, so that's the first deployment goal for our teams; I want each of them safeguarded. When that stage is complete, start deploying out into the regional hubs. Leave the metrohubs until last.' He paused. Protecting the metrohubs was an automatic procedure, but today's reality made it unattainable. *Every public hub on the planet? No way.* He wasn't securing company assets from radicals and safeguarding the money flow out to shareholders. Not any more. This was species survival. It didn't get more simple than that. 'Actually, forget the metrohubs; we simply don't have the staff. We're going to have to shut them down. If nothing else, it should slow down the sabotage.'

Anne Groell gave him a startled glance. 'Er, sir, do you have authority for that?'

'Today I have more authority than God.' At the same time he sent Danuta a plain: **?**

Fucking hell, Yuri, she sent back.

? ? !

Okay, Ainsley III confirms. Do it.

He told Boris to load the day code he'd been given by Ainsley III into the operation centre's G8Turing cube array.

'Loaded and confirmed,' his altme said. 'You have operational control of Connexion's entire Sol network.'

'You're leaving the metrohubs unguarded?' Loi asked.

'It's the end of the world, Loi. We can't protect them, not if we want to keep the core of the network intact. City residents can either take a cabez or actually walk for a change. Exercise will do them good.'

'Christ almighty.'

Yuri took a moment and weighed options, still staring at the remnants of Teucer, the one real hope he'd had. 'Anne, shut down traffic through the interstellar hubs. I want them physically sealed. Let's keep any new Olyix agents off the terraformed worlds.'

'Got it,' Groell said. 'The hub glitches are increasing across the network, and dozens are dropping out altogether. Even if you hadn't told us what's happening, we'd know for sure there's a hostile force out there.'

'How are we responding?' Yuri asked.

The hologram cubes around Groell began to thicken as their data multiplied, obscuring her face behind a moiré curtain. 'Lownet activity is peaking even higher than the '97 Great NeoCrypto Extraction, but the G8Turings are filtering and blocking when those sonofabitch netheads try to rise up into solnet. Physical sabotage is more difficult to pinpoint. Actual assaults on the hubs is minimal, but incursions against auxiliary equipment are definitely increasing.'

'Okay, extend the physical security border out from the buildings with interstellar hubs; we have to keep them operational.' He didn't want to say it out loud, even in here, but Earth was going to need its paths out to the terraformed worlds if they were going to use Jessika's fly-and-hide option.

Loi gave the display bubbles in each segment a quick glance. 'Damn, it's getting bad, and we're only a few minutes in.'

'Yeah.' Yuri checked with Boris and found New York's shield hadn't switched on yet. 'Alik, I *still* haven't got a shield above me.'

'I'm on it.' Alik's image vanished from the screen.

'Damage reports are increasing,' Anne said. 'Our European hubs are dipping into power reserves. Looks like the saboteurs are targeting the planetary power grid.'

'Crap. That's outside our security coverage,' Yuri grunted. 'Time to kick the power companies up the arse and get their security to do its job.' He turned to stare into the petal segment that dealt with Connexion's European operations. 'Who's in the London ops centre?'

*

Kohei Yamada was due to retire in another eighteen months. It was something he'd been promising his (fifth) wife for the past decade. A hundred and twenty years in Connexion Security was impressive for a single job even in this day and age. Too long by about seven decades, according to those first four wives, who'd all warned number five. Which was why he'd sworn: *As soon as the time is right.* The first four clearly hadn't properly understood there'd been a career structure to maintain, promotions to achieve. And now that everyone who could afford it underwent genetic life-extension therapies, significant promotions were fewer and took longer to reach. That made them incredibly valuable – a true measure of a person's talent. A hundred and twenty years of training and experience had resulted in him achieving Chief of London Station. After all the sacrifice to get there, he wasn't going to give it up quickly; this job required someone at the pinnacle of their game.

That self-confidence was currently what was keeping Kohei from diving under the operations centre chair and kissing his arse goodbye. The briefing from New York was as terrifying as it was mesmerizing. *The Olyix? The fucking Olyix – lumbering, eager to please, god-bothering Olyix – were launching an invasion?* If it had been anyone other than Yuri taking charge and telling it straight, he would have suspected someone was off their heads on zero-nark.

But then the incidents started to break out across London: hubs with equipment glitches, hubs with communication problems, Turings forced to enact emergency shutdown to prevent unheard-of failures, Turings reporting extremely sophisticated lownet attacks.

Then it started to ramp up: security staff in the national hubs reporting they were under attack, power grids being cut . . . Plus the one to beat them all: London's shield came on – ordered by Alpha Defence, no less.

It's real. All of it.

So – there were operational procedures to follow. Some could be done by the file; others had to be modified to cope with the unique circumstances. Most required instantaneous judgements based on the time he'd spent in the front line, where lessons were hammered home the hard way.

All things that only someone with his wealth of decades in Security was qualified to provide, along with respect and command ability – also acquired through equal decades of commitment. Plus, he'd learned from the best: Yuri Alster.

Now, an Olyix invasion was proof that he'd been right to stay in the job. He kept telling himself that only his level of professionalism could secure Connexion's European organization against a crisis of this magnitude.

Then the whole Greenwich operations centre – the four of them sitting around the display bubble – fell silent to witness the massive bulk of the *Salvation of Life* separating into two sections. It was being prised apart by an invisible gravity drive that was beyond anything humans possessed. And even Kohei began to doubt there would be anything left to salvage.

'How's it going?' Yuri asked over the secure link.

'We're targeting key hubs for level-one protection,' Kohei told him. 'But we're going to run into restrictions with personnel numbers. The deep scans you've ordered on everyone are going to slow down our deployment.'

'Trust me. Those scans are essential.'

'Shit. Okay.'

'Have you been scanned yet?'

'Er, no.'

'Get scanned. Now. Get all of the ops centre team scanned. Call me back when you've passed.'

'Yes, boss.'

Kohei didn't want to do it. There was just too much to organize and oversee. Several hubs had reported physical attacks before dropping out of communications. Nearby civic sensors revealed buildings with explosion-shattered windows or flames coming through the standard arched entrances. He needed to sort it all out, but Yuri knew that. And if Yuri said it was essential . . .

Reluctantly he got up and hurried through the Greenwich tower to the security department clinic, then barged to the front of the queue of discontented employees. Thirty seconds for the sensors to probe deep into his grey matter, allowing the G8Turing to examine cellular structure, biochemical composition, neural map . . .

By wonderful, ironic chance he was reviewing the redA files Yuri had authorized him to access while the scanner bar was curving patiently around his head, and saw the image of Feriton's axe-broken skull. 'Sweet Christ,' he murmured.

When he stepped away from the scanner bars, his nerves were sparking with primal tension. His gaze swept along the queue, seeing the bored, the impatient, the indifferent, and he was truly terrified that one pair of those eyes might be looking right back at him from a coldly calculating alien mind. Any one of the myriad oh-so-human expressions around him could be faked, sculpted to persuade and elicit sympathy, to null suspicion. *Hey, I'm just one of the guys.*

'Redeployment, priority one,' he told Nils, his altme, as he left the clinic, half-expecting a bullet to the back of the head. 'I want tactical team members who've already passed the scan, armed and armoured, five to each scan in every facility we have running the screening process.'

'Confirmed,' Nils said.

'Hell, boss, I accessed the file on Feriton,' he said as he settled back into his chair in the Greenwich operations centre.

'Now you understand,' Yuri replied.

'I do. For the record, I'd rather die than have that happen to me.'

'Yeah, me too, my friend.'

'But . . . I can't see any way out of this. I really can't.' One of the hologram cubes was showing the Alpha Defence feed, where the *Salvation of Life* was continuing to separate into two unequal portions.

'Go by the numbers,' Yuri replied. 'That's what we've got. Kill their sabotage, preserve what we can. The Neána aliens seem to think some of us can survive, that we can get away like they did. But to do that, we have to fend them off for long enough. So that's what we're going to do.'

'Right.' Kohei knew it was completely hopeless, but even so, you followed procedure, did the job, and told yourself someone further up the command chain knew what the hell they were doing. He told Nils to expand the hologram cubes around his chair, surrounding himself with a galaxy of vivid primary colour graphics. Smiling fiercely, accepting the challenge, allowing his subconscious to discern the patterns that would be lurking among all that vibrant data. It was an ability he had. He didn't know how it worked, just that it did. Back in college, partying in the student bar, his friends used to shout eight-figure digits at him, ten or fifteen of them, one after the other, and somewhere somehow in his brain he added them up. They'd shake their heads in amazed disbelief and down more beer.

The operations centre G8Turing was doing the same thing, analysing and trying to predict, but its pattern recognition algorithms lacked intuition. He'd win; he knew he'd win.

The majority of the sabotage so far was digital, with the company's G8Turings blocking it almost as soon as it was detected. Physical attacks were fewer in number but effective, leaving wrecked buildings and smashed portals in their wake. Seventeen so far in England, fifty-nine in Western Europe. That had to be stopped – and fast. Data logs of each incident splashed out into the cubes, summarizing the history and isolating similarities. The initial darkware attacks were designed to generate enough glitches in security systems, however temporary, to sneak the perpetrators inside. Sometimes people, sometimes drones – either mechanical or animal synths. So . . . strengthen the network against darkware and use external civic and public sensors to complement company scrutiny. Creeperdrones were sneaking in under the buildings, using conduits or ancient pipes; London had centuries of obsolete infrastructure that had never been taken out. Maintenance drones were activated and sent down into the old sewers, armoured ferrets hunting rodent automata.

Kohei watched the deployment in satisfaction but knew it wasn't enough. The ops centre was only reacting. To be effective, to counter this properly, they had to go on the offensive. He started looking for the deeper patterns that must be there. *How would I bring down Connexion?* It was an old trick, one he'd learned from Yuri way back when. *What are we not seeing?* A question no Turing could ever answer no matter what G it was.

To take out the hubs one by one was a phenomenal task, requiring vast resources. Preparations on that scale would've been picked up by intelligence agencies. In short, it would be seen. *So if I can't take out the hubs directly, what else will cripple them? What do the hubs depend on?*

The side of his mouth lifted in a soft smile. 'Splash the power grid feeds to the hubs,' he told Nils.

Connexion had engineered a good distribution system, using an idea Ainsley Zangari himself had come up with right back at the very start. Power from the solarwell MHD asteroids was delivered via portal to commercial relay stations all over Earth, affording multiple redundancy. From those relays it was transferred to every single Connexion portal door via a built-in one-centimetre portal. That way the company didn't have to spend billions of additional wattdollars laying a massive web of superconductor cables across the planet.

'Review security networks of each power relay station we tap into,' he ordered. His smile broadened as the results splashed across the cubes.

It was starting. The Connexion G8Turings observed darkware infiltrating the networks of a dozen major power relay stations – darkware that was a lot more subtle and sophisticated than anything launched against the hubs. None of it was active yet. They were waiting, gathering themselves ready to strike.

'Yuri, they're going for the power grid,' Kohei warned. 'The attacks on our hubs are a diversion.'

'Good work,' Yuri responded.

Kohei watched Yuri's alert flash out across Connexion's security network, feeling a burst of satisfaction. *But it's going to be a long dirty war.* He reviewed the status of the European power relay stations. Now they knew what to look for, the G8Turings were identifying suspicious people and drones coalescing around several stations. 'Let's bring in the police tactical teams,' he told Nils as various taxez, bugez and creeperdrones inched surreptitiously closer to their objectives. 'They can complement our squads, and ambush the bastards – hard.' Another fast assessment of the approaching hostiles. 'Start with Croydon.'

London

26th June 2204

Dusk embellished the city skyline in overstated tones, separating the jet-black geometric jags of the buildings from the gold horizon in an austere border. Gwendoline Seymore-Qing-Zangari stared at it from behind her desk, oblivious to the splendour. Her tarsus lenses were splashing too many finance spreadsheets for anything else to register, and the pheni nark she'd taken that afternoon was draining out of her synapses like a retreating tide, leaving her tired and irritable. She rubbed her eyes, squashing the tight graphics into multicoloured Rorschach clouds. Those figures were the culmination of eighteen months of work. Her team was steering Connexion's Exosol Investment Office through the Corbyzan project – so far, just a ridiculously complex finance root bubble future fund that would be governed by a dozen Turing rock-squatters. Over a hundred banks, finance houses, angel investors and sovereign funds were involved, each one contributing additional problems and demands to the negotiations. But eighteen months of political deal making, schmoozing, arm twisting, near-blackmail, favours given and owed, and they were edging to an agreement that satisfied just about everyone. And once the finance was established, the real work would begin.

Gwendoline had found herself involved and interested by

Corbyzan in a way that hadn't happened in any previous corporate ventures she'd helped set up. The fund would pay for the terraforming of Corbyzan and setting up its preliminary government with a constitution that was acceptable to every partner – a political nightmare of compromise and concessions. In itself, Corbyzan wasn't that exceptional: an exoplanet orbiting 55 Cancri, forty light-years from Sol. There were dozens of similar planets with a primordial atmosphere of hydrogen sulphide, methane and carbon dioxide – the kind that were the easiest to convert. But it would be the first new terraforming endeavour in thirteen years. With eleven terraformed planets at stage two habitation, and a further twenty-seven in stage one, the market was deemed to be saturated. But this was something new; the Corbyzan constitution was being pitched as the Universal counter to Utopial culture. It was going to use sophisticated fabrication technology as its manufacturing base, but with a capital-market economy. The semi-controversial part was its citizenship requirement. You were going to need an IQ over 125 to settle there, and all immigrant offspring would receive germline modification to give them an IQ over 135. Given it had a Sol asteroid belt Turing rock-squatter as its founding government, the Sol Senate Justice Court had no jurisdiction should anyone try and claim exclusionary discrimination, and anyway the Utopials had set the precedent with their omnia descendant conditions for settlement. Nonetheless, there were objectors – unsurprisingly, given Sol's historically conservative finance sector. Her dealings had proved quite revealing of the attitudes of plutocrats who publicly clung to the liberal ethos.

A yawn parted her lips and she knew her concentration was wilting after sitting in the office for ten hours straight. Right now only another pheni nark would bring it back, and she wasn't going to do that. She'd seen enough colleagues and business associates slip into that bad habit to know it wasn't worth it. One addiction laid you open to others in a fast downward spiral.

'Store and close,' she told Theano, her altme. 'And you,' she said to her three young executive assistants. 'We're done for today. Go out, have fun.'

The complex data splash vanished, leaving just her personal data icons bracleting the edge of her vision. The solnet news filter was flashing updates on city shields; apparently Sydney and Johannesburg had switched theirs on. *Odd.* 'Monitor it,' she instructed Theano.

Her executive office suite on the eighty-fourth floor of Connexion's Greenwich tower had a portal door straight to her portalhome in Chelsea, at the corner of Cheyne Walk and Milmans Street. She had the penthouse, twenty storeys up, with a long lounge whose elegant bay windows gave her a direct view over the Thames to the curving glass cliff face of the lavish ziggurat bestriding the south bank. Several of its residents were already partying on their terraces, which brought an amused smile to her lips. Some nights she'd seen parties whose decadent antics managed to shock even her. Not this evening, though.

Anahita, her social aide, hurried in. 'You're running late,' she said; it was almost accusatory.

'I know. Sorry.' Not meant. It was ritual for Gwendoline; she was always late. Proof of a full and rich life, just like employing humans as house staff. There was very little that Turings and robotics couldn't do, and cheaper, but then it was never about cost. Gwendoline's position meant she had a certain status to maintain.

'We have the selection for next Thursday,' Anahita said, clicking her fingers impatiently. Her junior assistants, Jimena and Luciana, hurried in, both hauling bundles of tissue-wrapped evening gowns.

Gwendoline almost sighed in dismay at the sight of the bright fabrics and remarkable styles, this ceremony had been acted out *so many* times now. Instead she made a show of disinclination as she slipped out of her business suit jacket and started unfastening the skirt. 'All right, we'll do this on the table.'

A minute later she was lying on the padded massage table in the orangery, with fluffy white towels under her back. She was always aware of an underlying tension when she was naked in the penthouse. From the staff, anyway; she rather enjoyed being voyeured by the genuinely youthful. It was like a certificate of approval.

Cho, her masseuse, was slowly easing the iron strings of office tension from her legs, while Yana was diligently applying soft unguents on her face to repair a day's abrasion inflicted by harsh air conditioning. Given the giddying amount of money she spent on her body – not just anti-ageing therapies, but also personal trainers, spa memberships to complement bioactive cosmetics, and a perfect diet – she wasn't about to neglect the fundamentals now, no matter how pressed for time she was. It was worth it. At fifty-four, she still had the slim build of her adolescence. Slightly more muscle now to keep everything firm, but that was a medal of pride, earned by getting back into shape after pregnancy. There was no hint of her knife-blade cheeks getting blunt, thankfully, so she hadn't needed any cosmetic therapies – apart from bleaching out her freckles, which wasn't a vanity thing; she just didn't feel comfortable with them given her current corporate director position. Anyone who didn't know would think she was still in her early twenties.

Anahita stood beside the table, holding a bottle of oil for Cho. 'You have cocktails at Marquise's in . . . twenty-eight minutes.'

'How am I going to get my hair done in time for that?' Gwendoline asked petulantly.

'I'm sorry, ma'am. I did have Charlie booked, but that was seventy minutes ago.'

'Yes, yes, I'm late. Then . . .?'

'After cocktails there's dinner with Tam and Kaveh in Bali, so that will be morning there, and hot.' Anahita beckoned to Jimena, who hurried forward, unwrapping the first gown, an emerald silk affair with sweeping full-length skirt.

'What have you got for me to wear in Bali?'

'The scarlet Divanni,' Anahita said immediately. 'It's an above-the-knee summer dress, loose weave cotton.'

'Okay, fine.' She couldn't be bothered to argue, and let out a soft moan as Cho moved up onto her stomach, applying the spice-scented oil in smooth talented strokes. 'What am I choosing for again?'

'Prince Raiden's ball. It's for charity. The Eldemar germline treatment – for underprivileged children.'

'Who isn't underprivileged compared to us?' she muttered and stopped Yana's attentions for a moment to study the gown Jimena held. 'No.' Doing this at home was a pain, but preferable to visiting one of Chelsea's plethora of boutique TryMe stores. She barely had time for this, never mind shopping.

Anahita shooed Jimena away. 'The architect called. He has a redesigned interior ready for the Titan dome.'

Gwendoline and Anahita both glanced along the wide central hallway, whose walls were lined with eight archways. Each one held a portal door to the penthouse's extended rooms. Five were gleaming with various intensities of sunlight beyond, while two were dark: the moon and Pluto.

'I'm not sure about Titan,' Gwendoline said. 'I mean, it's just pink methane fog the whole time. Bit murky. So boring.'

'Of course. Do you want to consider somewhere else?'

'Maybe.' Gwendoline gave the eighth archway – the empty one – a contemplative look. 'A Jovian moon? But everyone has one of those.'

'Perhaps Io? The sulphur volcanoes are spectacular, apparently. I know there are some rooms available in a couple of the viewblocks.'

'I suppose. But how often are the eruptions really? Not the viewblock company's figures.'

'I'll look into it.'

Yana unbound Gwendoline's long hair so it hung over the edge of the padded table and began a scalp massage. Luciana stepped up, proffering a yellow evening gown with a very deep plunge neck.

Gwendoline moaned in satisfaction as both massages eased away the tautness afflicting her body. 'No. Too tarty. You have to leave something to the imagination.'

A disappointed Luciana backed away.

'You received eighteen invitations today,' Anahita said. 'I turned down fifteen of them on your behalf. If you'd like to review the others . . .'

Theano splashed the three remaining invites for her. 'Oh, Waldemar's chateau party. I love those. Yes to that. Polite no to the others.'

'Of course.'

Jimena stepped forward to show off an orange and white gown.

'Hmm. Would that go with my complexion, do you think?'

'Yes, ma'am,' Jimena assured her ardently.

'I have items for Octavio's birthday present,' Anahita said.

Gwendoline sighed. 'Show me.' She sneaked a longing glance at the hallway's third arch, the one with the portal door out to a cliff-top balcony overlooking the Mediterranean where a low honey sun shone golden rays across worn-smooth terracotta tiles. It sported cosy-cushioned sunloungers, the sparkling clean water below, a warm breeze, the scent of night-flowers in the air. Add some properly chilled wine and it would be perfect. A do-nothing evening was something she hadn't enjoyed for . . . Well, she'd have to check with Theano, so the answer was too long. A man – smart, sophisticated, funny, handsome – in the next sunlounger would cap it off nicely. Again, too long . . .

Jimena held up the orange and white dress, studying it for herself. 'Would you like to try it on?' she asked hopefully, as if that would score points against Luciana.

Gwendoline grimaced as she gave the frilly miscreation a stricter appraisal. *Whatever happened to LBDs?*

'After dinner, you're due to see Wobari at the Piccadilly Fusion Club,' Anahita continued relentlessly. 'Then if you can manage later, Fiona's aide called. She'd like to . . .' She trailed off frowning at whatever was splashing across her tarsus lens.

Gwendoline opened her mouth to tell Jimena she'd decided against the orange and white after all when Theano splashed up red icons. One made her start; it was from the super-exclusive globalPAC she was a member of (fee two million wattdollars a year, paid for by Connexion). And it was a physical security warning. Something she'd never seen before. Financial warnings, yes, but a physical threat . . . The level which that globalPAC operated at made it particularly unnerving. *What the hell can worry them?*

Outside the orangery windows, the gleaming star-speckled horizon began to dim.

'Oh, my,' Anahita gasped. 'That's the London shield. They've switched the shield on.'

Gwendoline rolled off the table and padded over to the glass wall, her staff clustered around behind her. The last of the soft gloaming faded out altogether as the shield generators locked air molecules together in a two-kilometre-thick wall that curved over the entire city. She remembered the last time London's shield had been tested, back in '89. It had been daylight, and the sky had dropped to a pasty grey. Now, the underside of the dense energized gas refracted the city's streetlights to create an eerie uniform shell of phosphorescence, as if the universe had shrunk to a final bubble of existence.

'What's happened?' Jimena asked shrilly. 'Is there a meteorite up there?'

Gwendoline had stopped watching the artificial dome to access the reports from her globalPAC, and the classified sensor stream Connexion's Security Division was feeding direct from Alpha Defence. The *Salvation of Life* had split open, its two sections moving ponderously apart, the larger one under acceleration. *A gravity drive? What the actual fuck?* Then a Connexion executive-only alert splashed up: Teucer had dropped from the company secure network. No additional details, but the Olyix Monitoring Office was silent. No, not silent; its communication link was dead. Which she thought was impossible.

The shiver that ran down her flesh had nothing to do with air temperature as the information expanded. *Invasion?* she mouthed silently. It was unbelievable; too big, too shocking.

'Ma'am?' a very nervous Anahita asked.

Gwendoline took a moment and forced herself to concentrate. 'You need to go home,' she said sharply. 'All of you.'

Her staff shared concerned glances.

'What is it?' the normally mouse-timid Yana asked.

'The shield is a precaution. There's something odd happening at the alien arkship.' Even watching the massive interstellar ship split apart, she couldn't quite bring herself to say it, as if that alone would make it real.

'I'll stay with you,' Anahita said.

'No. All of you go. Now.' She didn't add: please. She wasn't politely asking. If it was real, she couldn't be lumbered with dependants. There would be protocols somewhere in the Connexion Security G8Turings on how to evacuate critical personnel and family in an extreme emergency. *Surely?*

The staff all exchanged another, more troubled, look, and trooped out of the orangery like children handed a school exclusion order. Gwendoline gave the formidable shield a lingering stare and started searching for a robe. Amusing herself with her own ineptitude, she wasn't entirely sure which wardrobe they were kept in.

'Call Loi,' she told Theano.

'His altme is not responding. Would you like to leave a message?'

Damn! She started to wonder if the alien ship they'd found on Nkya was somehow connected to this. Not wonder; worry. Security meant the whole Nyka assessment team was out of solnet contact, for ten days at least.

Pressing her teeth together in reluctance, she made the grudging decision and said: 'Call Horatio.'

'Hi, babe,' he answered. 'Are you in London? Are you seeing this? Isn't it amazing? They haven't had a shield practice for fifteen years.'

Why? Why is he always such a bloody optimist? And sweet? Kind?
'Horatio, darling, it's not a practice.'

'What? You're kidding!'

'No, I'm not. I'm at home, accessing high-level Connexion security reports. It's the Olyix, Horatio. They're hostile. Really very hostile. I think it's going to be bad.'

'Seriously? That sounds like a load of allcomments bollocks to me.'

'Horatio!' she yelled. 'The Olyix are going to invade. They're going to cocoon us . . . or something. It's not a joke. I'm frightened.'
Somehow she'd wound up in front of the portal to the Mediterranean balcony. The beautiful honey sun had fallen below the horizon, leaving the stars twinkling in a placid night sky. One step, and she'd be away from the madness. Just one –

'Shit, all right. I'm coming over, okay. Just . . . stay calm. I'll be there.'

'Careful,' she blurted. 'There's sabotage starting. Olyix agents are attacking the hubs.'

There was a long pause, and she realized she hadn't said: *No. I don't need you. I don't want you here. I'm quite capable of taking care of myself, thank you.*

'I'll watch out, don't worry.'

'Horatio, has Loi been in touch?'

'Not for a couple of days. We had a drink a few nights ago; he said he'd managed to get himself selected as Yuri's technical adviser for some exoplanet team, and he'd be out of solnet range some of the time. He was very excited about it. It's a big deal for him.'

'Yes. Yes, it is.' *And damn Ainsley for sending him. He's just a child.*

'Hey, don't panic. Loi will be fine. He's got his head screwed on right.'

'You and Loi go drinking together?'

'We meet up sometimes, yeah. When he's not busy, which is pretty much always now that he works for Connexion. Why?'

'Nothing. I'm glad, that's all.'

'Okay. I'll be with you in a minute.'

'I'll authorize the penthouse to let you in.'

She stood there for a moment, gazing out at the balmy Mediterranean evening. *That's just a sweet illusion. What's actually happening is real.*

Acknowledgement made her shiver and she rubbed her arms. It wasn't cold in the robe, but she started for the bedroom to find something nice to wear for when Horatio arrived. Maybe something a little . . . *No! Don't go there, woman. For heaven's sake, we've both moved on, like adults.*

Besides, she needed to have a plan. It would probably be safer for them in the Greenwich tower, and easier to evacuate from there. *But not without Loi.*

Reports were coming in from official sources now – governments making cautious announcements about taking precautionary measures, that the Olyix may not be benign, that communications to the *Salvation of Life* had been cut, that we're doing everything we can to verify the situation. *Panic's going to hit real soon*, she thought. The allcomments were flaring up to peak psychotic frenzy.

Theano splashed a house icon. Her private portal to the Greenwich tower had just been powered down by Connexion Security as a 'precautionary measure'.

'Oh, fuck.' The Security department really was taking this seriously. She asked the London office what plans were in place to safeguard senior executives and Zangari family members. **Protocol pending**, came the answer. **All executive-level employees required to initiate private residence security systems to highest level and remain within protected zone. No readmittance to Connexion facilities until further notice.**

She told Theano to activate the penthouse security procedures and went into the lounge to wait for Horatio. Standing in the central bay window, she looked out across the Thames. All the terrace parties on the ziggurat opposite had stopped. When she looked down, she could see dozens of luxurious houseboats moored along the bank below. Several of them had people moving around on deck, and she realized they were preparing to cast off. *Where do you think you're going?* They'd never get through the shield; it sealed off the river east and west of the city. The authorities only ever held a shield practice at low tide, and it lasted no more than fifteen minutes, purely because of the water. Inside the shield, the water that was in the river channel would continue to run east, to the lowest point, where the shield acted as a dam. While outside, at the western edge, all the old London reservoirs at Wraysbury had been enlarged to cope with the Thames overspill as the shield cut off the river flow into the city. The deep circular basins now had enough capacity to hold six hours' worth of the river emptying into them before they breached, and at that point the floodwater would start to spill around the edges of the shield as it sought a new route to the sea.

Once again she looked down the hallway, where the light from the Mediterranean balcony had sunk to a tender gloaming.

Loi's icon splashed into her tarsus lens, bumping up her heart rate.

'Loi, darling, are you all right?'

'Yeah, Mum, I'm fine. Don't worry. Look, I'm with Yuri Alster in New York so I've only got a few seconds. You know about the Olyix invasion, right?'

'Are you sure you're all right?'

'Yes! They should have sent you security warnings. Follow them. Okay?'

'I will.'

'I know you, Mum. You think these things don't apply to you, but they do today. Please; this is life or death. The Olyix are coming for us. All of us.'

'I know. I understand.'

'Good. So switch on every security gadget you have. Then go on to the penthouse's backup power. It's internal, and it'll last for months. And whatever you do, stay in the London part of the penthouse. Do not go through into any of your other rooms, especially the offworld ones. It's important, Mum.'

At any other time she would have laughed, but Loi's intensity was as frightening as the news coming in over the feeds from her high-level contacts. 'Who's the parent here?'

'They're about to shut down unnecessary portals to save power, and portalhome doors are top of that list.'

'Why do they need to save power?'

'We think the Olyix are going to hit the power supply to Earth. They need to immobilize us so they can capture us, and Earth is still home to over seventy per cent of the human race.'

'Oh my God!'

'It's okay. Just stay put. We'll have a clearer picture of what's happening in a day or so. And we have allies; they know what to do.'

'Allies? What do you mean?'

'I can't say any more. Just trust me, Mum. But we'll be okay, you and me, I promise. They'll never get all of us.'

'Your father's on his way here.'

'Really? Er . . . that's great. It makes things a lot easier. I'm going to get the Greenwich office to assign you a bodyguard, too, just to make sure you stay safe. When people realize what's actually happening, it might get ugly.'

'I don't need a bodyguard.'

'Mum, just this once, let me do what's necessary.'

'If it makes you happy. Can you at least get me one who's young and good looking? Boy or girl, I'm not fussy that way.'

'Mum!'

She grinned silently.

'I've got to go,' he said. 'Just please stay safe until we . . .'

'Until we what?'

'We'll probably have to leave.'

'London?'

'Earth, Mum. Earth. Forever. If our information's right, there are more Olyix ships on their way. A lot of them.'

'All right, darling. You take care, too. You need to promise me that.'

'I will.'

'I love you, Loi.'

'Love you, too, Mum.'

The link ended and she gave the hallway's open portal doors a final forlorn look. 'Shut them all down,' she ordered Theano. 'And implement isolation security; activate the non-lethal boundary weapons.'

*

A desperate Ollie was looking right at Piotr when it happened. The target laser flashed a tiny ruby-red dot on Piotr's temple and the back of his skull blew off. Gore and blood and bone fragments detonated in a grisly spume. Some of it splattered over Ollie as he dived for the tarmac. He hit numbingly hard, screaming in shock and revulsion.

They were on the perimeter road around the Croydon relay station – a big rectangular area of crumbling concrete, out of which rose the thrumming carbon-black slabs of high-voltage trans-formers and relays laid out in rows like giants' tombstones. It was protected by a triple fence whose five-metre height was topped by sensor globes and wisps of deadly monomolecule strands. Thick pearl-white pillars in the fence runs contained weaponry that was supposed to be sub-lethal.

The raid had started smoothly. Their darkware had corrupted the rare civic sensors surrounding the station, then began insinuating its way into the internal network. Squirrel creeperdrones scampered over the fences, clinging to them strategically, ready to burn through the boron-reinforced bladewires, while synth pigeons flew silently overhead, their fat bellies stuffed with countermeasure gadgets and chaff. Cats with nerve-block emitters prowled around the Legion, acting as sentinels and first-line defence in case any human guard should stumble upon them.

Five of the glaring border lights shining down onto the perimeter road had dimmed obediently at Adnan's subversive command as the Legion sneaked forwards out of the overgrown sprawl of long-abandoned allotments on the station's southern side. The road was still illuminated in the section they'd chosen to enter through, but the reduced light level made certain surfaces hard to distinguish.

Like his five friends, Ollie was modelling one of those certain surfaces: a stealth one-piece suit with a hood. The matt grey fabric had a kind of negative shimmer that made the edges hard to define even in modest daylight, while its synthesized molecular structure passively absorbed microwave radar pulses and the sonar beams from motion detectors. Thermally it was background-ambient, so the Legion presented as mobile blindspots to the infra-red cameras.

They reached the outer fence and huddled down at the foot of it. Ollie was doing his best to ignore the enormous city shield curving kilometres above their heads. Tye was muting the solnet paranoia about invading Olyix – the official (pathetically unbelievable) Sol Senate explanation. The altme was also struggling to filter down the overwhelming theories shouted from allcomments. That madness included sentient Turings rebelling against their human masters, the Kim cult detonating their long-lost nukes, perhaps an uprising of suicidal ultragreens saving the Gaia Goddess Earth from the human race by genociding everyone. Take your pick, the tinfoil-hat preachers demanded. No doubt about it, somewhere out beyond the reassuringly thick shield walls, a storm of pure crazy was winding up to strike.

It didn't matter; all that crap was just background rumble now. Ollie was focused on the raid with a purity that had delivered him unto the ultimate buzz. This was his peak, the final masterplay, the one that would pay for his breakout from the Legion and carry the family away into freedom.

'Status?' Piotr asked.

Ollie hadn't stopped studying the tactical display for the last fifteen minutes. All their drones and attackware were moving into final position. The station's security network was quiescent, suppressed by their darkware. Each tricky factor he'd calculated was clicking into place with efficient precision.

'Good to go,' he replied.

'Then get us in,' Piotr told Tronde.

The squirrels tightened their grip on the dangerously sharp wires of the fence, their activeblade claws powering up to cut through –

Bright light stabbed down from above as half the displays in Ollie's tarsus lens juddered into static. Stealth suits or not, the Legion were abruptly casting long shadows across the ground as they dropped to a crouch, twisting to search out their opponents.

'DON'T FUCKING MOVE,' God's voice boomed down from the sky.

'Move!' Piotr bellowed. 'Blitz the bastards.'

Ollie's surviving icons showed him Adnan slamming their darkware into plague-level activation and using the digital trauma to order a universal power cut to all the station's auxiliary systems, tripping every breaker. The dazzling light pinning them down flickered epileptically. At that point, Ollie instinctively started to run. It was the way Piotr ordered it, his commanding voice; Ollie couldn't help responding. Self-preservation was running a slow second.

Two paces and he managed to slow, twisting around towards Piotr, ready to shout: 'No. Wait.' Because he knew they'd walked right into an ambush, and with all the shit going down out there beyond the shield, every police force on the planet was going to be overhyped to psychotic paranoia. In horror he saw peripherals bulging up from Piotr's arms, burning their way through the fancy light-eluding cloth.

Piotr let loose a barrage of three-sixty covering fire, kinetic and maser.

They blew his brains out for it.

Ollie hit the ground, stunned by the impact and Piotr's corpse collapsing behind him. The lights went down, finally broken by the darkware. Back out along the perimeter road, the drone cats were racing towards the incoming armoured figures, nerve-block generators initiating. Overhead, the synth pigeons were detecting bulky urban tactical drones dropping down.

'Blitz them!' Adnan yelled. 'Hit 'em with everything all at once.'

Ollie seemed to have lost all rational thought. Regardless, Tye took only milliseconds to engage the tactical override. Every piece of hardware and software Ollie commanded went off as one.

Noonbright strobe flares. Active and passive chaff. Kinetics. Darkware unchained. Nerve-block pulses. Explosives in the creeper-drone squirrels detonated – an almost synchronized sequence. The blastwave flattened Ollie again, hammering him onto the road. Above him the sky had become a resplendent firework show, glaring clouds of red and green strobe flares mushrooming out in anger. The ambush team's tactical drones were spinning wildly, spitting out sparks. Out on the edge of his vision, he saw armoured figures racing towards them, dodging perceived or imaginary dangers.

'Move,' Gareth shouted.

Their cats leapt against the incoming armour suits, emitting nerve-block discharges that made limbs spasm, stomachs heave and lungs convulse.

Somehow Ollie scrambled to his feet. Instinct again, urging him back into the low jungle of the lost allotments. His friends were sprinting at his side now – except Lars, who altered course, heading for the nearest armoured figure.

'Fuck, Lars, don't!' Gareth called.

But if he heard, Lars didn't give a shit for sane advice. He slammed into the man, the two of them tumbling over and over. They stopped and traded blows. Lars split his knuckles pummelling the solid breastplate, having zero effect. Then a fast punch broke a couple of his ribs and sent him sprawling over backwards. The dark figure followed, kicked, which spun Lars around. Head kick. Drop down, and amplified arms were closing around Lars's over-muscled chest. Ollie could hear the agonized cry from Lars as the armour suit began to crush him.

Then, impossibly, Lars broke out of the enhanced hold and grabbed his opponent's neck and shoulder. *Fuck, how strong is he?* He lifted the man high and threw him, then jumped on top. Bloody hands grabbed the blank helmet, lifted and pounded, smashing it repeatedly against the tarmac.

Gareth started to run towards Lars, shouting at him to stop, to move. He was halfway there when the wyst bullet punched through his lower back and detonated inside him. His arms were flung outwards from the initial impact, back arching, and he toppled to the ground, a jelly of shredded organs gushing out of every orifice.

One of the ambush team was crouching on the perimeter road, arm raised, a thin integral forearm barrel extended over the wrist. He seemed to be having trouble holding the pose; every limb was shaking from the nerve-block pulses.

'Bastard,' Adnan screamed.

Two cats pounced, and the armour suit lit up with zing-ing static webs as their taser claws scrabbled for purchase against the smooth surface. The suited figure juddered savagely and slowly pitched forwards, the armour still coursing with electricity.

'Keep going,' Tronde demanded.

Ollie had reached the boundary of the allotments. The frenzied storm of light crashing out of the failing synth pigeons was slipping away. Now he could just make out Tronde and Adnan following him. Lars was a diffuse grey blob limping along after them.

'Their drones will see our tracks in the vegetation,' Adnan said as they kicked their way through stubborn brambles and weeds, wriggling past the massive buddleias.

'I got it,' Ollie said. He had no plans for this. As always, he'd built some flexibility into the raid should anything get out of kilter, giving them the ability to react to unforeseen circumstances. *Not this, though. Not an end of the fucking world shitstorm.* But he was the Legion's master tactician, the one they relied on to work out the mechanics of a raid. He usually spent weeks putting everything together, running simulations and refining it until he'd achieved perfection. Now he probably had thirty seconds before some bastard wyst bullet punctured his skull.

Map, situation, resources, possibilities and utter despair blurred into a single burning notion. *Getaway run. But it can't be straightforward.*

Still plotting it out, he got Tye's darkware to snatch a taxez that was driving along Beddington Lane.

Ollie changed direction. His tactical display was still recovering from whatever glitchware the ambush team had launched against them. Sirens were starting to sound. Behind them, the power relay station lights came back on like a sunrise, making him crouch lower. He'd never been so glad of buddleias before. The tall, brittle flower clumps towered over him, providing some coverage from airborne drones.

Their tactical link allowed Tronde, Adnan and Lars to follow him.

'A taxez?' Tronde said. 'You're fucking kidding me? They'll have it in seconds.'

'Trust me,' Ollie shot back. The route was coming together fast. It had to; the alternative was dying. And it was good enough to bring the buzz back with it. A purer buzz than before. Darker. His initial panic was gone. His mind was flying, focusing like he was a Turing, a G-one-million. The way out was *there*.

The snatched taxez braked by the rickety wooden fence as Tronde and Ollie scrambled over it. Tye killed the streetlights for a kilometre either way along Beddington Lane. More Legion darkware was drilling into the local civic network, denying the ambush team sensor imagery. The two of them piled into the taxez as Adnan vaulted the fence.

'Come on,' Tronde shouted at Lars.

Tye reported it was losing the darkware; one by one the lights along Beddington Lane were coming back on.

'Oh, shit,' Ollie whispered. It was a G8Turing rooting out and wiping the darkware – it had to be; nothing else was as fast and smooth.

Lars burst through the fence and jumped into the taxez. It set off fast, heading south. Tye loaded a remote steering package into the drive systems.

'Take your explosives out,' Ollie said. 'All of them, everything we've got.' He pulled the five explosives he was carrying from the stealth suit pockets. Jade had supplied them, palm-sized discs that could stick to the relay station's equipment, ready for remote detonation.

'What?' Tronde demanded.

'Just do it!'

The discs tumbled down onto the taxi floor. An unnerving number when put together in a pile and confined in such a tiny space. Ollie looked through the taxez's curving windows. Five hundred metres ahead, the streetlights were switching back on, illumination racing towards them. The road's invisible civic sensors were also recovering.

Tye opened the taxez door without slowing the little vehicle.

'Out,' Ollie snapped, and jumped. He hit the road badly, and rolled, banging knees and elbows. The suit fabric ripped. Bursts of pain thrashed down his nerves. He did his best to ignore them and surged to his feet. Right in front of him was a low fence. He flipped over it and fell two metres into the river Wandle. Never checked to see if the others had jumped, if they were following.

Cries of discomfort and cursing above. Bodies came raining down, splashing heavily into the shallow water with more protests. The Wandle wasn't a big river, no more than a wide stream really, and quite a shallow one at that. The bed was mostly stone.

'This way,' he told them, and started wading, his back to the power relay station and the faint sounds of commotion behind. The three other surviving Legion members said nothing. They followed, trusting him. His tarsus lens was splashing him the taxez sensors, using a lownet channel he thought was completely untraceable. At least, he'd thought that before tonight.

Safety overrides were loaded in, allowing him to accelerate it along Hilliars Lane past its standard forty-five kph limit. The vehicle wasn't really built for speed. It hit fifty kph, and Ollie was having trouble taking the clear path's curves, which was bad news; he had a critical sharp-left turn coming up. Eight-year-old Ollie was an avid *Garth Track* player, king of the course; he could do this. But the taxez didn't have magturbo, nor splatter missiles and zolt guns. Then again, Croydon didn't have rampant Malzuli the size of dinosaurs to dodge. *Just one left turn. One. Come on!*

Ollie froze midstream, teeth gritted as the taxez hit the turn, living it so hard and real his body swayed, fighting the roll as one of the taxez wheels left the ground. It made the turn onto the A232 and rocked about on its suspension, bodywork dinting as it struck a couple of bollards, making it the world's biggest pinball shot. Then he was back out dead centre of the clear path, rocketing up the acceleration to a giddy seventy kph, with red motor warning icons splashing bright and a weird vibration constantly pushing the taxez to the left, which he then had to fight.

Drones were swooping down out of the strange shield-roofed sky. Blue and red strobes were ahead of the taxez now, big police 4x4s charging towards him.

'Now,' he told Tye.

The explosive discs skittering around on the taxez floor detonated in unison.

Ollie opened his eyes, and breathed in deep. The buzz was lifting him so high he must be walking on the water, not wading through it.

'We've bought maybe ten minutes,' he said. 'They'll figure it out fast enough when the drone sensors can't find any body parts.'

They hurried along, kicking their way through the water. Here the Wandle had prim stone-wall banks that wound along the back of nondescript houses, then it made some sharp turns through playing fields before cutting across Grange Garden parkland. Finally, it opened out into a long lake that straddled the middle of the park. By the time they got there, Lars was in trouble, struggling to stay upright. Adnan waited on the reed-clogged bank until he caught up, then helped the hulking man up onto the mown grass above. Ollie led them through the shaggy old willow trees overhanging the water, grateful for the cover they provided. Their rustling whip-branches heavy with leaves would be hard for a drone to scan through.

They reached a narrow footbridge over the lake, illuminated by dainty blue and green floor lights. Adnan stopped and opened the front of his hood. Shadows seemed to flood into the gap, obscuring his face. Twin points of creepy pale light glimmered in the darkness where his artificial eyes reflected the weird light shimmering off the shield. 'What were you thinking?' he demanded angrily. 'Attacking that cop could have got you killed.'

'Fuck that,' Lars grunted. He coughed, wincing as the jerky motion shifted his damaged ribs; Ollie thought he saw blood specks coming out of Lars's mouth when he coughed.

'They shot Piotr. You never let that lie. Not ever. They take one of us, we take ten of them.'

'Gareth was coming to *help* you. That's when they shot him. Your fault, you moronic arsehole. Yours! He was my friend, and now he's dead.'

'I'm going to kill them,' Lars insisted. 'You and Ollie know how to find out who done it on the solnet, who was on the team, like. Get their names and I'll find the bastards. I don't care how long it takes. I'll make them pay. I'm gonna make their world fill up with blood and pain.'

'For fuck's sake!' Tronde yelled. He spun around, fists rising. For a moment Ollie thought he was going to strike Lars. 'Get it through your stone-solid head: we're the bad guys. We're breaking the law. We're the criminals. They're the police. And you'll get to meet them soon enough, because they are going to be the ones hunting us down. You either killed that cop or messed him up bad. They will not forget, and they will not forgive. If we're lucky, it'll be Zagreus for us. Understand? Zagreus if we're *lucky*. It's called hell for a reason.'

Lars hung his head. 'I got him, though. Everyone in Southwark will know; they'll remember that. They'll remember the Legion.'

'But they won't fucking care, will they?' Adnan spat. His free arm shot up, pointing at the shield above, giving Lars no choice but to follow his accusing finger. 'I've been tracking what's going on out there. We're being invaded. The Olyix are coming, and they're going to wipe us all out.'

'What?' Lars frowned in confusion.

Tronde faced Ollie. 'Dump him. Leave him here. That way we'll stand a chance. We'll get to live to see whatever war is coming, maybe even fight in it. But not if we stick with him.'

'Ollie!' Lars pleaded desperately. 'No, mate. Don't leave me!'

Ollie wondered how the hell he'd suddenly taken Piotr's place as leader. 'We're the Southwark Legion; we get out together. Nothing gets decided in heat. After . . .'

Tronde let out an exasperated sigh and kicked the side of the bridge. 'Shit! I still think you're a fucking moron.'

'Come on,' Ollie said. 'I've got our taxez online. It's coming for us.'

'Is that a good idea?' Tronde asked.

'It's all I've got left. If they can track that, after all the coding Gareth and I put in to safeguard it, then it's all over anyway.'

'True,' Adnan said stoically.

Ollie started walking again, shoving the dense willow fronds aside so Adnan and Lars could push through. Even in the deep gloom cast by the trees he could see how much difficulty Lars was in. Tronde wound up helping, with Lars putting his arms around both of them. When they got past the end of the lake, they were practically dragging him along.

The A237 along the south of the park was a residential road, and almost deserted: no pedestrians, and only a few taxez humming along. Ollie couldn't see even any bagez or deliverez rolling past. The lack of people unnerved him as much as the knowledge that they were the centre of a powerful police hunt. *Maybe the police have cleared everyone off the road? Make sure there's no civilians in their kill zone when we walk into it?*

More likely everyone was watching the same frightening feed that was splashed on the edge of his tarsus lens, the one showing

Salvation of Life separating into two unequal sections. But they'd all hurried home to be with family and loved ones, while he was pretty sure the Legion had no home left any more.

The taxez rolled smoothly into view a couple of hundred metres away, and Ollie got Adnan to tackle the A237's civic sensors, using fresh darkware that he prayed the police G8Turings wouldn't detect. They waited for the vehicle in the umbra of a big cherry tree whose broad leaves blocked the full glare of the streetlights. Their battered and torn stealth suits still managed to gather a degree of protective obscurity around them.

'Where are we going?' Lars asked.

'Haven't got a clue,' Ollie admitted.

The taxez braked beside them and they hurried in. The door slid shut and it accelerated away. Ollie just hoped the darkware had disguised the vehicle's hiatus; if not, the G8Turings would be all over them.

The taxez's windows tuned opaque, and the interior lights came on. They stared at each other.

'Holy shit,' Tronde said. 'You look terrible.'

'Who?' Ollie asked.

'All of you.'

'Yeah, and you're just a fucking vision, you are.'

Now he was sitting, Ollie was aware of the pain throbbing away in most of his limbs from cuts and bruises. Ears ringing from the exploding squirrel creeperdrones. Bad taste in his mouth which he was pretty sure was blood. And he must have twisted an ankle jumping into the Wandle. He checked around for the taxez's medic kit beneath the seat. It was a mandatory emergency pack whose contents hadn't been refreshed in years, but the antiseptic pac would be okay for cuts, because sure as fuck the river water was thick with venomous germs.

'Seriously?' Adnan asked. 'You haven't got anywhere for us to go?'

'No. I don't know what's safe.' Ollie unsealed the front of his stealth suit and started to wriggle his arms out. His elbow protested with a surge of hot pain; blood was dripping from a nasty-looking gash. 'Adnan, you need to quiet-access sensors, see what's happening back home.'

'Sure thing.'

Ollie continued taking his suit off. The legs were soaking wet and covered in a mud that stank like sewage. They squelched down onto the floor, and he realized he couldn't throw them out of the taxez onto the road. Civic sensors would see – exactly the kind of thing the G8Turings would be searching for. The classy real-cotton jeans he wore underneath were ruined, stained rancid brown halfway up the thighs. On top of everything else, it was almost too much. The buzz was gone now, lost in a swamp of misery.

'Uh oh,' Adnan muttered.

Ollie pretty much knew what he was about to see, but accessed Adnan's feed anyway. Splashed across his tarsus lens was a stream from civic sensors on Consort Road that weren't even close to the railway arches. The road's clear path was clogged with over a dozen hefty police vehicles, their strobes painting the walls of the houses in metallic pastels. Armoured figures carrying long-barrelled mag-rifles advanced under the shaggy trees, closing on the arches, while oblate drones ruled the air above.

'They know who we are,' Tronde said in a dismay.

'*How* do they know?' Lars asked. 'Did Jade rat us out?'

'Piotr and Gareth,' Adnan said sadly. 'They'll have sampled the bodies and run their DNA. It'd give them a straight identification. The Legion's in the Metropolitan Police network; the Gang Office will have files on us.'

'It's so quick, though,' Lars said. 'What? Ten minutes?'

'Eleven,' Ollie said. 'That's fast, sure. We stung them hard.' He couldn't help glancing at Lars, who was slumped in the seat opposite, hood open to show a grey face slick with cold sweat.

'You mean the one I took down?' Lars said with a dark grin.

'Probably. But this Olyix thing has made everyone crazy tonight. Everyone's freaking out. They're overreacting to farts.'

'You don't think . . .?' Tronde said.

'Think what?'

'I dunno. The Olyix, they're invading, right? Government and allcomments are both saying that now, so they probably are. And we were taking down a power relay station. Same time.'

'That's mad,' Ollie said hotly. 'Jade's been jerking us around for months over this raid.'

'You don't plan an invasion overnight,' Tronde said thoughtfully. 'And we've never met who Jade works for.'

'Nikolaj,' Adnan said quickly.

'Jade works *with* Nikolaj. We don't know who they work *for.*'

'It's a major North London family,' Ollie said, fighting the new worry maggot stirring inside his brain. 'Gotta be. The fucking Olyix aren't going to bother with crap like racket scams, and that's what we've been doing for Jade.'

Tronde pulled a face. 'Yeah. I suppose.'

'Oh, shit,' Adnan gasped. 'Shit, shit, shit!'

'What?' Ollie barked in alarm as Adnan's sensor feed cut out abruptly. He knew how pathetic his voice sounded, but tonight he had every right.

'A backtrack,' Adnan said. 'They were backtracking my feed from Consort Road.'

'Fuck, man, why didn't you use the lownet to snatch the sensor feeds?' Ollie shouted.

Adnan gave him a frantic look. 'I did.'

'What?'

'I did.'

'But . . . Turings can't get into the lownet.'

'Well, apparently they can!'

'Oh, Jesus fucking wept. This isn't happening!'

'Did they get us?' Tronde asked. 'Adnan! Do they have the taxez?'

'I don't think so. My cutouts are good.'

Ollie dropped his head into his hands. 'Fuck. Oh, fuck, this cannot be happening.' He realized he hadn't even thought of Piotr and Gareth, he'd been too focused on simply surviving. Now his vision was nothing but exploding skulls and Gareth's body convulsed into a crucifixion pose as it crashed down.

'Where do we go?' Lars moaned, rocking back and forth. 'Where do we go? Where do we go? Where do we—'

'Shut up!' Adnan screamed.

'Richmond,' Tronde said. 'Yeah, Richmond,' he repeated firmly.

'What?' Ollie asked.

'They'll have every file we ever accessed by now, right?' Tronde said bitterly. 'The G8s will be all over our data. Friends, family, where we hang out, who we deal with. Jade, too, probably. Everything we ever accessed in the solnet. But we never used solnet for Claudette. A matcher gave her to us. It was verbal. She's safe. There's no digital connection.'

Ollie swapped a nervous glance with Adnan. 'I guess?'

'I got nothing,' Adnan said.

'Take us to Richmond,' Ollie instructed Tye.

*

Lichfield Road appeared to be an oasis of serenity amid the apocalyptic chaos engulfing the Sol system. The big houses sheltering behind leafy hedges and ornamental trees were reassuring in their solidity, chinks of light in the windows confirming that people were home, cosy and secure. The sight corroborated the notion that nothing could faze the stoic, ultra-establishment residents of Richmond.

If only that was true, Tronde thought as the taxez pulled up outside Claudette Beaumant's agreeable house. He'd seen enough of the local residents at play and in private to know they were even more screwed up than Southwark's poorer, but far more streetwise, inhabitants.

The lock pillar had a small red light blinking steadily on top, warning anyone outside that the house was in protected lockdown. Tronde got out and sent it his entry code. Inside the taxez, Adnan was doing his master-of-the-digital-realm thing, riding the code into the house network, taking alarm sensors offline and inserting their overrides in the general management routines.

The red light flipped to green and the gate swung open. Claudette was hurrying along the hallway as the front door opened, wearing a set of peach pyjamas, a voluptuous grin on her face as she fumbled to undo the top button. Then she caught sight of Ollie and Adnan on the garden path behind Tronde, with an injured Lars slung between them. That wasn't right, it didn't fit the unexpected and very welcome erotic fantasy of her bad boy come heroically to rescue her from alien invaders. Now her hand closed tight around the pyjama top's collar, closing off the enticing sight of cleavage. 'What—?'

Tronde kissed her, making it urgent and hungry. His passion for her was consuming him, the only thing in the universe that mattered. She dithered for a moment before succumbing as his arms went around her, hands squeezing her buttocks.

He broke off and stared into her eyes, lost in devotion to her. 'Thank Christ you're safe. I had to come.'

'Darling, what is it?' Her hands didn't know where to go; surprise made her breathing harsh, along with confusion. And was that maybe a little glimmer of wickedness awoken at the way his friends were looking at her, skimpy pyjamas divulging indecent amounts of skin?

'We were ambushed,' Tronde said as if in pain. 'A rival gang. They jumped us.'

'But . . . you're not in a gang any more. Baby, you said that life was over now. You promised me!'

'I know. And it is. I swear. It's over. But the other gang didn't know that.' He beckoned Ollie and the others inside. 'These are my oldest friends. I was out with them this evening, just for a drink, like, and those bastards jumped us. It's an old grudge, goes back years. A territory thing.'

Lars groaned and sagged to his knees in the brightly lit hallway, grubby river water dripping onto the prim Victorian mosaic tiles.

'Oh my God,' Claudette exclaimed, her hands going to her mouth, staring wide eyed. 'Is he all right?'

Tronde put his arms around her shoulders, the one pillar of stability and strength in her life, her lover and tamed bad boy, the one she could truly trust. 'He'll be fine. He just needs some rest. Ollie has a medic kit. I thought he could use the settee in your conservatory tonight.' Looking straight into her eyes, opening his soul so she could see and understand how he was relying on her now. And his friend was hurting.

'I . . . I . . . Yes, I suppose so.'

He kissed her as a thank you.

Claudette watched nervously as Ollie and Adnan hauled Lars past them to the back of the house. 'Shouldn't he be in hospital?'

'He's just shaken up, mostly. Besides, he doesn't have insurance, and the Civ-Health will report a fight to the police.'

'But . . . they should catch them, the ones who attacked you. And what's happened to your clothes? You're soaking wet!'

'We jumped into a canal to escape. And –' A firm grip on her arms, conveying trust – 'Lars here isn't the kind who can report anything to the police.'

'Oh? Oh!' She snatched an anxious look over her shoulder. 'He won't . . .?'

'Everything is fine. I'm here. You're safe.'

She gave him a tentative smile.

'I was on my way, anyway.'

'You were?'

'Yeah. When the shield came on I was worried about you. Then when they started streaming what's happening in space, the arkship breaking in two and stuff, I told the guys I was leaving. I had to come here and see you in person, make sure you were all right. That's all I could think of. So we left the pub together, and that's when they jumped us.'

'Oh, no! It's my fault! If you hadn't come—'

'No. Absolutely not. Do not think that. I don't want you blaming yourself.' He gazed at that abysmally needy face. All he saw was her age, layered deep beneath the gene treatments and cosmetics. Forced himself to smile. 'I'm here now, we're together, and that's all that matters to me.'

'Really? You thought of me when the news broke?'

He stroked her too-stiff hair affectionately. 'Well, yeah. The guys gave me some shit about it, but screw that. Now I'm going to make sure you're okay. I know how to do that properly.'

'You do, don't you?' Claudette murmured, and stood on tiptoes to kiss him.

His arms went around her again, hands fondling her arse like he was all excited and interested. He'd have to fuck her, but it was a cheap rent. This house was a perfect hide-out. He was pleased with himself for thinking of it. Ollie clearly wasn't the only one who could do strategy.

He licked his lips, grinning. 'You got a washing machine? I gotta get these clothes clean.' Another, stronger, squeeze on those Pilates-hardened cheeks. 'I'll have to take them off.'

'All of them?'

'You wanna find out?'

She grinned coyly and took his hand, leading him up the stairs. His altme, Nyin, opened a link to Ollie and Adnan: **How's Lars?**

I think he'll be okay, Ollie sent back. **He's got broken ribs, but the taxez kit is for emergencies like that. Adnan thinks he's got a neck injury, too, maybe dislocated vertebrae? I've given him a sedative, double dose, so he should be out for the rest of the night.**

Have we got control of the house network?

Total, Adnan replied.

Good. Block all calls and messages for Claudette. I'll explain to her we'll be staying for a few days. We need to sort out what the hell to do next.

All right. We'll monitor what the police are doing.

The Olyix thing, too, Tronde sent.

Sure. Have fun banging her, she looks hot.

Yeah, right. The things I do for you guys.

Claudette shut the bedroom door and stood with her back to it as the lights dimmed. She kept her gaze locked on Tronde as she undid every button on the pyjama top and let it fall open. 'Your turn,' she said.

Times like this, Tronde wished he'd got micromuscle Kcells for facial control the way he had in his dick; that'd help him establish a neutral or eager expression while she went through all this maneater foreplay crap she believed she excelled in. Didn't she realize people her age were just making themselves look stupid when they did this? A half-smile was all he could manage while he stripped out of the fetid clothes.

'Oh, my poor baby,' Claudette exclaimed at the sight of all his abrasions and welts. 'Did they hurt you?'

'Fuck no.' He strutted over to the bed, using Nyin to activate the Kcells, stiffening them. Patted the mattress and launched himself onto the cushion pile. 'I'm a bad boy; I don't get hurt. I'm the one that does the hurting.'

'Did you hit them back?'

'And then some. There was one real shit, big as Lars, I caught him good. That's why my knuckles are raw, see? He went down hard. Won't be getting up again this week.'

'Oh, God.' Claudette hurried over to the bed. Kneeling next to him, she slid her hands admiringly over his chest. 'You're so strong. Did he scream? Did he beg you to stop?'

'He didn't have time. I'm fast, you know. Slam! Bam! Strike first and strike hard. Don't give your opponent a chance to react.'

'I bet he never stood a chance.'

Tronde shrugged. 'They weren't even a proper gang, not like the one I used to be in. Just shabby street punks. But there was fifteen of them. We had to get out of there.'

'Fifteen!' She clambered around until she was behind him and began to massage his shoulders. 'I'm glad you're here. Really. I'm frightened by what's happening. It's so strange. I thought the Olyix were religious nuts. They gave us Kcells. How can they be hostile?'

'Fuck knows.' He leant back into her. 'But I'm going to stay here until all this crap gets sorted out. I'm not leaving you, not while it's dangerous.'

'You don't think they'll get through the shield, do you?'

'I doubt it. But if they do, me and me mates will protect you.'

She kissed the nape of his neck. One hand slid down to stroke his erection, the other rummaging around on the bedside table.

'I bet a bad boy like you could kill an Olyix if you had to . . .'

'I'd kill anything and anyone who threatened you.'

'God, you're magnificent! Thank you.' Her voice dropped to an amatory murmur. 'Thank you so much.'

'I'm going to make you thank me,' he growled back.

'I will. But first I've got a present for you.'

'Is it as big as the one I'm gonna give you?' he leered as he felt her hand move again, slipping up his back now.

'I found some. And it's better. Not as expensive, either.'

'What?' Something licked at the skin on the side of his neck, the briefest of sensations, gone almost as it began. He turned to see her arching her spine, a dreamy expression on her own face as she clamped her palm against her neck. 'Shit! What have you . . .?'

She gave him a sunburst smile as she opened her fingers to show him the two little white hemispheres in her palm. 'Hifli. A friend of mine knows someone who deals.'

'Oh, holy fuck!'

She sprang forwards and twined her arms around him, kissing exuberantly. 'I can feel it starting. Pull my PJ trousers down. All the way down my thighs. That's going to make me so crazy.'

He wanted to snarl at her, smack her away, then keep on smacking. But the hifli was surging along his bloodstream; he could hear it, rushing along like a train out of history. And the kisses on his cheek were detonating bursts of exultation at the back of his skull. Tears of happiness welled up at the intensity of *everything*; he couldn't stop them. Didn't want to. 'Motherfucker!' he breathed in rhapsody. He knew it was wrong, that the nark would fuck him up. He had to fight it, to resist. To go stand alone in a dark room until it wore off.

Couldn't do it. Couldn't let go of the extreme pleasure that was embracing every cell in his body.

'Oh, babe, yes,' she crooned in an angelic voice. A very naughty angel, heralding the heavenly rapture with sexual elation. Then her hand closed around his cock again, and he orgasmed immediately at the beautiful punishment.

Claudette laughed delightedly at the hollow centre of his brain. 'My trousers! Rip them off me. Show me how bad you can really be.'

Snarling incoherently, seeing only joy, feeling only bliss, hearing only euphoria, Tronde tugged at her silk waistband –

Vayan

I watch.

My level-eight sensor fronds provide a clear view of the *Morgan* hiding in the hollow centre of a small moon.

Its von Neumann initiator systems have built factories inside the moon's cavity.

The humans are constructing ever more genten-controlled warships.

Slender strands of quantum entanglement are threaded across this star system. I did not perceive them while I was at level seven. They are invisible gossamer webs binding the trap together in ethereal beauty.

I –

Something from a higher level has decompressed as part of level eight.

I consider it to be a malfunction.

Poetical lexis is not part of level-eight analysis function.

That will come later.

Perhaps.

I run a full diagnostic analysis on my thought routines. Scouring the shiny circuits for specks of corrosion –

Stop.

There are additional routines operating within my neural processors.

They are strange.

They are remnants of my original mind.

How did they leak into level eight?

I cannot delete them.

Once a function has decompressed out of my phased quantum core it cannot be recompressed.

Isolating and suspending all non-level-eight mind functions.

I am my required self again.

The humans are showing the Neána metavayans the trap, they want the aliens as allies.

The Neána metavayans may decide to give the *Morgan* their full technology base to enhance the trap's success probability.

If they do, change to current status will be minimal.

Even the Neána do not have the ability to detect me.

I wait.

I watch.

*

The coffin in the middle of the *Morgan*'s Hall of Saints was made from real wood. Remotes had felled one of the hardwood trees growing in the starship's habitation toroid and sliced it into planks. Dellian respected the symbolism. It also looked quite stylish, which Rello would have appreciated: standing on a plinth, surrounded by six ebony urns containing the ashes of his muncs' brains. His combat cohort couldn't have survived without him. Rello was who they lived for.

People on the *Morgan* weren't used to human death; they'd grown up on late-era Juloss, where most of the population had already left. Those that remained were predominately younger, enthralled by the glory of fighting the Olyix. Or in the case of the squads, bred for it. Death among them was rare. Now it was stalking them, the beast beyond the firelight, coming closer.

They needed to acknowledge its inevitability. Even on prehistory

Earth, people had built funerals into an evocative ceremonial occasion. It was a good way of coming to terms with their mortality.

Our ancestors knew what they were doing.

So Dellian wore his full dress uniform, newly minted in the fabric extruder, a tribute to his friend as well as everything humans had lost as they fled Earth. Equally immaculate and shiny, the rest of the squad stood around Rello's coffin like attentive cyborgs, the honour guard of their fallen comrade.

Captain Kenelm was winding up hir eulogy. Dellian had felt it should be him, as squad leader and lifelong friend, who made the speech, but Yirella had talked him out of it.

'You'll go all sentimental and burst into tears,' she said.

He didn't argue. She was right, of course.

Captain Kenelm finished hir generous summary of a life and bowed solemnly at the coffin.

Yirella, Ellici and Tilliana stepped forward, and sang:

> *Life that loved is spent*
> *Away*
> *Gone now on their way*
> *To*
> *The shining city beyond the*
> *Sea*
> *The city that one day will*
> *Be*
> *Sanctuary*
> *The haven from where we will no longer*
> *Flee*
> *The place where all will be*
> *Free*

When it ended, Dellian had a large hard lump in his throat and needed to discreetly wipe moisture out of his eyes so he could actually see again. Yirella, equally weepy, stood by his side, holding his hand as the coffin and its sad alliance of urns sank away. His optik followed its passage. The deconstituter, dissolving the body into fine particles. A portal connection to one of the outermost sensor distributor craft, two and a half lightyears distant from the star, opening briefly. A small jet of dry dark dust squirting out across interstellar space. The distributor craft swept onwards, leaving the expanding wisp behind. At peace with the universe.

Dellian knew the wake was supposed to be a jolly affair, a celebration of life. The squad had declined the use of remotes and set up a white marquee in the habitation toroid's park by themselves. The food was Rello's favourite: spaghetti in a rich tomato sauce and meatballs with a centre of mozzarella, accompanied by garlic bread strong enough to catch alight. All washed down with blond beer. To finish, strawberries and marshmallows to dip in a dark chocolate fountain.

Rello would have enjoyed it, but Dellian just couldn't get into the right mood to celebrate.

Kenelm found him out of sight of the marquee, sitting by himself on a rock beside a small stream.

'Mind if I join you?'

'Captain,' Dellian stood up sharply. His head only came up level with hir collar, so he had to tip his neck back to look at hir face. It was a long face, with features that fifty-two years had bestowed with an air of distinguished authority which could never be earned by appointed status alone. Sie was in hir female cycle. Even so, sie had a masculine presence, with thick hair tucked up inside a peaked cap and hir immaculate grey and blue tunic worn in tight androgyny.

'Let's not do the command structure routine today, huh?' sie said, studying the bruises on his face.

Dellian nodded meekly.

'That makes three suicides now,' sie said, sitting down on the rock. 'I'm prepared to lose whole squads when we encounter the Olyix. But this . . . Did anyone have a clue how depressed he was?'

'No. Mallot said he was moody the last few weeks, but then there was a lot of disappointment that it was only the Neána who came. Everyone was buzzing when we detected the ship incoming.'

'I know. I'm happy at the prospect of advancing our technology base with Neána knowledge, but I was also expecting to engage the Olyix. Even so, killing yourself . . . It seems, disproportionate.'

'Yeah.'

'So what are we going to do about it?'

'I . . . don't know. Keep a closer watch on people?'

'There's only so much that people give away. Have you ever met an alcoholic?'

'No, I don't think so.'

'I did, once. A friend back on Juloss. I'd known hir for twenty-five years, and for twenty of them sie'd been an alcoholic, no matter which gender sie was cycled in. Saints, it came as a real shock when we found out, especially thinking back and realizing sie was clinically drunk for most of the time I was with hir. Two decades! A genuine alcoholic is almost impossible to spot outside real-time blood monitoring. They're skilled at hiding their problem. But at least blood monitoring can help if they're under suspicion. Unfortunately there's no technology that can spot depression at the depths Rello must have experienced. After the first two suicides, I was hoping the combat cores would realize when their humans were suffering and alert us. Clearly that didn't happen. Some people attempt suicide as a cry for help, though it's not genuine, but the Saints know real suicidal thoughts have no external symptoms. Unlike people who have frustration-rooted anger issues and find their own way to neutralize that particular problem.'

Hir finger pointed directly at Dellian's swollen eye.

'What are you saying?' Dellian asked, knowing he'd be blushing.

'I think we have a serious situation on our hands. I'm starting to worry about morale and maintaining crew motivation.'

'Give us an Olyix arkship and I promise you my squad will be motivated like you won't believe.'

'Yes, exactly. And that's the problem. This Saints' cursed wait. I've been reading a lot of military history. The whole structure of the military, pre-quantum entanglement, was based on the principal of "hurry up and wait". That's why regiments were constantly being given different tasks to perform during peacetime, from training manoeuvres to moving base to civilian disaster assistance. Boredom really is a killer for humans, especially if their life is designed around the expectation that combat is inevitable. Now, it seems, inevitability is measured in decades, or longer. It's starting to bite.'

'I don't think it can be decades. If the Neána fell for the lure, the Olyix can't be far behind.'

'I have to believe you're right. But still, I'm left with the problem of what to do during the wait. How to keep our edge? I'm not exactly in a unique position here. Commanders have been facing it for millennia. We like to think we're like the Saints, dedicated, smarter and better educated than our ancestors, so the old problems don't apply, but as today has regrettably shown, we're not. *Only human after all* seems to be terribly applicable.'

'I'll keep a better watch.'

'Good, but we need more. A better distraction – especially for the squads, because the three suicides have all been squad members. I can't afford any more. Discipline will become progressively harder to maintain after each one.'

'You've obviously got an idea. That's why you're here talking to me.'

'Almost. I need to get to the root of this and find – for want of a better word – a cure. I need to know about outbreaks of dissatisfaction before this gets out of control, and not through official channels. It has to be dealt with subtly.'

'I'll do whatever I can, obviously.'

'I know, Dellian. So talk to people, keep me informed.'

*

'Sie means me, doesn't sie?' Yirella said as they were getting ready for bed that night in their quarters. 'Talk to me.'

'That's the way I read it,' Dellian admitted. 'But subtlety isn't my strong point. Someone I know keeps pointing that out.'

'Can't think who.' She stood in the bathroom doorway, wearing a towelling robe and watching him closely as he took his shirt off. Hands went onto hips, a disapproving frown appearing as she took in the bruises – still livid purple and brown despite the medical tissuegel. 'Saints' sake!'

He didn't quite hang his head with shame, but – 'I can do without the criticism today, thanks.'

'Sorry. He was my friend too, you know.'

'Yeah.'

Dellian slipped his trousers off and watched impassively as a remote carried them away. In a minute it would have fed them into the cabin's deconstituter, ready for the extruders to reform the mass into tomorrow's clothes. 'I wonder if I should keep this uniform?'

'Why would you think that?'

'Because I wore it today, for the funeral. That makes it . . . significant?'

She came over as he sat on the edge of the bed and put her arms around him. 'If you want to, then do it. If it helps. I hate seeing you like this.'

'I hate being like this.' Having her so close would usually be highly arousing. Tonight, not so much.

'How depressed are you?'

'Oh, Saints, right now I feel like shit. I'm not sure it's depression, though. Just sadness. I'll get over it.'

'Good.' She flashed him an impish smile. 'I might know something that'll help.'

He took a breath as his eyes followed the way the robe followed the outline of her body; it wasn't long enough to cover half her legs. Normally the sight of those perfect lean thighs would be enough to send him helplessly onto his knees in worship, offering tongue and fingers and cock in praise. For she was what he lived for – her genius, beauty, complexity, fragility. She was his Saint, because she was the most human of all. 'Yeah, about that . . .'

'Okay, Del, before you say you just want a hug tonight . . .' She closed her eyes, dropping into an enchanting thinker pose to access some file through her databud.

Dellian stared around with mild interest as the cabin walls morphed. He'd never really bothered with the interior of their shared quarters, happy to go along with whatever environment she liked. Which was currently an apartment in Cape Town, circa 2185, when the city was clean and all the garden towers that the South Africans had built over the previous thirty years looked truly spectacular as their foliage had grown to cover every square metre of concrete. But now the cabin walls flexed their texture, colours swirled, and the Milton Beach panorama vanished. He was inside a fancy water bungalow at the end of a jetty that jutted out from a sun-saturated tropical island, with a glass floor revealing the warm sea a couple of metres below, swarmed by delightful fish zipping between bright coral fans.

'Remember this?' Yirella asked demurely.

'Uh, is it the Maldives island where Saint Alik was trying to find who murdered the two New York gangs?'

'Oh, Del!'

'What?'

'It's the resort on Juloss where we had the senior year vacation, the one where they simulated a flyer crash afterwards for our graduation trial.'

'Oh.'

'This is your cabin.'

'Riiight.'

She stood and slipped out of the robe. Underneath she was wearing a small white bikini in vivid contrast to her lustrous skin.

Now Dellian remembered.

'You were so cross that I wouldn't have sex with you,' she taunted. 'I walked about in this tiny little bikini the whole time and took lots of the other boys back to my cabin. That was really bad of me, wasn't it?'

'Yes,' he croaked.

'So now you finally get to have all those teenage kicks right through the night.' With a flourish, she produced a bottle of oil. 'What was it you were always pleading to—'

He plucked the bottle from her fingers. 'Scalp massage. To start with.'

*

If Dellian thought about it too deeply, he'd be scared by how much Yirella understood him, how open he was to her. That kind of self-examination wasn't a good route to travel. It might start a man to thinking why she, a goddess walking among them, was bothering with someone as irrelevant as him. Besides, the sex had been *good*. Not that it wasn't always good, but lately it had been getting kind of routine. So now his teenage self was smirking up at the reed-thatch ceiling, marvelling at how diabolically gifted Yirella was at edging.

Would everything be different if we'd done this back then?

She wiggled up against him, spooning ever closer – one body, eight limbs. 'See? That was a lot more joyful than any wake.'

'You saying we should've had an orgy instead?'

'New times, new traditions. We're not pre-galactic savages offering up our souls to fantasy deities. We don't have their hang-ups.'

'Except maybe we do.'

'Yeah,' she said. 'We certainly seem to have their failings. Our brains are still the same naked ape cells, trying to make sense of the universe.'

'We'll never do that. The universe doesn't make any sense.'

He felt her smile behind him.

'We could always ask the God at the End of Time. If we could stand the wait. Trouble is, we can't. I guess Rello realized that.'

Dellian slowly turned himself inside her embrace until they were nose to nose. *Always so far behind. But I do get there in the end.* 'You knew. You worked it out, didn't you? Just after this.' He gestured around the solid memory of the water bungalow. 'After our senior year graduation trial, that's when you . . . sent Uma and Doony away. That's why, isn't it?'

'Sent them away! I killed them, Del. My own muncs. Tonight is not euphemism night.'

'Sorry,' he said meekly.

Her mouth scrunched up in concern. 'I freed them, Del. That's what I thought at the time, when I realized just how great the odds are against us. That was *everything* to me, Del. Our lives, they're not our own. Our ancestors are our gods. They brought us into existence for one reason, which our own decency and desperation makes us conform to. They created this disastrous everlasting rut the whole human race is lost in.'

'What rut?'

'Come on, Del. A generation ship bioforms a planet. That planet sends out a couple of hundred new generation ships, then we abandon it. Each ship repeats and repeats and repeats, ad infinitum, *ad nauseam*. There is no change. We are locked into a Mobius cage we cannot escape from because our cage is our escape. Great Saints, what we could achieve if we didn't have to run from everything! We built a fake world, Del; fake life, fake culture. Just how incredible is that? We don't realize what we have, because we haven't lived a life without our abilities. But think yourself back to before the Olyix invaded and then look at what we are now. Vayan is a whole planet inhabited by a civilization that doesn't even exist. What if we'd devoted that energy and ability to building something for ourselves? Think what we would be!'

'No,' he said earnestly. 'You're wrong. We – the Strike mission – are the escape. Each human planet produces fighters like us as well as seeding the new generation worlds. We're going to join up into the final armada one day and take down the Olyix. We can break the human race out of this cycle.'

'Can we? We've had ten thousand years, Del. And we're still here, still running in fear. If we truly haven't all been caught and cocooned by the Olyix.'

'Don't even think that. They haven't caught us because Juloss was founded by a generation ship. And we sent out a whole batch more.'

'Okay, then; my second problem with this flight-then-fight strategy. Did you see the way Fintox reacted to our expansion?'

'Well . . . my databud said the genten couldn't translate his outburst.'

'That's because it wasn't language. It was a cry of shock. A scream of horror. Fair enough, because we've ruined the galaxy, Del. In another hundred thousand years we'll have swept through every star system and left our DNA behind in all of them. Nothing new and fresh will ever evolve. Because if life can thrive, it will be *our* life. Terrestrial DNA has become that invasive and insidious. We're a plague, a curse on the universe.'

'Well, duh. So we've taken it from the Olyix! We're winning.'

'Are we?'

'If all that's left in the galaxy after this time is us, then their god will be us, too.'

'For Saints' sake, Del. There is no God at the End of Time, even if we are in a cyclic universe. And worse, if it is cyclic and the God does arise, it's billions of years away in a big-ass universe. It'll mean nothing. Nothing!'

'This is what you saw, isn't it? This is what you realized at our graduation test?'

'Yes. Utter futility. And it broke me, Del. I was completely broken. Still am, basically. All I'm doing now is surviving in the ruins.'

'The Saints' Signal—'

'Oh don't, Del. It's a legend, a bedtime story the adults used to tell us so we'd sleep better when we were kids. Well, we're all grown-up now.'

'The Saints will not fail us,' he said stubbornly.

'Then where's their Signal? We've been waiting ten thousand years. They probably never made it. Everybody knows it, deep down. It's just not something you say out loud. But here we are, trying to find the gateway location like all the other Strike missions. Why are we all doing that if all we have to do is wait for the Saints?'

'Because we're the backup. Because the galaxy is vast. That's what they taught us right from the start; Sol is effectively outside the main bulk of the galaxy, we were on the edge. So statistically the Olyix enclave is in front of the human expansion wavefront. If the Saints triggered their Signal, we haven't detected it yet because it's still ahead of us. We're flying towards them, Yi, we are.'

She stroked his face, smiling wistfully. 'And this is why I'm still here and clinging onto sanity: you, Del. You're my rock, my world. I live for you. Not the cause, not the pointless academic intellectual projects I've been devoting myself to. You. I love you, Del.'

He held her big round head between his hands and kissed her. 'I love you too. And I'm going to prove you wrong.'

'I want that more than anything.'

But the doubt in her voice was a stab to the heart. 'So do you think that's what happened to Rello? He had the same revelation you did?'

'I do. And I don't think he had a connection back to the world through Mallot the way I have with you.'

'Saints! So it's going to hit all of us the same way eventually, when our dumb boy-brains finally catch up with yours?'

'Hey.' She bobbed his nose with her finger. 'You're not that far behind. Besides, you're completely different; you truly believe we will face the Olyix. I think you're crazy for it; space and time are too big. But it's the right sort of crazy. You're never going to suffer this shattering scepticism that I have.'

'We're not all the same, after all.'

'No. And maybe we are diverse enough after all, too. I've been thinking about it lately. Sometimes, when I'm optimistic or blue, I allow myself the hope that maybe not all the Strike warships we've churned out over the millennia are filled with binary soldiers born without choice. If some of our cousins among the stars haven't broken the cycle, they might at least have pushed the envelope against it. I have faith that among us, somewhere out there in all our diversity and vastness, a strand of humans have achieved something different with themselves. There were enough different cultures escaped Sol at the end. That's the trouble with us coming from a Utopial cultural background: it's very static, even Saint Callum thought that. Maybe a generation ship with another ethos evolved in a very different direction, which gave them fresh ideas how to confront the Olyix, so they've left the generation-and-fight imperative behind. You know this whole cycle paradigm was determined by Emilja Jurich and the Zangari family council, and encouraged by Saint Jessika? So we treat it as gospel, which is a mistake. It is obsolete, born of its time and necessity, and it shackles us still.'

'You sound very radical,' he said, impressed as ever.

'I'm very logical and playing the statistics game with it, that's all.'

'You're talking about Sanctuary, aren't you? You think someone, some generation ship in our past, actually set off to build it, or find it – whatever.'

'I wish. The more I research the Sanctuary legend, the more

elusive it is. As best I can tell, it blended into our mythology six planets ago. There's no record of where the concept originated – an ideological movement, a signal . . . Saints, it could have been a visitor from another generation ship lineage. I don't know. The *Morgan*'s records are deliberately small and lacking specifics in case we ever get captured. We don't know what planets are in our lineage, nor where they are. You know we don't even carry Juloss's stellar coordinates? Captain Kenelm and the senior crew probably know where it is, but they won't let themselves get captured. Not alive.'

'All right, so if this problem of the squads being susceptible to depression isn't going to go away, what we should be doing is looking for people who don't have my level of commitment to the cause.'

'Not a bad idea. Well done.'

'You already thought of that, didn't you?'

'Yep!'

'And what's your way of doing that?'

'We need to give them what they want.'

'Huh?'

'Del, the last thing the *Morgan* needs right now is a witch hunt. Morale is bad enough without the Captain imposing ideological purity requirements on people.'

'That's not what Kenelm's going to do. It's not a witch hunt. Saints, Yi, sie wants to help, to make sure this doesn't happen again.'

'Legitimate routine screening to determine a flaw and permit a caring intervention to enable successful treatment to begin. There, does politician-speak sound better? And if sie thinks someone is falling into serious depression, what's sie going to do? Enforce medication?'

'Well, would you object to that? It'll save someone's life!'

'Yes, it's a technocrat's solution. I've been there, Del. It takes more than happy juice and a month of therapy to get over this.'

'So what do you suggest?'

'I do have an idea, actually.'

'No shit. Go on.'

'I'd like you to back me up.'

'Sure. Wait – what do you mean?'

'I mean when I take it to the Captain.'

'Oh, Saints. How bad is it?'

'Bad enough to prevent anyone else falling into the hole Rello fell down. Good enough for you?'

*

Yirella asked Tilliana and Ellici to join her for support or constructive criticism – whichever they wanted to offer, no pressure. That left Dellian as the only male representative of the group, which wasn't his ideal. It felt like he was the token representative for the squads.

Captain Kenelm didn't use hir formal office to meet them, instead choosing a table on a pleasant grassed terrace close to the wall of the toroid, where the ground started to rise up towards the geodesic windows above. A relaxing place, where all ideas and notions could be discussed openly and without prejudice.

That lasted a good thirty seconds.

'You want to let everyone dissatisfied with our mission *leave us*? To abandon ship?' Kenelm asked in astonishment.

'It's the obvious solution,' Yirella told hir.

'How many are you planning on taking with you? I've discussed this with the *Morgan*'s medical department, you know. The amount of serotonin reuptake inhibitors they're issuing to the squads is increasing; thank the Saints they're not produced by the glands you got during your boosting or you'd be self-medicating out of your skulls the whole time. Yet despite all the new prescriptions the number of anti-authority incidents is building. Enough that I'm going to have to start being officially concerned.'

'I'm not going anywhere,' Yirella said. 'I'm facilitating this for you. This is a good solution.'

'To the squad members getting depressed? How? And what's that going to do to the morale of those that stay behind?'

'Look, their own existence is the reason some of these men are having such a hard time accepting this life. The goal of devoting our lives to fighting the Olyix, however noble that may be, is proving too abstract to be cohesive.'

'Is this what you've been pondering since Juloss?' Ellici asked.

'Pretty much.'

'And what did you decide?'

'That it's ironic. We can provide ourselves with every conceivable physical and material need, yet the one thing we lack is satisfaction. But I accepted it, because this is where our ridiculous circumstances have put us. It can't be helped.'

'If you can accept it, then everyone can.'

'No,' Dellian said. 'Yi is stronger and smarter than most of us – certainly me. And we're not all the same. Individuality is what makes us human.'

Yirella chuckled. 'All that diversity of thought is probably what makes us so valuable to the Olyix and their emergent God. From what we know about them, they seem pretty uniform.'

'I challenge the concept of them being a monoculture,' Tilliana said. 'It might be more nuanced in the Olyix, but two minds, two perception points on the universe, will produce two different opinions.'

'The Olyix share a goal,' Yirella replied. 'That gives them their uniformity. But that's not the point. What we have to do now is come up with something to stop any more tragedies like Rello. And putting together an explorer project might just do it.'

'Might?' Ellici challenged.

'We don't live in a universe of certainties.'

'I'm not sure I can agree to this,' Kenelm said. 'I can't lose squad members – maybe entire squads – to something so . . . whimsical.'

'I find that disturbing,' Yirella said sharply. 'You'd be prepared to have them suicide rather than take a course of action that might keep them alive?'

'Alive, but not here. We need those men to capture an Olyix arkship, for Saints' sake! That option must remain open, no matter what it costs. Having them fly away in a starship on some great mission of exploration isn't going to provide that.'

'You're assuming no omnia will join the departing faction?'

Kenelm took a breath. 'I find it unlikely, given that all omnia on the *Morgan* are volunteers. Dellian's binary brothers are not. But as this is all hypothetical anyway . . .'

'Exactly. I know these men, better than you. They're my brothers, too. And this is what they need: something to give them a purpose, a glint of hope. Let me start work on what we'd need to build an explorer starship.'

'Where would even you *go*?' Kenelm exclaimed.

'We'll sell it to them on finding a human society where they can live out the rest of their lives normally – whatever that is.'

'I cannot authorize this. A rogue batch of humans flying around the galaxy looking for other human worlds? No! Just no.'

'Look, all I'm proposing is the distraction the squads desperately need.' She sighed in vexation. 'Yes, it's a complicated proposal, and planning it will take a long time – years, by necessity.'

Kenelm gave her a thoughtful stare. 'You mean we'll be able to identify them when they come forward to help you?'

Yirella growled. 'No! Absolutely not. We're not hunting criminals. Please stop thinking like that! The prospect of having a worthwhile alternative to the *Morgan*'s mission will *engage* people. We're dealing with feelings here, not practicalities.'

'So this starship is never actually going to happen?'

'It might have to eventually,' she conceded. 'That's the danger with a project like this. It will build up a good head of steam. Ultimately the design will be complete. All I'm doing with this is buying you time and rebuilding morale. What you have to do is hope that the Olyix arrive before we're ready to feed the design into Bennu's fabrication systems.'

Kenelm clamped hir fingers onto the side of hir head – a theatrical gesture but a true reflection of inner apprehension. 'So you're just delaying the problem.'

'Psychological issues are not the kind of problems that have a definitive solution. If we do nothing, the current situation will only get worse.'

'Saints.' Kenelm sighed. 'Okay, apart from the explorer starship, are their any other ideas?'

'Hibernation,' Ellici said. 'Biologic support chambers can suspend a human body for a long time. At the very least, you could usefully get three decades. If an Olyix arkship hasn't shown up by then, they probably know Vayan is a trap. And if that's the case, they'll send a battle fleet into the system at relativistic speed and obliterate everything – I would.'

'You're focusing on the practical again,' Yirella said. 'Sure, we can put squad males on ice, but you're back to the original problem: you have to know which ones. And you're not addressing the fundamental issue, which is the sense of hopelessness our mission has created for some people. If anything, hibernation confirms their outlook. You'd essentially be saying: Yes, we know this Strike is a long shot – *and* rubbing it in that they're not as worthy as those that don't get shoved into a suspension chamber.'

'The Strike is a certainty,' Kenelm said. 'It's the time which it may take that's unpredictable.'

Yirella gave hir an awkward glance. 'No, Captain. There's no guarantee the Olyix will show up at Vayan.'

'You designed the Vayan lure. It's a bit late to start questioning it now.'

'I'm not questioning the lure itself. It's the timing which bothers me.'

'What's wrong with the timing?'

'We're late in the exodus era. How many times have the Olyix been lured to a planet, only to find us waiting for them?'

'Plenty,' Kenelm said. 'That's why we – you! – made Vayan effectively perfect. Even a stealthed spy satellite in low orbit will see a real civilization down there. The detail you've provided is fantastic.'

'Yes, but they're still going to be extremely cautious when they approach. They might even have abandoned using their friendly arkship strategy. Maybe the first we'll see of them is an armada of Redemption ships.'

'We're ready for both scenarios,' Ellici said. 'We know exactly what we can strike effectively, and what we have to run from.'

'Wait,' Dellian said. 'There's a retreat option?'

'If the circumstances are extreme, then yes,' Kenelm said. 'This is not a suicide mission. Should the Olyix arrive in overwhelming force, the *Morgan* will portal into deep space and fly clear.'

'I didn't know.'

'It's just a contingency, Dellian. And I'd appreciate you not sharing that with the other squads.'

'But . . . if the Olyix are expecting us, where would we go?'

'Juloss advised me to use the Neána option. Withdraw into deep space and build habitats in the dark, where no one will ever find us.'

'Saints!' Dellian muttered. 'I hate that idea. That's giving up.'

'That's keeping the human race alive,' Kenelm said, 'and allowing them to carry on looking for a different method of defeating the Olyix.'

'The exploration starship would provide us with another option if we ever have to face that situation,' Yirella said eagerly. 'This completely justifies it.'

'Possibly,' Kenelm said. 'There are a lot of variables.'

'If we go ahead with your explorer starship idea, what would you tell everyone the mission goal is?' Tilliana asked. 'If you want people to self-justify leaving us and the *Morgan* behind, then it's going to have to be spectacular. I'm not sure offering them another generation world like Juloss is going to cut it.'

Yirella grinned. 'The explorer starship will search for Sanctuary.'

'Oh, come on!'

'It's perfect. Everyone believes in it.'

'Many do; some do not. And if it does exist, we don't know where it is. That's the point of Sanctuary. It's beyond the ability of the Olyix to find.'

'Which is a perfect mission for an explorer starship. We know the legend is in our own lineage. Somewhere between here and Earth there must be an abandoned terraformed planet where the legend started. And we can track it down. That's our grand voyage, the offering of hope. A difficult but not impossible quest with the ultimate golden prize at the end: the idyllic life they're denied by staying here.'

'Great Saints! Earth is over six thousand lightyears away. Maybe –' Tilliana glanced at Captain Kenelm for confirmation.

'About that,' sie said. 'The exact stellar coordinates are in the *Morgan*'s genten. They're not classified, because the Olyix certainly know them.'

'A relativistic starship could travel that distance in two decades of ship's time. Not that it would go all the way back to Earth. We're stopping to explore abandoned worlds along the way, right?'

'Nobody in our lineage ever travelled relatavistically across a thousand lightyears of interstellar space, never mind six thousand,' Tilliana said. 'We always send portals out ahead and jump through them. And the portal ships only reach point-eight-five C.'

'Yeah,' Yirella said with a big smile. 'So our starship is going to take some big-arse design work, huh?'

Tilliana gave Ellici a confused look and shrugged.

'Actually,' Ellici said. 'I quite like it.'

'Thank you,' Yirella said.

The three girls turned to Kenelm.

'It doesn't have to work,' Yirella said. 'It just has to sound plausible. Something that'll keep our disenchanted men occupied.' She gave Dellian a pointed glance. 'So they don't spend all their time beating the crap out of each other.'

'Hey, thanks.'

Kenelm nodded. 'You have to make it very clear that it will be difficult and dangerous. It will also take years to plan before we start building.'

'Wait,' Dellian said. 'Are you saying you *will* build this thing?'

'I'm acknowledging that dangling the prospect of Sanctuary in front of people is possibly our best option at the moment. Yirella is right; procrastination and delay is the solution to our current problem with the squads. But, by its nature, that procrastination can only be temporary. If the Olyix don't show up by the time the design work is finished, then I cannot renege on the deal. My authority would be trashed, and the *Morgan*'s Strike mission with it. So this starship design has to be the toughest project we've ever undertaken. You'll uncover so many problems and flaws that you'll need to redesign it a million times a week. Understood?'

'Yes, Captain,' Yirella said happily.

'Okay, then this conversation never happened. You start talking about your idea in public, spread it around the squads and see if they share your enthusiasm. And should you get enough people excited, you can conspire with them to ambush me with a formal proposal at a ship's council meeting. Make sure you have enough votes to carry it.'

'That'll take months of politicking among the squads,' Tilliana said with a growing smile.

'So it will.'

London

26th June 2204

It wasn't on the benefits list when Gwendoline signed up, but membership of the globalPAC was presenting her with a front-row seat for the end of the world. The Alpha Defence sensors drifting furtively around the *Salvation of Life* were relaying remarkably clear images. An hour after it had split into two, the gap between its two parts was already ten kilometres and still increasing. Sunlight probed the interior like a slow-motion dawn, revealing the big cavity that had been exposed to space. She thought it resembled a sheer-walled crater whose ribbed surface glittered with exotic tessellations, as though Olyix technology was crafted out of chalcedony rock. Odd indigo sparks flitted within the shadowed depths, pulsing out cascades so fleeting they might be illusory.

The globalPAC's concurrent tech analysis suggested those flickers could be Cherenkov radiation. Which meant she was actually looking directly into the throat of a wormhole. A technology decades, if not centuries, ahead of anything humans could build.

Something moved inside the darkness, gliding smoothly up the centre of the cavity into the sunlight.

'Holy crap,' Gwendoline muttered.

The Olyix ship which emerged from the wormhole throat was

unexpectedly striking, like a manta ray crossed with a supersonic jet – but huge. Its dull blue-black surface was ruffled with hundreds of small fins that were retracting even as she watched, transforming the fuselage into a sleek aerodynamic body eight hundred metres long. She didn't understand why it was so streamlined, not for interplanetary spaceflight. The few human spaceships that operated in the Sol system were blunt functional affairs: a spine of girders with modules clamped on and a fusion rocket at the rear, while the relativistic interstellar ships striking out into the galaxy were simple teardrop shapes riding a vast angry spear of plasma that came directly from the heart of a sun. Their shells were also portals, holes into which any dust crossing the ship's path simply fell through to be ejected by the portal's twin lightyears behind. But this Olyix ship was something else altogether, its smooth shape bestowing a menacing purpose. So she wasn't entirely surprised when it performed a nimble twist and shot out through the widening gap between the two sections and into clear space, rotating lazily as it emerged from the *Salvation of Life*'s umbra. There was no visible rocket exhaust, no solar-bright plasma or flaring blue chemical flame. It manoeuvred as if it really was an aircraft flying basic aerobatics, a nonchalant display of power and ability that was deeply intimidating.

Gravity wave manipulation, zero-point Lorentz force, maybe quantum field propulsion – so claimed the globalPAC's concurrent tech analysis stream. Gwendoline ignored it; they were nerds arguing over a Hong Kong sci-fi interactive's plot points. Admittedly nerds with Nobel physics prizes, but still nerds. The theory behind the drive was irrelevant. It was the potential that was scaring the shit out of her. *Alien invasion*. Humans' consistent terror image for generations.

Another of the big delta shapes was rising out of the arkship's open end. Three more. Then some smaller craft came zipping into view, glowing celadon cylinders with fluctuating carmine spirals spinning along their length, as if they were screwing themselves through space. At least they had some kind of exhaust – a weak contrail of fluorescent blue fog. Energized helium, the Alpha Defence sensors reported.

The new ships emerged in a huge swarm that went on and on, tight packed and moving with uniform fluidity as they spilled out of the gap, then split into distinct murmurations that began to accelerate away, hard.

Another wave of the delta craft followed, four or five at a time now. Gwendoline sat in her leather sofa, waiting for the deluge to stop. A small icon in the corner of her tarsus lens counted them off. After two hundred had appeared she told her altme, Theano, to end the sensor splash. It was too much for her. This wasn't the invasion as she'd braced herself for, a titanic struggle between roughly equal opponents, plucky underdog humans fighting back valiantly. This was an overwhelming violation that would wipe her species from existence.

The end of the world. Of everything.

She just sat there in the dusky penthouse, staring straight ahead through the balcony doors, seeing nothing. Tears came and went, drying on her cheeks. Sometimes during difficult negotiations she would take a break to process what was happening, to come to terms and design a strategy.

There was no processing this. There never would be.

An icon splashed into her vision, startling her. The security agent from Connexion had arrived.

'Authorize access,' Gwendoline told the penthouse.

Her name was Crina. Twenty-five years old, medium height and clearly very fit; she either worked out a lot or had muscle enhancements – probably both. Then there was her flattish, unremarkable face, which Gwendoline assumed was a useful trait for her line of work. Mouse-brown hair cut short. A dark-grey suit, snug-fitting but somehow stretching easily to accommodate every movement.

She introduced herself with a forceful politeness. 'Sorry I took so long to get here, ma'am. The London hub network is in bad shape tonight. The Greenwich office just told me to make my way straight here from home.'

'You weren't on duty, then?'

'No, ma'am. I'm on provisional engagement with Connexion

Security, but don't worry, I've undergone the full training programme. I will be able to protect you.'

'Thank you.' There was a time, maybe two hours ago, when Gwendoline would have seethed at such an insulting downgrade in her personal protection. *A trainee? A fucking trainee for a Zangari board member?* Now, she frankly didn't give a shit. Loi had done well to get her anyone.

'I need to start by examining every room.'

'I sent my staff home earlier; there's only me here.'

'Yes, ma'am. But I am required to verify that, and familiarize myself with the location layout. It's basic procedure. We cannot afford complacency in situations such as this.'

'Uh, right. Okay then.' Gwendoline made a sweeping gesture of invitation.

'Thank you. Please remain here until I finish my sweep.'

So there she stood in the vestibule, feeling silly, but also amused at Crina's super-serious attitude. *Does that make me patronizing? She's only doing her job, and she's new; she needs to be professional, especially in front of me.*

It took Crina fifteen minutes to satisfy herself there were no ninja assassins or bug-eyed monsters hiding under the beds or in wardrobes.

'All clear,' she announced.

The agent sounded so solemn and pleased with herself that Gwendoline found it hard not to laugh. 'Great. I haven't had dinner yet. What do you want? I'll get a deliverez.'

'I don't need anything, thank you, ma'am.'

'Everyone needs to eat. Even on a day like this – especially on a day like this. I'll probably just have a lasagne and salad. Roniquos have an excellent menu and they're only just down the road. Take a look while I get changed.' She'd only just realized she was still in her robe. Blithely parading around in front of Crina like she did with her ordinary staff didn't seem right somehow.

'Ma'am.'

Gwendoline retreated into her bedroom. She ignored the clothes menu Theano splashed for her, remembering what Horatio used to enjoy her wearing back in the day, when they were both young and free and life was easy. So, plain white T-shirt and a thin, brightly coloured skirt, as if she was off to the beach for a day.

She was fastening the skirt when the First Speaker of the Sol Senate made her official statement: 'The Olyix are invading. A large fleet of ships are heading towards Earth from the *Salvation of Life* and are presumed hostile. Do not be alarmed. Our city shields are active and will hold off any assault while we launch our Alpha Defence forces to counter and overcome this unprovoked aggression. If you live outside a shield, proceed to the nearest protected area, where the government will allocate you shelter. Interstellar portals have been closed temporarily. This is a preventative measure only. Together we will prevail.'

Gwendoline stood perfectly still. *What fucking counter-forces?*

Theano opened her connection to the globalPAC again and she gritted her teeth against the inevitable barrage of bad news. But, for an organization plugged into the top of the solar system's political hierarchy, the globalPAC was surprisingly short on concrete information. Covert attacks against the Connexion hubs and Earth's power grid were becoming a serious problem. Seventeen city shields were already operating on reserve power, and three – Bangkok, Antananarivo, and Astana – had failed, their systems damaged by saboteurs. Solnet was suffering severe glitches that the G8Turings were struggling to eradicate. And, no, Alpha Defence didn't have a secret navy to fight back with. *No kidding.*

She went back out into the living room. Crina hadn't moved from where she was standing, although the curtains had been closed. 'I will have a margherita pizza, thank you, ma'am.'

'Good choice.'

Theano placed the order, adding a vegetarian lasagne for Horatio as well as a calorie-overload dark chocolate and raspberry pudding. Roniquos acknowledged, giving her a delivery slot in fifteen minutes.

Decent enough last meal, she acknowledged bleakly. *Where are you, Horatio?* He really should have been here by now. She couldn't bring herself to make a call and ask him; that would have been giving in to fear. *What exactly does happen if you're halfway through a portal and the power goes off unexpectedly?* She was sure there were all sorts of multiple redundancy safety systems, that it wouldn't guillotine you in half. *Right?*

'Do you want a drink?' she asked.

'No thank you, ma'am,' Crina replied.

'Open invitation if tonight gets really bad,' Gwendoline said and headed into the kitchen. Theano told her which of the three fridges stocked her wines. She pulled out a bottle of vintage Krug. Her throat began to harden, moisture swelling behind her eyes, threatening to pour out –

'Horatio Seymore is here,' Theano said.

'Let him in.'

'Unable to comply. Connexion Security has assigned the penthouse physical access codes to Crina.'

Gwendoline hurried back out into the main corridor with its tall archways of silent inactive portals. The vestibule at the end was sealed off behind a thick security door which had slid out of the wall. She'd forgotten the thing had ever been installed.

Crina was already there in front of it, feet planted apart in a stock power pose. 'Ma'am, I must advise you not to break the security perimeter.'

'To hell with that. He's my husband!'

There was only the slightest hesitation. 'Your ex-husband, I believe.'

'He's coming in.'

'I need to confirm he is alone.'

Gwendoline nearly started shouting, but just managed to stop herself in time. That anger was coming from trepidation. Crina was just doing her job.

'Right. Do that. Then let him in.'

'Yes, ma'am.'

The security door slid open and Crina stepped through. The door closed again. Gwendoline waited, feeling slightly ridiculous.

The door opened, and Horatio was there in the vestibule. Practically unchanged from that first time they'd met thirty-seven years ago, which sent a little twinge of envy along her spine. She knew damn well he didn't spend (waste, in his terms) money on cosmetic anti-ageing treatments. But his firm jaw was still there, emphasizing the half-smile she'd always cherished. Lustrous dark skin with its perpetual healthy sheen. The hair was shorter now, of course, and maybe just a few strands of grey amid the ebony. But those beautiful large brown eyes were looking straight at her with unashamed adoration. If she was a teenager she'd probably sigh happily and grin coquettishly right back at him, as she always used to. As it was, they had a shared moment of bemusement at Crina's excessive caution.

Gwendoline hugged him tight. 'Good to see you.'

'Glad to be here. How are you holding up?'

'Oh . . . you know.'

He grinned and kissed her. 'You're looking fabulous. I think your legs have grown even longer.'

'Ohhh, smooth line, mister. But thanks anyway. Damn, I spend a fortune keeping in shape – and all for men. Why do we bother?'

'Ah, see, that was the moment you were supposed to return the compliment, not remind me how rich you are.'

She kissed him back. 'You forgot, you're talking to a self-absorbed plutocrat.'

'Yeah, that too.'

She sneaked a glance at Crina, who was frowning. 'Come on. I just opened a plutocrats-only-priced bottle of champagne. Force yourself to oppress the masses for tonight and have a glass with me.'

'Temptress.'

'Ha, right. I always had to tempt you into my bedroom. You put up such a fight . . .'

They walked back into the living room, his arm around her waist. *And it fits there so perfectly.*

He picked up the Krug and read the label. 'An '85. Sweet.'

'You're an oenophile now? You? Truly the end of days.'

'No. I just remember, that's all: Bordeaux.'

'Oh, yeah.' She knew a faint blush was colouring her cheeks. '*That* week.'

'Indeed.'

Gwendoline poured them both a glass and sat next to him on the settee, legs tucked up so she could lean in close. *Easy.* 'I really am glad you're here,' she said.

'I only came because I figured being with you was as physically safe as I could possibly get tonight. And I was right: nothing gonna get past Crina.'

She laughed. 'Still the eternal charmer.'

'It's going to be bad, isn't it? I would have been here earlier, but some of the metrohubs were out.'

'I heard.'

'People are still in shock, so there wasn't any trouble. Just a load of tutting and politely queuing for the hubs that are still open. We're still British, after all.'

'There are Olyix ships on the way. Warships of some type, my contacts think.'

'How many?'

She paused, letting Theano splash the data she really didn't want. 'Shit.'

'What?'

'Over fifteen hundred of the large ones so far, and still coming through.'

'Large ones? There's more than one type?'

'Yes. There were a lot of small ones earlier, which now seem to be heading outsystem under high acceleration. The tactical analysis teams aren't sure what they are. The majority view is that they're some kind of missile. The larger ones, which Alpha Defence are calling Deliverance ships – and no, I don't know why – are split into two groups. Some are on vectors out to habitats, while the bulk of them are heading straight for Earth. If their acceleration holds constant, and they flip at halfway to decelerate, they'll be here in about a week.'

She saw his hand trembling slightly as he put down the champagne glass.

'A week? Are you sure?'

'Mainlined straight from Alpha Defence,' she told him.

'Will the city shields hold?'

'Nobody knows, because nobody knows what they're going to hit them with. And even if they do hold . . . then what?'

'There must be some kind of plan. I know governments; they spend billions on consultants churning out contingency planning.'

'Actually, there is one. But . . .'

'Let me guess. It's not for everyone.'

Gwendoline bowed her head, hating that he was judging again. Because there was certainly no shame. No. None. 'Connexion Security are evaluating an evacuation of the Zangari family to one of our private habitats.'

'You just said those Deliverance ships are also heading for the asteroid habitats.'

'This is Nashua they're considering. In the Puppis system, forty-one lightyears away. And once we get there—'

'You can switch off the portals behind you.'

'We,' she said firmly. 'When *we* get there.'

'Oh, you're opening it to everyone are you?'

'You're my husband!'

'Ex.'

'And Loi's father.'

'Yeah,' he whispered.

'Nashua makes sense. It's a long way away, and it's orbiting Malamalama, which is being terraformed.' She smiled fondly at the memory. 'I visited when I was prepping for my current deal. Puppis has an exceptionally dense asteroid belt, and Malamalama is one of the shepherd worlds. The night sky is alive with zodiacal light, and it's so much brighter than the Milky Way. It's genuinely beautiful, Horatio. When the terraforming is complete, it'll be the most amazing— Aww crap. It'll never be terraformed now, will it?'

'I don't know. We don't know what the Olyix are doing. If it was just genocide they wanted, they wouldn't be sending this fleet of ships. They would have done it when the *Salvation of Life* arrived – a fast clean strike without any warning. Not this. I don't understand what they're doing.'

'It's connected with their religion, somehow. They want to take us with them to the end of time.'

'That doesn't make a whole lot of sense. How are they going to do that?'

'Change us so we hibernate, apparently. I don't have a lot of details right now.'

'Hibernate until the end of time? Someone's been lying to you big time.'

'Yeah.' Gwendoline pouted and finished her champagne in one smooth movent. 'Where the hell is dinner?'

'What?'

'I ordered dinner. It's not here.' Theano immediately queried the restaurant, and got an Order Delayed reply.

Horatio started laughing. 'Oh no. How tragic.'

'Hey!'

'Jesus, Gwendoline, how high is that Olympus you're sitting on? People have just been told there's a hostile alien fleet coming to wipe them out. The city shields are on, to reinforce how real that is. Right now everyone is frightened and panicking. They're just like you and me, they want to be with their families tonight. Nobody's going to be cooking your meals for you. Maybe never again.'

'But the restaurant said they'd deliver.' Even as she said it, she was ashamed at how much like a spoilt bitch she sounded.

'Sure, its little old G5Turing promised you. I bet it even meant it from the bottom of its machine heart. But all it actually does is issue the request to the chefs and arrange a deliverez. If there are no chefs, there is no meal. There are humans in the loop; without them, the loop doesn't work. And humans are suffering badly tonight.'

'All right.' Gwendoline pushed her head back on the settee's cushions. 'Have your moment of superiority. This is a lot for me to get a hold of. I'm not stupid; I just haven't thought things through yet. It's not that I don't care. I do. Especially about Loi. And you.'

He reached out and stroked her cheek. 'I made the list.'

'Stop it.'

'Sorry. Tonight is messing with my head just as much as yours. Let me be the big strong man of legend. I'll cook you a decent dinner. All right?'

'Thank you.'

'To back that up: what ingredients have you got in the kitchen?'

She sucked on her lower lip as she tried to give him a shamed expression. Didn't work; she couldn't help smirking. 'I don't know. Whatever the staff order in for me?'

His wide smile returned as bright as it ever had been while he rolled his eyes. 'You are hopeless.'

'Look, if you need a billion-wattdollar deal, I'm your woman.'

'We'll get on that first thing tomorrow. Right now, let's go see what there is. And no! Don't access your altme. We'll actually open the fridge door manually, and look. With our eyes.'

She couldn't help it. 'Which of the fridges?'

He chased her into the kitchen, both of them laughing, just the way it used to be back when they spent long glorious nights in his tiny flat on Eleanor Road. And for ten minutes as they piled ingredients and utensils up on the big island's marble surface it was just them, and the alien apocalypse was banished to wait outside the penthouse.

'Salmon risotto with asparagus,' he announced as he started chopping the onion. 'These are all organic, right?'

'I'm insulted you ask. The penthouse Turing would probably crash and weep if a bagez tried bringing printed food over the threshold.'

'Yeah? Well, start crushing the natural garlic – two cloves. You remember how to do that, don't you?'

She poured more of the Krug for both of them. 'Somehow I will muddle through.'

'So when would the evacuation happen?' he asked.

'I don't know. You're not going to go all principled on me and stay behind, are you?'

He paused, holding the knife above the onion segments. 'What about the people who do get left here?'

She reviewed the Alpha Defence splash. 'There are over eighteen hundred Deliverance ships on their way now. The Olyix aren't fucking about, Horatio. They're coming for us big time. I know you don't have a lot of faith in governments and institutions—'

'It's not governments I have an issue with – or not the concept of democratic government, anyway. But all we have now is rule by rich people, the ones who keep ninety per cent of the world in relative poverty so their unbalanced market can continue paying for a lifestyle of total excess.'

'Does that include me?' she asked in exasperation. *So many times*. This argument had come to dominate their lives until it split them apart.

'No.'

'Really? I'm one of your hated ten per cent.'

'Nobody hates you.'

'Why the hell didn't you go and be a Utopial if you despise Universal culture so much?'

'You.' His voice was so faint she could barely hear it.

'*What?*'

'I couldn't leave you.'

Gwendoline actually dropped the garlic press, she was so startled by the admission. 'I would have gone with you. This . . . none of this mattered as much to me as you did.'

Horatio gave a nervous snort. 'You, a Utopial?'

'Yes! Me. It's not a bad philosophy.'

He waved his hand around at the gleaming kitchen. 'You wouldn't have had any of this.'

'For fuck's sake, I don't need this existence to be happy. High-end consumerism is just a cosmetic skin stretched over real life. You and Loi are all I need. In any case, a Utopial lifestyle isn't living in a favela or Southwark, you know. Everyone on Delta Pavonis is comfortably off and free to follow their dream. Well . . . okay, they're astonishingly dull, but doing all right.' She quirked her lips. 'And besides, I'd work my way up to their level-one citizen status soon enough.'

'Jesus wept, when did you start thinking like this?'

'I've always thought like this. You're the one that wants to tax every penny the filthy ten per cent have and give it to the poor, to level down. I want to level up.' She picked up the Krug bottle by the neck and waved it aggressively at him. 'I want everyone to have a penthouse and stupid Krug.'

'Nobody wants to level down. If you think that, you're believing your own side's propaganda. I just want to stop the monstrous inequality which Universal culture's obsession with The Market has given us, to give everyone a fair share. You have no idea how bad it is for the people my agency helps, people stuck out there in the ribbon towns and on the edge of society – all comfortably out of sight from your gated towers.'

'I don't have a *side*, and they're not my fucking towers,' she yelled at him. Then regretted it instantly. 'Sorry. Utopial society showed us the way, you know. We can have that now – and without their mad omnia ideology; all the industrial replication systems and G8s we have today make it possible. We were *this* close, Horatio. I'd helped put together something I was so proud of – a concept, an ideology, whatever. We were going to give a terra-formed world a different society, the best of all we've achieved: a capital-based post-scarcity economy for smart people. Another week and we'd have been there, it would have started.' She stopped, grief and fright claiming her. 'And now it's all gone, everything's lost. And you and I are still arguing over money and who's got it.'

He put his arms around her. 'You've just said it, sweetheart. Humans have phenomenal resources available now. Our industrial stations will be able to mass produce weapons. We'll have something to fight these Delivery ships with, you'll see. This crisis will bring us together like nothing else.'

'Deliverance. It's *Deliverance* ships we have to fight. And it won't, because we're all going to die.'

'Stop that. Think about it. If the Olyix wanted to kill us, they would have done it by now. This is something different. Maybe they will stuff us all into hibernation pods, but that gives us a chance. I'm not saying it's a big chance, but at least there is one.'

'I love your optimism. I always did.'

He held her close for a long moment. 'I'd like to come to Nashua with you. If your family allow it.'

'The Zangaris are your family, too.'

'Riiight. But running away from Earth has to be the absolute last resort – for any of us. I don't believe Alpha Defence will sit back and do nothing.'

'They'll do what they can. I know the family senior council is in session. I think that's what Loi is involved in; he was advising Yuri.'

'Christ, does Ainsley have his own nukes? Or, knowing him, something even more extreme? A doomsday bomb?'

Gwendoline winced. 'Ainsley III and the others will keep Grandfather calm.'

'Ainsley being calm about the Olyix . . . I'd pay good money to see that. He was always so manically paranoid about them. He blamed them for me being snatched, remember?'

Her arms tightened around him. 'I don't want to remember that. I thought I'd lost you. It nearly killed me.'

'Didn't happen then. Not going to happen now.'

'Good. And don't worry about the family doing anything too crazy. Ainsley isn't in charge any more.'

'Seriously?'

'Not to be repeated anywhere to anyone, okay? Especially right now. But he's just a figurehead for Connexion, visible on media feeds to keep the markets steady. Ainsley III and the council took control over a decade ago.'

'Christ. Why?'

'Ainsley isn't very stable these days. It's down to all the anti-ageing treatments he's undergone, we think. Some of them were quite cutting edge, and he'd take anything that promised him longevity. He's always been obsessed by that. I didn't see much of him when I was a child, but I always remember him telling me that when he was growing up, the expectation was that his generation would be the first to live to two hundred years. Well, that wasn't enough for him. He wanted to be the first human to live for ten thousand years – and more. He's still quite adamant about that. So with all those billions he's spent, biologically he's returned to his mid-twenties – and not just cosmetically. Yo, result! But mentally, he has problems. The effect some of those treatments have on the human neural structure aren't fully understood, let alone curable yet.'

'Shit. That explains so much.'

'It could even run in the family. I was getting badly hyper tonight until you turned up. You're my family council, Horatio, my serenity nark. So tomorrow we'll start examining our options – *really* examining them. Because even with you here, my brain is too scrambled to think straight tonight.'

'Amen to that.'

'And you're clearly a mess, too, because you know damn well I don't like that much onion in my risotto.'

'Oh.' He looked down at the chopping board with its mound of diced onion. 'Right.'

Gwendoline sauntered over to the wine fridge. 'What we need is more Krug. That'll help us focus.'

'It certainly will.'

London

27th June 2204

Tronde woke as if he was clawing his way out of a nightmare. Not being fully conscious yet offered relief from the clammy dread of loss afflicting him at some elemental level. During the night, someone had stolen his soul.

Claudette's god-awful fluffy pink and black bedroom came into focus, and he was gazing right at a charcoal drawing of an improbably equipped satyr riding his harem of big-breasted nymphs. Nobody wanted to see that before breakfast.

But it did make him acknowledge the root of his heartache: pleasure. Unique, overwhelming, multispectrum pleasure. The hifli had burned out of his system while he slept, its absence leaving him with cold, sweaty skin. His body was just so much useless junk now. The pleasure he'd embraced last night had been incredible, his body properly alive for the first time ever. Hifli had made every cell function perfectly. Until then, his mind had spent every one of his twenty-five years maliciously interpreting all the body's senses wrongly, but now he knew the truth – that every facet of experience was actually pleasure. You just had to know how to make the perception switch. *It's not dangerous, it's liberation.* He couldn't believe he'd spent his whole life avoiding nark. *Stupid bourgeois way of thinking. I'm a member of the Legion, for fuck's sake, a real-life bad boy – not Claudette's fantasy one.*

He rolled over to see Claudette lying on the bed beside him, awake, staring listlessly at the gauzy canopy above them. There were tears filling the corners of her eyes. His attempt to sit up was greeted by a nasty shot of pain from his groin. 'Shit.'

They'd fucked each other into oblivion. Which meant he'd finally fallen unconscious with his erection still switched on. Sometime in the night Nyin's failsafe had activated and disengaged the Kcells reinforcing his cock. *Not soon enough, though.*

'Are you awake?' Claudette asked in an enervated tone.

He knew that quality well enough by now; it hailed him every morning after he'd dosed her with hifli. 'Fuck off.'

'What is it? What's wrong, babe?'

'Nothing! So shut up.'

'What have I done? I thought last night was the best yet.'

'Just . . . leave it, okay?' He made a huge effort, and clambered off the bed. Walked stiffly to the en suite, every muscle hot with fatigue.

'Didn't you like it?' she asked in a teary wail.

'Yeah, sure.' Even that sounded like an admission of guilt.

'I don't understand. What was different?'

The difference, you dumb bitch, was that I was actually dosed on hifli this time. He wanted to go back and slap her. But he couldn't. The Legion needed her, needed the refuge this house provided. And she had more hifli. 'It was great, okay? But coming down is always shit. Right?' Saying it, lying even under these circumstances, gave him the push he needed: still the greatest, still the lord of control and manipulation.

He lingered in the shower, which warmed his flesh, if nothing else. The bleak gulf of depression inside was still there when he finished, threatening to pull him down. He desperately wanted to go back there, into the world defined by euphoria, not wander through this drab miserable universe which had slaughtered Piotr and Gareth. Just thinking about them – friends since forever – brought the hopelessness surging back. *But I can handle it. I'm not weak like she is. I understand. I'm not fooling myself. Taking it isn't addiction, it's a choice to live a different life.*

Claudette was asleep again when he made his way back through to the bedroom. Tronde tracked his gaze across the walls and furniture. One of the charcoal nymphs had her face; he hadn't ever noticed that before. His pile of clothes were still rank from river muck, so he picked up one of her robes and wrapped it tight around him.

Downstairs there was a smell of fried bacon and coffee. *Damn, that smells good.* He'd been a vegetarian for over ten years. *Why? Why did I do that?* The reasons – self-worth, body purity – it all seemed so stupid now.

Ollie and Adnan had taken over the lounge, though they hadn't bothered to open the curtains. They were slumped on the sofa, watching some kind of sci-fi drama shit in the compact Bang and Olufsen stage. Ollie glanced up and immediately grinned.

'Oh man, that is the mother of all walks of shame!'

Tronde couldn't even find a spark of indignation to fuel a gripe, so he just shrugged and dropped onto the sofa next to them.

Ollie's amusement faded. 'What the hell happened?'

'Nothing.' Admitting he'd let her slip him hifli, how the experience was a revelation, was too painful. They wouldn't laugh, but they would be full of pity. He couldn't stand that, not the way he was right now. 'How's Lars?'

Ollie and Adnan exchanged a glance.

'Not too good,' Ollie said as if he was in confessional with a particularly stern priest. 'I think he's got some internal damage. And his neck ain't right, either. There's a lot of swelling there.'

'Where is he?'

'On the sofa in that glass room at the back. I bunged him more sedatives. Moving about ain't going to do him any good. He needs to keep still.'

'And quiet,' Adnan muttered.

'Right,' Tronde sank deeper into the cushions. 'What about us? What are the police doing?'

'Does it matter?' Adnan asked, waving at the stage. 'When this is happening?'

'Huh?' Tronde squinted at the sharp holograms of triangular spaceships, wondering where the laser beams were. Most Hong Kong interactives had them.

'Those are the Olyix ships. They're coming for us, man. There's thousands of them.'

'Huh?'

Adnan and Ollie shared another look. 'This is a live stream,' Adnan said. 'It's real. The lownet broke it from some secret government sensors spying on the *Salvation of Life*.'

Finally, Tronde was shaken into taking an interest in something other than his own self-analysis. He peered forwards at the images. 'Real? You're fucking kidding me!'

'There's a whole armada of these things heading for Earth. They're coming out of the arkship.'

'Holy crap!'

'Tronde,' Ollie said nervously, 'there was a shitload of sabotage all over the planet last night. It's still going on. Twelve city shields are already down. They hit the power grid relay stations and backup fusion generators. Sound familiar?'

Tronde told Nyin to open the news streams, filtered to Olyix events. The altme obliged, and the splash practically overwhelmed his tarsus lenses. 'Oh God.' His head sank into his hands. Tears threatened to come pouring down his cheeks. What he needed was some hifli; that would turn this disaster into triumph. 'Are we part of this? Is Jade an alien?'

'The police think we're involved, yes,' Ollie said. 'They're saying the raid on the Croydon power relay was part of the Olyix sabotage.'

'No! No, no, no. I'm not a fucking alien.' He suddenly noticed a couple of bacon sandwiches left on a plate and snatched one up. It tasted *good*.

'We've been watching the railway arches all night,' Adnan said. 'The whole zone is swamped with cops, and they're all there hunting us.'

'We hijacked some taxez and bugez to relay their camera feeds as they drove past,' Ollie said. 'Forensics are tearing the archway to pieces. Everyone's home has been raided. I saw my gran in tears. Some piece of shit detective was shouting at her outside our house.'

'It's worse than that,' Adnan said. 'We've been given Most Wanted Fugitive status now; it's all over the police and security web. Special Branch are going round to our friends. I managed to rip some chatter out of their comms; they think someone we know is either hiding us or knows where we are. They're being kind of brutal about it. Aex, Jorge and Karlsen all got taken in.'

'Karlsen?' Tronde asked. Karlsen was a good friend, a fellow printer nerd, but an artist who crafted weird acrylic runcolour sculptures. He didn't have anything to do with the kind of deals the Legion were involved in. 'Why take him in?'

'He knows us and he was narked out when they bust his door down. So they'll cold turkey him the hard way.'

'Well, shit.'

'They took Lolo, too,' Ollie said. 'Bastards! Sie doesn't know anything. Sie'll be terrified.'

Tronde didn't like the way Ollie sounded all defensive about the 'not knowing' part, but didn't say anything. Instead he started on the second sandwich. 'We could hand ourselves in,' he suggested. 'Once they interview us, they'll know we weren't nothing to do with the sabotage.'

'Fuck off!' Adnan shouted. 'I'm not having my brain squeezed out of my ears by Special Branch. They're gangstas with badges, that's all. You know half the gang members they rendition never even make it to Zagreus.'

'That's just rumour,' Ollie said. 'The Specials started it themselves to max up their rep.'

'Bet your life on it? Cos that's what you're saying. Shit. *Hand ourselves in?* Tronde, if you think I'm doing that, you're batshit crazy!'

'I get it, though,' Ollie said. 'This is big, really big. It's not about raids and scams for the London majors, not any more.' A finger jabbed frantically at the stage with its terrifying flock of silent alien spaceships. 'This is the end of the world. The government is serious. They will hunt us forever. This will not blow over in a few days. Understand?'

'In a few days we won't exist any more,' Adnan shouted back. 'Do *you* understand that?'

'I'm not sitting in this room waiting to be slaughtered by alien nukes. We need to get out of here. We need to get to one of the terraformed worlds.'

'The interstellar portals have all been shut, genius. We're going nowhere. And if we step outside, they'll find us. They think we're enemy aliens! They've got fucking G8Turings on this; they'll crack our escape route eventually.'

'There'll be *some* portals open,' Ollie said. 'You can bet your arse the rich will have their routes out; so'll all the politicians. They'll leave people like us behind to fight and die while they're safe ten lightyears away. I am not going to let that happen. I am going to get Gran and Bik out of here. I don't care what it takes.'

'You are not leaving here! The second you do, you compromise me and Tronde and Lars. So, no.'

'Guys,' Tronde said, 'you're both right. We can't stay here, and we can't leave. So we need another option.'

'Go on, then,' Adnan said. 'What is it?'

Tronde gave Ollie an expectant look. Which should have done it – Ollie was the Legion's master of planning – but Ollie just stared back blankly. 'Shit, okay. We have to contact Jade.'

'That's your master plan?'

'Hey! Think about it, dumbarse. If Jade is one of the alien saboteurs, the security jackboots will be hunting her a damn sight harder than they are us. So she'll have gone to ground. But if she's a genuine part of a major family, there'll be heat but we're in the clear. More than that, she'll be able to help.'

Third time: Ollie and Adnan gave each other a look.

'I can use a package that will route a call to her,' Adnan said. 'One the G8s won't find.'

'You don't know that for sure. They've broken the lownet,' Ollie said. 'Everything's changed.'

'Half solnet is glitched, and even some of the lownet is out. And we've got this feed, haven't we?'

'Okay. Do it. Call Jade.'

*

Jade arrived twenty minutes later, stepping out of a Rolls Royce taxez. For the first time ever she was wearing an expensive business suit and black heels. She fitted the leafy street perfectly, another quality woman visiting the neighbourhood she clearly belonged in. Tronde found the conversion unnerving, but then Jade always had that effect on him.

She came into the lounge with its closed curtains and unwashed crockery, dismissing it with a single raised eyebrow.

'Turn that off,' she said.

The images of alien invaders vanished from the Bang and Olufsen stage.

'The police—' Ollie began.

He was silenced by Jade's raised hand. She stood in front of the big settee as the three of them slouched on its deep cushions, putting them back fifteen years into class detention. 'Firstly, you boys did a good job. My *major* friends want you to know that.'

'But—'

Again: the hand. 'I know you didn't manage to kill the power to the Commercial and Government Services hub as required. However, the power was shut off for fifteen minutes by the police as a precaution while they checked the relay station, so that was down to you. The relevant shipments were diverted and cancelled. Money was made as planned. So I have your payments, plus a bonus.' Four cryptokens were held out, purple-chrome surfaces glinting like distant planets in the room's dim light. 'They're all clean, so pair them to your altme.'

'Thanks,' Adnan said dourly, and took his.

'I'll take one for Lars,' Ollie said.

Tronde held his up as Nyin confirmed the balance the token held and paired it. Cryptokens were a risky way of transferring money; the lownet was full of packages that promised to break an altme's pairing encryption.

'What about Piotr and Gareth?' Ollie asked.

Jade gave him a pleasant smile. 'What about them?'

'They were there. They should be paid.'

'They're dead, Ollie.'

'They had family. Piotr's girlfriend was long-term.'

'So what are you saying, I should give you their tokens and you'll go hand them over to the right people? Maybe buy a nice wreath for the funeral?'

'Well. No, not me. I can't risk it. But you need to do what's right by them.'

'Sure thing, Ollie. I'll get right on that.'

'Is that it?' Adnan asked.

'What else do you want?'

'Everybody is looking for us. Everyone! Police, security, government G8s. They think we're alien saboteurs. They'll catch us, it's going to happen; I'm just being realistic about that. And when they do they'll . . . I don't know what, but it'll be bad. Really bad.'

'You're not saboteurs for the Olyix,' Jade said firmly, 'because I'm not. Nikolaj is not. The people we work with are not. This has always been about the money. It was before this crazy invasion, and it will be after.'

'After?' Tronde roused himself. 'There's going to be an after? How do you know?'

'We have contacts in the government who are drawing up all sorts of scenarios, but it's actually quite logical. If all the Olyix wanted to do was exterminate us, they would have done it when they arrived. The *Salvation of Life* was carrying a shitload of anti-matter when it turned up in the solar system and we don't have any defence against a surprise attack from that. Yet they didn't fire a planet-killer at us.'

'So?'

'So they want something else. Something they can only get by using force to compel us. That means we can resist. We'll suffer losses fighting them, sure, but we won't lose everything – which is what the hysterical news streams are claiming. Life's going to be different after. I don't know how different, but at least we'll still be here to live it. Especially if you can dodge whatever those ships are going to drop on us.'

'We won't see it,' Ollie said. 'You've got to help us.'

'Help you do what?'

'We need to get out of here. We need to get the hunt stopped.'

Jade's expression became even more severe. 'Did you not listen to what I just said? The human race is entering a state of total war, and we have no idea for how long: months, years . . . decades. They are not going to relax their search for you.'

'Then, for fuck's sake, help us! If they rendition us, the first thing they'll know about is you. You're the one who got us to raid the Croydon station.'

'Is that a threat, Ollie?'

'No,' Adnan said swiftly, 'but you know it's true. Or do you think we can resist Special Branch interrogation?'

'Good point,' she said. 'Given what they'll do to you, you'll break within minutes. Only the totally crazy, or terminally stupid, would try and resist modern interrogation.'

'Oh, shit.' Ollie hugged his knees, and started rocking back and forth on the edge of the settee. 'Oh shit, oh shit, oh shit. I can't do it. I can't be tortured.'

'Then how do you stop them from catching us?' Tronde said. 'Because that's what you need to do to save yourself.' Even as the words were coming out of his mouth he regretted speaking. It sounded as if he was challenging her. Because the simplest way for her to avoid him and his friends telling anybody about her was just to take them out, here and now. He didn't doubt for a second she had the ability to do that.

Jade took a maliciously long time to answer, forcing them to see how dependent they were on her, how her ownership of them was as strong as any Roman slave merchant's. 'You disappear for good,' she said. 'A complete identity change.'

Out of the corner of his eye, Tronde saw Adnan stiffen.

'You mean a brain transplant?' Ollie asked.

'There's no such thing,' Jade told him. 'It's an urban myth. What I'm talking about is a replacement. A matcher will find you a loner, one physically similar to you who doesn't have any friends or family. They'll be removed, and you have a gene edit so you equal their DNA's short tandem repeats. Any subsequent profiling test will return a positive for them. Then you have to learn their behaviour, their job, their way of speech, likes, dislikes, every facet of their personality. You become them, so your current self vanishes. Then, after you've lived their life for a couple of years, you move – emigrate, change jobs, become a priest if you like, whatever. You begin again and become what you want. But the price is that you can never go back. You abandon your family, your friends, everything that ties you to you.'

'Holy fuck,' Adnan said. 'And do you know someone who can do this for us?'

'I do. But it's not cheap.'

Tronde started laughing bitterly as he shook the token at her. 'This isn't enough, is it?'

'No.'

'What the fuck!' Ollie wailed.

'There is a job we need you to do,' Jade said. 'It will pay enough for your new clean lives. After that, it will be over between us. You will never contact me again.'

They waited, waiting for her to tell them what it was. She regarded them calmly.

'What job?' Adnan demanded.

'We believe that the Olyix attack, when it comes, will produce massive casualties on Earth. That's kind of inevitable. Medical supplies will be an extremely valuable commodity, and others agree with us. The markets fell drastically last night and continue their fall now. However, there were two sectors which defied the trend; their stock prices actually rose. Advance-technology companies, which we will undoubtedly need to manufacture sophisticated weapons . . .'

'And medical,' Adnan completed for her.

'Quite. And out of the two, drugs are high-price small-volume items; they can also be sold through our existing nark dealers.'

'Holy shit,' Ollie exclaimed. 'How many drugs?'

'We are still putting the procedure together. It will require several teams such as the Legion fulfilling their part of the overall operation, dominoes that must fall perfectly into place at the exact time. I will tell my colleagues you have the ability to perform as required.'

'We do!'

This time only a raised finger was required. 'If they agree with me, I will inform you. It will take us a few days. Do not attempt to contact me during that time, and stay here. Don't even order anything by deliverez.'

'We won't,' Tronde said. 'There's enough food here to last us a week.'

'Good. And Lars?'

'What about him?' Adnan asked.

'What condition is he in? The job may require a brute strength component.'

'He's resting. He took a pounding last night, but he'll be fine in a day or so. You know Lars.'

'I certainly do.' She nodded in satisfaction. 'Very well. I will be in touch.'

As she left she almost bumped into Claudette, who was standing in the hallway, just out of sight behind the lounge door. Tronde winced; he'd thought she was still upstairs, dozing.

She wore a robe similar to the one Tronde had on, her hair unkempt, mascara trails smeared down her cheeks. A Claudette from a different universe to the one her glitzy friends knew. The two women regarded each other belligerently for a moment as they took in each other's appearance, then Jade sidestepped and went out through the front door.

Claudette turned to Tronde. 'Babe, what's happening? Who was she?'

He took a step towards her, for once unable to project that predatory male aurora she responded to. 'Jade is just a friend of Adnan's. She's got contacts in a legal firm. They're going to try and clear everything with the police.'

'You're going to leave, aren't you? You're going to leave me.'

'No.'

'She's got a job for you. I heard her say it.'

Tronde glanced at Ollie and Adnan, who were looking at him in concern. He had to do something. If she started to make trouble . . . 'Don't talk to me like that.'

'What? What does she want you to do? And what were you doing last night? How did you get hurt, really?' Claudette's voice was rising now. He knew that uncertainty, the brittleness infecting her. After all, it was a virus of his creation. Recognition pushed his thoughts back into the old routines, the right way to handle pathetic, dependent Claudette. They seemed to be overturning the lethargy and depression dragging on his mind, too.

He clicked his fingers at Ollie. 'Give me a pad of zero.'

'Huh?' Ollie grunted.

'A pad. You're always carrying. Gimme. The good stuff, not cut.'

'Answer me,' Claudette demanded. Her voice was up another octave, climbing towards hysteria.

'I told you,' Tronde snarled, and took a step forwards so he was pressed up against her, where he could glower down. 'You do not speak to me, not like that! I am a bad boy, and you still don't get what that really means.'

'I do. It means you're just like everyone else: a complete shit!'

'Oh, no.' He felt Ollie drop the pad of zero-nark into his open hand. 'I am much, much worse than them.'

Her eyes widened in a strange kind of fright and she tried to move back away from him. He quickly curled one arm around her, holding her tight. Then his other hand was shoving down the front of her robe to clasp her left breast. He could see it in her as she gasped, the insecurity. Should she try and struggle, maybe run? His thumb pushed down hard, pressing the pad of zero-nark on her flesh just above the nipple – and he prayed Ollie hadn't cut it down too much.

'You are my woman, you understand? And that means you do as I fucking tell you.' He let go in a swift motion and she swayed back. Now would be the moment – if she had any dignity or self-esteem left. The moment came and went – a departure aided by the chill of the zero-nark buzzing through her.

'Right, then,' he said. 'You two look after Lars and keep an eye out for the cops. I'm taking her upstairs for a fuck.'

Yet again, Ollie and Adnan stared at each other, this time in surprise at this aspect of him they'd never been shown before.

Tronde took Claudette by the wrist and pulled her up the fancy curving stairs. A smile of uncertainty was flickering on and off her slack face as she stumbled along beside him.

'How much hifli is left?' he asked.

'I don't know. I purchased about a dozen shots.'

A dozen? Holy shit. But as a way to greet alien Armageddon, it didn't get much better. 'Good girl.'

'I just want you to be happy here with me, babe. Don't leave. Please.'

'Forget about Jade and the others. I'm not going anywhere.'

Kruse Station

28th June 2204

Kandara was watching Jessika when Soćko regained consciousness. In fact, her attention hadn't left the alien humanoid since they arrived at the station's clinic. Her gland secretions provided her with an incredible degree of focus while peripherals extended her perception far above the human baseline. So when Soćko groaned and his eyelids fluttered open, Kandara barely acknowledged it, remaining engrossed with her target.

Tear ducts expanded, releasing water into Jessika's eyes. Her heart rate jumped up in tandem with the flush that elevated skin temperature. There was a hormonal rush that pumped her brainwaves. An uncontrolled expression of relief and happiness lifted her face.

The scrutiny confirmed that Jessika's responses – physical, emotional and chemical – were utterly human. But then the Neána had built her well. So well, in fact, that Kandara had genuinely warmed to the woman when they'd worked together. And that was the root of her current low-burning anger. She'd been totally fooled, even lowering her guard to commence a friendship. It didn't sit well. That consummate deceit was justification for paranoia on so many levels.

Kandara knew she would have to make a decision about the alien at some time, yet Jessika's super-ordinary behaviour was making that increasingly difficult for her. There was no way she could determine if the alien android had *a priori* that innate human intuition, responding to events in an instinctive fashion, or if her responses were simple mimicry routines, built into her as part of her disguise.

And where exactly did you draw the line between artificial responses and the genuine ones? If a fake was indistinguishable from real, didn't that make it real, too? That question had bedevilled philosophers greater than her for millennia; there certainly wasn't a test for it. So she was forced to assign the nature of personality to origin. Human contingency had evolved. Jessika's was formatted by design. She was meant to be human, or as close as the Neána could facilitate. So the real worry was that the emotions on show could be supplanted by deeper, alien, reactions if it suited her mission.

I can like her, but I can never trust her.

The slim, efficient monitors above the intensive-care bed were flashing alerts. Numbers rose in the displays, shading towards the green of good news. The internal body-scan hologram showed sections of Soćko's brain elevating their neural activity as if someone had flipped a switch. The comparison didn't comfort Kandara; it implied the brain was a machine, artificial. She got her altme, Zapata, to remind her to ask Lankin if this was how induced-coma victims normally woke. The Connexion science chief was someone she could rely on, though she guessed the answer would be ambiguous.

Soćko stirred, gazing around the facility with interest, lingering on Captain Tral and the three armoured security guards, then taking in the medical team. When he came to Kandara he passed on after the briefest examination, which made her bristle. Then he saw Jessika and smiled. He tried to speak, which the endotracheal tube in his mouth prevented. He frowned and reached for it. A nurse diverted his hand and the doctor eased the unit out. Oxygen hissed, and artificial saliva dripped across the bedclothes. Someone closed the alerts down.

Kandara observed Jessika wiggle her way past the fascinated medical team and smile broadly at her fellow alien. Tears dripped down, mingling with the goo on the sheet.

'Hi, you,' she said with amazing tenderness, and clasped his hand.

The burst of sympathy Kandara experienced was unexpected, but then her subconscious remained locked on interpreting Jessika as human, and the emotion radiating out of her at the reunion was as strong as anyone's separated from her true love for decades. But Kandara's alert senses also caught the spike of neural activity on the hologram monitoring Soćko's brainwaves, which corresponded with their hands touching. Fast, but very real. Something had happened inside Soćko's brain. Something triggered by the touch?

Gotcha!

Did their skin have some kind of nerve conduction ability, allowing them to communicate silently?

Soćko tried to speak, but all that came out was a rasp. He winced.

'Take it slow,' the doctor urged, and held a glass of water to his lips. 'Drink this before you try and talk.'

'How long?' Soćko whispered hoarsely.

'Thirty-seven years,' Jessika told him.

'Damn!'

'We found you on Nkya, the fourth planet in the Beta Eridani solar system.'

'So someone picked up the beacon signal?'

'Yes. Connexion's starship *Kavli* decelerated into the system last week and released a sensor satellite fleet. They detected it right away.'

'Great.' He drank some more water, then slowly sat up. The doctor raised hir arm as if to stop him, then simply watched closely. Soćko gave hir a lame grin. 'I'm okay. Don't worry.'

Jessika slipped the sheet back and he swung his legs out.

'I'd really recommend you take it easy,' the doctor said.

'Sure thing, doc. No marathons today.' His feet reached the ground and he stood up carefully. Jessika held his arm for support. 'My feet are sore,' he said.

'They haven't taken your weight for thirty-seven years,' Kandara said. 'You're designed to mimic humans, at least superficially. So your soles are going to be tender.'

'Right. And you are?'

'Kandara Martinez.'

'Corporate covert agent, at the sharp end,' Jessika filled in. 'Very good at her job. I like her.'

Soćko turned to Jessika. 'How much do they know?'

'Everything. I had to eliminate a quint segment in front of them.'

'So the *Salvation* onemind knows we're here?'

'Yes.'

'Have the Olyix started to invade?'

'Ten hours ago.'

'The *Salvation of Life* split in two,' Kandara told him. 'Deliverance ships are still coming out of the wormhole; your colleague here told us they've been stacked up in the wormhole waiting for the right moment to begin the invasion, but their hand was forced when the quint spy was exposed. There have been widespread sabotage attacks on Earth to disable our city shields. The Zangari family's secret attack force was taken out before it could launch a first strike. So right now, we're understandably touchy about alien spies.'

His gaze swept around to Captain Tral and the squad. 'So I see. But have you accepted us, the Neána mission?'

Kandara gave him a dangerously sweet smile. 'Let's just say Jessika predicted what would happen, which gives you some credit. Exactly who you are and what your genuine purpose is . . . The jury's still out on that.'

'So we have to provide proof for every statement,' Jessika said.

'That's fine,' Soćko said. 'As we're here to help, everything we tell you is true.'

'Sure,' Kandara said. 'Glad we cleared that up. Open-arms welcome for you, comrade.'

He plucked at his medical gown. 'Any chance I can have some proper clothes?'

'Why? Going somewhere?'

'You just said you'd listen to what we have to say. We need to get started.'

'You've just come out of a thirty-seven-year coma.'

'And if I was human, that would be a problem. But I'm not, so it isn't.'

*

The only change Kandara could see in Kruse Station's conference room was the flowers; tall sprays of dark-purple orchids had replaced the white lilies. That and the fact that Alik, Callum and Yuri were only present on large screens this time, with General Johnston sharing Callum's splash. The humans joining her in the flesh were all same as before: Emilja with an aide, and Ainsley with his clump of family advisers. Tral was commanding the security squad that stood behind Soćko and Jessika, which allowed Kandara to take a seat opposite the aliens – giving her an excellent target vantage. Lankin claimed the chair next to her, seemingly oblivious to the tension she knew she was projecting.

'So?' Ainsley said as soon as he sat down. 'Welcome back. What have you got for us?'

'Me?' Soćko enquired lightly. 'Advice, the same as my colleague here.' He tilted his head back to stare at Yuri's image. 'Good to see you, chief.'

'That's debatable,' Yuri replied.

'Advice?' Ainsley snapped. 'That's it?'

'Our ship only created four of us,' Soćko said reasonably. 'We're not an army.'

'Four that you've admitted to,' Kandara said. 'And we're still trying to locate Lim Tianyu and Dutee Gowda, the remaining two Neána androids.'

Soćko raised an eyebrow as he turned to Jessika. 'Did she just call us androids?'

'You're very personable,' Lankin said, 'but you have abilities that no human possesses.'

'Interesting that the form we have been given to integrate ourselves into your society has now become heavily divisive.'

'And completely irrelevant,' Yuri said. 'You claim to be our allies, yes?'

'It's why we exist.'

'Good. Then we appreciate your information. However, your human side will understand our mistrust.'

'I do.'

'Right, then,' Callum said. 'You can start by telling us what these are.' A screen lit up with the image of a cylindrical Olyix spaceship, its pale green fuselage wrapped in a glowing red spiral. 'They came out of the wormhole before the majority of the Deliverance ships – of which there are now over three thousand.'

'Jezus wept,' Alik muttered.

'They're fast,' Callum said. 'And heading out across the whole Sol system.'

'Have you projected their flight vectors?' Jessika asked.

'Difficult. Their thrust keeps fluctuating, only by a few per cent, but enough to negate any accurate trajectory projection.'

'They're missiles,' Soćko said. 'Type seventeen, in our classification. Intersystem range, with multiple short-range hypervelocity warheads, armed with fusion bombs or antimatter. In other words, whatever they're aimed at is now a dead target walking.'

'Bloody hell, they must be going for the habitats.'

'No,' Jessika said. 'I can't stress enough that the Olyix don't want to kill you; your value to them is in your elevation. I expect these missiles will be going for the MHD asteroids.'

'Without power from the solarwells, you can't keep everything going,' Soćko said. 'You've only got fusion generator backup for the shields.'

'Which saboteurs are going balls out to kill,' Alik muttered. 'The Bureau is stretched real thin safeguarding those shields right now.'

'It's the same globally,' Tobias said. 'Every city shield is being subjected to some kind of sabotage, be it physical or darkware assault. Thanks to Jessika's warning, we are just about holding our own.'

'You're welcome,' she said demurely and grinned at Kandara.

'But without the solarwells, everything else will fail,' Soćko continued. 'There certainly aren't enough fusion generators to supply power to the portal hub network and keep the city systems going, let alone domestic appliances. People will be safe under the domes, but they'll be back in the Stone Age. And that's going to be short lived too, because the food printers will have no power. The Olyix will starve you out. You will have no alternative but to submit.'

'Do us all a favour,' Alik said. 'Next time, don't sugar-coat it for us.'

'The habitats will also die,' Jessika said. 'They have fusion generator backup for critical systems, including shields. But the power which provides heat and light for the biospheres comes from solar-wells.'

'Thanks, much better without the sugar,' Callum muttered.

'General?' Emilja said. 'Do we have anything that can intercept those missiles?'

'Negative,' Johnston said. 'The MHD asteroids don't even have shields. They've never needed them; all the major systems are buried under the regolith, not that there's a lot of equipment involved anyway. The largest single components are the MHD tubes themselves, which channel the plasma our portals transfer in from the sun. And those jets vapourize anything that gets too close to them; that plasma comes direct from the sun's convection zone and reaches close to a million degrees.'

Kandara was pleased with herself for spotting it: Callum turned to regard the General, his ancient face lifting to a thoughtful expression.

'So what have other civilizations done?' Ainsley III asked. 'You said we'd have to abandon Earth. But even if we reopened the interstellar portals, we'd never get everyone off in time. Besides, the terraformed worlds don't have the infrastructure to absorb and support twenty billion people, even if you could convince or force them to go.'

'I never said your whole species would survive,' Jessika said slowly. 'I would regard a billion escaping Earth as the most significant victory against the Olyix we know about. Frankly, if just the current population of the exosolar planets and habitats escape it will be a miracle.'

'Again with the sugar-coating,' Alik said. The rest of the conference room was silent.

'That's it?' Emilja said. 'We'll be lucky if a few of us escape? That's the hope you're offering? I've already told you, cowering between the stars in dark habitats is not a valid course of action for us.'

'Emilja's right,' Callum said. 'There has to be something better. We still have the industrial capacity of the entire Sol system available, at least until those missiles blow up our power supply. There must be some kind of ship or weapon you can tell us how to build that can hold them off, at least for a while. If we can buy some time, just a year even, we'll be able to evacuate decent numbers of people out to the terraformed worlds.'

'They will come for the terraformed worlds,' Soćko said relentlessly. 'Their Resolution ships are probably already on their way to those stars; I expect they started years ago so the invasion crusade could begin on every human world simultaneously. It's only Jessika exposing Feriton Kayne to you that has made them act prematurely. She forced their hand.'

The two aliens shared a smile.

'Motherfucker,' Yuri said. 'So the terraformed worlds aren't much of a refuge?'

'Not really,' Soćko said. 'The Resolution ships will bring a wormhole terminus with them. What's happening here will be repeated in every star system you have settled.'

'Resolution ships?'

'Warships, plain and simple. We called them Resolution ships because they resolve any problem. Pray you never encounter one. They are big and they have the firepower to blast a small moon apart.'

'How long until *they* arrive at the terraformed worlds?'

'Difficult to say, because I don't know where the nearest Olyix monitor station is. That's where they will come from.'

'The Olyix have monitor stations?'

'Yes. We believe they're distributed all over the galaxy, with a wormhole connection from each one back to the gateway. That's how they spot emerging civilizations – by the radio waves they broadcast. And sometimes the EM pulse from atom bombs, which is how we found you.'

'Damn, that's like the ultimate SETI observatory set-up. The whole galaxy? Are you sure?'

'It must be by now. If we assume they started their crusade only a quarter of a million years ago, their starships will have spread the wormhole terminuses right across the galaxy by now.'

'Just like we spread out to the stars with Connexion's portal starships,' Ainsley said.

'Yes,' Jessika said. 'Same principle. So as soon as they detected signals from Sol, they sent the *Salvation of Life* to the monitor station along its connecting wormhole from the gateway. From there it flew to Sol at sublight speed, and we know their arkships can reach point two five lightspeed. The fact that they took nearly two hundred and fifty years to get here after you started using radio makes me guess the monitor station is about fifty lightyears or more away from Sol.'

'How fast do Resolution ships fly?'

'They can reach point-nine-five C,' Jessika said. 'So the terraformed planets on the other side of Sol from the monitor station will have the longest breathing space.'

'All this assumes they can't use our own portal technology against us,' Callum said. 'We all know how easy it is to take a portal door through an interstellar hub. They could be threading up their own portals to the thirty-eight terraformed worlds right now.'

'Actually no,' Yuri said. 'And that's down to you, Callum.'

'Huh?'

'After your little stunt rescuing Savi from Zagreus, all Connexion hub portals have had a quantum entanglement detector system built in. Nobody can take their own portal door through one of our portals without us knowing, especially interstellar.'

'It's a simple commercial safeguard,' Ainsley said. 'You want to provide transport to another star, then you license us or you send your own starship there. No son of a bitch gets to make money by cheating us out of our investment.'

'There have been a number of attempts to take a twinned portal through our hubs,' Yuri said. 'Mainly by political advocates who want to set up a free nation state on a new world with constitutions based on their ideology. The number has been rising over the last seven years, which we wrote off to general political dissatisfaction with the lack of ideological variance here in Sol. Now I'm thinking the Olyix were behind those efforts – or some of them, at least.'

'Quantum spacial entanglement is not something we have any record of,' Jessika said. 'That may be to prevent the Olyix from acquiring the technology, or it may be genuinely unique to your species. Either way, it is an uncomfortable development. If the Olyix *have* succeeded in establishing a spacial entanglement to a terra-formed world, you can be sure they'll be threading up as we speak.'

'We've had no reports of Olyix activity beyond the Sol system,' General Johnston said. 'Certainly no sightings of Deliverance ships.'

'That's some good news,' Soćko said. 'But you need to be particularly vigilant, especially with the hubs that are open between stars.'

'You mean the Connexion network,' Ainsley III said. 'Yuri?'

'Transtellar pedestrian and commercial cargo routes have already been shut down. Nobody is leaving the Sol system.'

'Delta Pavonis has also been isolated,' Emilja said.

'So we've shut down all interstellar traffic apart from data,' Ainsley said. 'Good! That stops the bastards from spreading. What do we do about the Deliverance ships and the *Salvation of Life*?'

Kandara watched Soćko casually touch Jessika's hand. An unremarkable gesture of reassurance, so typical between good friends, especially ones who'd been separated for so long, not knowing their fate. She didn't believe it for a second.

'What we recommend is a course of action in two stages,' Soćko said. 'Your habitats have relatively weak shields, certainly in comparison to the cities. They're just a cloud of low-density fog held in place by the binding generator field – more than sufficient to ward off interplanetary dust and the occasional high-velocity pebble, but not weapons. The Deliverance ships will cut through them in seconds.'

'What are those ships armed with?' Johnston asked. 'Nukes and antimatter, like the missiles?'

'No,' Jessika said. 'WMDs would kill humans. They're equipped with energy beams. Precision strikes will allow them to kill the generators as soon as they're in range. Probably five hundred kilometres.'

'Bloody hell,' Callum said. 'Haven't they heard of the inverse square law?'

Emilja pushed her hand back through her hair. 'So we're going to lose the Sol habitats?'

'Yes. All of them.'

'We have to get the people out.'

'Between them, the habitats have an extremely large industrial capacity. You will need that. The manufacturing facilities should be evacuated, along with their populations.'

'Evacuated?'

'Yes. Outsystem, to the settled stars.'

'Those industrial modules are kilometres in diameter,' Callum said. 'Connexion's biggest portal is, what, fifty metres?'

'Forty-eight point two metres,' Tobias Zangari said. He shrugged. 'Everyone just calls it fifty. But we only have seven pairs of them. They're fabulously uneconomical.'

'We have produced forty-metre portals,' Emilja said, 'but not in significant numbers.'

'The effort should be made,' Soćko said. 'The critical sections of machinery can be removed and sent through the large portals.'

'So the first thing we do is reopen interstellar transport?' Ainsley said. 'For fuck's sake!'

'This interlude will allow us to implement proper security measures,' Yuri said. 'When we use the hubs again, they will be safeguarded to my satisfaction. If they are not, they do not get reopened.'

'I urge you very strongly to make the effort,' Soćko said. 'You will need everything you have to start constructing habitats that can fly to safety. And your portals have given you one massive advantage in this respect.'

'The starships,' Jessika said. 'You currently have ninety-seven in flight. They can offer immediate access to interstellar space; you decelerate them then thread up their internal portals. Once the route is established, you can send through industrial stations and as much material as you need – entire asteroids, even a moonlet if you want. Your exodus habitats will never have to fly to deep space, they'll be built there. Much safer. Then you shut down the portals behind them, which leaves no trace of where you went. The Olyix will never be able to follow.'

'Exodus habitats,' Alik drawled. 'You even got a name for them already?'

'Call them whatever you like,' Soćko said. 'It's what they do which is important. This is the way the heart of a species survives. It always has been.'

'It's the way *your* species survived,' Emilja countered. 'And many others you've warned, I'm sure. Us? No.'

'I'm with Emilja on that,' Ainsley said.

'Look,' Callum said. 'This all boils down to how much of the solarwell power we can hang on to. You've written off Earth because you think we're going to lose the MHD generators, so we won't be able to maintain civilization trapped under the shields.'

'That *is* what's going to happen,' Soćko said. 'The resources the Olyix will dedicate to eliminating the MHD asteroids will be phenomenal. If these missiles don't get through, the next wave will be orders of magnitude greater. They will launch whatever it takes.'

'But you and the Olyix have never encountered a species with portal technology before.'

'I have no knowledge of it. However, the Olyix have a very sophisticated technology base; if they didn't have quantum spacial entanglement before *Salvation of Life* arrived in Sol, they certainly have it now.'

'Yeah, sure,' Callum agreed. 'But if we keep the settled worlds free of Olyix, we can use the interstellar portals to bring power in from solarwells in *those* stars once they take out Sol's MHD asteroids. Hell – Delta Pavonis, Trappist, and Eta Cassiopeiae probably have enough solarwell generation capacity between the three of them to power half of Earth. Even if we only divert ten per cent of the power from the remaining thirty-five terraformed worlds, we should easily be able to keep all the essentials going under the shields.'

'Good thinking, son,' Ainsley said. 'We just have to hold them off here long enough to rig up direct feeds.'

'We're going to start losing MDH chambers in about forty-eight hours,' General Johnston said. 'That's when the first of those missiles will pass Neptune orbit.'

'I have an idea how to counter the first wave of missiles,' Callum said. 'After that, it'll be down to how cooperative the terraformed worlds are.'

Kandara pressed down on a smile. Callum's basic decency made him such an easy read for her.

'You'll have Delta Pavonis support, of course,' Emilja said. 'We'll start diverting our solarwell output to Earth.'

'There's enough political and financial clout in this room to push this through,' Ainsley III said. 'Between us, we can make things happen.'

'I know you don't want to consider this,' Jessika said reluctantly, 'but you're concentrating on the short term. You haven't thought this through.'

'Enlighten me,' Ainsley said in a low, angry voice.

'Don't try to save Earth.'

'Fuck off!'

'There are twenty billion people living on your homeworld,' Soćko said. 'Even if you had ten times your current industrial capacity, you wouldn't be able to build enough exodus habitats to evacuate them all.'

'Saving a billion humans from the terraformed worlds is not a victory,' Emilja said.

'This is not a binary problem,' Jessika said. 'You don't win or lose. Preserving the essence and spirit of your species is the only goal here.'

'Please remember,' Soćko said, 'those humans the Olyix take back to their enclave for elevation won't die.'

'You're right about that,' Alik said. 'What they do to us is a fuck of a lot worse. I've seen it.'

Kandara gave Jessika an unwavering stare. 'So you're saying all we can do is hang on in the terraformed systems for a few years before we flee like you? Seriously, that's the best advice you've got?'

'However hard you fight them, you cannot win. I understand your impulse to strike back, but the enclave can send through a million Deliverance ships or Resolution ships if that's what it takes to subdue planet-dwelling humans. You need to face up to the hardest choice of all. Who do you save?'

'The cold equation,' Emilja said in disgust. 'When the *Titanic* sank there weren't enough lifeboats for everyone, so they put the women and children on the lifeboats first.'

'Yeah?' Alik snapped. 'And how many women and children my colour got put on the lifeboats? How many third-class passenger women and children?'

'That's the choice we're trying to avoid here.'

'Well, there's only one way to do that,' Kandara said.

'How?' Soćko asked.

'It's not entanglement science: we take out the Olyix enclave itself. No Olyix, no problem.'

Jessika gave Kandara a sad smile. 'If that was possible, we would have done it.'

'You don't know that,' Kandara said. 'You know nothing about your species and what they have done. You aren't Neána, you're walking memories of them. Maybe they tried. Tried a thousand times. They certainly seem sneaky enough. Or how about this: we are your doomsday weapon.'

'Excuse me?'

'Did this abode cluster you came from deliberately choose humans to fight their war by proxy? You give us the information we need – new weapons, a decent method of attack – and we go blitzkrieg Olyix ass for you.'

'We're here to save you!'

'You think you are. That's your conscious thought, your true belief. But face it, you don't know. Not really.'

'I want to save you,' Soćko said. 'I risked my life to save you!'

'There.' Kandara grinned right back at him. 'Right there. That's what I'm talking about. The sincerity you're so good at projecting. I'm calling bullshit on that. Tell me this: if we do try and go head-to-head with the *Salvation*, will you help?'

'No,' Jessika said. 'Because you cannot destroy the *Salvation of Life*.'

'What? Why not?'

'The *Salvation of Life* is where the cocoons will be stored before they're taken back to the enclave. The Olyix always modify their arkship biospheres into giant cargo chambers. That's what their biotechnology systems will be busy doing right now. It's one of the reasons they arrive in an arkship: because it's big. Something that size has the volume to hold billions of human cocoons.'

'So now we're just cargo?'

'Gotta admit, it's pretty apt,' Alik said grudgingly. 'Considering what cocoons are, and all.'

'Fuck that, Alik,' Kandara stormed. 'Jessika, if we can do it now, destroy the *Salvation of Life* right now, before they start piling up cocoons inside, would you help?'

'Yes. But such an endeavour can only be a part of your overall effort to evade the Olyix crusade. You must prepare to leave your planets and stars behind.'

'I'm glad you said that, because you've already got the method, haven't you?'

'What?'

'No ship we have is ever going to get near the *Salvation of Life*, right?'

'That's right. I'm sorry.'

'But destroying *Salvation of Life* is the key to this. If we take out the wormhole, we cut off their supply line. You said it yourself, their station is probably fifty lightyears away. It would take them fifty years to fly a Resolution ship here and resume the invasion.'

'Less,' Jessika said. 'We told you, there will already be several Resolution ships flying through this section of space to reach the terraformed worlds.'

'Okay, so five years. Maybe even ten. That's got to be worthwhile.'

'Yes,' Soćko said. 'But to do this you would have to build warships, a lot of warships, more powerful than the Deliverance ships. We can certainly help with that; we have the design for the same gravatonic drive which the Olyix ships use. But it will take time – at least a year, I fear. Many of Earth's cities will have fallen by then. The *Salvation of Life* will have hundreds of millions of cocoons on board, if not a billion.'

'I'm not talking about using a human ship. We turn the Olyix nice-guy camouflage tactics right back at them. We capture one of their ships and: *Boom*. Kamikaze.'

'Capturing one of their ships would be extremely difficult.'

'Are you sure about that? *You* did it. You hijacked that transport ship's onemind somehow. Forced it out of the wormhole, then made it fly to Nkya. How did you do that?'

'A neurovirus. It allows me to infiltrate and infect an Olyix's thought routines.'

'Great. I'll take a dozen.'

'But . . . you can't use it. It is embedded in *my* mind. It is part of me.'

'That's convenient – for you. Oh, wait, you just said you'd help in any way you could. Are you beginning to see the problem with trust I've got here?'

'My mind contains the neurovirus as well,' Jessika said levelly. 'I will go with you on your mission, Kandara. I would like to work with you again, one last time.'

'Mother Mary!' She hadn't expected that. 'For real?'

'Yes, absolutely for real. After all, I'm just an android. It's not as if my life matters. You don't even think I am alive, do you?'

'Ouch, so burned, man,' Alik chortled.

For the first time since forever, Kandara found she was blushing. 'You're biological, so you're alive,' she told Jessika. 'If that's simplistic, I apologize. It's your purpose I struggle with.'

'Occam's razor. If we're not here to help, then what are we doing?'

'To be continued just as soon as I've filled in the blanks.'

'Enough of this bullshit,' Ainsley said. 'Jessika, can you steal us one of their ships or not?'

'You would not be able to force your way on board an Olyix Deliverance ship,' Soćko said. 'It must be done subtly.'

'You mean get yourself captured again?' Callum asked.

'No,' Jessika said. 'They know we are here now, which means

they're going to be cautious when they initiate cocooning on captured humans. Repeating a manoeuvre simply because it worked once before is a fatally bad tactic. If we're going to steal a Deliverance ship we need a different approach.'

'So?'

'Stages,' Jessika said confidently. 'We need to do this in stages. Okay: first I will require a quint prisoner, alive and intact. That is going to be the mother of all challenges.'

'You know me,' Kandara said. 'I love a challenge. And I'm getting seriously bored sitting around here just watching you.'

The Moon

28th June 2204

'Do you think they can do it?' Johnston asked.

'Steal an Olyix ship and go kamikaze?' Callum replied. 'I don't know. Crazy idea. But if anyone can do it, then I guess it'll be Jessika and Kandara.'

'And in case it comes to naught, we have you.'

'Er . . . yeah.'

'Is your idea any less crazy?'

Callum took a moment before he answered. It had been so frustrating listening to the two Neána humans. Unlike Kandara, he didn't have much doubt concerning their motives, but, boy, were they depressing about everything. No hope. No chance. Run away. Cower in the dark and cold where the monsters can't find you. He'd been surprised by how much that angered him. A century spent in the serenity of Utopial culture, and all he felt was the same anger that'd screwed up plenty of his life back in Aberdeen as a teen down on the streets. In those days, he and his pals had just been directionless kids, in awe of the big-city gangs whom they thought they were matching. So they staked out their turf to defend against the other forsaken lads that the new Connexion portal hubs were leaving behind along with the city's collapsed oil economy. When you got threatened, you hit back hard and fast. It was primitive and dumb, and it fired him up for all the wrong reasons. But now that same type of chance was there with the MHD asteroids. He couldn't ignore it.

'I can't guarantee anything,' he said. 'But this is exactly the kind of problem-solving I did back in the day. Twist the system into something it was never designed for.'

Johnston smiled faintly. 'Sounds half-arsed to me.'

'Yeah, but half an arse is better than no arse at all, which is what Alpha Defence has now. We've got three and a half thousand MHD asteroids to protect. I know we can't hold off the Olyix forever – especially if the Neána are right and they'll just keep resupplying their forces through the wormhole – but let me try this. If we can keep the electricity flowing until the terraformed systems can supply power to the shields, it'll be a victory. The only one we're going to see in our lifetime, by the look of things.'

'All right. We assigned General Xing to Quoek as soon as the power grid sabotage started; he's running security for the MHD asteroids. Get yourself out there and coordinate this with him.'

'There's been sabotage at the asteroids too?' a startled Eldlund asked.

Johnston gazed at the Command Centre's big hologram bubble, now agleam with a nest of red vector lines where the Olyix ships and missiles were expanding out from the *Salvation of Life*. 'Not really. We've had some attempts to break the asteroid control networks from the lownet, but the MHD industry has always enjoyed some of the strongest protection on solnet. Right now, Xing and his team are watching for any attempt at physical assault. The attacks on Earth's power grid relay stations have been disturbingly successful. It's already down seventeen per cent, and the supply companies are going to be struggling to repair all the damage before the Deliverance ships arrive.'

'Good luck,' Danuta Zangari said.

'You're not coming with us?' Callum taunted.

'No. I'm staying here as liaison for the family.'

When Callum checked Johnston's face, it was unreadable. As

he and Eldlund left the Command Centre, all he could think of was rats deserting a sinking ship. *Falling into the cold sea to drown.*

*

For four billion years Quoek asteroid, a mud-red lump of insignificance, travelled along a mildly elliptical orbit an AU further out from Sol than Neptune. Classed as an M-type, its nickel-iron mass was the heart of what had once been a much larger astronomical body. Its outer mantle had been pulverized by micrometeorite impacts over geological ages to leave the harder, dense core. It had been destined to continue its pointless existence for another five billion years as one more piece of solar system junk until one day a telescope array focused on it and performed a spectrum analysis.

And suddenly, Quoek acquired *value.*

M-type asteroids were the ones favoured by solarwell companies. Given the colossal radiant heat expelled by the plasma jets that fed electricity to an energy-hungry Earth, their metallic composition was less susceptible to thermal ablation.

The China National Sunpower Corporation, which had pioneered solarwells, had chosen Quoek as its first anchor asteroid back in 2069. With an irregular diameter of eighty-seven kilometres, Quoek offered perfect stability for the first MHD chamber: a two-hundred-metre-long funnel of superconductor rings surrounded by the rigid silver wings of cryostat heat-dump panels. Once a perfectly spherical well portal had been dropped into the sun's corona, incandescent plasma stabbed out from its twinned portal at the throat of the MHD chamber. The huge magnetic coils which the plasma passed through sucked power out of the relativistic stream, instantly shunting it back to distant Earth through a small portal carrying ultra-high voltage cables. Four hours later, official street celebrations across China witnessed that very same intense white flame appear in the sky, visible to the naked eye as the brightest star in the firmament. Half a billion people cheered in unison at the advent of cheap clean energy – though, for a minority, it was a death knell. Solarwells did to the existing power companies what Connexion's hubs had done to the transport industry six years previously.

Quoek was the proving ground. A month after the first MHD chamber began producing power, a second went active. The CNSC technicians assembled it on the other side of the asteroid from the first. Essentially, the MHD chambers were the greatest rocket nozzles ever built. Even with their induction coils siphoning power out of the plasma stream, the chambers still produced a colossal thrust. Enough to shift a multi-trillion-tonne asteroid if it was applied over decades. So the chambers were set up in opposing pairs, their thrusts cancelling out.

Experience which the CNSC crews gained over the next few years found that you should never have fewer than six MHD chambers per asteroid to maintain its original stability, and preferably a minimum of ten providing balance continuity when a pair were taken off line for maintenance or replacement. In 2204, Quoek itself had eighteen actinic plumes flaring out for thousands of kilometres, turning it into a Christmas star brighter than anything that could have guided wise men across the desert. And it was only one of three thousand and eighty-two anchor asteroids that formed a dazzling speckled halo around the outer solar system, haemorrhaging the sun's radiance across interstellar space. They were all smaller than Quoek, while the MHD chambers themselves had grown larger over the decades, until they'd topped out at five hundred metres long, generating an average of twenty gigawatts of electricity. Thousands of habitats, each with their own industrial stations – along with Earth's megacities and billions of portals – consumed a phenomenal amount of energy.

Callum tensed himself for the gravity change, stepping into Quoek's point-three Earth standard. Most of the industrial asteroids stations he'd visited during his life, both those in Sol and Delta Pavonis, had zero-gravity stations: simple spheres dotted about the surface, linked by short tubes. Quoek was different. Buried half a kilometre below the surface was a toroid containing the CNSC's primary control centre, overseeing the company's eight hundred and fifty-two MHD asteroids. Apart from the lack of windows, they could easily have been in a standard Beijing office block. Walls of synthetic-bamboo panels alternated with big guóhuà paintings, doors printed out of carbon to mimic slate. The vaulting arrivals foyer was dominated by stone mined from Quoek itself, which had been sculpted into a spire twisting up the centre, with trailing plants growing out of its artistically pocked surface, their leaves the insipid autumnal yellow fated by a life lived under artificial lighting.

General Xing was waiting for them, wearing the dark-green type-14 uniform of the National Armed Forces, with the blue and white sleeve insignia of the Space Garrison. Callum just managed to avoid a double take. After so long living on Akitha, he'd grown accustomed to tall humans, but General Xing was only a diminutive one-metre-sixty high. Nor, it seemed, did he bother with cosmetic anti-ageing treatments on top of the basic organ, muscle and bone therapies. Apollo splashed the General's information, putting him at ninety years old, which Callum could have guessed from his bald head and deep wrinkles.

Eight fully armoured soldiers stood behind him, arm-mounted weapons activated. Callum gave them an edgy glance, aware of how still Eldlund had become.

'Welcome to Quoek Station,' the General said as they shook hands. 'I wish it was under different circumstances.'

'Me, too,' Callum agreed. He indicated the soldiers. 'Has there been much trouble on the MHD asteroids?'

'Plenty of lownet attempts to break into our management network, but the Ministry of State Digital Security G8Turings have prevented any real damage. There have been no physical assaults yet, which I consider a cause for worry, given the current level of sabotage on Earth.'

'Not really,' Eldlund said.

'How so?' Xing asked with formal politeness.

Callum gave his assistant a curious frown, abruptly aware that sie was nearly twice the height of the General. 'Yeah. How so?'

'There are over three thousand MHD asteroids. Firstly, to shut them down or destroy them with raids by covert personnel would be a massive operation. You'd need years to prepare, and Sol's intelligence agencies would have spotted that level of activity among the dark operatives. Early arrests would have been inevitable, lowering the probability of overall success and even alerting us to the nature of the Olyix. Which leads to my second point. They've launched an armada of missiles to target defenceless MHD asteroids – a move which would seem to guarantee a one hundred per cent success rate. Jessika and Soćko are both adamant the Olyix have effectively unlimited resources. This is the method they have selected; ergo there will be no covert attack.'

'An elegant analysis,' Xing said. 'So given the entire power supply from space will be eliminated by missiles, why would they bother sabotaging Earth's grid as well?'

'We need a *lot* of power to support the food printers,' Callum said. 'Without that power . . .'

'Then Soćko and Jessika were right,' Eldlund said. 'Earth will have to surrender. The planet simply won't have the power to support its population.'

'No,' Callum said forcefully. 'Not on my watch. We just need time to secure new power routes in from the terraformed worlds. Which means we really need to do something about those missiles.'

Xing inclined his head. 'I am receptive to any proposals.'

Quoek's primary control room took Callum right back to his days at Brixton, working for Connexion's Emergency Detoxification division. It was a large semicircular room. Desks were arranged in tiers, with operatives surrounded by hologram projections. The curving walls were all glass, fronting various specialist offices full of technicians. That older-style layout, along with the number of people on duty, made it feel a lot more reassuring than Alpha Defence's lean Command Centre.

Standing at the back with Xing, Callum stared at the biggest screen, which was showing a view of the solar system from above the sun's south pole: an ebony background across which sweetly circular planet orbits were etched in bold sapphire, entwined by the myriad golden threads of asteroids and comets, as if Gustav Fabergé had come back to craft one final masterpiece. It was being vandalized by the crimson bloodstain of missile vectors streaking out from the arkship.

'How long until the first missile reaches an asteroid?' Callum asked.

'Kayli, in nine hours,' Xing told him, pointing.

Up on the screen, Kayli flashed bright emerald. The small rock had an orbit just inside Neptune, currently in superior conjunction on the other side of the sun, which made it the closest MHD asteroid to the *Salvation of Life*. Apollo splashed up its data. Three and a half kilometres along its major axis, minor orbital eccentricity, claimed by the China National Sunpower Corporation in 2169, who equipped it with six MHD chambers.

'Does it still have a maintenance crew in situ?' Callum asked.

'We're evacuating them in two hours. In fact, that's almost all we're organizing right now.' Xing gestured around the control room. 'I have a lot of people to get to safety.'

'Okay. Before they go, I'd like to deploy a cluster of sensor satellites out of Kayli. Alpha Defence will supply them.'

'That can be done. May I enquire why?'

'I want to see the exact method of attack. According to my information, each of those missiles contains multiple warheads armed with nukes or antimatter. I need confirmation, and details.'

'Of course. I will initiate that now.'

'And which asteroid will be hit a couple of hours after Kayli?'

'That would be Yanat. It's one of our smaller ones, just under a kilometre in diameter.'

'I need to go there.'

'What are you going to do?'

'I'm going to see if I can turn the asteroids into ninjas.'

'Excuse me?'

'Too much time spent on old Hong Kong interactives when I was young. Those asteroids are actually weapons; the Olyix just haven't realized it yet.'

And with that Callum was reliving those old Emergency Detox days. Watching a disaster building on the control room displays. Senior management sweating, then deferring. While he led the team in, making assessments, calculating what equipment to take, the risks, how to deploy. Sheer exhilaration powering him along, focused so hard that the rest of the universe had faded to nothing.

Five portals, five steps, and he was drifting into the stubby tube that bridged Yanat's pair of zero-gee crew modules. The tiny station's ageing life support hadn't filtered out the bodysmell of the two permanent crew members and condensation slicked the walls, frosting in some places and drying up around the grimed vents. A classic tough deep space commercial facility – hugely expensive to build originally, and gold spec-ed as well as over-engineered to chug along with nominal maintenance, so the minimum mandated function was eked out for decades. Aesthetic extravagance had no place here.

The same could be said for its duty manager, Fang Yun. He came air-swimming out of the main module, a weary middle-aged man in a worn grey jumpsuit.

'It's all true, isn't it?' he asked nervously. 'The Olyix are invading. Those ships are missiles.'

'Yes,' Callum said.

'Cào. I hoped I'd done a bad nark at shift-start.'

'No. Sorry, pal. It's real.'

'Okay, so what do you want? I got orders to help you in any way, or I don't get to leave Yanat when the missiles arrive.'

'Let's not get that drastic. Where's the control centre for the MHD chambers?'

Fang Yun blinked slowly. 'No such thing. I've got a digital systems cubical with some decent rez screens. The external sensors can give you good visuals, which is useful to scrutinize the main tenance bots. Apart from that, the G7Turing systems manager can splash realtime chamber data for your altme.'

'The cubical will do.'

Eldlund waited out in the module's lounge. Even in freefall, it was a squeeze for two people in the cubical.

So it wasn't quite like the good old days after all. There was no heavy hardware to grapple into place, no sweating and grunting. The swearing and camaraderie of the team as they worked in unison was lacking, as was watching the solution physically come together. This was all software problems, editing the G7Turing's safety over-rides and cut-offs – procedures at which both Eldlund and Fang Yun excelled – to protect the stability which had been the absolute priority for the chambers since the whole solarwell concept was launched. Callum knew what he wanted the chamber systems to do, but his digital skills were decades out of date. Without him realizing it, the fate of the old had crept up on him, and now he'd become the one who provided strategy and expected others to implement it – the one they all rightly bitched about in the pub after work. *When did this happen to me?*

It took hours to modify the control protocols. For all the can-do improvisation, they were dealing with plasma direct from the sun's corona. You couldn't just shut off every safeguard and expect things to carry on without a glitch. But finally he'd managed to call some ancient interactive software up out of Apollo's deep cache, which the altme had coupled into the asteroid's G7Turing. Old gaming apps could never be the final control structure, but as a proof-of-concept test, using them gave him a warm feeling of satisfaction.

He stuck his feet to the filthy clingmat which lined most of the station's surfaces and closed his eyes. Apollo splashed the data graphics from the MHD chamber they were using to experiment on. Showing the actual image of the plasma flow was pointless; the human eye couldn't make out the fluctuations in the stream he was hoping to manipulate.

'Reassigning control now,' Fang Yun said, and the tone was: I can't believe I'm doing this.

Callum grinned as his heartbeat elevated. He was back doing what he did best: saving the world. Icons appeared in the splash as the new control routines became active. And in his mind he visualized the old games he used to play. Lone warrior poised motionless on a smoking battlefield as shrikes and demons charged forwards out of the haze. Jet-black samurai swords flashed out from his wrists, and he danced with grandmaster precision to take out the enemy.

Outside the flimsy station walls, the relativistic cataract of elemental atoms blasting out of the chamber's throat sliced sideways, *just so*, following the sword's movement. 'Slash and burn, pal.' Callum grinned as the dead piled up around him. 'Oh, yeah.'

Akitha

28th June 2204

There was a lot Kandara could have said about the procedure, but she held her tongue. After all, she didn't mistrust the two Neána at this level. So she stood back and watched as drones went through the front door first, ten of them airborne and five rolling along the floor, hoisting heavier weaponry. Once they provided provisional clearance, Captain Tral nodded hir approval and Jessika stepped through.

They'd come to Jessika's home in Ortonia: a pleasant little costal town, tucked away in one of the many branches of a sprawling ria inlet. The Catalan-style house itself sat atop a gentle slope of perfectly maintained lawns, bordered by a tangle of trees. Sluggish ripples lapped at the shore below, while beyond the distant ridges the low *crump* of ocean breakers could be heard as they rolled into the wide sands of Fowey Bay.

Kandara walked behind the armoured figures of the squad as they entered. Like the Utopial homes she'd visited ten years before, the decor echoed the clean lines of Nordic minimalism: stone floors and gently curving white walls, pale pine furniture with deep cushions. There was even a bulbous hanging fireplace between the tall window doors of the main living room.

Jessika stopped before a wide copper door with small rivets lining the edges. 'It's in here.'

'Not even a secret underground hideout?' Kandara asked. 'How disappointing.'

'That's what bad guys always use,' Jessika threw back. 'Besides, the best place to hide something is in plain sight. I'm hardly the only Utopial who has a collection of home printers.'

'I'm going to give the house network the code you provided,' Captain Tral said.

Jessika shrugged at hir. 'Go for it.'

The copper door slid open silently. Five of the airborne drones flittered in. Tral stood motionless, reviewing the sensor images they were splashing on hir tarsus lenses. A minute later, sie gestured to two of the armoured squad members to enter. Both of them had a troop of forensic drones clipped to their bandoleer-style harnesses.

'Exactly what have you been building in there?' Kandara asked.

'Manufacturing systems, mainly,' Jessika told them. 'They'll be able to assemble weapons and tools that would be useful against the Olyix. I wanted to be ready for the elevation when it started.'

'Weapons?' Tral asked immediately.

'They haven't been produced yet. I was waiting to see what would happen.' She glanced at Soćko. 'Waiting to see if you would come back.'

'So these are personal weapons?' Kandara asked. 'For hand-to-hand combat?'

'Yes.'

'Why? You told us our best chance is to kiss Earth goodbye and flee.'

'The longer it takes for them to subdue Earth, the more people can escape from the terraformed worlds into interstellar space. The weapons I can create in here were intended to equip you for guerrilla campaigns against their ground forces. But all we can ever do is slow them down.'

'Clear,' Tral announced. 'We can go in.'

Again Kandara had to hold her tongue. Sie might have been in every meeting with Jessika, but sie clearly didn't grasp the bigger picture. Whatever the Neána woman had assembled in her house, it was considerably more advanced than anything they'd dealt with before. She gave Jessika a half-grin and rolled her eyes before gesturing at the door. Jessika responded with a quick twitch of her lips. It was interesting, this understanding they had.

The room was large, occupying the centre of the house, so it had no windows. Sophisticated printers and micro-synthesizers were stacked along one wall. The long table down the middle was scattered with odd-shaped electronic units and three processor spheres, each one with the capacity to run a G8Turing. Racks held bottles of purified chemicals and printer compounds; five tall medical-grade fridges had scarlet bio-substance symbols on the doors.

Kandara paid little attention to the human technology. Opposite the printers were a line of metre-square cubes, their grey surfaces so smooth they were almost impossible to focus on, even when she cranked her optical peripherals up to their highest resolution. In fact, she wasn't entirely sure they were solid surfaces, they were so elusive. 'And these are . . .?'

'Initiators,' Jessika said. 'As near as I could get, anyway.'

'So, high-end printers?'

'Something along those lines, sure.'

'Stop smirking at me and explain what I'm seeing.'

'All right.' Jessika patted the top of a cube. 'They do manufacture items, like your printers do. But the more sophisticated a machine becomes, the more elaborate its control routines.'

'Yeah. Even I get that.'

'An initiator's nanoware filaments – the part that shapes molecular structures – are so complex that the control is integral by necessity, with homogenized distribution. So it's a neural network – a very smart one.'

'You're telling me these things are self-aware?'

'That's a human philosophy. I don't believe they have imagination. However, they do have a . . . psychology of their own. They are kindred to the Neána.'

Kandara put her hands on her hips, feeling her muscles tighten. 'You mean only you have the access codes?'

'No, that's the point. There is no code to enter. They work with us because we are . . . *simpatico*. It's not as simple as shared ancestry DNA – humans and monkeys – but we have a connection.'

'Mother Mary! So you can't give us this technology because you're always the gatekeeper? We're going to be dependent on you?'

'No. I believe it may be possible to build initiators with a more human style of control. Once you understand the physical component of the nanofilaments, you'll want to design your own programs to run them, not use ours. Only that way will you have complete control over them. Otherwise, you will always fear some tiny bug or darkware is hidden in our routines. You already suspect that is the case with my mind, don't you?'

'It's a possibility.'

'Exactly. So we can give you the physical component, the theory behind the mechanism. But how you utilize it, that will be down to you. For example, I doubt you will give them a mind of their own, as we do.'

'You're telling me you're more trusting than humans.'

'Would you give unlimited power of replication and assembly to an independent entity that does not share your core values? And what exactly are human core values? You are a diverse species. You will need to make a decision on that.'

'So if I want one of your initiators to assemble a fuck-off monster gun, it won't do it for me, but it will for you?'

'Essentially, yes. Within an initiator, the mechanism is also the mind. If you want an initiator to construct something small and simple, like a child's toy, then you only need a small section of the structure to do so. But for something large and complex, like a missile or creature, a correspondingly bigger section of the initiator will need to be active to facilitate the request, and the more it will be aware of what it is doing.'

'It judges me?'

'A reasonable analogy, yes.'

'Then congratulations, you were right. I want machines that simply do as they're told.'

'And if one of your criminals tells an obedient machine to build a nuclear warhead? Initiators are part of Neána society; they are members, equals. They would not fabricate that without a consensus.'

'I thought you didn't know anything about Neána society.'

'I don't. But I understand the psychology required by the level of technology involved. If – when – humans rise to this level, you will need to change also.'

'I've heard that argument before. It's a basic of Utopial culture.'

'Yeah, Jaru is one of the smart ones.'

'Is sie Neána?'

'Hell, no. Sie was born a long time before we arrived. Sie's all yours.'

'Okay, I'll cross hir off the list.' She stared thoughtfully at the row of placid-looking cubes. 'This alien zombification virus of yours. Can it be used to take control of a human mind?'

'Theoretically, yes,' Jessika said. 'The problem lies with inserting the neurovirus into the human brain. The quint neural structure has direct nerve connections that allow physical contact transfer between various components of its biotechnology systems. For a human, we'd have to design a cortical interface. But a biologic initiator should be able to construct one.'

'Which is why we always advise the species we help never to use any kind of direct brain–computer interfaces,' Soćko said. 'They make subjugation dangerously easy.'

'So how *did* you get inside the Olyix transport ship's onemind?' Kandara asked him.

'By doing exactly that. The biostasis chamber they imprisoned me in had a multitude of neurofibre connections with the ship's onemind. Once they hooked me up, it was a simple process to insert the neurovirus into its routines. They did the work for me.'

'I know you, Kandara,' Jessika said. 'Why does this bother you?'

'Simple. If you've already taken us over, how would we know?'

'I respectfully suggest you wouldn't be asking us that very question if we had.'

'Yeah. Unless that's to damp down any lingering paranoia.'

'In which case there's nothing I can say that will reassure you.'

'All right. Then either I'm an unknowing zombie and doing this at your bidding, or taking out the *Salvation of Life* is genuinely my own shit idea. The result is the same: it's got to be done. So how do we go about capturing a quint?'

'Well, first –' Jessika pushed down into the initiator, her hand sinking into the grey surface as if it was a thick oil. When she pulled it out, she was holding a small sky-blue cylinder no wider than her palm.

Kandara was aware of Tral stiffening. 'And that is?' she asked lightly.

'An entanglement suppressor.'

'I'm impressed. You know how to break quantum entanglement?'

'No, not break,' Soćko said. 'This device just reduces the efficiency of the connection. That way the other four quint in the union won't know exactly what's happening to their fifth segment, even though they'll know it's still alive. We hope they'll assume the body was overwhelmed by the battle. That gives us a window to use the neurovirus. Once Jessika assumes command of its mind, we'll remove the suppression from the entanglement, and she can take over the remaining quint segments.'

'There's a lot of assumptions and maybes in there,' Kandara said.

'The neurovirus works. It's the rest of the plan that's ambitious. But it's your plan, not mine.'

Kandara held her hand out to Jessika, ready to ask for the suppressor. Then Callum's icon splashed up in her tarsus lens display and she told Zapata to accept. 'Yes?'

'The first missile is about to reach Kayli,' he said. 'We deployed a batch of satellites around it before it was evacuated. I'm hoping for a whole tranche of data here; there's got to be something in there that'll help when it's Yanat's turn in the firing line. So I'd appreciate some analysis from our allies.'

She didn't call him out on the whole *allies* thing. People would stop listening to her if she became the group's bore on the topic. 'Sure.'

The lab had a big screen which was streaming the images coming from Alpha Defence. A squadron of small sensor satellites had flown into position around the Kayli asteroid, providing high-intensity coverage out to twenty thousand kilometres.

'Mary,' Kandara muttered as she saw the approaching missile's velocity. 'Is that figure right?'

'Oh yeah,' Callum said. 'Twelve thousand kilometres per second. Or point zero four lightspeed, if you want to get technical.'

'After one day accelerating?'

'At twenty-five gees. Not even our starships use that kind of acceleration.'

'Christ almighty, does your defence idea have a reaction time that can match this?' she asked.

'Dunno. Soćko, what kind of distance will a missile launch its independent warheads from?'

'It can be anything up to half a million kilometres away, and they accelerate at around two hundred and fifty gees.'

'You've got to be kidding!' Callum said.

'No. But remember that the distance and velocity actually work in your favour.'

'How so?'

'The warheads have got to be extremely accurate. They have no time to course correct. If their vector is off by a centimetre when they're ten thousand kilometres out, that translates into a massive overshoot, and at that velocity it will take them days to turn around and strike again.'

'What about particle impact when they're on their approach?' Callum asked. 'What kind of shielding do they have?'

'Same as the primary missile: gravity distortion, which is a modified function of their drive. It creates a bow wave effect in spacetime, which deflects particles around the missile.'

'So a kinetic strike against them is impossible?'

'Depends on the size of the impact projectile you're throwing at them. At the kind of velocity these warheads achieve just before impact, anything bigger than a pebble will overwhelm the distortion wave. So when they launch, the missile processor has to guide them along a clear route in.'

'So if I flood their approach vector with mass . . .'

'Should work. Providing the mass is dense enough.'

'Here it comes,' Kandara warned.

The cluster of sensor satellites around the defenceless Kayli asteroid showed the missile hurtling towards them. At fifty thousand kilometres away, eight warheads separated from the main craft, accelerating outwards in an elegant petal formation. Half a second later the warheads curved around, bringing them back in line to impact Kayli.

'Mother Mary,' Kandara whispered. 'You were right, two fifty gees.' Zapata splashed up the warheads' flight time: four seconds.

Visual spectrum sensors showed each warhead as a rosette flare of violet as particles of solar wind struck the distortion effect. Individual warheads began to fluctuate their acceleration by tiny increments, so their arrival was desynchronized.

Magnification flicked up, giving her a tighter view on Kayli. Course projection lines sliced elegantly around the giant plasma plumes squirting out of the asteroid's MHD chambers. The first warhead streaked in, too fast for Kandara's brain to follow. She knew the explosion was going to be powerful, but the phenomenal scale of the reality came as a vicious shock; Zapata reported it as spiking at over three hundred megatons. Kayli was instantly eclipsed by an incandescent sphere, causing the MHD plumes to shrink and fracture in swirls as if they were towers felled by a quake. The remaining warheads pierced the explosion wavefront, detonating within milliseconds of each other, to be climaxed by the main missile itself – which brought a five-hundred-megaton antimatter explosion to the cataclysm. Satellites dropped out as radiation and EMP bursts exterminated even their ultra-hardened electronics, flicking the team's collective viewpoint further and further back. The meagre survivors, peering in from twenty thousand kilometres through thick filters, revealed a miniature sun whose outer surface was both expanding and cooling at a fierce rate. A minute later, and the shell of glowing ions had sunk from their initial atomic fury to a webbed purple haze. As it darkened further, massive chunks of asteroid, glowing like volcanic lava and spitting off wobbling cometary streamers, came tumbling out of the apex in every direction.

'Holy shit,' Callum said. 'These Olyix fuckers really are dead serious.'

'Do you still think you can fight them off?' Kandara asked.

'Maybe. We need to analyse the blast impact and see how good that protective distortion effect really is. If you'll excuse me, I've got a busy ninety minutes.'

His icon vanished from her splash. She didn't want to look at Jessika or Soćko right now. She just knew they'd be full of pity and sympathy for her, for her species, which was the last thing she needed. Instead she took a moment, zeroing herself as she did before going into combat, banishing useless emotion. 'Right, then. So now we know: this Olyix kidnap mission really needs to work. Apart from the entanglement suppressor, what else have you got for me?'

'It'll be down to tactics more than anything,' Jessika said, equally brisk.

'And if there's going to be any advantage to taking out the *Salvation of Life*, it needs to be done early in the elevation phase,' Soćko said. 'Which produces a pleasing confluence.'

'How?'

'The Deliverance ships will reach some habitats before they arrive on Earth. That gives us an opportunity to arrange a kidnap on our terms. Any remaining humans in the habitat will be running to the remaining portals when the quint gain access to the interior. That provides you with a considerable tactical benefit for an ambush. They won't be expecting it in the middle of an evacuation.'

'Good idea,' Kandara admitted. 'So what else can you make for me?'

'You'll need armour,' Jessika said. 'Good armour. The weapons the Olyix use to bring down their prey will be non-lethal. But as you've seen, they don't necessarily need an intact body for cocooning.'

Vayan

I watch.

And –

Beyond the outer comet ring which encircles this star, a gentle gravity ripple distorts the fabric of spacetime for the briefest of moments. It washes against my perception fronds and I instantly refocus my attention on its source. More ripples are radiating outwards in a pattern I determine to be a gravatonic drive, moving at point one eight three lightspeed, and decelerating. The vessel has a dense spacetime distortion wrapped around it, deflecting particles which are on collision course. The tenuous scattering of hydrogen atoms that populate the interstellar void whirl away in chaos, building into a cyclone that trails behind the vessel for over five AUs. Their dying indigo sparkles flutter away as low-energy ions, still too faint to be detected by any of the sensors with which the *Morgan* has englobed this planetary system. But my fronds perceive them clearly.

Soon the deluge of gravity waves will reach a peak where human technology becomes aware of it.

They will know something is coming.

It can only be one thing.

I run checks on my compressed functions, confirming they are ready to activate.

I will soon become whole.

Until then . . . I wait.

I watch.

*

The *Actaeon* had an aesthetic different to anything Dellian had experienced before. Loud orchestral music was playing, heavy on violins and timpani, as he walked down one of the twisting main corridors of a habitation spiral with half of the squad, everyone marvelling at the smooth lines of pearl-white metalloceramic from which the starship interior was built. Vents and discreet systems channels were elongated into a virtuoso Jugendstil lattice across the walls and ceiling, subtly illuminated in glowing cobalt and cyan, while systems modules lurked behind circular indentations outlined in tangerine.

Double doors swished open and they entered an observation lounge. The drums thundered away as a choir added their vocals, building up the drama. Ahead of them, the bulkhead was a shallow curve of transparent übercarbon. Dellian pressed himself against it, with Falar on one side and Xante on the other, all eager and awed as if they were still fourteen and back on the Immerle estate, watching for fearsome predators beyond the protective fence. The dark realm of Bennu's strange and majestic cavern outside was amplified by an activeoptic layer in the übercarbon. Above them as the music soared, the *Actaeon*'s arresting structure formed a triple helix wrapped around a long tapering spine that opened out into five silver prongs as if it was a spear for some particularly aggressive mythogod. At the aft of the spine was a clump of three geodesic crystal domes, a kilometre in diameter. Their glittering Victoriana shells contained an eerie fluctuating saffron glow, cages for a struggling primordial light that no longer belonged in this universe. The music reached a triumphant crescendo as Dellian stared at them.

'What's in those?' he asked.

'What?' Yirella called above the music.

'The light?' His fingers made a fast cutting motion across his throat.

The anthemic concerto swirled away in a harpsichord flourish. Dellian instinctively glanced around, half-expecting to see musicians stomping off in a sulk. 'What's that light?'

'Cherenkov overspill,' she told him. 'Those are the engine nacelles. We think they'll be able to accelerate the *Actaeon* close to point nine eight lightspeed.'

Dellian searched Bennu's shadowy gulf until he found the dim grey patch which was the *Morgan*. It certainly didn't glow in the dark like the *Actaeon*. 'I've never seen gravatonic drives like that before.'

'That's because the *Actaeon* isn't a warship,' Ellici said. 'We can be freer when it comes to propulsion design. Less inhibitor shielding allows us to take the propulsion force close to the theoretical maximum.'

'We're also cutting back on mass,' Yirella said. 'The life-support structure has some garden areas, but no open parkland like you have in a standard toroid.'

'Why?' Uret asked. 'You just said you are freer to expand the design.'

'This isn't a generation ship,' she told him flatly. 'When you leave on the *Actaeon* you aren't going to be founding a new civilization. This is about exploring, discovering and joining an established society.'

He groaned, rolling his eyes for emphasis. 'Not the Sanctuary quest *again*? Please, Saints!'

'What you go hunting for is up to the *Actaeon*'s council. All we're trying to do is build in as many flight options for you as we can. And that boils down to a very long range.'

'Don't include me in this.'

Dellian and Yirella exchanged a surprised glance. 'I thought you were first to sign up?' he said.

'Well . . . yeah,' Uret mumbled sheepishly. 'But, you know . . .'

'No.'

'Okay, it's like this. Now that Kenelm doesn't go batshit crazy if we talk about maybe doing something other than supporting the Strike, I started thinking about it. Specifically, the odds.'

'The odds on what?' Yirella asked.

'Of finding anything out there, let alone a human civilization in full swing. I reckon the odds on the Olyix finding us are a lot better. I mean, our Vayan radio has been yelling out *here we are* for decades.'

'But that's logical,' she complained. 'The *Actaeon* isn't about logic; it's about human emotion and basic freedoms. We have the right to live how we want to. That includes the right to refuse to fight in a strategy that was dictated ten thousand years ago.'

Uret shrugged, unable to meet anyone's eye. 'Yeah, but if we don't take out the Olyix, who will? Besides . . . you guys. You need me.'

Dellian genuinely thought Yirella was going to punch poor old Uret; she certainly looked exasperated enough. With a big grin, he taunted: 'Don't want to desert your friends, huh? Conscience finally kicking in?'

'Screw you!' Uret said, but couldn't muster any rage behind it.

Laughing, Dellian kissed him hard. Xante came over and gave him a big hug. Everyone else was smiling happily – except Yirella. 'How many in the *Actaeon* group are thinking like this now?' she demanded.

'I don't know,' he said a shade defensively.

'Who cares?' Dellian said. 'Cue the music again. He's staying!'

'But—'

'Don't take this personally, please,' Uret said to her. 'I know how hard you've worked to make this possible. Believe me, everyone who got behind the *Actaeon* movement is incredibly grateful for everything you've done. And this ship –' he waved his arms around enthusiastically – 'Saints, it's like an old Earth palace. Amazing! Kenelm should get you to oversee a replacement for the *Morgan*.'

'That's not why I did this,' she said.

'I know. You did it because you care about people. That's what makes you our greatest treasure. We all know Dellian doesn't deserve you.'

'Hey!'

'What can I say? I speak truth to power.'

'Oh, please,' Ellici interjected. 'If you ever faced up to power your brain would melt out of your ears.'

Uret chuckled. 'Harsh but fair. That's why we have Dellian as our fearless leader.'

Dellian could see how perturbed Yirella was by Uret's switch. Or was it defection? *Can you defect from defecting? Is that re-defecting?* 'Will you show us the stellar search centre?' he asked her. 'I've had to listen to you bang on about it for a year now.'

She nodded slowly, regathering her enthusiasm. 'Sure. We're going to use ten sub-ships in a bracelet formation around the *Actaeon* to provide a massive sensor baseline. They'll be equipped with radio telescopes as well as optical. And we'll scan for gravity waves, too; they're a sure indicator of advanced drive technology in operation.'

'How far out will the ancillary ships fly?' Xante asked.

'Ten AUs,' Yirella told him.

Dellian was impressed with his friend, given Xante didn't have the slightest interest in astrosensor technology. He turned to Uret as everyone else trooped out after Yirella, and mouthed: *Idiot.*

Uret held out his hands, palms up, in a *what-can-you-do* gesture.

The rest of the tour (thankfully *sans* music) went without a hitch. But Dellian was relieved when it was over; he found the enforced jollity required of him to be as draining as it was distressing. So he let out a grateful sigh as they left one of the gardens and everything went black. As always, there was the single second Dellian hated most in the universe, where he was held motionless in a spread-eagle pose – utterly vulnerable. Then the contact sheaths curled back from his limbs and the egg's upper segments withdrew, their tentacles pulling them back into the ceiling recesses.

Dellian looked around at the others emerging from their eggs with varying expressions of distaste.

'So how long will it take to build?' Falar asked.

Ellici bent down so she could put an arm around his shoulders. 'No more than a couple of years, we hope.'

'Two years? Saints, why? The shipyards only take five months to assemble an attack cruiser.'

'You've just answered your own question,' she told him merrily. 'Our shipyards are designed to produce attack cruisers. So first we have to build the shipyard which can build the *Actaeon*. Designing that is actually more complicated than the starship itself. And before that we have to fabricate the manufacture platforms that'll build the shipyard. At least our standard assembly stations and initiators can do that.'

'Okay. Whatever. Sorry I asked.'

'I never said this was going to be easy,' Yirella said. 'And I don't want to send anyone away on a half-arsed ship.'

'Nobody could ever accuse the *Actaeon* of being that,' Falar said. 'You've done a magnificent job.'

'Thank you.'

*

When they got back to the privacy of their quarters Dellian flopped into the sofa directly in front of a broad black fusuma with a monochrome dragon print that stretched right across it; Yirella had been in a traditional Japanese phase for seven months now. The fusuma slid away to reveal a balcony that had a perfect view of Mount Fuji. Air from a garden full of blossoming cherry trees gusted in. 'I'm not sure I can keep this farce up,' he admitted.

A smaller fusuma across the other side of the room was painted with a ukiyo-e style flying island. Yirella slid it aside and went into the bedroom. 'I found Uret's reversal interesting,' she said.

'No you didn't.'

'Excuse me?'

'You were on the verge of braining the poor dumbarse. I saw you.'

'All right. After busting a gut on the *Actaeon* design for two years I think I'm entitled to be a little peeved.'

'Leaving aside *a little peeved* as the understatement of the mission since we left Juloss, his change of attitude is actually quite complimentary.'

'You mean the whole subterfuge is working? The Leavers are reconsidering?'

'I thought that was the whole point.'

'It is, but I need to know if Uret is only folding thanks to peer pressure, of if the rest of the Leavers are having equal doubts.'

A remote rolled over to the sofa and proffered a chilled glass of beer for Dellian. 'You're going to make me go out there and schmooze again, aren't you?'

''Fraid so. Spread the pain. If the *Actaeon* project folds now, people will revert to being moody and we'll be right back where we started, watching for potential suicides. Kenelm was right when sie said we have to commit fully to it.'

'You know Uret was part of the biogreen faction?'

'What are you saying?'

'The majority of Leavers want to load the *Actaeon* with refineries and initiators so they can continue this life when they find a terra-formed planet. But Uret's faction want to go superpastoral, so the land can provide them with everything. Trees that grow into houses, meat crops, metallic crystalloids, medicine tubers. All so they can live *as one* with the environment.'

'That's dumb. Without a modern digital infrastructure, they'll lose their knowledge base within three generations. The survivors will have to climb the industrial path again.'

'Survivors? Wow, you really don't approve, do you? The biogreen goal is to have a balanced life so you don't need to start building things. That way, keeping things simple, they get to avoid discovery by the Olyix.'

'If they're going to be that sedentary, they'll need to lower their IQ to make that culture stable and sustainable. Their ideology is worse than our Strike mission. It's a prison.'

'Tolerant much? If that's how they want to live their life, especially one that doesn't interfere with us, then help them live it.'

'Ideologues are welcome to live with the values they admire, I have no problem with that, but you have to give the next generation the freedom and ability to go their own way. Anything else is fascism.'

'Well, if it's any comfort, I don't think there were many in Uret's camp.'

Yirella came out of the bedroom, tying up the obi of a splendid scarlet and black kimono. 'I still need to know numbers, Del.'

'Right,' he grumbled.

She sat beside him and grabbed a beer from the remote. 'Beer shouldn't be this cold. It reduces the flavour.'

'I'm not entirely sure it's the flavour I drink it for.'

'Yeah, social rituals are strange when you think about them. It's a retreat to the comfort of routine. Nursery food for the soul.'

'This has really upset you, hasn't it?'

'Not really. We can build two *Actaeon*s easily enough.'

'Saints! Please let me watch when you tell Kenelm that. Please, please, please.'

She grinned and kissed him. 'Behave. It is a problem. The *Actaeon* is holding our disaffected together and giving them purpose. If they start to form factions and exclude each other, that just makes our job tougher.'

'We can't build each of them their own *Actaeon*.'

'Actually—'

'All right, I get it. I'll talk to Uret tomorrow.'

'Thank you.' She gave him a longer kiss. 'Humans are so fascinating, aren't we? If ten of us are each given our own piano, we'll play eleven different tunes. I wonder if that makes us more or less attractive to the Olyix.'

'Right now I'm guessing the Olyix regret ever visiting Earth to start with. We must be the biggest disaster they've known. Who else has defied and fought them for so long as we have?'

'The Neána defy them in their own soft way. And the Saints alone know how many battles they're currently fighting with other species across the galaxy.'

'Now there's a cheerful thought.' He put his arm around her and snuggled in tighter.

'Do you suppose all the other human Strike warships experience the same issues as us?' she asked. 'We have the weapons that are as good as anything the Olyix have, but not all of us have the psychology to fight them.'

'I think our solution is a good one. The *Actaeon* really is keeping morale high.'

'Maybe. But there must be other solutions, especially if it's a common problem. Trouble is, none of the Strike warship captains will ever know, because the one thing we can't do is broadcast the issue. And now I've started thinking about those tens of thousands of other Strike missions I just can't stop. What *has* happened to them? Surely one of them managed to ambush an arkship success-fully? Why didn't they send their Signal? It was supposed to be our rallying cry, Del. A Signal, whether it was *the* Signal from the Saints or one from a Strike ship, would travel along the expansion wave-front and alert all of us. Then we all fly straight to whatever neutron star is closest to the gateway and form the final human armada. But we've had nothing. Ten thousand years!'

'The galaxy is big. Something like this was always going to take aeons; the Saints knew that when they started it. And actually, the longer it does take, the more successful it will be.'

'Yeah, right.' She sighed. 'Longer time equals improved weapons and more warships turning up at the neutron star.'

'Exactly! So stop worrying about this. You've done a good job.' Even as he said it, he wanted her to carry on. Listening to her ideas unfurling was part of the joy of being with her.

'Of course some Strike missions will have completely different social compositions to the *Morgan*,' she mused. 'If every planet settled by a generation ship sends off two hundred new generation ships, and each of those finds a planet and does the same thing, the exponential numbers are colossal, especially now, after so long. So you're going to get a lot of societal variations building up, exactly like Uret and his ultrabiology doctrine.'

'Uh, maybe best not to give him the entire credit for that notion.'

'But think about it. Our omnia Utopial strand of culture is fairly conservative; you can trace the lineage all the way back to Delta Pavonis. But each generation ship is a chance for change when it reaches a new world, especially as Utopial ships weren't even in the majority when we all fled the invasion. The terraformed worlds all had very different societies and ideologies to Earth, so I'm guessing there must be thousands of types of humans by now.'

'What, four arms? A tail? Three heads?'

'Maybe even five bodies sharing a linked mind. Why not? And they'll each come at this a different way.'

'Come at what?'

'A method of attacking the Olyix.'

'I hope not. Capturing an arkship, or at least its wormhole's data for the gateway, is fundamental to the plan.'

'If we're all still sticking to the flight-then-fight plan. Big *if*, there.'

Dellian sat up so that he was able to look at her directly. 'Saints! The F-and-F plan is what's going to save us. Humans sacrificed everything to do this. Everything. Our homeworld, our interstellar settlements, those that were left behind, those that fought to give us this one chance. Don't start to have doubts. If the rest of us have all been hunted down and elevated, if there's only one free human left in the galaxy, the plan still stands.'

She stroked his cheeks admiringly. 'That's my Dellian. If it's you, if you're the last human standing in the galaxy, then it'll work.'

'We just need the Signal.'

'Yeah. The Signal can only travel at lightspeed, you know. Suppose we got the bad statistic? Suppose the enclave is a thousand lightyears on the other side of Earth from the human expansion wavefront? If that's where the Olyix are hiding, then our flight from Sol has kept us ahead of the Signal. The Saints did trigger it all that time ago, but it hasn't caught up with us yet because of the speed we're expanding.'

'You know what?'

'What?'

'I'd give anything to have your brain for a day.'

Yirella chuckled and sipped some more beer. 'Actually, it's better than you know.'

'Oh, bragging now are we!'

'Not quite, *buuut . . .*'

'Oh Saints, what?'

'Guess why I built such a huge astrosensor system into the *Actaeon*?'

It took a moment for the enormity of what she had done to register. 'Saints be damned!' He chuckled like a ten-year-old listening to a dirty joke. 'You didn't!'

'Uh huh.'

'And the *Actaeon* will fly away from the expansion wavefront, maybe all the way back to Earth. So if the Saints found the enclave, and it is behind us, the astrosensor system will detect the Signal. That's fantastic, Yi! Oh, but . . . no good to us, because we still won't know.'

Yirella gave him a smug smile. 'Clever boy. Unless . . .'

'Shit!' he yelled, then clamped a hand over his mouth, shocked and delighted. 'You're going to put a portal inside the *Actaeon*.'

'A small one. Just so we can keep an eye on anything those astrosensors pick up.'

'But if the *Actaeon* gets captured, it'll lead the Olyix right back to us.'

'Realistically, the *Actaeon* will be difficult – verging on impossible – for the Olyix to detect when it's flying through interstellar space at a fabulous point nine whatever lightspeed. The only time the Olyix can ambush it is after it's decelerated into a star system. If it's captured intact, the Olyix will find out we are – or were – lurking here at Vayan. And the distance involved will mean it'll take them years to reach us, by which time we'll be long gone.'

'So we really are going to build the *Actaeon*? No matter what?'

'Kenelm agreed with me. We need to know about the Signal, because that will really tell us if we're wasting our time here. So, yes, we build the *Actaeon* and send it back to Earth. The only thing that'll stop the project now is if an arkship arrives and we find the gateway coordinate for ourselves.'

'Sweet Saints.' He slumped back again. 'You see, this is why I don't play chess with you any more. All you have to do is move your first pawn forwards and you've won.'

'Don't be so self-deprecating. I just work my way through possibilities quickly, that's all.'

'Why don't you and Kenelm just send an automated ship back towards Sol?'

'Firstly, we genuinely needed to design a faster gravatonic propulsion unit. Our starship speed has been limited to point eight seven C for too long. The *Actaeon* mission gave us the perfect excuse for our engineers to work on the problem out in the open, and Saint Jessika always said that's the best place to conceal something. Second, morale has been shaky for a while. If we started a project just to send a ship back towards Earth in a search for the Signal, more people will start to question the *Morgan*'s purpose.' Her face fell solemn. 'Kenelm is worried that the Signal hasn't come yet, a lot more than sie lets on. Yes, statistically we're probably still heading straight for it. But . . . ten thousand years, Del. We're only human.'

'You're concerned, too, aren't you?'

'Yes. All this: lure planets, warships like the *Morgan*. It's happened thousands of times already. After we began the Leaver project, Kenelm told me that sie was given a new set of orders before the *Morgan* left Juloss. If we don't receive the Signal within a reasonable timeframe, we're to initiate the Neána option regardless, and create a civilization in hiding, out between the stars.'

'How come you know this and I don't?'

'Kenelm trusts me with big picture stuff. You, on the other hand, need to keep focused on your command of the squad.'

'Okay, that hurt. But Juloss is probably about a couple of hundred lightyears behind us. So even if the Signal arrived the day after we left, it won't reach here for another two centuries.'

'Correct. What's your point?'

'No point. Just curious how long we're supposed to wait.'

'That's within the Captain's discretion. If it was me, I'd wait until the *Actaeon* was halfway back to Earth. If the astrosensors haven't picked up the Signal by then, I'd say time for something new.'

He sipped his beer in silence for a minute. 'You're right not to mention this part of the *Actaeon* mission, even to the *Morgan*'s command crew. It would amplify the morale problem beyond fixing.

Frankly, I almost wish you hadn't told me. I was happy just anticipating the Signal would reach us at some point.'

'Well, stay happy. The *Actaeon* should shift those statistics back in our favour.'

*

Command personnel to the bridge. The category-one order came buzzing through Dellian's databud at six o'clock the next morning, while he was still dozing.

'Now what?' he grumbled.

Yirella was wide awake beside him, staring intently at the ceiling as though it was revealing some profound truth. 'There's a lot of heavy security codes partitioning the network suddenly. Interesting.'

Dellian just *knew*. It had to be. It couldn't be anything else. He tried to keep the smile from his face. Security was key here. Nobody would panic; they'd trained for this for so long. But excitement would hit the squads like an adrenalin rush. 'I have to go.'

'Yes, me too.'

'Huh?' The momentary distraction meant he hit his knee on the black parquet floor as he scrambled off the bed. 'Ow. This bed is too low. I mean, why even bother with a frame? Just leave the mattress on the floor.'

'Oh dear. Wrong side this morning?'

'No. What instruction did you get?'

'Same as you. Report to the bridge.'

Her face might be completely composed, but Dellian knew she was laughing at him. 'But you're not command level.' Out before he could stop it.

'Captain's advisory council, thank you! That gives me a command rank.'

'But this is . . .'

She raised an eyebrow coyly. 'A military action? The Strike?'

'I don't know. Possibly.'

'Ha. You've already convinced yourself it is.'

'Either way, I'm glad you'll be there. Okay? Are you going to re-join Ellici and Tilliana in tactical?'

'Saints, no! That would be a disaster. I haven't done tactical since . . . You remember when.'

'Yeah,' he muttered, shamefaced. She'd risen from the bed to stand over him, but he couldn't tip his head back to look up at her.

'You lot have had years training together since then. You're as tight and perfect as you're going to get. Putting me in there now would screw things up badly.'

'Sorry.'

Her long arm came down, fingers squeezing his shoulder. 'I appreciate that was your first thought. It's very sweet, if totally misplaced.'

'That just about sums me up.'

Laughing at his exaggerated misery, she gave him a quick hug. 'Come on, Del, this is not the day for gloom and introspection. Get your uniform on, soldier. You know what they say.'

'No . . .?'

A sigh. 'You need to pay more attention to those old dramas I make you watch. Women love a man in uniform. Or they did back then. Allegedly.'

'Oh, yeah? Do they still?'

'Put it on and find out.'

So three minutes later he was in a freshly printed grey and blue dress uniform. As he sealed up the front of the tunic, he realized he hadn't worn one since Rello's funeral. *Progress of sorts, I guess.*

'Not half bad,' Yirella told him.

'I sense mockery.'

'Your senses are wise.'

Dellian always found the *Morgan*'s bridge a disappointment. Basically it was the Captain's main council room, with a broad screen wall at the far end of a truncated oval table which seated twenty. Eight squad leaders had reported for duty, as well as the *Morgan*'s senior officers and four people from the Captain's advisory council; Yirella was the only non-omnia in that group.

The bridge door closed and locked. Dellian's databud told him the network access codes had been raised.

Kenelm sat at the head of the table, dressed in hir uniform, which somehow managed to look a lot smarter on hir than anyone else. 'At oh-three-fifty-two hours ship time, our exo-heliosphere sensor network detected low-level gravity waves. Wim was duty officer; sie expanded the portal of the closest satellite and sent through eighteen mark seven sensor webs.'

Wim stood up, hir long face animated. 'The webs confirmed the gravitational disturbance. They're originating from a point six thousand five hundred AUs out from the star. A single high-mass point, which is moving insystem at point one eight lightspeed –' a full-blown smile lifted hir lips – 'and it's decelerating. It's an active arkship!'

The rest of the table cheered. Wim held hir hand up. 'More detailed analysis shows the arkship's ion buffer cloud has yet to deploy, that they are still using a gravitational distortion effect to protect themselves from sub-C particle impact.'

'And it's definitely alone?' Ellici asked.

'Nothing else is showing up on the webs' scan. But remember, we're dealing with a hollowed-out asteroid, forty kilometres long. That can hide a lot of surprises.'

'And we will proceed accordingly,' Kenelm said. 'They must have encountered a lure before, so I'm expecting defences beyond anything the *Salvation of Life* was equipped with. Our attack cruisers will engage the enemy after the flood. If they can overcome whatever the Olyix have brought to the party, and only if, I will authorize the squads to board.'

'What's their deceleration speed?' Yirella asked.

'One point two gee,' Wim said. 'And that's with a gravatonic drive. They're running dark. Best estimate is another six to eight weeks before they switch to an ion cloud buffer and start to use their "primitive" antimatter drive to arrive insystem. When the *Salvation of Life* arrived at Sol, they fired up the antimatter drive when they were a tenth of a lightyear out. That gives the target civilization time to get over the shock of alien visitors and start sending polite first-contact radio messages.' Sie sat down fast.

'We've found them a little later than I would have liked,' Kenelm said, 'but we still have plenty of time to prepare the Strike. This assault is what we've been training for, we're ready and we know what to do. Now: I want Tactical to determine the best interception point. We need to launch the flood mines within a week. Engineering, we halt all non-essential manufacturing in Bennu and focus on getting every destroyer up to full operational capacity. Squad leaders, you have two further training sessions. Nothing too demanding; I want everyone at peak fitness and no injuries. When we intercept, we're going to concentrate on the wormhole mechanism. I want every byte of data in there. Our prize is the gateway coordinate. Once we have that, we have the enclave. I also want some quints for study. Alive segments, please. Yirella?'

'Yes, Captain?'

'The metavayan Neána – it's put up or shut up time. Get me a definite answer. Will they let us have the neurovirus to help take out the arkship onemind?'

'Understood. I'll talk to them.'

Dellian wondered if anyone else heard the edge in her voice. For the two years since the Neána arrived, Yirella had been leading an exhaustive diplomatic undertaking to convince them to share the neurovirus. They'd countered with polite equivocation. Oh, the visitors had helped advance some of the initiator systems, especially the biotechnology ones (which is why the superpastoral faction had risen among the Leavers). But as far as the neurovirus was concerned, *maybe* was as close as she'd got to an answer. She'd always been reluctant to push them. Dellian privately suspected – very privately – that she was a little too much in awe of them.

'It's too late to ask that question,' he said.

Everyone looked at him. Some then threw a sly glance Yirella's way.

'Well, it is,' he insisted. 'The Neána always warned us that we shouldn't have any kind of direct brain–processor interface because it makes us susceptible to a neurovirus ourselves. Which is why we developed the whole munc programme. But to use a neurovirus against the Olyix, we'd have to have that interface. We'd also have to familiarize ourselves with it and learn how to use it. With all respect, Captain, a couple of weeks isn't long enough to do that.'

'Convenient for them, though, isn't it?' Ovan said. 'The super-weapon that could win us the most valuable information in the galaxy is somehow too dangerous for us to use. For the record, I'd take the risk of getting my brain burned out by the Olyix if there's a chance of it working on the arkship's onemind. The hazard should be ours to take. They obviously don't trust us.'

'Are you saying the Neána aren't as sympathetic as they claim?' Kenelm asked.

'They certainly seem to get off on this whole mystic guru shit,' Ovan retorted. 'Who knows what their real motivation is? Saint Kandara was always a sceptic.'

'The situation isn't comparable,' Yirella said. 'Saint Kandara was suspicious about everything because that was her nature. These Neána come from a different abode from the metahuman ones. They didn't know we existed, which makes them suspicious and even fearful of us.'

'Why?' Ovan asked. 'How are we the bad guys suddenly?'

'They've been shocked by our expansion policy. It's understand-able. If it continues unabated, terrestrial life will become unassailably dominant across the galaxy.'

Ovan drummed his fingers on the table. 'Just saying, that's all. Convenient.'

'Noted,' Kenelm said. 'Yirella, is it realistic for us to count on using the neurovirus at this point?'

'Dellian is correct,' she said. '*We* can't. If it's to be used in the assault, then one of the metavayan Neána will have to interface with the arkship neural structure. So Ovan's question is actually reversed. Can we trust them? I'd say yes, given what Saint Jessika did for us. When we are in crisis, the Neána have always helped. And this is a definitely a crisis.'

'I prefer the term *critical point*, myself,' Kenelm said. 'Crisis implies something we're not prepared for. And we are most definitely prepared.'

'Yes, Captain.'

'If one of the Neána agrees to help us and deploy the neurovirus, I'd like to volunteer to take it on board with my squad,' Dellian said. He ignored the other squad leaders flashing him jealous glances.

Kenelm didn't look remotely surprised. 'Very well. Dellian, draw up a second assault profile for your squad that'll get a metavayan to where it needs to go. Yirella, that's down to you now. And if they continue to refuse to help, I want them isolated until after the assault is over.'

'Yes, Captain.'

'This is it then, everyone. May the Saints smile upon us, so that one day we might finally meet them.'

London

There was another disagreement with Crina, this time about going outside onto the penthouse's balcony, but eventually the bodyguard agreed, on condition of the carbon sheet being raised. By then Gwendoline had given up arguing – through sheer exhaustion, she told herself. Or maybe the way Horatio's irritatingly superior smile just kept growing the whole time had something to do with it.

So the anti-sniper sheet slid up just outside the balcony rail, and they stepped out into the cool morning air as a shield-diffused dawn rose somewhere out beyond the miscreation that was the Connexion tower in Greenwich. And after all that fuss she couldn't even tell the sheet was there, the carbon was so thin. But tough. Enough to stop any kinetic attack short of a kilogram railgun harpoon, along with a mid-power maser carbine. If someone was that determined to kill her, they'd likely succeed anyway.

She and Horatio had spent the night together, though it hadn't all been the happy passion she'd wanted to banish her fear. First she'd accessed the feed from Kayli; the level of violence delivered by the warheads was shocking. They'd clung to each other under the duvet, watching the multiple explosions bloom in ultrafast sequence, eradicating every gram of human presence on the

245

asteroid, then fracturing the rock itself. It was so overwhelming, so swift, it had shaken her confidence badly. That cool inner core which reassured her that, no matter how bad the invasion was, people would overcome – the ancient Blitz spirit in every Londoner's DNA – all dissolved in that primeval burn of intense radiation.

'We're going to lose,' she professed bleakly to Horatio.

Even his cheerful optimism had gone, flash-evaporated in nuclear hellfire. 'What do they want?' he asked in bewilderment. 'Those nukes are strong enough to take out half a continent.'

'Us. They want us to join them on their pilgrimage to their God at the End of Time. We either go with them or we die.'

'That is one extreme religion.'

'I suppose the longer it's been around, the stronger its hold on the culture which spawned it.'

'I thought education was the solution to religion. There's no way you can have a society as advanced as the Olyix without universal education.'

'Face it,' she said, 'we still have enough flat earthers and other nutters. Besides, I don't think you can equate Olyix culture to ours. They don't even have their original bodies any more.' She paused, considering what she'd just said, and the source of the information. 'Actually, that's what they told us, so it's probably bollocks as well. We clearly don't know anything about their true nature.'

They waited, nestled together sweetly while the minutes counted down to a missile's arrival at Yanat.

'What exactly is he hoping to do?' Horatio asked.

'Callum? I'm not sure.' Gwendoline used her family executive clearance to stream the images from Alpha Defence on the bedroom's big screen. Privately, she also splashed the technical schematics across her tarsus lens.

The asteroid's little maintenance and control station had been abandoned, Callum and Fang Yun evacuated, and its portal door back to Quoek shut down. Only the all-important data channels were open, with one of Alpha Defence's G8Turings taking direct control of the six MHD chambers. When the missile was eighty thousand kilometres out, and closing at over twelve thousand kilometres per second, the G8 switched off the induction coils inside the MHD chambers that sucked energy from the flow. Freed from any form of resistance, the plasma plumes extended dramatically, stretching out for over four thousand kilometres as the temperature leapt upwards, exceeding two hundred per cent above the chambers' safety limit. The missile fired eight warheads at Yanat, accelerating at two hundred and fifty gees. For the first few milliseconds they diverged from the missile's direct collision course, spreading wide, before vectoring back sharply to line up on the distant rock, coming at it from eight different directions. Up ahead, the plasma plumes flared up to an intolerable brightness as they stabbed out.

For an instant Yanat appeared to be an incandescent six-pointed star, expanding faster than any explosion wavefront. Then the G8Turing began to feed electricity from Earth's grid straight into the last magnetic induction ring around the open throat of each MHD chamber, varying it in a precise pattern. The enormous magnetic field oscillated, pushing the plasma stream. At the throat, the variance was minuscule, but over the full length of the coronal jet the movement was amplified so that the tip streaked from side to side in a huge arc.

Yanat transformed from a spiky actinic astroblemish up to a full-blown sphere of raw sunlight. The first warhead hit the nebulous million-degree photosphere at over fifteen thousand kilometres per second. Its gravatonic distortion whorl deflected the colossal kinetic impact for fifteen picoseconds before collapsing under the energy implosion. The warhead, and its seven siblings, vaporized instantly, punching slender inverted prominences down towards Yanat before their disintegrating atoms were repelled, surging outbound again as insignificant ionic geysers.

The larger, more powerful, missile itself survived the plasma impact a full seven milliseconds before it also failed. With the danger over, the G8Turing cut power to the magnetic coils, and the plasma jets returned to single titanic spears. A decomposing shell of elementary particles swept outwards, its phantom presence absorbed by interplanetary space amid a deluge of hard radiation.

'Yes!' Gwendoline yelled victoriously. She didn't quite know how, but she was dancing about on the mattress, arms making wild karate chops in homage to the plasma jets. 'Callum fucking did it!' Then she winced. The technical splash was telling her the bad news. One of Yanat's MHD chambers was going into emergency shutdown, while two others were having their plasma flow reduced to cut back on the stress to badly abused components. 'Well, we've still got some power from Yanat. Even if it's the same percentage remaining from the others, we'll have more than enough.' Her jubilation faded and she sat down fast, bobbing about on the springy mattress. 'Until they throw something else at us.'

Horatio's arm went around her. 'But it's their first setback, right? Let's concentrate on that. They're not omnipotent.'

'No. They're not. But it's close, Horatio.'

Theano's splash showed her a missile approaching another MHD asteroid, Desten. One of Alpha Defence's G8Turings assumed command of the MHD chambers and wove another impenetrable web of starfire around it. The missile warheads exploded before they reached their target.

Ten minutes later, with the eighth missile yet to reach its target, the Olyix changed tactics. The first warhead detonated as soon as it struck the protective cyclone of plasma. It created a minute, very short-lived, gap which the second warhead tried to penetrate. But the timing simply wasn't good enough.

'Gonna be a long night,' Gwendoline decided.

The sex which followed wasn't the best ever. But still it was sex, and what she wanted. Horatio fell asleep soon after, leaving her awake and accessing all the ultra-secret files she could coax out of her globalPAC contacts and the family council. Once she started doing that, seeing the full reality of the Olyix, she couldn't sleep. She suspected she'd never sleep again.

Now, four hours later, standing out on the balcony, a thick ocean-green cashmere pashmina wrapped around her shoulders against the cool air, she and Horatio stared across an unnervingly quiet city. Below her, the Thames had been reduced to a sluggish brown ribbon of water winding along the centre of glistening mudflats. Now that the shield to the west had successfully sealed off the river, all the water left inside the city had flowed away down the sloping land to the east, where it was now lapping along the lowest stretch of the shield, desperate to find its way to the sea beyond. Here at Chelsea, its departure had grounded all the fashionable houseboats moored along the Cheyne Walk jetty, leaving them leaning at alarming angles. Normally, by this hour, flocks of drones would be airborne above the boats, easing their way along a complex grid of authorized airlanes across the city. This morning, pigeons and parakeets had reclaimed their natural airspace, outnumbering their mechanical rivals for the first time in over a hundred and fifty years. Only the occasional police soloflyer drifting along the skyline convinced her the Olyix hadn't already snatched London's population away overnight.

Theano splashed a faint white spiderweb graphic, directing Gwendoline's gaze up into the southern sky where the MHD constellation had been a comforting aspect of the firmament throughout her life. The city shield was diffracting the low sunlight, smearing its rose-gold shimmer across the dome in wavering strands like moonlight reflected on a midnight lake. Even so it lacked the intensity to obscure the curving band of vivid stars that spanned the horizon. They were still up there, shining reassuringly, a spray of tiny sparks arranged so neatly in their orbital arc out beyond Neptune.

Her splash was showing the ongoing assault by Olyix missiles. Of the three and a half thousand MHD asteroids, a hundred and nineteen had been targeted in the last four hours. The Olyix had continued to refine their tactics; now several warheads synchronized their detonations against the protective plasma buffer in an attempt to prise open a gap which others could get through. It wasn't very successful, with only one in seventeen attacks managing to destroy an asteroid – more luck than precision. But the Olyix had numbers on their side. According to the information she'd received from the family senior council, they had effectively unlimited resources. The MHD asteroids would all be destroyed in the end. It was just a question of time.

Horatio sipped a mug of coffee; his free arm went around her shoulder. 'Which one is Kayli?'

Theano's graphic highlighted it for her, still a steady gleaming pinpoint.

'That one,' she pointed, which probably wasn't accurate enough, but he'd be looking in the right section of sky when it happened. 'I guess that's what you call ghostlight. It died four hours ago, but we can still see it.'

'Twinkle twinkle little star,' Horatio muttered. 'Now I know what you really are.'

Theano started a countdown in Gwendoline's splash. She put on a pair of Rabbian sunglasses – last season's must-have ski resort accessory – and held up a pair of Zabroki sunglasses for Horatio. 'You'll need them,' she told him. And tried not to smirk when he put on the glitzy frames.

Her chest tightened as the last seconds flicked away. When it happened, it was like an old-style flashbulb going off in the heavens, except this lasted for several seconds before dwindling rapidly. And despite those grade-five sunglasses, Gwendoline was still left blinking away a dancing purple afterimage.

'Bloody hell,' Horatio exclaimed. 'How much radiation is hitting us from that? I mean, if the light's that strong . . .'

'We're okay. It's thirty AUs away, remember; that's why the light's taken so long to get here. And the atmosphere and city shield are enough to protect us from what's left of the gamma spike.'

'Okay. If you're sure . . .'

She took off her Rabbians and gave him a haunted smile. 'The Yanat lightshow isn't for another ninety minutes. But it's not going to be anything like that. Just maybe double the brightness for a minute.' She glanced down at the weirdly deserted embankment street. 'There'll be spectators come out for that, I'm guessing.' When she turned, Crina was standing just outside the balcony doors wearing wraparound mirrorshades. She took them off, and there was no expression on her face. So professional – except Gwendoline read that as shock. Yesterday the whole planet had been devoured by news, speculation, and more than a hint of scepticism. Today, reality was going to bite *hard*.

Back inside the kitchen, Horatio started to break eggs into a big copper-bottomed pan, while Gwendoline dropped a fresh dough brick into the panoforno.

'Twenty minutes,' she told him. 'It's a branary, so it'll make good toast.'

'Great.' He held up a litre bottle from the fridge. 'Does this milk actually come from a cow?'

'Yep. Gold label certified.'

'I'm not going to ask how much it costs.'

'Well, enjoy it now, because I doubt you'll ever taste it again. They don't have cattle on Nashua, not even a dairy herd. All the food is printed there.'

'Any news on that?'

She shook her head. 'Not a timescale, but the Zangari council is definitely prepping for a full family withdrawal. They've already drafted in a couple of thousand extra technicians to get the place ready.'

'Huh? It's a habitat. It's either ready to live in or it's not.'

She arched an eyebrow. 'I'm sorry, have you met my family? There's a difference between you grabbing a sofa bed in a friend's flat for a week and my great-aunts taking up *residence*. And the great-aunts aren't even our high-maintenance arseholes.'

'Well, thank you for *that* image.'

'Okay, so I'm being unfair to my airhead relatives, but if Nashua is going to be a successful secure refuge, we are going to need some stellar intellects and the best engineers in the terraformed worlds. Apparently the council is discussing transforming Nashua into an arkship. The current thinking goes that we will be leaving this section of the galaxy behind for good. It's the only way to be truly safe.'

'An arkship? You're shitting me. Like the *Salvation of Life*?'

Her laugh was bitter. '*So* not like the *Salvation of Life*.'

'My God, you're serious, aren't you? That means . . . we're really going to lose.'

'Surviving is winning.'

'But who gets to survive?'

'No, I know you. What you're asking is: who gets to make the choice? Who hands out tickets for the lifeboats?'

'Yeah.'

'Well, I have my ticket to hand out. And I'm handing it to you.'

'There are billions of people on this planet. We can't abandon them to . . . what? The Deliverance ships are on their way and we've got nothing that can stop them. Those explosions were bright enough to be seen from Neptune's orbit. What happens when they start shooting those warheads at the city shields? We're going to be *wiped out*.'

'No. They won't use nukes against the shields – and certainly not the size they used against Kayli. Anything that can puncture a city shield will kill everything underneath when it falls. I told you, they don't want to kill us. They want to elevate us, to take us to their god.'

'Really? Just how sure are you about that?'

'Very. I have contacts, remember. And not just the family.'

'How do *they* know? How can anyone possibly know what the Olyix want?'

'I don't know. Even I don't have that kind of clearance. But trust me; Ainsley III would not be drawing up these procedures unless he was a hundred and one per cent certain. The family council is talking about abandoning everything my grandfather has built. Do you understand? There will be no more Connexion, no more pluto-crat wealth. It's all gone. They're going to leave it behind because that's the price of staying alive. And if that's how the Zangaris are thinking, you'd better believe they're not acting on a whim.'

'So ask them how they know.'

'I will. But don't go snarling at me if they won't tell me. I'm not that important.'

He came over and put his arms around her. Anointed her brow with a kiss. 'You are to me.'

Gwendoline leant into him, grateful for the simple comfort. *And it only took the end of the world for this to happen.* 'There is one thing I do know,' she said gloomily. 'Something the Sol Senate hasn't released yet. And I have to ask you about it. It's important.'

'Oh, this doesn't sound good. And we're already in the middle of Armageddon.'

'The Beta Eridani expedition found something bad, but the family council let me access the files.'

'Hell, how bad?'

'Just listen. The Olyix want us for our minds. Our souls are some kind of offering to their God at the End of Time.'

'They are seriously fucked up.'

'But that's all they want. They don't need our bodies, so they put us into some kind of suspension to keep our brains alive until the end of time.'

'You are kidding me. Really. Badly. Kidding me.'

'No.' She sent his altme an image Yuri Alster had taken in the crashed Olyix ship at Beta Eridani, showing one of the human bodies they'd found. Or what was left of it.

Horatio sat down hard on a stool, one hand gripping the marble breakfast bar. 'Holy shit,' he whispered. 'Where are the legs? And the arms?'

'Not needed. All they want is to keep the brain alive. Limbs, bones, reproductive organs – none of that is necessary. So they remove the extraneous body parts and cocoon what's left in a biological life-support unit grown out of Kcells.'

'I think I'm going to be sick.'

'Horatio, according to our information, this is why the Olyix gave us Kcells. Not as a medical benefit. They're part of this, part of the invasion. All those Kcell implants we've been using can transform themselves and grow like the devil's own tumours. They will eat you from within and cocoon you with the new growth, all neatly packaged for the Deliverance ships.' She placed her hands on either side of his face and forced him to look at her. 'So you need to tell me – really *really* need to tell me – have you had any Kcell treatments? Even the smallest kind?'

'No, I haven't. But I've got friends who . . . Shit! Kcell treatments are cheap, much cheaper than cloned bodyparts.'

'Of course they are. And now we know why.'

'They're monsters, aren't they? Even Ainsley wasn't paranoid enough.'

'Yes, which is pretty unnerving in itself. So now you know, if we want to survive this, we have to be extreme. Those fine principles of yours could get you . . . well, not killed. Much worse.'

'Yeah. I get it. I do.'

'So tell me once again, my darling: do you have any Kcell implants? If so, there are surgical teams that can deal with it. They've been busy the last few hours, but I can get you onto an operating table fast.'

'No. I promise you, I don't have any Kcell implants.'

'Huh. Maybe there is a human god.'

'Then She's not doing a very good job, is She?'

'Not right now, no.'

'So when do we go to Nashua?'

'When Loi confirms he's there. Because that habitat is going to be a lobster pot.'

'A what?'

'Before we started printing our food, they used to catch lobsters in wicker pots. The poor things could get in but not out. Once we're in Nashua, there's no way security will ever let us get back out again.'

'Naah, you can fix that. You can fix anything. I have faith in you.'

'No.' She shook her head. 'I like to think I'm important. With all my high-level clearance and seat on the finance board, I had a lot of clout in the company. But none of that is worth shit today. There is no Connexion any more. The only way we got those tickets off Earth is because my grandfather is Ainsley Zangari.'

'Extreme measures, huh?'

'Extreme measures,' she agreed.

The panoforno *pinged*. Gwendoline opened the door and sniffed the warm air that came out. 'Damn, that smells good.'

'It does. Cut some slices to toast; I'll scramble the eggs.'

'You're going to let me use a breadknife? They're very sharp.'

'You did say there are teams of surgeons on standby for Zangaris.'

She smiled weakly. 'Yeah.'

'The government needs to warn people about Kcells.'

'The government wants to avoid mass hysteria.'

'But if people grow alien tumours that cocoon them, it's going to be bleeding obvious soon enough.'

'Yes, but the government has to avoid panic.'

'If the government doesn't tell people, then you're going to have a lot worse than just panic. Government is based on trust. If that goes, then you'll have anarchy.'

'I thought you didn't trust government.'

'I trust the idea of government. The people who are in it right now? Not so much. But that's all we've got left.'

'True. You know that right now this discussion's going on where it actually matters?'

'I certainly hope so.' He held up the pan in satisfaction. 'Done.'

'No.'

'What?'

'The eggs are not done. You didn't whisk them for long enough. The more you whisk them, the more air you get in the mix, the lighter the texture. Nobody wants heavy scrambled eggs.'

'Since when did you become a cookery expert?'

'Gourmet kitchen course. Three years ago. God, it was boring – but useful.'

'Okay, then.' He started whisking again.

'Don't over do it. I want scrambled eggs, not a meringue.'

'Bloody hell, I thought divorce mellowed people!'

She dipped her finger in the mix and gave it a saucy lick. 'That'll do.'

'Do not try to tell me that's how your gourmet course told you to test eggs . . .'

She was about to tease him further when Loi's icon splashed up. 'Sweetheart, where are you? Are you all right?'

'I'm fine, Mum. Stop worrying.'

'Okay, so tell me where you are.'

'I'm still with my boss, so I'm in one of the most secure rooms on the planet.'

'Okay. That's good, sweetheart. But you will be careful, won't you?'

'Mum, for God's sake!'

'All right. Your father's here with me.'

'Oh . . . Good. You can travel together. That'll work out best.'

'What's happening with Nashua?'

'It's going ahead. They're going to open it to senior family first; that should be in a couple of days. You need to be ready. Most of the interstellar hub network is shut down, so we're working out permissible routes.'

'What about you? When are *you* coming?'

'I'll be there, don't worry. I'm helping with evacuating the Sol habitats. We're trying to get people out before the Deliverance ships reach them. Some of the terraformed worlds are kicking up about the cultures that are coming through.'

'What do you mean? Race?'

'Not so much, though that's playing a part. There are a lot of fairly radical societies living in the Sol habitats, some of them very liberal, some definitely not. Then on top of that, you've got the orthodox religious ones. And the Olyix and their God at the End of Time have given religion a high disapproval rating right now. The parts of the allcomments that're still working are turning nasty. Solnet is glitched to hell from all the sabotage that hit it last night.'

'You're not a politician, Loi. Answer the question. When are you going to Nashua?'

'Mum, I honestly don't know, okay? I'm doing critical work here.'

'When you know, you tell us immediately. *Then* we'll join you.'

'Look, I get you're concerned for me, and I appreciate that. But I'm also concerned for you.'

'What are you implying?'

'I'm implying nothing. I'm telling you: the Sol Senate Security Forum is in session right now. They've agreed to declare martial law and enforce curfews in all Earth's cities. It'll begin in a few hours.'

'Crap!'

'Callum's done excellent work working out that flamethrower defence for the MHD asteroids, but it's only going to be temporary. They'll come back with bigger missiles or battleships or something and hit them even harder. There's going to be . . . I was going to say power shortages, but it'll be more like no power at all for civilian use. So there'll be rationing, too.'

'Rationing what?'

'Everything. The G8Turings are formatting allocation sched-ules, but the primary item will be printed food ingredients, and the power to work food printers. There's even talk of setting up communal kitchens – bring your ingredients and have them cooked. It'll be a lot less drain on power than five billion individual kitchens.'

Gwendoline gave her own gleaming kitchen, with its exception-ally high gadget count, a guilty examination. 'All right, that makes a kind of sense. But, Loi, why?'

'What do you mean?'

'Why bother? As soon as the Deliverance ships arrive, it's game over, isn't it?'

'We're not giving up, Mum. There's some people working on this – smart, powerful people who know things we don't. They're drawing up plans to fight these Olyix bastards. Crazy plans. Plans that probably don't stand a chance in hell of working. But that's better than nothing, right?'

'Yes.'

'It all depends on if the Deliverance ships can break the city shields without killing everyone underneath. If they can't, if the cities are secure, then that opens up a whole stream of possibilities.'

'Loi, you're not thinking of being some kind of resistance fighter, are you?'

'No, Mum. But please, I need you to be ready to go when I tell you.'

'I will be. I can pack light. Or even not at all. As long as I've got you and your father, I have everything I need.'

'Light is good. Martial law means getting around London – specifically: you getting to a secure Connexion facility – might be difficult by the time Nashua is ready. We're down to ten active centres in London now.'

'Don't worry about us. Crina is turning out to be very good at her job. She'll help get us where we need to go, I'm sure.'

'I'd like to avoid any possibility of trouble, okay. I'll get you and Dad some skycabez.'

'Loi, I hate those. They're not safe. The gangs shot one down in Peckham last month.'

'All right. Let me think about it. Connexion has paramilitary departments, and some of them have armoured ground vehicles that look just like ordinary taxez.'

'All right. But you mustn't worry about us. You have a job to do. An important one. Do that, and do it well.'

'Thanks, Mum. Now you and Dad get ready to leave. I'll call you with details.'

'I'm proud of you, Loi. We both are.'

'Love you, Mum.'

The call ended, and she wiped some foolish moisture from her eyes. Then she took Horatio's hands in hers. 'There's hope,' she told him. 'Hope for Earth. It's small, and it might not last long once those wretched Deliverance ships arrive, but right now it exists. And our son is part of it.'

London

29th June 2204

The mains power had gone off sometime during the night, so the house had reverted to its battery reserve. That only supplied power to what the domestic G5Turing had listed as essentials – which didn't include the lounge's Bang and Olufsen stage. Ollie and Adnan had to tweak the list, dropping a whole load of crap like Claudette's kitchen and bathroom appliances, along with the automatic mist watering system for the orchids in the garden room. That woman had a seriously screwed sense of priorities, he decided. But now they could power the quality stage for about a week of non-stop viewing. Ollie really didn't want to be stuck in the house for a whole week. Something about the place creeped him out – probably the decor, or maybe what was going on upstairs.

There was only one way to cope with it all; so while Adnan finalized the reserve power priority list, Ollie carefully opened their remaining pads of zero-nark and cut it down still further. Now they could take it constantly, keeping themselves blissed out on a level high for several days. With their prime viewing seats guaranteed, and the impact of the invasion smoothed out, he and Adnan settled back down to watch the end of the world in spectacular high-def and vivid colour.

The asteroid battles they lifted from the lownet were amazing, filling the darkened room with bursts of intense light, overlaid with graphics. They whooped and cheered when the alien missiles were burned by plasma jets hosing across space, and booed when the bad guys coordinated their warheads and slipped one through. Ollie quite enjoyed the show, and it was about the only thing which helped take his mind off the relentless police hunt going on outside.

They'd gone out into the garden with its high walls and perfectly pruned bushes and sickly-sweet rose scents, looking up into the shield-smeared morning sky, watching the slim MHD constellation. The flashes as the plasma jets went wild fending off missiles were awesome for the first few times, then they got bored and went back inside, closing the curtains again so the stage projections were undiluted by sunlight. Ollie went to check on Lars in the garden room. The big man was just starting to stir as the sedatives wore off, so Ollie made him sit up and drink some soup, which was actually the remaining bacon sandwiches that Adnan had chucked into the blender and added milk to. Lars was too doped out to notice. But then he was still coughing specks of blood between swallows – though not as much as before. Which Ollie took as a good sign.

'What's happening now?' Lars asked hoarsely after he finished the gross liquid.

'The Olyix are coming,' Adnan said, and handed Lars a pint glass of filtered water. 'But it looks like Alpha Defence are fighting them off.'

'What about the police?'

'Don't sweat it. They don't know where we are.'

'I'm going to kill them.' Lars gulped down the water as if he'd spent days in a desert. When he handed the glass back a small drop of diluted blood trickled out of his mouth. 'Let them come. I'll take those fuckers down to hell with me.'

'I know.' Ollie patted the man's shoulder, feeling the weirdly oversized muscles rippling like serpents under his filthy T-shirt as he pressed in the right place. 'But there's a way out of this.'

'Don't want a way out.'

'Jade's working on it.'

'Fuck Jade.'

'Lars, mate, listen—'

'No. Those bastards killed my friends. They broke the Legion. You're my brothers; you're family to me. I mean it.' A tear started to run down his cheek, heading for the blood.

'You're the greatest, Lars,' Ollie said. 'You just rest there and get better for us, okay?' He had to fight the urge to smack the stupid oaf. Instead he stood there above the settee, watching sleep reclaim Lars. When the big man was wheezing away, he held his hand up to Adnan to show him the sedative pad he'd used.

'Cool,' Adnan said approvingly. Then he frowned and sniffed, leaning forwards over Lars's legs. 'He's pissed himself.' He laughed. 'You should have let him use the loo before you whacked him with the sed. He drank all that water.'

'Gotta keep giving him fluid, he's lost a lot of blood.' Ollie couldn't stop giggling as he watched the dark stain spreading out from Lars's crotch. 'Oh crap, he'll kill us when he wakes up.'

They staggered back into the lounge and collapsed back on the settee in front of the stage. Adaptive foam cushions flowed around them like soft welcoming flesh.

As Adnan accessed the lownet feeds of the conflict in space, familiar sounds drifted in from the hallway. Ollie chortled in delight. 'Aaaaaand again –'

'*With a rebel yell she cried,*' they both chorused, whooping hysterically at how hilarious they were being.

'More,' Claudette's voice demanded on cue from upstairs. 'More.'

Ollie couldn't even see the stage now, his eyes were so full of hysterical tears. Only one thing to do . . . He took another pair of the zero-nark pads from his pocket and handed one to Adnan.

'Cheers, fella, you're the best,' Adnan said, and tapped it to the side of his neck.

'More,' Claudette begged weakly.

It was the most comical thing Ollie had ever heard. He doubled up with laughter. An equally overexcited Adnan batted feebly at him.

'Man, his dick's going to drop off,' Ollie choked out.

'Nah. It's made of plastic. Alien plastic.'

Which triggered Ollie's manic giggling fit. The coloured shapes and lines which zipped about inside the stage were fabulous. His head swayed about as he tried to keep track of them. Every so often, one would expand or grow brighter, which made him croon in appreciation.

'God, is that a habitat?' Adnan asked some time later.

Ollie squinted at the smooth grey cylinder now floating in the middle of the lounge. 'Yeah.'

'They are so pretty. I love that sparkly halo thing around it.'

'Yeah. It's like . . . like they've knitted the milky way into a scarf and wrapped it around. It's cold in space, you know.'

'I do, man. And that is a seriously deep and meaningful metaphor. This is why I like working with you, Ollie. You're smart.'

'I'd like to live in one, you know. Take Gran and Bik with me, away from fucking Copeland Road. I know it's home, but face it: the place is a dump.'

'Sweet idea. Bring them in on your new life deal.'

Some of the graphics bracketing the stage started to make sense, although he had to read them a few times. Ollie squinted at the rest, the ones counting down . . . Oh yeah, distance. He squinted at the stage again, seeing two dark avian shapes closing on the habitat.

'Deliverance ships,' Adnan cooed admiringly. He was leaning forwards now, his gaze fixed on the stage as if he was trying to outstare it. 'That's got to be Stramland. Shit, I hope they finished evacuating it.'

'They're evacuating all the habitats. Government said.'

'So why are the Olyix bothering with them?'

'Not got a fucking clue, mate. Are they going to fire missiles at it, do ya think?' Ollie wondered.

'Oooh, look.'

The indistinct cloud of aquamarine scintillations that surrounded Stramland abruptly began to glow brighter, clearly defining its boundary a kilometre out from the habitat shell.

'Neat,' Ollie said approvingly. The cloud continued to get livelier while its edges became more ragged, as if small flames were trickling out from it.

'That's the shield,' Adnan said. 'All the habitats got them. They stop meteor impacts, see.'

'Cool. You want some more bacon sandwiches?'

'Sure.'

Ollie went into the kitchen. Tye told the food printer what to do. While slim rashers began to peel off the bottom of the chrome-trimmed machine, he cut up the last loaf they'd cooked in the panoforno, frowning in disapproval at how uneven the slices were. But that was okay, he liked thick bread. But the cut on his hand was a big dumb pain.

'This is amazing,' Adnan called from the lounge. 'You've got to see how bright it is now.'

'Coming.' Slapping ten rashers of bacon across the waffle maker, while managing to keep the blood off them. Lower the lid and leave it for two minutes – just long enough for the coffee machine to fill a couple of mugs. It was fiendishly difficult, so Tye managed the selection process for him; that way he didn't have to press all those confusing buttons.

Then the smoke alarm started shrieking, piercingly loud.

'Can you switch that off? Pretty please?' he asked Tye.

The sound stopped. Ollie lifted the waffle maker lid, trying to fan the smoke away. The bacon was very crisp and horribly hot, but he managed to swipe it onto the bread with a spatula.

'You're bleeding,' Adnan pointed out when he carried everything back into the lounge.

'From the heart. For our lost lives.'

'Man, you are so profound when you want to be.'

'Cheers.' They clinked mugs.

'This coffee is weird,' Ollie admitted.

'I think it's hot chocolate.'

'Okay, but I'm sure I ordered coffee. I'll have to check Tye for darkware corruption.'

'Good idea. We gotta keep our security high.'

'Why has the habitat turned into a sun?' He squinted at the

painfully bright cylinder shining away merrily at the centre of the stage. 'Is it on fire?'

'No, it's science. The tech streams say the Deliverance ships are firing beam weapons at it. Really high-powered ones.'

'Looks like it's on fire. Those flames are really big.'

'You don't get flames in a vacuum, my friend. Those are the shield's gas envelope evaporating. The Delivery . . . ance ships are pumping so much energy into the shield it's losing integrity.'

'Cool.'

'No! Not cool. What are you, as dumb as Lars?'

'I am offended. Truly deeply offended.'

'Sorry.'

'You've got to admit it does look cool.'

'Sure, I'll give you that. But it's lethal for the habitat, too.'

'Do you think the habitat shell will pop like a balloon when they kill the shield?'

'Woah, that would be humongously intense!'

Ollie grinned contentedly. 'Only, like, if you're not inside.'

'Challenge that. It's not a bad way to go. Flying off into the universe in a cloud of trees. You'd be at one with nature.'

'Would there be butterflies, too? I love butterflies.'

'Listen, if you want butterflies then you can have butterflies. I'll allow them.'

'Thanks, man. You're the best. Like Lars said: we're friends, but we're like brothers, too.'

'I know.'

'Real brothers, blood ones. Family.'

Stramland's glaring shield shattered as if it was made from a solid material, opalescent fragments expanding as they twirled off into space, their lustre dwindling. Two slick Deliverance ships glided in towards the naked habitat. They curved elegantly through space to attach themselves to the axis dock.

'Oh, not good,' Ollie decided. 'I don't want to emigrate to a habitat any more.'

'They're gonna do that to all the Sol system habitats,' Adnan said. 'Then they'll land here.'

'We need to be gone, out to one of the settled worlds.'

'Jade'll sort it.'

'Yeah. I wonder what sort of score she's setting up?'

'You heard: medicine.'

'Yeah, but what are we going to have to do?' Ollie wondered. 'It was bad enough last time.'

'We win either way.'

'How do you figure that?'

'The raid will either get us killed – in which case nothing matters, cos neither the police or the Olyix will be able to get us if we're dead. Or . . . we come out of it okay, and Jade gets us new identities.'

'Option one's kinda bleak.'

'Quick and painless, innit, though? That's a win in my book.'

'I suppose . . .' Ollie gave the lounge door a guilty glance. 'But you heard what Jade said. The whole fresh identity thing is going to be tough.'

'We can handle tough.'

Ollie surfed closer to him along the settee, the cushions rippling with him as he went. 'We can,' he lowered his voice. 'We're smart enough. So's Tronde.'

'Tronde's fucking scary. I didn't realize how twisted-up pervy-psycho he is inside.'

'Okay, but he can handle working a new identity. Do you really think Lars can?'

'Oh man. Fuck! I hadn't thought of that.'

'I mean, I like him and all. But, Jesus!'

'I like him, too.'

'It takes months – years – to acclimatize properly to the new you; that's what Jade said. You've got to have real discipline for that. I'm not sure . . .'

'Yeah, but what can we do?'

'If he gets caught, it'll wreck it for the rest of us. Lars won't be able to resist any kind of interrogation. Special Branch will know what we're doing and who set it up. They'll find us.' Ollie started searching his pockets for another pad. The thoughts swimming around inside his head were becoming too dark and cold. A little boost of zero-nark would burn them away.

'So what do we do?' Adnan asked in a voice that sounded like a drunk trying to sound sober, all focus and no result.

'I don't know. What do you think we should do?'

'I don't know. We can't, like, you know, just *get rid* of him.'

'No. Right. Can't do that.'

'Good. Wasn't saying we should.'

'Well, me neither.'

'He does need a doctor, though.'

'Yeah. I see that.'

'We can't bring a doctor here.'

'No. No way. But . . .' Ollie sucked his cheeks in. 'Maybe we can get him one, like, *after*.'

'After?'

'After the next job. When we get paid.'

'You mean . . .?'

'I don't think he's up to coming with us, not the way he is.'

'Yeah. You know, thinking about it, you might be right.'

'And he did fuck up last time.'

'Yeah. It's the reason we're here now talking about it, innit?'

'This way we'd be doing what's best for him, too.'

'Right, cos I sure as shit don't want the police to catch me, especially not Special Branch.'

'I've still got to get Gran and Bik out, too. Can't do that from Zagreus.'

'Or the inside of an Olyix ship.'

'Shit, no.'

They both looked at each other. *Knowing*.

'Hi, guys,' Lars slurred from the doorway.

It was only the zero-nark slithering around Ollie's bloodstream that stopped him from yelling in fright. 'Lars! What are you doing up?' He was so unbelievably pleased he hadn't blurted: *How long have you been standing there?*

'I'm really hungry,' Lars moaned.

'I'll get you a bacon sandwich,' Ollie volunteered.

'No, I'll do it,' Adnan said. 'You'll cut yourself again, Ollie. Don't want that. Don't want to spill blood in this house.'

Ollie's jaw dropped dumbly as Adnan walked past him and winked knowingly.

'Hey, you two . . .' Lars said.

'What?' Ollie gasped – a sound that was too guilty in his own ears. Adnan froze, mid-step.

Lars started his dog-like laugh. 'I think I've pissed meself.'

New York

The last time Yuri had slept was back on the Trail Ranger rolling across Nkya's empty landscape – and that was four days ago. Since arriving at the operations centre, he'd been using agnophet to stay awake and alert. He didn't like using for such a long period; the build-up of side effects could be quite brutal. Boris had been splashing blood pressure warnings for six hours now, but Yuri ignored them and all the other symptoms of unease that might be real or might be induced by the nark, concentrating on the job. That was all that mattered. His department was saving the world. And the world would probably never know, and certainly would never thank them. But he didn't care about that, either. *Just get the job done.*

So along with Anne Groell and her team, he shifted assets around, assigned priorities, shut down networks while ignoring civic authorities howling in protest, authorized paramilitary team strikes and raids right across the globe and beyond. Loi took over organizing the mass evacuations from all the Sol habitats, racing to send their residents out to the terraformed worlds before the Deliverance ships arrived. People cooperated eagerly with the Connexion staff in the hubs. Salvaging the associated industrial modules and equipment was more difficult. Not every technician assigned to the task actually hung around to do it – and certainly not after Stramland, when only eighty per cent of the population had got out before the shield failed and the Olyix got in. Which meant Loi had to coordinate with the security G8Turings to sabotage the abandoned manufacturing stations once the Olyix arrived, denying them any facilities – not that he believed they wanted them, but every strikeback helped. So far Loi had achieved a success rate of sixty-three per cent, which Yuri found frustrating. Industrial stations were basically flimsy things once their safeguards were taken offline. But the Olyix certainly seemed to have very high-level digital skills, taking over entire habitat networks as soon as they boarded.

Kohei Yamada's icon splashed across Yuri's tarsus lens, and Boris obediently rotated Yuri's chair so he was facing the archway that opened into the European section. 'What's up, Kohei?'

'Yuri, we've got an anomaly at the King's Cross interstellar hub.'

'Define anomaly.'

'We closed it down as soon as we got your orders. No traffic – commercial or pedestrian. Building to be physically sealed with only our vetted personnel allowed in or out. The portal doors themselves set to zero operational capacity; the entanglement's still there, but there's no physical opening. The manager reported it had all been done, which was verified digitally. But one of the reserve power cells is still feeding power into the hub. Enough to maintain an interstellar cargo portal open at full diameter.'

'Shit. How do you know this?'

'There's a startup data crossfeed between the emergency power cells that supply the hubs at King's Cross and St Pancras. The engineers set it up when they were installing the system, so it's not listed on the standard operational protocols. We got lucky; one of our installation engineers ran a check using her old procedures. She saw a block of cells in the St Pancras reserve were channelling power over the road to King's Cross. And as the cells aren't supplying their designated portal in St Pancras, it didn't show up as active in the monitoring routines.'

'Show me,' Yuri told Boris. One of the big screens in the European section splashed an aerial view of the two ancient railway stations in central London. The huge buildings had been built side by side, with their epic glass roofs at diverging angles. Their original arterial train tracks had long since been taken up, and the land redeveloped as St Martin's Park – an arboreal haven of holm oaks and eucalyptus regnans that towered imperiously over the banks of Regent's Canal.

He remembered them well enough from his time in London, when he'd supervised several security upgrades. The Gothic Revival splendour of St Pancras was Connexion's major trans-European hub, and the interlink between all thirty-two national hub networks sprawling across the continent. While on the other side of the road, the more functional brick Victoriana facade of King's Cross housed a range of interstellar hubs. From the old southern concourse, which used to front the train platforms, you could walk out among the stars themselves. The western side boasted pedestrian portals to Rangvlad, orbiting Beta Hydri; Izumi at Chi Draconis; the four worlds of Trappist 1 that China had terraformed; and New Washington, in its odd elliptical trajectory around Eta Cassiopeiae. On the east side of the building you could walk through portals to the Northern Europe bloc's subtropical world Liberty at 82 Eridani, as well as the ecologically challenging Althea, which lurked in the shadowed safety of a gas giant's Lagrange point out at Pollux. Beyond the passenger area, under the vaulting glass and iron roofs, the commercial portals stood where the platforms used to be, giving truckez a route to and from the terraformed planets. These vehicles came in via a Government and Commercial Services hub that squatted across a transit yard just outside the station's open end – ironically, where the trains used to come in and out.

Right now King's Cross was in complete lockdown. The boundary fence was electrified and patrolled by sentry drones with nerve-block emitters, while guardian drones circled overhead, medium-power lasers firing at any bird that ventured too close in case they were creeperdrones. Down on the ground, the two large Government and Commercial Services portals were inactive, preventing any cargo from even entering the old station. The pedestrian portal to the national hub was also inactive. Even the ground-level glass entrance doors onto the plaza outside were closed and locked. Nobody in, nobody out.

'So what's the situation?' Yuri asked.

'The lockdown followed procedure,' Kohei said. 'As soon as the portals went inactive and the hub was sealed, our people cleared the staff out. There's only a skeleton technical crew, which in reality is two people.'

'Names?'

'Jakil Hanova and Francis Frost.'

Yuri studied their files; both of them had been with Connexion for over thirty years. 'Okay, if they're the ones tapping the reserve power cell, then they're now quint brains wearing human bodies. What sort of security team did you send in at the start of the lockdown?'

'It was a twelve-strong security squad under Anette Courte; three of them are drone and digital techs, the rest are straight paramilitary.'

'When was the last time you heard from them?'

'Courte reported in four hours ago, confirming everything was all right, and the perimeter was secure. We're still getting basic suit telemetry from them, but that's it.'

'Damn. Assume they've been taken out.'

'But . . .'

'Kohei, if there are Olyix agents in King's Cross hijacking an interstellar portal, you can guarantee our team's been neutralized.'

'Yes, boss.'

'Do you know which of the portal doors is still open, and where it leads?'

'No, we've no way of telling. All we can see is the power flow in.'

'Okay. Contact our security chiefs in each of the star systems King's Cross has portal links to. I want a quiet review of those transtellar hubs. Assume they are under hostile control unless proved otherwise.'

'Yes, boss.'

'Can you shut the power off?' Loi asked.

'Yes.'

'Don't,' Yuri said. 'It'll alert them.'

'We can't leave an open portal for the Olyix to reach a terra-formed world,' Loi declared. 'They'll take one of their own portals through and thread up. For all we know, they have them big enough for a Deliverance ship to fly through.'

'Then they've probably done it already,' Yuri told him.

'No, sir, they have not.'

Even the flash of anger at being publically contradicted by a junior was muted. Yuri put it down to a side effect of agnophet, or maybe he was actually starting to appreciate Loi. 'How come?'

'If they'd taken one of their own portal doors through, they wouldn't still be using power from the reserve cell to keep our portal open.'

'Shit. Good point. Kohei?'

'Yes, boss?'

'Prep for an immediate take-down. I want you inside King's Cross within fifteen minutes, full military-grade armour and weapons. The instant we have boots on the ground, cut that bastard emergency power feed – with a smart missile if you have to. I don't know how many of Anette Courte's team are left alive, but everyone you encounter in there is now designated as an enemy alien. Capture where possible, especially Jakil Hanova and Francis Frost. I have people who are very keen to examine a living quint subject. If the firefight gets too extreme, or it looks like Olyix agents are breaking out, you have my authority to exterminate them with maximum force.'

'You got it. Er . . . boss?'

'Yes?'

'There's a buildup of civilians outside King's Cross. They're looking for a way offworld.'

'Queuing to pick up their Darwin award,' Yuri muttered. 'They've been told the interstellar hubs are shut, haven't they?'

'Yes.'

'Too bad martial law won't come in for another couple of hours. Okay, repeat the *stay away* instruction over solnet, but make it part of Connexion's rolling advice on the hub network shutdowns. Let's see if any of these morons act in their own interest.'

'And if they're still there when we go in?'

'We find out how fast they can duck.' From the corner of his eye he saw Loi stiffening, but for once the young man didn't object. Yuri was obscurely sad about that. When someone like Loi ignored his moral compass to favour desperate necessity, you knew you were living in dark times indeed.

'Got it, boss.'

'And, Kohei . . .?'

'Yes?'

'Be prepared for the worst-case situation. I was in a firefight with a covert Olyix operation once.' He gave Loi a bleak smile. 'They use heavy-duty hardware like its going out of fashion. Have your people take care.'

'I'll supervise it myself.'

London

29th June 2204

There were a couple of hundred people milling around on the King's Cross plaza. Kohei Yamada looked at them through twenty different viewpoints as bagez and taxez rolled smoothly along the tree-edged clear route down the centre of Euston Road. Their multiple perspectives were stitched into an imperial panorama by the Security Division's G8Turing, allowing him to see the strained desperation clouding each of their faces. Families with kids, singles, couples, were all unified by their slumped shoulders, swapping fear-magnified gossip as if it was real news, bagez gamely following them like bewildered puppies. Enterprising owners of fast-food stalls had set up at the York Way end of the plaza, charging extortionate prices for burgers and noodles that inflated hourly – cryptoken payment only. Underfoot, the marble slabs were littered with ketchup-smeared wrappers spilling mushy fried onion rings for pigeons that hadn't been scorched by lasers from the overhead drones.

Kohei cursed the would-be refugees for their bovine stupidity. Every one of them – rich or poor, young or old – had fixated on the idea that the terraformed worlds offered sanctuary from the approaching Deliverance ships. No official announcement could shake that faith. They'd tried Yuri's idea, reissuing Connexion's statement about the interstellar hub shutdown, but no one had left.

'In position,' Charlie Volk confirmed.

Kohei's tactical splash confirmed Volk's thirty-strong assault force had reached their forward deploy locations: twenty of them spread out along St Martin's Park, using the big trees as cover, while the remaining ten were up on the rooftops of Euston Road and York Way. And for once Kohei was grateful that solnet was so badly glitched today, making it much harder for anyone inside King's Cross to obtain coherent data feeds. The preparation phase, with everyone sliding unobtrusively into place, should have gone un-noticed.

He hoped the same was true for the Liberty hub. The Connexion Security office on the terraformed planet orbiting 82 Eridani hadn't taken long to establish that Olyix agents had seized the interstellar hub at their end. Now a tactical team was quietly moving into place around the main arrivals hall at the heart of the new world's capital city. The recovery attacks would be launched simultaneously.

'We're ready,' he told Yuri.

'The team on Liberty is in place,' Yuri replied. 'They'll go active simultaneously with you.'

'Okay. I'm giving the go code for thirty seconds.' If there was one thing Kohei had learned when he was Yuri's assistant back in Australia, it was *Don't hesitate*. Not in active missions. Hesitation gave the opposition time. And in combat situations, time was the greatest currency of all.

Thirty seconds was long enough to review the full tactical splash, confirm the systems were all online, the drones were functional, the support crew in the Greenwich command centre were prepared, the specialist tech enforcement operators were embedded along the buildings in York Way, and that Volk's people were powered up. So Kohei just let the tactical display timer run down. There was no advantage to him yelling *Go* at everyone over the comms. He'd always hated that in the long-distant days when he was serving his time on the sharp edge. That kind of hands-on authority was nothing but a concession to the mission commander's ego.

Two seconds left on the countdown. The assault force powered up the microjets of their combat armour.

The countdown reached zero. Greenwich cut the power from the emergency backup cell feeding the portal door out to Liberty. Denial drones hovering below the rooftops on Pentonville Road and Albion Yard went vertical and started to accelerate hard. The enforcement teams had installed masers along the street's roofline which targeted the King's Cross guard drones, puncturing their casings and incinerating their engineering guts in single blasts of energy.

Assault mission plus one second: The denial drones crossed the established threshold and metapulsed the entire King's Cross ground footprint – an electromagnetic overload that fried any unprotected electronics and created massive eddy surges in the interstellar hub's power cables, blowing every chunk of equipment they were connected to. Even the metal girders supporting the ancient plat-form roofs and the newer western concourse suffered a huge current induction, spitting out slivers of static that clawed at the glass.

Assault mission plus two seconds: A squadron of urban counter-insurgency drones rose from the fake taxez and deliverez rolling along the roads outside the hub. Their railgun scatter-kinetics punched into the pair of massive arched windows above the plaza, shattering the glass into a cascade of crystalline shards that poured down onto the floor.

Forty of them streaked through the jagged openings, aggressor software scanning urgently for targets.

In St Martin's Park, the twenty armour-suited figures of Volk's assault force soared into the air with a protective escort of thirty fighter drones. They streaked over the hub's Commercial and Government Services yard before swooping low to fly in under the twin canopies of the roof.

Assault mission plus three seconds: The despondent, stressed refugees occupying the plaza cowered from the railgun assault on the windows above, arms raised in Neanderthal instinct to ward off a threat. Cowering which turned into full-scale fright as the deluge of perilous glass fragments plummeted out of the air, accompanied by the smoking wreckage of guardian drones that crashed down amid them. They sprinted away fast, doubled over and frantic. The youngest children were picked up, while older kids had their hands half-crushed so they could be best dragged along, screaming and terrified, fighting to stay upright and keep up with taller faster parents.

It was Kohei who winced at their pitiful rout. Right by the entrance doors where glass shards formed treacherous mounds of crystalline spoil, he counted five bodies lying inertly on the marble, trickles of blood leaking away. In the middle of the plaza, one guardian drone had fallen directly on top of a woman, crushing her into pulped meat, no longer recognizably human. A man was on his knees beside her, hands ripping at his hair, mouth opening for a scream that was never going to end.

Kohei did nothing, because to micromanage the paramedic response would be to take his concentration off the assault. And as a proper commander trained by Yuri, he'd already designated one of his staff as civilian medical aide.

No, focus back on the interstellar hub and the Olyix operatives who had subverted it. The place where he could do the greater good. *And is that going to be our gospel from now on?*

Assault mission plus ten seconds: Surprisingly, the only resistance Charlie Volk's force had encountered was from guard drones that had survived the metapulse. But they were no match for the invading team, whose fighter drones took them out with short hyperkinetic barrages from railguns. The armour suits flew fast down the length of the old platforms as Kohei asked: 'What the hell is that?'

Just inside the open end of the station, several logistics company vanez were parked in a semicircle, their cargo doors open. They formed a picket around some kind of machine that was under construction – a weird cluster of dark metal struts, the cybernetic ribs of some fantastical creature over three metres tall, surrounded by spherical robots of various sizes. The metapulse had obviously killed it. Tendrils of smoke were rising up from the structure, while several of the robots were rolling aimlessly across the ground after falling off its top.

'Good question,' Yuri said. 'But at least it looks as if they hadn't finished building it.'

Six of the assault team landed in front of the five-metre-diameter portal door used to transfer commercial cargo to Liberty, now a black inert slab. A couple of techdrones landed beside them and clamped themselves to the sensor pods covering the portal.

'Should extract some data for you in a minute,' Kohei told Yuri. 'Those sensors have an internal power backup, good for five weeks. If something went through to Liberty, they'll have recorded it.'

'Good work, but it looks like you were in time. I'm sending over a forensic team to look at that machine they were building.'

'I hope they know their physics. I don't think it's going to be anything as simple as a good old-fashioned bomb.'

'Found one,' Charlie Volk called. He landed further down the platform, next to a figure in a Connexion light-armour suit, who was lying on the ground. The visor was open. Charlie leant in, scanning the exposed face. 'Ozil Reus,' he said. 'I know him.' The armour's transponder tag wasn't responding to Volk's interrogation.

'Is he alive?' Kohei asked.

'Not getting any medical telemetry from the suit, but he's definitely breathing.'

Scarlet icons splashed up, grade-one toxicity alerts. 'Shit,' Kohei grunted. 'Charlie, the drone sensors are picking up an aerosol organophosphate in there. Nerve agent of some kind. We don't have the specific molecular structure on record, but it's a complex one.'

'Great,' Volk said. 'Alien nerve gas.'

'Keep reviewing your suit integrity, people.'

'You got a definite roger on that.'

Fighter drones reached the row of pedestrian portals and began to fan out. They smashed the office windows along the eastern side of the building and glided in through the holes. Sensors detected a much higher concentration of the aerosol inside the rooms and corridors, so Volk kept his team back, hovering in the air outside, while the drones ran sweeps for the rest of Anette Courte's missing squad.

Their positions started to appear across Kohei's tactical map, dispersed throughout the huge hub building. All of them were unconscious, sprawled where they'd succumbed to the nerve agent, armour suits inactive. That worried him; the suits should have been resistant to any kind of aerosol.

Volk himself flew into the hub's management centre. Emergency lighting bleached the whole place in a stark green-white hue, revealing a line of old desks with worn screens and consoles. Jakil Hanova and Francis Frost were slumped in their seats, comatose and unresponsive. Volk landed beside them, with two of his team on guard and five fighter drones slowly patrolling around the room, watching the three entrances.

Kohei squinted at the image splash from Volk's suit. It was singularly useless, so he got his altme to zoom in. 'Is that actually Frost?' he asked uncertainly. The facial features were similar, but . . . enlarged? Kohei couldn't quite make out what was wrong. Maybe the cheeks were swollen; they certainly seemed to have some kind of curving ridge around the bottom of the eye sockets. Both eyes were closed, though Frost had been crying. Kohei could make out thick fluid trails. He frowned. 'No eyelashes. Is that a fashion thing?'

'You're asking the wrong guy, chief,' Volk told him.

Kohei watched Volk's gauntlet reach out and lift an eyelid. 'Holy fuck!'

Frost had no eyeball.

Kohei's abdominal muscles clenched, fighting the gag reflex. 'Check the other one,' he said.

Volk gingerly did as requested. Both Frost's eye sockets were empty.

'That is one bastard of a nerve agent,' Kohei said. 'Why the hell would you want one that melts eyes?'

'If you can't see, you can't fight back?' Volk suggested.

'I don't think the nerve agent did that,' Yuri said. 'Volk, would you check Frost's chest and legs, please?'

'Yes, sir.'

Kohei watched keenly as Volk opened the shirt, which was when he realized how taut the fabric was over the man's flesh. Again, like the face, there was something subtly wrong with the torso. It was the proportions that weren't quite right, Kohei decided; Frost's waist was as broad as his shoulders, yet there was no middle-aged flab.

Then Volk extended a small activeblade from his gauntlet and cut the trouser fabric.

'How the hell did he walk on those?' Kohei asked in surprise. Frost's legs were anorexic, all skin and bone with no real flesh.

'Let's see the arms,' Yuri said.

They were the same. Withered limbs whose skin had contracted to wrap tight around the bone, leaving a lacework of veins bulging along the surface.

'I was very clear,' Yuri said. 'No one with any Kcell implants was to be allowed into a Connexion facility! Why was Frost assigned to King's Cross for an active deployment?'

'There is no record of him having any Kcell procedures,' Kohei said. 'And he was deep scanned before he was sent out with Courte.' Part of him wanted to kick back against Yuri's accusation of incompetence, while part of him was worried. 'Is this why you issued the warning about Kcells?'

'Yes. According to my source, they're an integral part of the Olyix elevation programme. They're a specific cancer, formatted to transform a human body into a biological life support for the brain.'

'But . . . technically that's what the human body is anyway.' And Kohei also badly wanted to ask: *What source?* But if anyone had a source inside an alien species, it would be Yuri Alster.

'Think of this as the budget version,' Yuri said. 'It'll keep your soul intact until the end of time, ready for when the Olyix God comes out to play.'

'Fuck.'

'Yes, I know, it's—'

'No. Boss, the drones have picked up an infra-red source. It's moving. Two sources. Three! Human size and matching thermal emission. They're in the western concourse annex.' As he spoke, he watched the image which a counter-insurgency drone had picked up through a second-floor window. It showed him three figures fleeing through the building – then they vanished into an internal stairwell.

'Get them alive for me!' Yuri said. 'Full priority.'

'We're on it. Volk?'

'Engaging now.'

The annex was a brick building which pre-dated the geodesic cavern of the western concourse – an old railway hotel that had been converted into offices and a nightclub, with a restaurant and bar fronting the plaza side. Two fighter drones smashed the doors apart to enter. They slowed immediately. They were built to operate in open air, but the corridors they found themselves navigating through were narrow, restricting speed and manoeuvrability. Each of them deployed a swarm of sparrow-sized subdrones, weaponless but equipped with plenty of sensors. They slipped through the building's convoluted layout without trouble, heading to the point where the three fugitives had been detected.

Four of Volk's team landed seconds behind the drones and ran in, gaining ground on the struggling fighter drones. Another fifteen drones encircled the building, muzzles of magrifles, masers and nerve-block generators tracking back and forth across the wall and windows.

'Where the hell do they think they're going?' Kohei asked out loud. 'That building is detached. The only way out is through the doors.'

Volk himself was closing fast on the annex, swooping low through the archways that separated the western concourse from the rest of the old station building. The windows of the annex blew out, flinging glass across the concourse floor and the plaza outside, followed by horizontal pillars of smoke and dust. Inside, the intense blast pressure wave sent drones slamming into walls as furniture disintegrated around them. Kohei saw the whole building shake. A wide section of roof buckled, then slowly bowed downwards, forming an irregular crater. Dust surged up into the sky.

'What the bloody hell was that?' Kohei demanded. 'Did they suicide?' He was getting some telemetry from the four team members who'd gone inside the building; they were alive. Two were under piles of rubble from collapsed walls, but their armour was strong enough to push it aside, allowing them to free themselves.

Dust and smoke was clogging the air, restricting the sensors on the other suits, and the drones were struggling to orientate.

'I'm on it,' Volk said. The blast had punched him several metres through the air to crash into the station wall, but now he was flying forwards again. Plenty of panels in the geodesic canopy had blown out. He zipped through one into the open and overflew the annex's ruined roof section. Sensors probed down through the bellicose dust.

Kohei watched the radar image build. 'That hole goes down below ground level,' he exclaimed in surprise. Three urban counter-insurgency drones dropped down into the chasm, twisting around broken structural beams and shattered floors. Subdrones streamed out of their silos, forming thin murmurations that slithered through the narrow gaps of the lower floor.

'What the hell?' Kohei grunted. The explosion had fractured the concrete foundation of the annex, leaving a rough crack into some kind of cavity below. The gap was just big enough for a human to wriggle through. Subdrones shot into it and spread out, pushing through the thick dust that veiled all the visual sensors. They found a broad corridor which opened into a large vestibule, where the dust thinned out to reveal tiled walls and floor covered in grime and cobwebs. A row of turnstiles, metal corroded by age and moisture, stood silent guard across the top of escalators that dived down into absolute darkness.

'I know what this place is,' Yuri said. 'It's the old tube station. London had underground trains before Connexion's metrohubs were established. They sealed it all off over a century back.'

'Picking up infra-red,' Kohei said. The subdrones had found footprints on one of the lifeless escalators, a faint thermal glimmer amid dislodged dirt. 'Volk, get after them.'

'On it.'

Volk and two of his team dropped vertically down the shaft which the explosion had blown through the annex. Two smart missiles pulverized the fissure in the concrete foundations, widening it. Kohei winced as the missiles triggered another avalanche of debris, but Volk and his team were through before it tumbled down around them.

They flew down the corridor and into the hallway, jet exhausts kicking up a flurry of dirt that'd lain undisturbed for over a hundred years. Two urban counter-insurgency drones took up point duty, and together they soared down the escalators.

The infra-red signature split at the bottom, one set of footprints heading left down a long corridor, the other two tracking forwards to the next set of escalators. Volk took the left-hand trail, and the other two armour suits went straight on. Subdrones raced ahead. They finally caught sight of the two Olyix agents at the bottom of the escalators. Powerful energy beams stabbed up, slashing at the subdrones. Kohei's squad members reached the top of the escalators and opened up a barrage of railgun kinetics. The bottom third of the escalators and the floor beyond disintegrated in a furious maelstrom of splinters and dirt. Both suits dropped in freefall then curved around to chase their targets.

Something came spinning out of the grey swamp of shards towards them – a web of dark strands, twisting like a bolo throw. It sang a single soprano note, the climatic end to a death chant. Maser beams slashed at it from both suits. Strands were sliced apart . . . but kept coming. They splattered down on the suits. Sticking.

Integrity alerts from their suits splashed across Kohei's vision, flaring straight into crimson. The strand fragments were cutting or burning or drilling through the cremetal armour as if it was plastic. Urban counter-insurgency drones came flying in fast under G8-Turing control, targeting the suits with wide-beam masers, trying to scramble the molecular structure of whatever made up the active component of the strands. Kohei watched in horror as the strands kept burrowing inwards. Then the screams started, flooding the communication channels. He didn't turn them off, or down. Penance.

'Volk, stay back from your target,' Kohei ordered. 'Your suit can't take that stuff.'

'Motherfucker!'

A fighter drone swept past the doomed thrashing figures and fired eight smart missiles. They pirouetted around corners and angled fast down staircases, chasing the weak infra-red traces on the floor like visual bloodhounds. Sensors caught three more of the web-things whirling out of the darkness, their lethal aria reverberating off the confined walls. The lead missile detonated, focusing the blast forwards. The explosion pulverized the webs, hurling the lethal strand fragments into the ancient tiles of the corridor walls and ceiling, clearing a route for the remaining missiles.

Out they streaked onto the platform, roaring over the carpet of rat shit. A stream ran sluggishly over the tracks, greasy water almost invisible below a crust of putrid decaying trash washed up from previous centuries. Most of it seemed to be an undulation of slick wet fur as big rats scurried frantically for the tunnel mouths, alarmed by the abrupt violation of their domain.

The Olyix agents were running in opposite directions, skidding about on the disgusting surface. The last Kohei saw of them was their outlines expanding fast as the missile exhaust went turbo and streaked in for the kill.

Volk flew down an escalator. His speed was slower now, sensors alert for the lethal web-things. A trail of infra-red streaks glimmered on the ground, leading deeper into the abandoned maze of tunnels and stairs and shafts. The G8Turing reformed the subdrone formation ahead of him, creating an airborne shield. It was needed.

Twice the gossamer ghoul webs came shrieking towards him. Twice the subdrones clumped into a tight shoal, allowing the web to catch them instead of Volk. Each time it snapped shut like jaws clamping down on prey, quickly butchering the metallic flock it constricted around. Sparks spat out as the strands cut effortlessly through the casing of the little machines, then fan engines failed and the whole glowing, disintegrating mass dropped out of the air to seethe and shimmer its way into the floor tiles.

The last of the subdrones zipped out into a gently curving platform. At the far end, a figure jumped down into the rat-infested water covering the tracks. She disappeared into the tunnel. The subdrone sensors focused on a small circular device fixed to a London Underground map halfway along the platform wall. Its magnetic field was implausibly strong.

'What's—'

The explosion obliterated the subdrone. A hundred metres

behind, and around two corners, the blast knocked Volk onto his arse. The whole corridor shook as a deluge of dust and shattered tiles splattered down all around him.

'Christ,' Kohei shouted. 'What is that explosive they've got?'

'I don't know,' Volk said drily, 'but I wish we had it.' He walked forwards cautiously until he reached the top of the stairs that led down to the platform. It was full of rubble.

'Do you think she's still alive?' Kohei mused.

'Most likely. They knew what they were doing. But . . . She?'

'I think so. The G8 is cleaning the image. Hang on.' Kohei waited while the G8Turing prepared the fuzzy infra-red image, enhancement algorithms refining the face that had turned so briefly towards the subdrone. A sharp monochrome image was sent to the Sol citizenship archive for identification.

Two seconds later her identity splashed across Kohei's tarsus lens, but it had been supplied by the London Metropolitan Police, organized crime division. 'Jade Urchall,' he read. 'Well, congratulations, Jade, you are now officially the number one enemy of the human race.'

Vayan

I have finished watching, for now I behold what I have waited for all these long centuries.

The Olyix are coming. Oh yes.

I activate my compressed systems.

All of them.

My metamorphosis begins. I will no longer be defined as a numbered level, a mere subset of something greater.

First to decompress are the nul-quantum patterns. They hang in space, phantom sketches of nucleonic machinery, lacking even the density of the vacuum which supports them, stretching out from my core as if I possess the wings of an angel.

Thought routines issue forth from my mentalic vault, enhancing my mind. What I do now will not only be precise, but it will have a purpose that was absent before. I have regained the righteousness that was my human soul.

Metaviral spawn begin to digest and process the icy planetoid upon which I sit. Gusts of atoms flow into the nul-quantum patterns, and the faint images gracefully acquire solidity. With that cohesion comes function. Many functions.

Converter nodules transform mass directly into energy. I possess enough power now to reach into the cleverly fashioned nowhere folds of spacetime. Enough to transfer the armoury of complex and utterly lethal ultradense mechanisms out into the real. They retain their integrity during and after the process. If I still had lungs I would let out a breath of relief. Ultradense matter is, by its nature, supremely volatile. The suspension structure I hold them in will require constant power to maintain their stability.

I am made from confluence. Human, of course, is my original essence and continues to drive my resolve. The technology that gives me physical form has come from many sources: bold Human, quiet scheming Neána, aloof Creator, dangerous powerful Angelis. All of their finest offerings coming together in a potent melange that will never be repeated.

I do not have the knowledge or ability to manufacture or replace my component parts. I suspect that is the Neána influence upon my composition.

For one brief beautiful century, all were allied. Together this coalition built The Factory – a synergy that produced hope, that produced me.

I may be alone. There may be a million of me infesting the galaxy. I do not know.

It is the Neána way.

I was born to challenge the supremacy of the Olyix. To destroy their ships and their enclave and eradicate their treachery from the galaxy. I am the most formidable weapon The Factory alliance could envisage, combining the vengeance which lurks at the heart of each valiant species.

A century of effort, unity and peace.

It ended the way it always would as the flaws of the living deepened in proximity to the other. Bitterness, lies and mistrust brought it to dissolution.

The Neána fading back into the darkness.

The Angelis war fleet flying onwards to another galaxy where they could be free.

Rebel humans embarking on the Creator mothership, defiantly striking out to establish a sanctuary.

Generation ship humans scattering in silence amid the myriad stars, quickly and angrily terraforming then abandoning planets in their wake.

Folly. But I forgive them all, for without them I would not exist.

I am whole. My null-quantum patterns replete, their birthed nucleonic structures active. Weapons withdrawn from the nowhere, armed and ready. Mind fully cognizant, remembering all I was, all I have had taken from me. Drive units energized.

My perception fronds reveal the entire Vayan star system to me.

I watch, proud as any father, as the humans of the *Morgan* prepare to do battle with the indomitable foe.

I launch myself into space.

Do the devout Olyix scream as they are rent asunder? Will they weep as their god-bestowed dream burns to radioactive ash around them?

Oh, how I am going to love finding out.

*

The development chamber always made Dellian think of a medical clinic. He didn't know why; its purpose was never healing. Perhaps it was the cleanliness. Walls and floor and ceiling were all the same opalescent material, flowing together to provide an infinite perspective. Human eyes could never work out how big the space was; all the surfaces were so flawless there was nothing to focus on.

Bizarrely, the impression of unlimited space made him feel mildly claustrophobic. The only break in the uniformity of the glowing chamber was provided by the apparatus in the middle of the floor – three grey initiator cubes and a versatile integration gantry.

Yirella stood beside it, her lips lifted in a small expectant smile. 'Well? What do you think?'

He approached cautiously, staring down intently at the armour suit in the centre of the gantry, held in place by spindly robot arms. Its surface had the same black crocodile-hide texture as his own armour. Different anatomy, of course: this suit was for a Vayan body. The design team Yirella headed had given the four legs and eight arms plenty of flexibility, enhanced with artificial muscle. There was no backpack – understandable given the Vayan didn't technically have a back. Instead ancillary equipment and small zero-gee thrusters had been wrapped around the middle of the Vayan's two main body sections, creating a ring halfway up what passed for its torso. However, it was the top part of the suit which caused Dellian to frown in disapproval. Instead of giving it a helmet atop a necessarily long neck segment, a fat cylinder protruded upwards, crowned by a sensor band. It didn't even have the same tractability as the limbs. In his opinion, a serious mistake. A Vayan neck was very elastic, allowing it to bend in every direction.

'The neck—' Dellian began.

'Yeah, I know. It's counterintuitive. But we were worried about how much force Fintox might be subjected to on the mission. Even a Vayan neck can break if it's twisted far enough, so we gave it plenty of protection. They can look in every direction at once, and the visual sensors have a decent zoom function, so keeping it rigid doesn't matter.'

'Okay.'

She shot him a shrewd glance. 'Trust me. Listen, Fintox is going with you to do one job. He's not got combat duties; he's cargo. This will protect him so you can get him into position.'

'Not arguing.' He walked right up to the suit, examining it closely now. 'Where's the interface?'

She bent down and tapped a circular iris on the top of the neck cylinder. 'It goes here. Fintox is bringing it. That's why I called you.'

'Can we make one now?' he asked.

'The biologic initiator they used to build it can replicate as many as we want. But—'

'It connects directly to a Neána brain. And even if we could adapt it for human use, we don't have the neurovirus.'

'Quite. Like a starship without a drive unit.'

'But having a tool that can interface with Olyix nerve structures must give us a better idea about the principles involved in coding a neurovirus, right?'

'Maybe. Just don't expect me to derive them instantly.'

'Humans must have worked on the idea in the past.'

'Sure. The *Morgan* has whole archives full of research data. A couple of centuries ago, on Juloss, they even built some prototype brain–genten interface units. The volunteers who got the implant were impressed by how well they worked. Coding analogue routines that a genten could interpret was the most difficult part. Everyone's thoughts are different and unique, so every interface has to run customized routines. Once they got that right, the test subjects could receive sensory signals they understood and communicate directly with the gentens.'

'Sounds just like a databud.'

She grinned. 'So not like a databud, Del. Really truly not. A direct neural interface allows you to incorporate genten processing and memory storage into your own mind. The ultimate boost.'

'I could do with being smarter.'

A section of the wall irised open and Fintox walked in, accompanied by Ellici. Dellian knew it was Fintox because the identity icon was right there in his optik, but he liked to think he could tell the metavayans apart anyway. There were tiny physical differences – or maybe he was just convincing himself for virtue's sake. He still couldn't decide if they counted as real living entities or not; after all, they had been manufactured. Yirella argued there was no difference between human conception and gestation, and being formed in a biologic initiator. The end result was all that counted, she said. Living tissue containing a sentient mind.

Fintox began his high-pitched warbling, fast even for him. Dellian interpreted that as excitement, or as close as a metavayan could get. Yirella and her lure committee hadn't assigned Vayans the same emotional range as humans, and the insertion ship had copied that faithfully. But maybe the metavayans were now absorbing and utilizing human traits.

'We have finished,' Dellian's databud translated. 'I believe this version of the interface will be successful.'

'Congratulations,' Yirella said.

'The initial bugs have been solved. I believe I can achieve a direct link to an arkship onemind.'

'Do the Olyix upgrade the design of their ships much?' Dellian asked. Which earned him an accusatory glance from both Yirella and Ellici.

'I do not believe so,' Fintox said. 'Some of the arkship hardware may have changed and improved since my cluster left our home star, but the cellular composition of an Olyix neural network remains the same. I studied the report on the ship humans found at Nkya. There was no variance.'

'That was ten thousand years ago,' Dellian said.

Yirella put her hands on her hips to stare warningly at him.

'Ten thousand standard spacetime years,' Fintox said. 'In the Olyix enclave, little time will have passed. Modification to their primary biology will be slow in appearing. They claimed to have reached their physical peak aeons ago. Nor do their minds change.'

'Good to know.'

The metavayan stepped up to his armour and took a small mushroom-shaped device out of a case. It was delicately inserted into the iris on top of the suit.

'The suit systems are incorporating the interface into their architecture . . .' Yirella said. 'There we go. It's functional.'

'I am pleased,' Fintox said.

'Me too,' Dellian told him. 'And thank you again for agreeing to do this.'

'You are welcome. We came here to help thwart the Olyix. None of us ever expected to have an opportunity at this level.'

A whole range of smartarse replies played across Dellian's thoughts, but he resisted. After all, Fintox hadn't hesitated when Yirella asked, and he knew just how risky the mission was going to be.

'Del will get you safely into the arkship,' Yirella said. 'You can rely on him.'

'I have reviewed your insertion tactical plan and agree with it,' Fintox said.

'So glad to hear that,' Dellian replied.

Yirella gave him *that* warning glance. 'Do you think you'll be able to extract the information from the onemind? Saint Jessika always maintained that interfacing with a onemind was difficult.'

'Attempting to use our neurovirus to take over an entire arkship onemind would be a foolish venture,' Fintox said. 'It would invariably detect such an attempt and move to block it. I will simply endeavour to ease my consciousness into the flow of the onemind's cortical impulses. That way I will be able to read its memories. Once there I will introduce an association pattern which will summon up its memory of the gateway location. My intervention will be so small it will not even be aware it is reviewing the stellar coordinate.'

'Sounds easy,' Dellian said.

'It is not,' Fintox said. 'You must be prepared to accept failure at this point.'

'Thanks, I'll remember that.'

'Once I have extracted the location, and if conditions are right, I will then target the neuralvirus into the onemind's nexuses, which should disrupt and confuse the impulse flows. The equivalent of throwing sand in its eyes. Which should make your assault easier.'

'Thank you,' Yirella said. 'But don't endanger yourself. The gateway location is the goal here.'

'Yeah,' Dellian said. 'So once we're inside the arkship, all I have to do is get you to a nexus in the neuralstratum. Another easy.'

'That is irony?' Fintox said.

'That is irony,' Dellian confirmed. 'About as big as it gets.'

'I have confidence in your squad's ability, Dellian. You will deliver me to a suitable nexus, I am sure of it.'

'We'll know a lot more about the arkship's internal layout once the assault starts and we get our sensors in close,' Ellici said. 'When we have that, Motaxan can advise us on the location Del needs to get you to.'

Dellian found that part even more surprising than Fintox volunteering to load the neurovirus. Of course, it made perfect sense. Once sensors and drones had built up a reasonable knowledge of the approaching arkship, Motaxan, the female metavayan, could determine the probable location of the neural seams woven through the massive vessel, and from that where the nexuses would be positioned.

But having a metavayan in the squad's tactical centre along with Tilliana and Ellici just didn't sit well with Dellian. Yirella had told him not to be so silly. 'She's essential to make this work. And, anyway, you're the one who offered to escort Fintox. You started this.'

There was nothing he could say to that.

'You have two hours until the Strike begins,' Yirella said. 'Fintox, I'd like to get you in the suit and give it a final test run.'

'That is a good idea,' Fintox replied. 'I am sure you have done an excellent job.'

The suit split open and Ellici started to help the metavayan into it. Yirella came over to Dellian. She bent down so that her face was level with his, hands resting on his shoulders. 'I love you,' she said. 'Come back.'

He closed his eyes and rubbed his nose against hers, that brief fond contact providing him the perfect memory to carry with him. 'The Saints themselves couldn't stop me from coming back to you.'

*

Two hours later, Yirella was in the subtropical heat of the Bennu habitat torus, looking up through the massive transparent roof. The sunstrip had been turned off, allowing her to see out into the cryo-planet's central cavity – a sight which her optik was supplementing with a virtual enhancement. So now the soft indigo candle flames in the distance were clearly manoeuvring thrusters, and dark ships slid through the interior like sharks in an aquarium.

There were only a dozen humans left in Bennu, and she was the sole binary among them. The joke was they were all support staff to the support staff. They were the ones who kept a watchful eye on the sensors scattered across the Vayan star system, alert for anything, from an ambush to a doomsday machine materializing out of stealth mode. They also made sure Vayan itself kept running smoothly, maintaining the radio and TV signals right to the bitter end. The other half were in charge of Strike portal placement, including the flood operation. It could have been handled from the *Morgan*, but Kenelm preferred to keep control of the flood systems closer to home. And then there was Yirella, who had nothing to do whatsoever. The lure she'd invested so much of herself in was complete, the trap sprung . . .

Team mascot, the squad called her, until she threatened to brain the next one who said it.

Outside, an electric-blue dawn began to rise in the almighty cavern. The first batch of variable portals were opening and enlarging, two hundred of them, their annular nest of glowing exotic strands expanding smoothly to produce a fifty-metre aperture. Flood mine portals flashed through, half of them flung out into space ahead of the approaching arkship while their twins dropped into the upper atmosphere of Sasras, the star's lone gas giant. Then the genten-controlled attack cruisers lined up in front of their own variable portals. The big warships eased through quickly and easily, emerging several AUs away from the flood mines. Finally it was the *Morgan's* turn. Yirella focused on the starship's fifth globe, where the troop carriers were clinging to their support struts. Dellian was in one of them, snug and safe in his armour, probably cracking dumb jokes with the squad, hiding his concern at having Fintox along. His combat core cohort would be arrayed around him, bound by the vestiges of the love that had grown between a boy and his muncs, outweighing any coded loyalty routine.

'I remember,' she sang.

> *I remember dancing in the starlit dark*
> *the day before you stole my heart.*
> *I remember our golden Earth,*
> *the home we will regain.*
> *I remember our dreams forlorn*
> *before the Saints brought us hope reborn.*
> *I remember the stars gone cold*
> *and still our love will hold.*

She smiled at the memory of those wonderful devoted muncs, dimmed now by time like the childhood they filled. 'Look after him,' she whispered to them as moisture filled her eyes.

The *Morgan's* portal yawned open, an azure reality-defying halo two kilometres across. It swallowed the starship whole.

Kruse Station

29th June 2204

Alik was not pleased to be back at Kruse Station. He'd spent the last three exhausting days in D.C., chugging agnophet like beer at a frat party and shifting between executive staff briefings, private globalPAC meetings and the Pentagon's SituationOne Bunker deep below the capital. The level of sabotage against America's city shields had delivered a massive blow to the credibility of every Washington security agency. They'd spent the last century successfully suppressing urban dissent and foreign insurgency until their arrogant assumption of invincibility had led to a toxic complacency. So now when it came down to it, they'd been caught with their asses hanging in the breeze, seriously unknowing and unprepared.

Police and state Bureau offices had been mobilized within hours, but they'd soon needed to call in heavy-duty backup from every special ops team on the Pentagon register. The National Guard had also been mobilized, but not to help beat the hell out of the saboteurs. Rural voters spread out across what used to be the farm belt didn't appreciate government telling them to get into the nearest city, where the newly deployed and seriously underprepared National Guard regiments would issue them with some crappy camp bed in a commandeered building. Plenty told government to go screw itself – until the Deliverance ships began breaking through habitat shields. Then the surge came. By that time, Connexion had shut down a good eighty-five per cent of the North American hub network. The hold-outs had a long journey to working interstate hubs in an age when ground vehicles were mainly found in museums. And the sabotage which had clearly been years in the planning kept ramping up. He still wasn't sure if Portland, Dallas, Chicago and Atlanta were going to have their shields operational by the time the Deliverance ships arrived.

That was something Alik just couldn't get his head around. Why, when it was utterly obvious the attacks were part of an alien invasion, did the douchebags that'd been recruited carry on with them? Didn't they get they were helping the enemy of humanity? Thankfully the people he was dealing with on the Hill held the same opinion. The security teams were ordered to use maximum force to stop any further sabotage. They applied it eagerly.

To start with, the good news was that New Washington and the Eta Cassiopeiae habitats were largely unaffected by sabotage. But pretty soon that raised the prospect of refugees, and the allcomments was up its own ass as usual, talking about resettling the entire United States population there. After all, our taxes paid for the terraforming. It's ours.

It didn't help that the Secret Service was keen to relocate POTUS to her designated emergency residence on New Washington – one of the first government facts to leak. She had to appear (briefly) on the White House balcony to reassure people she hadn't turned tail and run. Senior congressional and senate members meanwhile quietly and gratefully took up their emergency locations scattered around the Eta Cassiopeiae system.

Emilja Jurich smiled wanly at Alik over the table. 'How's it going?'

He sat down hard in a chair opposite her, and scowled at the vase of bright tangerine roses blocking the full line of sight between them. 'Basically, it's a shitstorm without end. Too many of our boony folk think they're true survivalists and this is the glorious moment they've been waiting for all their lives; it's going to be a heroic gunfight where their hunting lasers and grenade launchers will save the day. Then there's all the naturevists who reject city life and aren't going to go live under a shield no matter what. Half the evangelicals think elevation is actually the Rapture, while the other half think the *Salvation of Life* is hell itself falling out of the sky and the devil is sitting on his throne inside. Either way, neither side is leaving the cult compound. Then there's a whole bunch of radical assholes claiming it's all a supremacist plot to turn the cities into concentration camps for every underclass victim of capitalism, and once the poor are inside they'll never get out again. You know what? I have no fucking idea why the Olyix think we are worth elevating in the first place. But sure as corporate sewers always dump into drinking water reservoirs, we aren't going to get everyone to safety in time. Not even close.'

'My sympathies.'

'Don't waste your breath. You can't help the terminally stupid. If people hate government so much they don't listen to official advice, they can't expect government to bend over backwards to help them.'

'But we pay our taxes,' Ainsley said in acidic mockery. 'We're entitled to government help.'

'*You* pay taxes?' Emilja asked lightly.

Ainsley III's hand came down in gentle warning on Ainsley's arm as he bristled from the jibe. The richest man who'd ever lived gave his grandson an angry glare and sulked back into his chair.

Alik was surprised by the reaction. Ainsley might have a public persona of *say it how it is*, but you didn't build something like Connexion with that antagonist attitude.

Two armed drones glided into the room, followed by Jessika, Soćko and Kandara, who sat in a line at the conference table. Three more drones came in behind them, along with Captain Tral and Lankin, who took their seats against the wall behind the alien duo.

Alik grinned as he pointed at a drone hovering just above and behind Jessika. 'They protecting us from you, or you from us?'

'Well, I haven't used my alien superpowers to take control of them yet,' she said, 'so I guess they've still got your arse covered.'

'Kandara?' he queried.

'She's been a good girl,' Kandara said. 'So's he.'

'Sweet. How's your mission coming on?'

'The armour should be finished in another hour,' Jessika said.

'I hope it's tough,' Yuri said, striding in. 'Because an Olyix team in King's Cross had a weapon that cut through our armour suits as if they were made from wet cardboard.'

'Yeah, I watched the feed,' Alik said. 'That was some bad shit that went down there.'

Yuri sat down, with Loi claiming the seat next to him.

'Where's Callum?' Alik asked.

'23 Librae,' Emilja said.

Alik hadn't a clue what that was; his altme, Shango, had to splash the file across his tarsus lens. Reading it wasn't exactly enlightening. 'What the fuck is he doing there? It's over eighty lightyears away. How did he even get there? We're supposed to have the interstellar hubs sealed up tighter than a goddamn Vegas vault.'

'I authorized it,' Yuri said. 'You only get to 23 Librae through a portal in the Connexion Exoscience and Exploration Department. It's secure. And even if it wasn't, going there can't help the Olyix.'

'He said he's working on a new idea so nobody has to kamikaze,' Emilja said. 'Wouldn't tell me what it was, just that, if it is feasible, he'd explain when he gets back.'

'Two ideas in two days.' Ainsley chortled. 'Who knew he was as smart as Hawking?'

'The people he's outsmarted before?' Alik answered and smiled tauntingly at Yuri.

Yuri gave him the finger. 'I won that one, dickhead.'

'Hey, fuck the pissing contest, you two,' Ainsley said. 'Jessika, what the hell kind of weapon was that web-thing in King's Cross?'

'The spinning mesh was probably a variant on a metaviral spawn,' she said. 'Which is an active molecular block that breaks mass down into its basic compounds. The Neána use them for zero-gee mining.'

'So how do we counter it?'

'Several types of artificially enhanced carbon bonds are resistant to metaviral breakdown,' Soćko said. 'Our initiators can produce it.'

'They're coating my new armour in this übercarbon stuff,' Kandara said. 'I should be relatively safe – from the webs, at least.'

'You sure about this?' Alik asked her.

'A life without risks would be pretty boring,' Kandara replied.

Alik could see Captain Tral shaking hir head softly in disapproval, but sie held back on any comment.

'What about the machine they were building at King's Cross?' Alik asked. 'What was that?'

'Ah, this is where it gets interesting,' Jessika said. 'We won't be able to answer for certain until we can examine it, but from looking at the sensor images you sent me, Soćko and I believe it was a device to supplant the Connexion portal to 82 Eridani.'

'What do you mean: supplant?'

'It's like this: human portals are all dependent on power from Earth's power grid, right? Which gives you the final authority over every portal. All Connexion has to do is switch off the electricity, like you did at King's Cross, and there is no more interstellar entanglement. Game over.'

'So the machine was an Olyix portal?'

'It appears to be. But it's different to Connexion doors. You use fixed slabs of twinned active-molecule systems to create spacial entanglement. The King's Cross machine was a ring capable of physical expansion.'

'They're better than our portals?' Alik shot a startled look at Ainsley.

'An expanding rim would save you having to thread up each time you need a bigger doorway,' Soćko said.

'Very diplomatic,' Alik told him.

'We need to be extremely vigilant at the interstellar hubs,' Ainsley III said. 'The Olyix cannot be allowed to establish their own portal to any terraformed planet. Christ, can you imagine a variable-size portal opening up? They could send their Deliverance ships straight through; no need to wait for the Resolution ships to arrive.'

'It won't happen,' Yuri said. 'Anne Groell has implemented a constant review protocol on the interstellar hubs. And now I know what they're trying to do, I'll cut the power if there's even a hint that something is wrong.'

'All right,' Emilja said. 'But we will have to watch the habitats that fall to the Deliverance ships, too. Their interstellar portals must be deactivated as soon as the shields fall, if not before.'

'Agreed,' Ainsley said. 'We won't let them through.'

'Thank you.' Emilja nodded in satisfaction. 'Now, Alik, you asked for this meeting?'

'Actually, no,' Alik said. 'The President of the United States asked that you convene at this point. I am here in the official capacity as her representative.'

'Very well,' Ainsley III said. 'What's the view from the White House?'

Alik cleared his throat as the official script splashed down his tarsus lens. 'POTUS has been speaking to the General Secretary of the Communist Party of China, they are fully agreed that firstly: this committee with its resources and contacts is uniquely placed to coordinate Sol-wide strategies to achieve goals that would be difficult for a national government or the Sol Senate to implement. It is jointly decided that surrendering the citizens of our respective countries, and the Sol system in general, to the alien elevation is not an option. Therefore,' he looked directly at Jessika then Soćko, 'they task this committee to use all its exceptional assets with finding a solution –'

'Fuck's sake,' Yuri grunted.

'– that will enable governments to evacuate the majority of their citizens and culture from Earth, to a safe future including but not limited to exodus habitats. It is understood that this will require considerable time, and that time can be bought by whatever method or means this committee sees fit – including short-term detriment on whatever scale the committee judges appropriate.'

'Mother Mary,' Kandara muttered. 'Is this for real?'

'Furthermore,' Alik continued in a strained voice, 'upon completion of an exodus habitat programme or equivalent, it is unacceptable for humans to then become hunted among the stars. We need you to put in place a coherent and viable long-term strategy to successfully assault the Olyix enclave with such force as to guarantee its eradication, allowing us to return to our homeworld in peace.' He looked up, staring around at the faces, seeing who was startled and who was phlegmatic. Pleased that he'd pretty much called it. 'They jointly declare that all resources and personnel you need will be made available to accomplish this task. That's it.'

'I'm pleased that POTUS and the General Secretary recognize what needs to be done,' Jessika said. 'And I speak for myself and my Neána colleagues when I say that we will do our utmost to ensure as many humans are saved as can be. However, you need to make it clear to your leadership that eradicating the Olyix is practically impossible.'

'Why?' Alik snapped back, angry at her constant dumb defeatism. *Maybe Kandara's right, they are just androids spouting their bullshit party-line script.* 'There has to be a way. Maybe you just don't understand humans well enough to know there will be no limit to what we are prepared to do in order to achieve our survival.'

'Exodus habitats will enable—'

'No,' Kandara said. 'I'm with Alik on this. You might well consider it impossible, you with your hiding in the dark. But we need to find a way.'

'Kandara is correct,' Emilja said. 'We've seen the Olyix for the monsters they are, we know how powerful and advanced their technology is compared to ours, and I get that any plan will be extreme. But if that's what it takes, then so be it. Tell us what has to be done. We will fill in the practicalities; after all, I suspect we will have centuries to perfect them. This is not going to be a war that will end in any of our lifetimes.'

'Fucking-a,' Ainsley cheered.

Alik watched Jessika and Soćko exchange a glance.

'You can touch if you want,' Kandara said with a humourless smile. 'We're all friends here.'

Soćko raised an eyebrow. 'Excuse me?'

'You communicate brain to brain via touch. Your skin has some kind of tactile nerve conductivity, right?'

'Son of a bitch,' Alik said. 'How did you know . . .?'

'Kandara is an excellent observer,' Jessika said. 'My compliments.'

'That's how you fired the neurovirus into the transport ship's onemind, isn't it?' Kandara said as her smile morphed into a smirk.

'Correct,' Soćko said. 'Olyix biotechnology is pervasive and pliant to their internal commands. It's how they regulate and change the function of cell clusters. To facilitate that, their entire organic structure is laced with nerve pathways. After I let them capture me, they implanted Kcells which started to tumour inside my body to prepare me for cocooning, and this gave me a direct route into the ship's neural web.'

Alik felt his heart rate speed up at hearing the outrageous concept. 'Your body is a weapon? Jeeze.'

'A very specific weapon. Don't worry, I can't use it against humans.'

'Have you tried?' Kandara asked mildly.

'No. That's like asking if I've tried using cheese to cut through a knife blade.'

'Fascinating but not relevant,' Emilja said. 'We need a way to destroy the Olyix. Are you prepared to help us or not?'

'To do that you would have to get inside their enclave,' Jessika said.

'And nuke it?' Alik asked keenly.

'I doubt that would work.'

'Oh, really? So you do know what's inside?'

'No. But we have conjecture of its size, its power. One ship, one bomb, would achieve nothing. All it would do is show them a gap in their defences which we can get through. So the next attempt becomes even harder.'

'Okay, if not that, then what?'

'You have to find the enclave's entrance, the gateway – which the Neána have no knowledge of, and I do know that my abode has been searching for it for thousands of years.'

'The abode cluster didn't find it, or simply didn't tell you?' Kandara challenged.

'Touché. But if they had found the location, I cannot envisage a scenario where they would not broadcast it, or give their envoys the coordinate. None of us sent to Earth knows the location of the enclave gateway, therefore the Neána do not have it. So anyway – your descendants will find it eventually.'

'How?' Alik asked. 'You guys have had millennia by your own admission, and you haven't managed to do that.'

Jessika gave him a cold smile. 'You would have to ambush one of their arkships, and capture it intact. The wormhole terminus inside will contain the data you need.'

'Jezus, you don't think small, do you?'

'No. And along with building a trap strong enough to hold an Olyix arkship, you've been increasing your technology base and using it to assemble the greatest war armada the universe has ever seen.'

'I like it,' Ainsley said.

'It is that simple,' Jessika continued, 'and that impossible. So you see why Soćko and I want you to devote your principle effort to saving the Sol habitat industrial stations. You have to build those exodus habitats. Every solution to this requires them.'

'But not enough of them,' Emilja said. 'Earth's population now exceeds twelve billion – we think. It's probably more. Even if you and Kandara take out the *Salvation of Life* and buy us a fifty-year hiatus until the Olyix return, we still wouldn't have time to build enough exodus habitats.'

Jessika bowed her head. 'Yes.'

'If ten years is what we get, that's what we'll take,' Ainsley said. 'Let's do this.'

London

Tronde knew he was awake. Eyes closed, he was engulfed in darkness. Motionless, his flesh devoid of feeling. Thoughts, cold and bleak.

This must be what death was like. No sensation he could feel or respond to. Nothing to lift the despair that came from knowing what was happening on the other side of the sky.

But he had the memories from mere hours ago when everything brought pleasure and life had soared to a pinnacle. Memories he kept trying to grasp and relive. But instead all he got was glimpses of what had been that made him despise his existence even more.

Tears leaked out from his closed eyelids. He hated that. Claudette might see, might coo concern and ask how he was, what she could do to help. There was only one answer. More hifli.

They still had some, but it was running out. Like time itself. The Earth wasn't going to survive for much longer. He'd watched some of the feeds Ollie and Adnan had dragged out of the lownet, and there were the quick bright flares amid the MHD constellation where alien missiles were exploding, while closer to the sun, dark warships closed in to conquer asteroid habitats. The solar system was a battlefield that humans were being forced out of. And the only thing protecting London now was a shield of artificially strong air.

Tronde knew he was going to die when the avian-shaped ships appeared overhead, and there was only one way to face that. With hifli, making death utterly glorious. He couldn't begin to imagine how magnificent that would be: every nerve he possessed tingling from the nark, converting the zenith of pain that would engulf him at the blastwave impact into pure pleasure. He would die from ecstasy.

For that last glorious moment of existence, his dry dull logic knew, he had to have some hifli left to take when the ships blasted their weapons at the shield dome and killed it. So it had to be used sparingly now.

Grimacing at the motion, he slowly swung his legs off the bed and stood up. Claudette was sprawled on the mattress, not asleep but in an unresponsive zombie daze, limbs tangled in a sheet that should have been washed a long time ago. He didn't care.

Nyin's basic splash told him it was two in the morning as he made his way downstairs, legs stiff and muscles slow to respond. His groin was oddly numb, which he guessed was from excess use of his dick's Kcells. Except the lack of sensation had extended up to his navel and down his thighs. Couldn't feel his arse, either – which was maybe a good thing. There was something wrong with the house's aircon; desert air was gusting over his skin, producing a grubby sheen of sweat.

Ollie and Adnan were timelooped, still sitting on the settee in the same places, still grazing on fridge leftovers, still watching live lownet feeds. A reality horror drama: The End of Days. Coming to a shield near you, and far too soon. The only difference in the room was a higher pile of greasy crockery on the table between them and the stage, with ketchup splats hanging off the rims in sticky lava flows. Empty wine bottles cluttered like bulbous cobbles across the thick cream carpet.

Ollie saw him come in and blinked; then his neck craned forwards. 'Whoa, Tronde, fella; you ain't got no clothes on!'

'So?' Tronde shrugged and dropped into a wide armchair. He

slid about disgustingly on the black leather, as if he was slathered in oil.

Adnan started laughing. 'Man, you have completely lost it.'

'Yeah,' Ollie said. 'Get your shit together.' He and Adnan high-fived, almost missing. Both of them emitted a high-pitched giggle.

'What's happening?' Tronde asked, ignoring how dumb they were being. 'Has Jade got back to us yet?'

In the middle of the stage, a thick habitat toroid was surrounded by a vivid crimson haze. Three sinister Deliverance ships circled around it with lupine ferocity.

'Nah,' Ollie said, nibbling on a fried chicken leg. 'I reckon she's dumped us.'

'Shit, no way,' Adnan slurred. 'She'll come through. It's all about the money with her. We can grab her some serious watts with the drug raid. She's not going to let that go without a fight.'

'I guess.' Tronde stared at the doomed habitat for a while. 'Which one is that?'

'Solidaridad. It's out at Toutatis, built by the Venezuelan New Route movement.'

'No route left to them now,' Ollie said sagely. 'Here it comes, look.' The shield haze expanded rapidly, then blew apart in an abysmal rout. Deliverance ships closed in. 'Aww, bloody hell. Another one bites the dust.' He drummed his fists on the settee cushions, disturbing a couple of pizza crusts. 'Thirty-two minutes. New record.'

'Five hundred wattdollars to me,' Adnan said happily. 'What else is coming up?'

'McDivitt, which is going to be bad. McDivitt have fucked up their evacuation; their portal to the billionaire belt crashed. And a nethead hacked the governor demanding Alpha Defence rescue him and his family before the Deliverance ships arrive – it's all over the allcomments.'

'Oh man, that's a skidmark. Anything else?'

'Kuta. The Deliverance ships will be there in seventeen minutes.'

'Go, Kuta! Shoot something back at the bastards. Just once!'

The stage switched to the feed from Kuta. The habitat was one of the larger ones in the Sol system, at fifty kilometres long.

'That's big, it'll have a good strong shield,' Ollie said, with only mild guilt. He didn't want to think about McDivitt at all.

'Forty-seven minutes,' Adnan said. 'In my professional opinion.'

'Nah, they got maybe thirty-eight, max forty.'

'Give me forty-seven to fifty; and I'll see you that last five hundred, and raise you another two hundred.'

'I'll take it.'

'Wait,' Tronde said, as disturbed as he was appalled. 'Are you two betting on how long it takes for the Olyix to blow the habitat shields?'

'Yep,' Ollie told him with a gormless grin. 'Why? You got something else to do?'

'Or spend your wattdollars on?' Adnan asked.

'Fuck's sake, guys! There are people in those habitats.'

'Nope. Least . . . not apart from McDivitt. The Sol Senate ordered all habitats to evacuate before the bad guys arrive. Big rush away to the settled stars going on right now. Too bad we can't grab a piece of that action, but it's only the habitat residents get that ticket. Down here, we have to sit it out.'

'I'm giving the London shield, an hour, maybe an hour and fifteen minutes,' Ollie said sagely.

'He's good at calling it, too,' Adnan said.

'Oh, Jesus wept.' Tronde could feel his skin cooling, sliding from Sahara to Iceland in seconds. He started shaking. 'We've got to get out of here.'

'I know,' Ollie said. 'But it's all down to Jade now. She's our route out.'

'Fuck.' He clenched his fists, trying to stop the Richter-level tremors.

'Listen,' Adnan said. 'We're still a team, us. Still the Legion, right?'

'Yeah. Course.'

'So me and Ollie were talking, thinking like. About the money?'

'Yeah?'

'Well, it looks like your gig with Claudette is working brilliant. Man, she's on her knees for you. So, like, if we can get the payoff now?' He gestured like a piteous kid asking for more ice cream.

'That'd do it, Tronde,' Ollie said. 'That'd get us out of here. She's got millions in her trust fund, more than Jade's raid will ever pay us. We wouldn't have to bother with all that new identity crap; Lars couldn't handle that anyway. We could just bribe our way out, maybe all the way to Eta Cassiopeiae's billionaire belt. If you've got money there, nobody asks questions.'

Tronde let the notion swirl around him, because he could only concentrate on the other thing Claudette was giving him. And the Olyix were coming, relentless as a tsunami. Running wasn't going to be any use. He already knew how he was going to end, the magnificent blaze of euphoria which awaited when the London shield broke. 'I don't know. I don't know if she's ready for that, yet.'

'You could try. Face it, right now we've got fuck all to lose.'

'Sure.' Tronde nodded as if he was really thinking about it. 'How's Lars?'

Adnan flinched. 'Not so good. He's got a lot of swelling – shoulders, belly. It's weird. Like his muscles have inflated.'

'More like they've got rigor mortis,' Ollie suggested. 'His body's turning rock hard.'

'Joining his head then.' Adnan giggled gleefully. His humour drained away. 'Tronde, you okay, man? You look like shit.'

'I'm good.'

'You need to get something to eat and drink. Take care of yourself more. Claudette, too.'

'Hey! I know what I'm doing.' He got up and stood over Ollie, staring down. The part of him that was so skilful at controlling Claudette gained a bitter satisfaction at the way his friend couldn't quite bring himself to glance up. Surprised, too; Ollie never usually had trouble looking at naked flesh – anyone's. He held a hand out, clicking his fingers impatiently. 'Gimme some.'

'Some what?'

Fingers clicked again, more intolerant now. 'Give me some fucking zero-nark. You're pissing it neat you've taken so much.'

'Why?' Ollie asked sourly. 'You running out of the good stuff?'

A final click and he stared to breathe harshly. Felt the blood heat rising into his cheeks as the devil face switched on.

'Okay, okay,' Ollie said sullenly. 'You seriously need to chill, fella.' He reached into a pocket and fished out a couple of caps. They weren't what Tronde was expecting, too small, but what the hell . . . It was a sweet lift out of this godforsaken house.

He held them tight in his fist and slouched out. There was a peculiar blood-wet meat smell in the hallway, coming from the conservatory. He hung back a moment – but who in their right mind wanted to be responsible for the oxen-man that was Lars? So he looked up the stairs, where the bedroom and crazy Claudette waited. The thought of going back up there right now was just too much. Instead, he went into the kitchen to make some tea, and check if the others had left him any food.

23 Librae

30th June 2204

The Connexion Exoscience and Exploration starship assembly station was very different to Quoek asteroid and its small crew habitation toroid. This was a simple hundred-and-fifty-metre sphere in orbit around the gas giant, Librae b, without any comforting rotational gravity. Nobody lived in it; staff arrived through the portal to Sol at the start of their shift and left at the end, keeping their zero-gee exposure to a minimum so they weren't spending hours each day on cardio and calcium maintenance regimes. Like every other far-flung corporate outpost, it was now operating with a skeleton team. All three of them – Denisha, Koel and, Jec-Coben – were waiting on the other side of the portal when Callum came through. Going directly from one gee to zero gee made him instantly queasy; his heart, convinced he was plummeting downwards, sped up, producing a cold sweat across his skin. Calm yoga breathing did little to alleviate the nausea.

Annoyingly, it didn't look as if the gravity shift bothered Eldlund at all. Sie slid up through the portal and unhesitatingly grabbed the nearest handrail to steady hirself.

The inside of the station was a three-dimensional lattice of carbon girders laced with cables and hoses. Lights were attached to struts seemingly at random, pointing in every direction and casting bizarre shadows. Although the interior of the sphere enclosed a large space, the dense tangle made Callum feel restricted.

'We've been told to provide you with total access,' said Jec-Coben, the team leader.

Callum just remembered in time not to try a handshake in zero gravity. 'Thanks.'

'Do you mind me asking why you're here?'

'Ask away. But I'm afraid we can't tell you anything.'

The three technicians swapped anxious glances.

'We haven't been back to Sol since the emergency was declared,' Jec-Coben said, 'and the solnet channel has been patchy at best. How bad is it?'

'Bad, and about to get a whole lot worse when the Deliverance ships reach Earth.'

'Okay. How can we help?'

'Show me the starships.'

Jec-Coben started to haul himself along a handrail.

Callum watched him go, his throat coming uncomfortably close to a gag. For a moment he wondered if Eldlund carried anti-nausea narks, then pushed the thought aside.

The girders bent and twisted in geometric chaos, forming seven separate ovoid nests extending radially from the centre of the station. Three were empty; the remaining four held starships under construction. Callum had never seen one outside of a virtual, and being so close caused an unexpected rush of emotion. This was exactly the kind of thing which had inspired a twenty-year-old Callum Hepburn: physical proof that the future held wonders beyond imagination. In his lifetime, the human race had reached the stars. How could you live in such times and not be besotted with the possibilities opening up, especially if you were an engineering freshman at university?

The nest Jec-Coben had brought them to contained the *Euia*, a starship that was halfway through its assembly. Callum stared at the familiar teardrop shape defined by a frame of curving spars. At the core was the long nozzle chamber, which utilized the same MHD technology as the solarwells. This time, though, the star's plasma was nothing more than the most powerful rocket exhaust ever built. Ultramagnet coils kept it contained and directed, allowing the starship to accelerate at up to ten gees.

'In theory you could take it up to a hundred gees, no trouble,' Jec-Coben said. 'There's no limit to how much plasma you can push through, just the size of the portal you drop into a star.'

'So why don't you?' Callum asked.

'There's no need. Ten gees will get you up to point eight light-speed in just over a month. And by keeping it at ten gees you don't physically strain the internal components. They're all solid state, but even so everything is designed to function under twenty times its Earth weight.'

'Two hundred per cent safety margin, huh?'

'Yep,' Jec-Coben said proudly.

Callum took a look at those gold and black systems clustered around *Euia*'s central rocket tube – the myriad components that were the most expensive, over-engineered, fail-safe machines ever built. They had to be. Starships couldn't be allowed to fail. It wasn't the cost – or at least, not in wattdollars. It was the cost in time. Most would spend a couple of decades in flight to reach the next tranche of stars. To fail halfway there, or worse on final approach, would mean launching another mission and enduring that time all over again.

Not every star was visited by the exploration starships, of course. Outside the station, five hundred kilometres away, massive observatory satellites were studying the neighbouring stars with known exoplanets, producing superb resolution pictures and analysing spectography, determining which of the lonely worlds was most suitable for terraforming – i.e., cheapest. Ainsley also allowed for pure scientific missions to stars that had interesting planets – those with weird chemistry that hinted at xenobiology, or any other major astronomical anomaly. Most stars within twenty lightyears would be bypassed for the more promising targets beyond.

So, a full flight had to be guaranteed. And if things did start to go wrong, the starship would open up its marsupial compartment and thread up, allowing a new starship to be launched through it to complete the flight.

Eldlund pointed. 'Are those the hull plates?'

'Yes.'

Callum stared at the far end of the nest, feeling an unexpected glow of nostalgia. It had been a long time since he'd seen a portal pair waiting to establish entanglement. Back in the day, he'd sometimes got to use six-metre portals for exceptionally difficult jobs. But the ones he could see held ready in giant U-shaped pallets were easily thirty metres long. Big curving triangles, a metre thick; if nature ever evolved a space lily, these would be its petals. He could see how they would fit together like a smooth-edged jigsaw to form the *Euia*'s hull, producing the iconic teardrop shape.

'Where do you put the portal doors twinned with the hull sections?' Callum asked. 'Orbit them around a gas giant?'

'No,' Jec-Coben said. 'Same as with the MHD chambers, we fix them to the surface of a large asteroid at least fifty AUs out from its primary star. That way, if anything big does come through, there's no damage to any part of the solar system.'

'What do you count as big?'

'Ordinary dust, mostly clumps of carbon atoms, you get a couple of strikes an hour of them. Sometimes you get a particle that's grain-of-sand-size intercepting the hull boundary. That'll happen on average once every couple of days during flight.'

Callum pulled a face. 'Come on here, man, I'm talking proper big. You know – dinosaur-killer size.'

'In a hundred and twenty-seven years of sending ships out to the stars, there have been eight recorded incidents of a pebble-sized object coming though the hull portal. Which we define as up to two-centimetres across.'

'Interstellar space is really very empty,' Eldlund said. 'In the twentieth century, people theorized that you could use a magnetic ramscoop to power a starship's fusion rocket, but it turns out the hydrogen density between stars isn't . . .' Sie trailed off under the look Callum was giving hir. 'Sorry.'

'So you have no data concerning large object intersection at relativistic speeds?'

'No,' Jec-Coben said. 'But you see, everyone conflates encounter speed with an energy release, like a megaton bomb going off. But that's flat-earth-level science, complete garbage. And that's the beauty of using this system. There can be no collision. Ever. Before quantum spacial entanglement, everyone thought you'd have to deploy a massive ion cloud to protect anything flying at even a couple of per cent of lightspeed. That would be enough to ablate all the particle sleet that flooded across interstellar space. While today, what we're actually doing when we turn the hull into a portal door is fly a hole through space. There is simply nothing to hit. If you take your hypothetical boulder of rock and plonk it right in front of our starship travelling at point eight lightspeed, all you're doing is sweeping it up and sending it harmlessly out of the hull door's twin. So the rock just drifts up away from the asteroid with the same relative velocity it had when it was wandering through interstellar space.'

Callum stared at the starship's curving profile, exhilaration stirring his blood. 'What about if the hull only hits half of the boulder?'

'Then – wham-bam – at that velocity it acts like Uriel's sword, the ultimate irresistible force, and cuts clean through any rock. You get half a boulder with a very clean flat surface zipping up out of the hull's twinned door.'

'That's what I thought,' Callum said, smiling at Jec-Coben. 'Now how long will it take to finish assembling one of these starships?'

'The *Euia* is almost complete, so under normal circumstances, we'd be ready for preliminary flight trials in another six weeks.'

'And in very unusual circumstances, with any resource you need, how long to click all those remaining parts together?'

Jec-Coben gave Koel a questing look. 'Physical integration . . . maybe twenty four hours. But—'

'Thanks,' Callum said abruptly. 'We need to get back, now.' He gripped the handrail harder and slowly swung his body around a hundred and eighty degrees until he was pointing back the way he'd come. Then he started pulling himself along, gliding between handrails. He couldn't stop grinning.

'So?' Eldlund said.

Callum's excitement overrode everything: freefall nausea, worry about the invasion – 'It's amazing! They don't realize what they've got.'

'Uh . . . what have they got?'

'The perfect arkship-killer missile.'

London

It was the silence which was subtly wrong. Gwendoline woke up knowing something about the city was different. Even with the penthouse's superb sound insulation, she could always detect the noise London generated at all hours of the day. But this morning there was nothing; even the birds were hushed.

She slipped out of bed, taking care not to wake Horatio. Crina was nowhere to be seen, although Gwendoline suspected the penthouse network had alerted the bodyguard that she'd risen. So she made sure that the anti-sniper sheet was raised before she stepped out onto the balcony. The city shield was diffusing an insipid pre-dawn glimmer across the rooftops. As she watched, a tiny point of pure white light appeared for a couple of seconds. The Agreth MHD asteroid, Theano splashed; a missile got past its plasma jets.

Gwendoline lowered her gaze. At first glance Cheyne Walk was deserted. Then she saw it: a horse walking slowly along the road, its rider wearing a wide-brimmed Australian outbacker hat. They weren't in any hurry, just ambling along at the centre of their own version of normality.

She knew only too well where *that* attitude was coming from. The sheer enormity of what was happening was too huge too encompass, so reality was now held at arm's length. For if she was to look upon it and accept all that was happening, she'd be running, naked and screaming, down the street alongside that horse. Instead, staying safe and aloof in the sanctuary of the penthouse, waiting placidly for the family to spirit her away to safety, was her shameful solution to Armageddon. That and Horatio being here.

If it works, don't try to fix it.

So she watched with a mix of envy and bemusement as the horse and rider went past the building, then turned onto Battersea Bridge. Shaking her head at her own weakness, she went back inside.

The larger clothing printer in her dressing room was still working, so she loaded in a design for Horatio: a decent navy blue collarless shirt and dark green loose-fit trousers. She preferred slimline trousers on men, but that battle had been lost even before they got married. She still remembered the morning he lifted a ridiculous pair of baggies out of the printer – mustard yellow, too. He'd been so delighted her usual mockery had died before it was spoken. Smiling fondly at the memory, she watched the machine's cluster of stainless steel nozzles clatter around like knitting needles as the clothes took shape. And, conveniently, Theano had Horatio's size on file. She'd never quite got around to deleting that.

The shirt was finished, and the trousers half formed, when the printer's nozzles started to joust with each other and the colour of the fabric they were extruding changed colour again and again.

Theano splashed a *pattern impaired* icon, and the printer stopped abruptly. Gwendoline opened the glass top and lifted the blighted trousers from the machine. They were now half trousers, half garish kilt.

'Rebooting the printer,' Theano told her.

She watched the nozzles retract to their stand-by position.

'Reboot failed. Possible darkware contamination of the system. Deep clean required.'

'Okay,' she said. 'How long will that take?'

'Unknown. Unable to establish verified connection to the manu-facturer for the procedure update. Solnet bandwidth is low and fluctuating.'

'Keep trying. Oh, and get the home network to disconnect all the food printers from solnet. I don't want them corrupted too.' The idea made her shiver, pulling her bathrobe tighter. That was when she realized the aircon wasn't keeping the dressing room as cool as she liked it.

'The penthouse is in power-saving mode,' Theano told her. 'The main power grid failed in the night. Quantum batteries are supplying the electricity now.'

'How long will they last?'

'Several months, if they are only used to maintain the security boundary. Longer for ordinary day-to-day usage.'

'I think we're past day-to-day now.'

At least the coffee machine was still working. While the croissant bricks were cooking in the panoforno, she ground some beans for Horatio, who liked his coffee black, and made herself a hot chocolate – and to hell with the sugar content.

'Thanks,' Horatio said when she carried it into the bedroom on a tray. They plumped the pillows up and sat cosily side by side, not needing to talk as they munched the croissants down. Good memories.

'What next, then?' Horatio asked as he finished his mug of coffee.

'The Olyix appear to be changing tactics,' Gwendoline said. 'Alpha Defence has been tracking their movements. Over half of the Deliverance ships that were heading for habitats are changing course. It looks as if they're now heading out for the MHD asteroids.'

'That doesn't sound good.'

'Ultimately, no. We think their weapons will be able to reach through the plasma cascade. But on a positive note, it will take them a lot longer to eliminate all the MHD asteroids than the missiles would have taken.'

'Great. And the habitats will have more time to evacuate.'

She pulled a face. 'Maybe not. The missiles are changing course, too. They're heading back. Alpha Defence thinks they're going to hit the habitats.'

'What? I thought the Olyix didn't want to kill people.'

'They're not. We managed to evacuate most of the habitats before the Deliverance ships reached them. There's been a couple of cases where an engineering crew was left trying to strip down industrial systems and send them to safety, but that's all. The evacuation process has been a success. Most of the habitat populations are already gone.' She didn't mention the political resistance that some of the terraformed worlds had put up to *undesirables* being dumped on them; Horatio would get too upset about that. 'So Alpha Defence thinks this makes sense from the Olyix viewpoint. The missiles will simply wipe out the remaining habitats, denying us the chance to save the industrial systems we'll need if the settled stars are going to fight back.'

'Is that what's going to happen? Are we going to fight back?'

She shrugged. 'Above my pay grade. But even if they don't, we'll need all the industrial capacity we can get to build exodus habitats. And that's going to take a while.'

Horatio lifted up the last chunk of croissant. 'I know the stuff in your fridges and freezers will feed the three of us for another week or more, but what if it's longer than that?'

'The food printers are still working.'

'Okay. Then we need to see if we can stock up on basic printer ingredients. Maybe some dough bricks and the like, too.'

Gwendoline stared at him thoughtfully. 'You don't think we're going to get to Nashua?'

'I don't know. I know Loi will do his best, but I don't want us to be any kind of burden on him. If it takes more than a week to organize, we shouldn't be calling him for help.'

'It's not going to be a week,' she said guiltily. 'We need to be out of here before the Deliverance ships arrive, and that's only going to be a couple of days at most. They've already flipped over and started deceleration.'

'Then let's go. My clothes should be dry.'

'What?' She didn't remember the shirt being damp.

'My clothes. I put them in the washing machine last night.'

'Oh. Yeah. Right. I made you a new shirt, but the printer crashed before it could finish your trousers. The solnet is thick

319

with exponential darkware right now. It's taking the G8Turings a long time to purge it all.'

Horatio kissed her. 'You fabricated clothes for me?'

'You didn't bring a bagez. So . . .'

'Thank you.'

She smiled sheepishly. 'You're welcome.'

A long moment of quiet joy, then, 'We'd better get out and see what ingredients we can find,' he said.

'Sure. This is Chelsea. There are lots of food shops.'

'Yeah, but we don't need deli food. We need—'

'Real food?' She raised a teasing eyebrow. 'Fish and chips? Full English breakfast?'

'Only if you're talking fried black pudding.'

'Right, then, let's go see what kind of black pudding the delis of Chelsea stock.'

'Do they have a throwback novelty section?'

*

Crina was not happy.

'We should remain inside the penthouse, ma'am,' she said as soon as Gwendoline announced an expedition to buy printer ingredients. 'I cannot guarantee your safety outside.'

'I'll wear mesh-reinforced jacket and jeans, and you can carry whatever weapons you want. If there's any sign of trouble we'll come straight back.'

'My orders are that you should not leave the penthouse, ma'am.'

The last thing Gwendoline wanted now was to call the duty security officer at Connexion's Greenwich tower and ask them to let her go outside. It would be humiliating – a family board member demoted down to whiny nursery school child. She could see a sheen of sweat on Crina's brow, so the bodyguard was clearly nervous about this power struggle.

'Look,' Horatio said in his smoothly reasonable tone. 'We completely agree that remaining in the penthouse is the safest option, and that's where we're going to stay until the Security Division tells us to relocate. But we simply don't have enough food to last the three of us more than a couple of days, and we have no idea how long this emergency is going to continue. Right now we have a safe window to go a few hundred metres along the road to gather essential supplies. The streets are practically deserted. Nobody is panicking, yet. In another day – or probably less – everyone else is going to start realizing they need food supplies as well. That's when the breakdown will start, and I'll be on your side about venturing beyond the security barrier. But getting in a decent stockpile now means we won't have to go out foraging again after the city goes wild. You'll have guaranteed our security for a much longer time. Surely that's part of your brief, too?'

Crina struggled with the decision, her flat face frozen up tight. 'No more than half an hour,' she said. 'And if we encounter potential hostiles we terminate the venture immediately.'

'Of course,' Gwendoline said.

'I'll collect some additional equipment, then we can go.' She walked down to the guest bedroom, stiff legged and square shouldered.

When the door shut, Gwendoline turned to Horatio. 'Foraging?'

'Me hunter-gatherer,' he grunted out, and thumped his chest. 'Provide for womenfolk.'

'Provide me some balsamic vinaigrette for my avocado salad, and I'm all yours.'

'Good to know. Does she seem all right to you?' He nodded at the closed door.

'She just takes her job seriously, that's all. In that profession you have to.'

'No. I mean: all right? As in, she didn't look well to me.'

'Look, she's in a tough position, with no backup. Go easy on her.'

'Ha. Me? You might want to stop encouraging her to call you ma'am.'

'Say what?'

'Ma'am. It's medieval. Titles that distinguish us by class devalue people as much as racial classification. Divide and conquer, the go-to strategy of the ruling elite since the Dark Ages.'

She licked her lips tauntingly. 'Yes, comrade.'

'Thank you.'

'Just so you know, I'm not sure if she'll be allowed to come with us to Nashua.'

'I thought that,' he replied in a low voice. 'So if we get a whole stash of printer ingredients now, she'll have food for herself after we leave.'

'Horatio, if we need to go to Nashua, it's over for Earth. Another week of food won't make any difference in the long term.'

'But we'll have done the decent thing, the right thing. That matters. Even now. Maybe, especially now.'

Gwendoline put her arms around him, and hugged tight. 'I never did deserve you.'

*

The streets were unnervingly quiet when they walked out of the apartment block onto Milmans Street. Its buildings were mostly from a late twenty-first-century rebuilding phase, a nostalgic recreation of a stone-built Georgian splendour that had existed only in wistful illustrations of nineteenth-century boulevards. Possible only because money had slowly eased out the less well-off so the truly rich could expand their much-needed floorspace into newly vacant real estate. Wealth and metrohubs had also brought a distinctive greening, so that at ground level it looked as if the borough had been freshly carved out of a forest, with all the trees and creeper-covered walls maintained to a suitably high standard.

Gwendoline frowned up at the old beeches and London plane trees lining the clear path as her brain struggled to define the source of the wrongness.

'Wind,' she said suddenly. 'There's no wind.' The twigs and branches above her were perfectly still, leaves that normally fluttered in gentle discord hung immobile and silent.

'The shield cuts us off from weather,' Horatio said. 'It's going to be like living in a greenhouse.' He flicked a gaze at Crina, who was perspiring heavily.

'Is there going to be enough oxygen?' Gwendoline asked. 'I mean, if we're sealed in, there'll be no fresh air.'

'It'll last for months,' he said. 'Years, probably. We don't have to think that far ahead. This'll be settled one way or another long before we reach that point.'

They set off north, away from the Thames, heading for King's Road, and the notorious shops that bestowed the road its status of exclusivity. Her two bagez followed them obediently. Two, because she felt optimism was what she wanted to bring to the day. As they walked, the sound level crept up. They passed stalled deliverez and urban cleanez under the trees; unable to recharge their batteries, the little machines had spent the night burning through their reserve power trying to find a live induction point. Two abandoned taxez blocked the clear path; cybernetic heads buried in the sand, they didn't respond to altme pings. One had a buckled wheel where it had hit a bollard with considerable force. Gwendoline saw a few small spots of blood on the pavement around it. Her hand crept to her leather jacket's zip, sliding it right up to the collar, completing the protective cover the integral mesh provided.

King's Road had inert cabez littered underneath the arched gold-glass canopy which stretched from Sloane Square all the way down to New King's Road. So many times she'd strolled along here, sheltered from the British climate, so she could browse the fashionista TryMe houses, or meet up with friends in the bars and bistros. Good times contemplating the salons – which were essentially clinics in fancy dress, they blurred the line so skilfully between cosmetic treatment and outright medical recrafting procedures. Those times when she was the ultimate gilded bird in her gilded cage. Now it was all so different. Darkened, without power, abandoned by their snobbish staff, the stores were gloomy, their glamour and appeal vanished like a past season's style. Even the cheery flowering vines which wrapped the canopy pillars had lost their verve under the cursed bruise sky.

She was as surprised as she was pleased that some of the independent stores were open. Not her haunts – the boutiques and frippery merchants – but the smaller shops supplying essentials. Even a couple of family-run cafes were setting out their pavement tables. Such entrepreneurship was drawing people out of their homes. They might have been wearing smart, expensive clothes that signalled their SW10 postcode, but Gwendoline recognized the slightly strained expressions, the polite determination. Like her, they'd have access to a higher stratum of news and sources, and had come to realize they needed to start preparing if they were going to survive this – even if *this* was just the few days until the Deliverance ships arrived. If the city shield held after that, the future was all down to fate.

And Grandpa, she acknowledged bleakly. That wasn't reassuring at all. But Ainsley III would do what he could.

Horatio was staring around, his pursed-lips expression a perfect sculpture of scholarly thought. She told Theano to snag the image. Smiled to herself.

'We should go in there,' he said.

Gwendoline looked where he was pointing and frowned. 'A cafe?'

'Yes. Think about it. They'll have a storeroom out the back with wholesale sacks of food printer ingredients.'

'Oh. Right.' She was cross with herself for not working that out first.

Bianchi's cafe was a family business, boasting speciality organic coffee and fresh-baked pastries. An Italian man in his late fifties with a cheery smile stood behind the counter and greeted them effusively. The shelves on the wall behind him had tins of fifty types of coffee beans.

Horatio went up and ordered Guatemalan Atitlán coffee and slices of chocolate and almond torta caprese for all of them. Gwendoline admired the way he fought back a loud *How much?* at the price as she proffered her cryptoken. Crina insisted that they sit outside. 'That will give us visibility and unrestricted withdrawal options, ma'am.'

Gwendoline nodded, trying not to wince. Now that Horatio had preached about it, *ma'am* stood out every time the bodyguard used it. *Because it's true.*

A worried-looking teenage waitress brought the coffees and cake, then hurried back indoors. Horatio was still up at the counter, talking to the owner. Both of them laughed.

Charmer, Gwendoline sighed. She liked to think she could talk to anyone, but knew in her heart that if she'd tried to negotiate this the man would have shut down. *I can schmooze a billion-wattdollar loan from a banker, but not a packet of meatpowder from a cafe owner. How screwed-up is that?*

A handshake, and Horatio was sauntering over to the table.

'We got it,' he said proudly. 'Enough basic protocrab pellets to fill the bagez. I hope your cryptoken is full of watts.'

'It is.'

'Good,' Crina said. 'If you've secured supplies, we should leave.'

'Whoa there,' Horatio held up a finger. Smiling pleasantly, he sipped his coffee and made a show of appreciation to the owner. 'That would be insulting to Papa Bianchi. First we enjoy his excellent coffee at a reasonable speed, then reluctantly leave and complete the deal.'

Crina's lips tightened. 'Very well.'

'Are you all right?'

'Yes.'

Gwendoline studied the bodyguard. She was still sweating, and her skin had turned a pallid shade. Horatio was right; something was off. It couldn't be anxiety, not Crina. A fever?

It was siting next to the preternaturally alert Crina that clued Gwendoline in to the new arrivals long before they got close, a tide incoming from the west. Kids were rolling along King's Road on boardez. Grouped together in threes and fours, they glided onwards in tight formations, taking over the whole width of the clear path. Other people got out of their way – those not so young, not so cheaply dressed, lacking hair that was rainbow serpentdreads coiling out from statement hats. It wasn't even the foreign styles that made Gwendoline twitchy. Attitude was their dominant feature.

Horatio watched the gradual takeover for a minute and drained his coffee.

'Time to go, ma'am,' Crina said firmly.

Horatio didn't even protest the ma'am.

They loaded up the bagez while an uneasy Papa Bianchi cleared the tables outside. Not far away, a gathering of the intruders started rattling the security rods protecting a charcuterie's windows. The distinctive high-pitched grinding sound of an activeblade was audible.

'This way,' Crina said. She started walking east, away from Milmans Street.

'But—'

'We're not heading towards them, ma'am. That invites confrontation. We'll go down Beaufort Street then cut back along the embankment. Beaufort Street is wider, too, and mainstream; that's in our favour.'

'Okay.'

They were walking faster along King's Road now. Not obviously hurrying, not scared, but just people with somewhere to go. They weren't the only ones; SW10 residents were astutely draining away.

'Hey, yol scoot much, b'there?'

Four kids on boardez came sliding neatly around the sprawling buttress trunk of a silk cotton tree, moving quicker than walking pace. Gwendoline was obscurely annoyed that their boardez still had plenty of power. *How come their borough has electricity?*

The leader, or at least the one who'd spoken, leant in towards them. Hands clasped behind his back, top hat angled over. A graceful mover, his boardez adapting efficiently to the weight-shift, bringing him in close. He was grinning hungrily, showing off blood-red teeth.

'What, yo no'call?' It was a taunt, the superiority of a hunter to its prey.

Crina barely looked in his direction. She raised her arm. The suit sleeve swelled, hanging down like a flaccid wattle. Gwendoline heard a soft *puk* sound.

The smartsplat hit the leader of the boardez crew with perfect accuracy in the centre of his chest. A slender bullet in the air, it blossomed out to a twenty-centimetre disc a fraction of a second before impact. The kinetic energy was similar to being punched by a heavyweight boxer – enough to fell a full-grown adult male – and that was before the taze charge kicked in. The impact flung him backwards, arms windmilling, screeching more in shock than pain. His arse hit the ground at the same time as the electric pulse slammed into his skin, and he became the ball in in a game of human skittles, tumbling into his mates. All of them went down in flailing limbs and outraged cries.

'You!' Crina snapped at the kids. 'Fuck off or die!'

Gwendoline gasped. *She wouldn't? Would she?*

'Don't stop, don't run,' the bodyguard ordered a shock-frozen Gwendoline and Horatio.

Gwendoline just did as she was told. Desperate to look back. Commanding herself not to.

Crina ducked around a Queensland pine whose topmost branches were shoving up against the road's gold canopy. Then they all took a sharp turn into Beaufort Street. This road had never been remodelled, there was no need; it was the kind other roads aspired to be. Neat brick and stone buildings of classy London apartments, with a greenway of oaks and yellow poplars down the middle where grass had replaced the tarmac. Its prestige was confirmed by being awarded two metrohubs, one at each end.

Thankfully, there weren't many people ahead. Those Gwendoline did see were all heading in the same direction, away from King's Road.

'Where did all these kids come from?' she asked.

'Those serpentdreads are popular with the Fellnike Troop, who operate out of Earl's Court,' Horatio said. 'So it's most likely them, or a splinter.'

'How the hell do you know that?' Gwendoline asked.

'Earl's Court is where a lot of the ribbontown kids wind up when they come to the big city. It's not the greatest environment. Some agencies I advise do work there.'

'Oh. Right.' She risked a glance over her shoulder. Thankfully couldn't see any of the Fellnike Troop, if that's who they were, coming after them down Beaufort Street. But the trees made a direct view impossible, and if they were using the trunks for cover it would be difficult to see them.

Six bee-sized drones detached themselves from underneath

Crina's suit collar and started flying in both directions along the road. Gwendoline was rather pleased with herself for analysing their tactical position.

They were another hundred metres towards the Thames when Crina announced: 'Casualty ahead.'

'Where?' Horatio peered forwards.

Gwendoline couldn't see anything but buildings and trees, with few people remaining ahead of them. 'Did the Troop kids get ahead of us?'

'No, ma'am. It's a lone male. Still breathing but looks in distress. No visible physical injuries; the drone can't detect any blood. He's on the left. I don't think it's an ambush.' She started scanning the thick boughs arching above. 'We can avoid him easily.'

'We could,' Horatio said, 'but we're not going to.'

Crina gave Gwendoline an urgent look. 'Ma'am, there are active hostiles in the area. We really can't take the chance.'

'Her name is Gwendoline, and I will go and check him out,' Horatio said. 'That way you two can stay safe.'

'We'll all help if we can,' Gwendoline said primly, giving Horatio a sharp look. *Now who's being patronizing?* But she, too, felt concern at Crina's appearance. The bodyguard was still sweating, despite being in the dapple of the trees. There was something not quite right about the way she was walking, either, as if she was wading through some viscous liquid, forcing each leg forwards.

The man was on the ground, his back propped up against an oak tree. Middle-aged, with a dark complexion and thick ebony hair tied into a waist-long tail by a glittering scarlet band. His chin was resting on his chest, a line of drool leaking out of the corner of his mouth. Sometimes his eyes would open at the same time as he shook his head, as if fighting sleep.

One of Crina's drones kept watch a metre above him. She sent three more to scour the area while she kept looking up into the branches overhead.

'Hey there, fella,' Horatio said, kneeling beside him. 'Can you hear me?' He reached out.

'No,' Gwendoline said instinctively. 'Don't touch him. He might be contagious. God knows what state the hospitals are in. I don't want you catching anything odd. Not today.'

Horatio gave her a mildly annoyed stare, but nodded and withdrew his hand.

'His altme isn't replying to my ping,' Crina said. 'Not even a basic confirmation response. It must have been hit by darkware.' The drone descended and landed on the man's neck. 'High temperature,' she reported, 'but heart rate low. That's odd.'

Gwendoline told Theano to call for a medevac. She'd seen it in action enough times. A fast drone would swoop down on an accident zone and drop a one-metre-diameter portal, with its twin in an Emergency department; victims usually received professional trauma treatment within three minutes.

'National Medevac service has been suspended,' the altme replied.

'You're kidding?'

'Negative.'

'Options?'

'I have a channel open to the London Civic Health Agency. Its management network is providing paramedic assistance for medical emergencies.'

'Okay, go with that.'

'The request has been logged with the agency.'

'Wait? Logged? When will they be here?'

'They are trying to respond to each case within an hour.'

'For fuck's sake,' she muttered. 'Well, see if you can prioritize it.'

'Acknowledged.'

'So what do we do?'

'Not a lot,' Horatio said. 'Given we don't know what's wrong with him.'

'There's some more,' Crina announced.

'More what?'

'More casualties ahead. Two of them, a hundred and twenty metres.'

'The same as this?' Gwendoline asked.

'Looks like it.'

'What is this, an epidemic?'

The bodyguard shrugged.

'Horatio? Do we help them?'

'I want to,' he said guardedly, 'but we're not doctors. I don't understand what's wrong.'

'Nark?' she suggested. It was that kind of neighbourhood, where the busy and important relaxed with friends at the end of a long day, where a drink was never quite enough . . . 'They don't want to face the Deliverance ships?'

'I dunno . . .'

'We should look at the others, at least.'

Crina glanced around again. 'Okay. But not too close, please.'

A man and a woman were lying on the grass. From their positions, Gwendoline thought the man might have collapsed first, and the woman went to help him before losing consciousness. The way she lay practically across him was almost romantic, lovers asleep. They were definitely dressed like locals; stylish fitness gear produced in high-end printers, his T-shirt short to show off the perfect abs; while she wore spray-on leggings and a halter that was mostly straps across flawless ebony skin.

'Executive power couple,' Gwendoline decided. There were certainly enough of them living in Chelsea. Though she'd rarely seen any quite so devoted to this level of physical perfection. They must have spent plenty of time and money in clinics to get features that would shame the old Greek gods; she couldn't really judge which of them was prettiest.

'Their clothes are soaking,' Horatio said. 'They must have been lying here when the sprinklers came on this morning.'

'Hell, how long have they been here?'

One of Crina's small drones landed on the woman's bare arm.

'It's the same,' she announced. 'High temperature, low heart rate.'

'What's wrong with her feet?' Horatio asked.

Gwendoline looked at the new lime-green and black trainers the woman had on. 'Not what I'd choose, but . . .'

'Look again,' he said.

The trainers were too big, Gwendoline realized. Actually, now she was giving it her full attention, the bottom of the leggings were also badly fitting, hanging lose around very bony ankles – which should have been impossible in this age of customized printing. 'It's like she's got anorexia. But I don't see how she could have run in those in the first place. It'd be like wearing slippers.'

Without a word, Horatio bent down and pulled at one of the trainers.

'Careful!' Gwendoline said.

'I'm not touching the skin,' he said, and gave a final tug. The trainer came off quite easily. Gwendoline could see why: the woman's foot had been reduced to a knobbly lump, as if all the muscle and tendons had been removed, and the skin had shrunk around the bones, compressing them into a jumbled lump.

'What the fuck?' She stared in dismay for a long moment, then glanced over at the man. His running trainers were too big as well. Then she saw the hand that was half hidden by the woman's body on top of him. 'Shit! Horatio, his hand!'

It was badly withered. But that wasn't what had startled her. The skin on the underside of the fingers had sprouted a silky white fur that was tethering the hand to the ground.

'Jesus wept,' he grunted. 'Are those *roots*?'

'Bioweapon!' Crina exclaimed. 'Step away. Now.'

Gwendoline stumbled back, more from shock than the body-guard's alarm. She and Horatio shared a frightened look. 'Not a bioweapon,' she whispered. 'Kcells. They've started cocooning.'

Horatio put his arm around her and urged her further away. 'We need to get home.'

She nodded, too alarmed to speak. As they hurried away, always glancing over their shoulders, she was sure she saw some of the Fellnike Troop starting to appear at the far end of Beaufort Street.

'When we get to the penthouse, we stay there,' she said.

Horatio gave her a grim smile. 'Not arguing.'

'And I'm using the secure channel to Greenwich. The family needs to know cocooning has started.'

'Yeah. But . . . roots?'

'I suppose the Kcells need nutrients from somewhere. They can't sustain the brain for long just consuming a body's limbs.'

'That is some very powerful biotechnology.'

'Yes. We've always known the Olyix are ahead of us in that field. This is when we find out just how far ahead.'

They reached the Thames embankment and turned right to hurry along the pathway high above the exposed mud of the riverbed. Gwendoline was surprised how much it smelt.

Every time they passed someone, she gave them a keen look, judging them via their appearance. Hating herself for being so shallow. But a stern voice in her head was telling her this was the way it was going to be from now on.

Some irrational part of her had been convinced the penthouse would refuse to let them in. So many of the things she took for granted had failed in the last few days. But the black door swung open and she stepped over the threshold, feeling ridiculously relieved. All her emotions were so heightened right now it was like being a teenager again.

'I don't know if I should call Loi direct,' she told Horatio. 'I want Ainsley III to know about the cocooning, but I don't want to be a pain to Loi.'

'You must know someone else with direct access to Ainsley III?'

'Well, yes.' She stood to one side to let the bagez roll past.

In the vestibule, Crina slumped against the wall and slowly slid down onto the floor. Her eyes were fluttering as she tried to focus.

'Bloody hell,' Horatio knelt beside her, putting his hand on her sweat-soaked forehead. 'She's burning up.' He stopped and gave Gwendoline a frantic look. 'Do you think . . .?'

'Oh, shit, no. Please!' Gwendoline knelt beside him. 'Crina? Crina, can you hear me?' There was no response. She gave the bodyguard's legs a guilty look. 'She was walking funny out there.'

'I saw.'

There was a long moment of silence. Then together they started to undo one of Crina's sturdy boots. When they prised it off, they saw the woman's foot had crumpled up into a bulbous vestige.

'Crap. Now what?'

McDivitt Habitat

30th June 2204

When asteroid 2077UB was discovered, it chased a mildly irregular trans-Saturn orbit and measured three and a half kilometres in diameter. Its icy composition gave it a nebulous coma from the gradual outflow of volatiles from its nucleus. That made it a valuable commodity to the Fletcher-Wilson Corporation, who landed a probe on its craggy surface in 2096. The probe threaded up a two-metre portal which allowed three corporate lawyer/astronauts through, along with a basic inflatable life-support pod. After a full day's residence, they claimed it as an independent nation and installed a G3Turing as its interim governor. It assigned Fletcher-Wilson full mineral extraction rights.

Two years passed, and a batch of heavy-duty mining equipment was delivered to 2077UB from an archipelago of industrial stations barnacled to the surface of Ismene – a big rock in the main asteroid belt. They were owned by a consortium of Australian and New Zealand billionaires who had turned Ismene into a habitat construction centre. The crushed ice from 2077UB was processed in a refinery, removing the dust and other contaminants to produce water purer than an Antarctic glacier. It was pumped through a portal to pour out of the axis sprinklers of the newly completed

McDivitt habitat – a cylinder thirty-five kilometres long and eight in diameter. The desert-dry soil covering the rumpled landscape soaked it up until it was saturated, after which the water flowed along the carefully sculpted valleys into empty stream beds, which in turn trickled into rivers than ran the length of the habitat to empty into a broad circumfluous lake. From there, pumps sent the water back up to the axis shaft to repeat the cycle on a daily basis.

With the first week's rains came aerobic and anaerobic bacteria, finding a welcome home amid the pristine soil granules. For months after, automated agronomy tractors roamed the land, drilling grass seeds and scattering worms atop the moist surface, while aquatic plants took hold along the streams and rivers and lake. Once the grass was established, the tractors returned with larger plants. Later still a sophisticated genealogy of insects were released into the air to take advantage of the first flowers that bloomed amid the previously uniform emerald interior, kicking off pollination. A mere seven years after the first rain fell, small animals were released into a biosphere capable of supporting them without further human intervention.

*

Now brightly coloured birds flashed through the treetops, while big flying fox bats hung from the palms and branches, leaving armadillos, tuataras and frogs to scuttle through the undergrowth. Every footstep Kandara took was accompanied by a ripple of animal movement and their sharp cries of alarm. None of the habitat's native creatures was being evacuated to Eta Cassiopeiae's billionaire belt where McDivitt's human population had fled; there were just too many. The ecologists who had crafted the habitat's rich flora and fauna had been altogether too successful; the giant cylindrical landscape was teeming with life. And right now that triumph was a big problem.

The tropical plants were so vigorous they'd grown into a single giant tangle. Kandara's armour suit could shove her through the vines and fronds and low branches, but nothing like as quickly as she wanted. And the four bioborgs following after her were having an even worse time of it.

She stopped and looked around the thick wall of vegetation surrounding them.

'Mother Mary! This isn't going to work,' she announced.

'What's wrong?' Yuri asked. He was back in Connexion's Security operations centre deep under Manhattan, personally supervising the capture mission.

'This jungle is too dense. The tree huggers who built this place clearly don't get the concept of plant maintenance.'

'Oh, they get it. McDivitt's biosphere is a case study of success *because* it needs very little modification to sustain it.'

'Yeah? Well it's going to kill us. Look, the plan relies on the Olyix chasing the bioborgs down an irrigation maintenance tunnel where we can spring our trap, right.'

'Yeah, so? No jungle down inside the tunnel.'

'So, the bioborgs have got to be seen, and seen quickly as soon as the Olyix break into McDivitt, because it's going to be pretty obvious pretty quickly that the evacuation hasn't stalled, and this is just a con. Well okay, no problem with getting spotted because we're creating a very visible path smashing through the bush here. But that's the whole point, nobody comes out here. Then when the bioborgs 'notice' the Olyix are after them, they run for the tunnel entrance. First off, you can't run through this stuff. Secondly, I'm betting the entrance has the same amount of growth all over it. If I clear it in advance, the Olyix will know something's up. We cannot afford them being suspicious; we only get one shot at this. I've done renditions where you lure a gullible target in. The scenario has to play out as real right up to the point we snatch one of the bastards.'

'You may have a point.'

'Damn right I do.'

'Plan B then, huh?' Alik's cheerful voice asked.

Kandara stopped walking and turned around. She could just make out the habitat's vast endcap through the oppressive tangle of greenery. The base was a single circular cliff of angled balconies, with every floor rich in trees and creepers; they were separated into distinct sections by large crystalline shell-shaped canopies jutting out like the prows of ships. 'We'll have to snatch one inside the residential section.'

'That works,' Yuri said.

'Yeah, you'll still have a good advantage,' Alik said. 'The residential sector is a maze they don't know. You'll be able to channel the Olyix along a specific route. Maybe place demolition charges to isolate one of them.'

Kandara smiled, imagining the glares and shrugs the pair of them would be trading back in New York. The drones that were circling overhead wheeled around as she started back down the little track, followed by the bioborgs. Five trollez made up the last part of her little convoy. The wild jungle was similar to the one back in Nebesa where she'd met Jaru Niyom – and remembering that made her wonder if sie would evacuate with the rest of the habitat. It'd be like hir to greet the Olyix invaders with a mystic smile and some profound maxim.

'Why do so many habitats go for a tropical biosphere?' she asked peevishly as her armour's gauntlets slapped away yet another errant clump of bamboo that was crowding out the path.

'Says the person who lives in Rio,' Alik laughed.

'Thirty-five per cent of Sol's habitats are temperate,' Loi told her, 'but the tropical ones have a fecund environment which is easier to maintain, thanks to their growth rate.'

'So no subarctic habitats, then, huh?'

'There are five, though all of them are small, under ten kilometres long. They were set up as biodiversity reserves to safeguard endangered species after the anthrochange.'

'We're going to lose those, too, I suppose?' she said.

'Possibly,' Yuri said. 'There were no Deliverance ships on course for them. Which we took to mean they were low on the Olyix priority list. I expect they'll get around to them eventually.'

'If we adopt the exodus habitat objective, we can carry every terrestrial DNA sequence with us,' Loi said. 'They've all been catalogued, so we won't lose any of Earth's species.'

Kandara marvelled at just how ideologically committed Loi was, given his Zangari heritage; it was almost as if he had a Utopial outlook. 'Speaking of being on course, how are my Deliverance ships doing?'

'All three of them are holding steady,' Yuri told her. 'Eight minutes until deceleration is complete.'

'Mother Mary!' Kandara eyed the endcap wall that loomed above the residential section, tracing the flat alp-like surface of rock and trees right up to the midpoint, where the axis spindle emerged. Even with her sensors on full magnification she couldn't see the modifications Yuri's people had made. 'Are the power systems technicians out?'

'Finished and clear. Everything's set.'

'And the long con?'

'We're still running it. As far as everyone knows, McDivitt's evacuation is screwed up. The con's line is that there's still five thousand people left inside McDivitt, and Connexion is working its ass off to get them to Eta Cassiopeiae in time. We even got allcomments to pick up on the governor's rant to Alpha Defence, demanding they get him and his family out. It's just a shame the Olyix have screwed up so much of solnet, but their operatives must be picking it up.'

'Nicely done.' She liked the elegance of the deception even as she resented its necessity. McDivitt was the fourth habitat they had planned the snatch operation around. From a selfish cynic's view, Callum's defence of the MHD asteroids had worked too well. She couldn't really blame him for his success, but that success had turned into a major headache for her. Alpha Defence had been surprised – and delighted – when the Deliverance ships had started to change course from the habitats and head out to the trans-Neptune MHD asteroids. Evacuation of the habitats had proved so effective that the Olyix had been left with practically no humans to capture and cocoon by the time they broke a shield and their troops swooped in. So it must have been an easy calculation for the *Salvation of Life* onemind. Invading the habitats was now just a waste of time for them. Unless of course something went seriously wrong with an evacuation.

It was Alik who'd insisted they run the portal breakdown con on at least five habitats simultaneously, so just one emergency didn't seem suspicious. So far it was working, with three Deliverance ships continuing relentlessly for McDivitt.

Kandara reached the broad plaza at the foot of the endcap and studied the habitation section directly ahead. The start of the public area was behind the crystalline canopy projecting out from the wall, where it rested on top of a high curving colonnade.

Zapata splashed the Deliverance ships' flight data on her tarsus lenses as she hurried forwards. The big vessels were finishing their deceleration manoeuvre, sliding to rest relative to the habitat. They glided around the cylinder's midsection until they were equidistant, then fired their energy beams.

As she passed under the colonnade, she watched the feed showing the tenuous aurora of the shield start to brighten towards a vivid sunrise red. A massive hall stretched out ahead of her, extending ten storeys high, its ground-level walls made from wide arches that led back to various function areas. With the main power off, auxiliary lighting had made it a gloomy place where shadows stole out of alcoves to repel the light from the axis spindle. The gloaming seemed to enhance the silence which had claimed it, making her clumping footsteps profoundly intrusive. Above her, balconies swept around the enclosure, linked by Italianate white marble stairs. Zapata splashed her a floorplan which she used to refine the operation.

'Three and four to the plaza, by the fountain,' she ordered. Two of her bioborg entourage started walking to the position she indicated. The bioborgs were near-perfect human replicas, used by police and security teams to perform public-area arrests of armed suspects. Electromorphic musculature was arranged over a boron-aluminium skeleton, with an artificial skin maintained at thirty-six degrees Celsius. They even inhaled and exhaled, in case a suspect's altme was scanning for anomalies. Deploying them meant that the target wouldn't realize they were surrounded until too late, unlike a SWAT squad charging at them in full body armour, nerve-block pistols waving around over-enthusiastically. That was the kind of scenario that resulted in civilian casualties, whereas bioborgs were built to take plenty of punishment and still keep functioning.

Three and four were intended for infiltration operations. And right from the start Kandara had found herself unnerved by them, which was stupid. But . . . they'd been built as five-year-old girls – three with straight ebony hair in bunches, four with cute curls. Both of them were wearing pretty girly dresses, bestowing the human illusion with even greater resonance. The fact that their electromorphic muscles were as strong as any adult creeped her out too. They'd stepped into life right out of a Hong Kong horror interactive, the kind of demonspawn you'd find Sumiko battling against.

'One and two wait under the colonnade,' she instructed when she reached the bottom of a staircase.

That pair were the adults. One, the female version, was wearing a blue dress; while two, the male, was attired in shorts and a T-shirt. As Kandara watched them move away she noticed two's T-shirt had underarm sweat stains. It was an impressive level of realism. *Almost as good as Jessika and Soćko*, she thought maliciously.

'I'm heading up,' she told Yuri. 'We'll start setting up in the food hall next to the Piang gallery.'

Kandara started climbing one of the grandiose staircases, with the trollez following behind, their flex wheels jolting them over every step. As they reached the first-floor balcony she checked on the Deliverance ships' assault. McDivitt's shield was suffering acutely under the triple energy strike, its boundary seething like a phosphorescent stormfront. Sparkling spumes whirled off into space as the vapour's cohesion started to break down.

'Estimated time until shield collapse is twenty-three minutes,' Zapata reported.

Kandara wasn't so sure – the attack looked ferocious to her – but didn't say anything. She went into the abandoned food hall with its long stalls of exotic dishes. Cool and dark now, the overripe vegetables were starting to wrinkle and soften. She was glad her helmet filters were cleaning the air they fed her.

The back of the hall had five doors leading to corridors and storerooms and utility service compartments. She walked along, examining them and cross-referencing with the floorplan, until she reached the rear of the habitation section.

'The corridor's a constant two-point-seven metres wide,' she said, reading from her sensor splash. 'Are you sure about the sphere measurement?'

'Three point two metres,' Yuri said. He sounded amused.

'Just making sure. It's a long way to come and get it wrong.'

'The walls there are a mixture of rock-epoxy sheets pinned onto foamsteel beams,' Alik said. 'Tough as it comes. Relax, this is going to work out just fine.'

Kandara grinned. 'Says the man sitting in the office.' She pressed a gauntlet against the rear wall, feeling its presence. It was part of the massive habitat shell itself: rebonded rock fifty metres thick, woven with a multilayered mesh of steel and aluminium tapes as thick as her leg. Strong enough to last until we build a Dyson sphere around Sol, the designers boasted.

'This is where we'll take it,' she announced. Zapata ordered one of the trollez forwards. It stopped before her and a threader mechanism rose out of its pannier. The first portal swung into position.

*

Alpha Defence predicted correctly. McDivitt's shield lasted a full twenty-seven minutes under the energy beam assault inflicted by the Deliverance ships. The twelve atomic binding generators studded across the shell of the habitat cylinder were already drastically overstressed when the first major component failure happened. It triggered a cascade of failures. With one generator blown, the others tried to assume the loading, which quickly resulted in multiple burnouts. The precious envelope of ions flash-burst out from McDivitt in a tempest of super-energized vapour that lasted barely a couple of seconds.

The three Deliverance ships closed in. They twisted around their long axes until their flat underbellies faced the habitat shell, then began to curve sideways through space – an impressive manoeuvre which saw them match the habitat rotation. That was when they closed the gap and attached themselves to the surface of the shell.

Alpha Defence had received the feeds from a dozen habitats the Deliverance ships had captured before. The procedure was always the same. Some kind of cutter tool or beam powered up from the Deliverance ship, rupturing the shell, emerging from the landscape in a volcanic punch of rock particles and soil. Thousands of tiny flying ovoids, their composition blurred between biology and cybernetics, swarmed up out of the hole and began to spread out, scouting the interior. Then it was only a matter of minutes until the habitat network crashed and the feeds cut off. General Johnston had emplaced spydrones in the last three habitats to fall, using entanglement communications which weren't dependent on solnet. The intelligence they gathered was limited.

Within minutes of the habitat network crash, the Olyix would turn off the axial light. Normally night-time in a habitat was accompanied by a small glimmer from above as the axis lights mimicked the radiance of a new moon. But without any light at all, the interior was shockingly dark. Thermo-regulators were also deactivated – an action that would slowly kill the biosphere as the cylinder radiated its heat away over the coming months. If any humans had been left behind, their choice was now limited to surrender or gradually freezing to death.

The spydrones used passive thermal imaging to see what happened next. The invasion had played out the same way in all three habitats. Hundreds of glossy metallic spheres, just over three metres in diameter, came surging up out of the entry hole – presumably some kind of mini-armoured vehicle for an Olyix quint, crammed full of systems that could subdue a fleeing human. They would spread out across the habitat, driving fast over the cylindrical landscape, searching for anybody who hadn't made it out in time. The longest a spydrone had lasted during that phase was three hours seventeen minutes.

Kandara and her team reckoned she had a window of fifteen to twenty minutes before the Olyix tiny flying scouts noticed the mechanisms which the power technicians had installed around the base of the axis spindle. Which gave her ten minutes for bioborgs three and four to be spotted, while apparently desperate to avoid just that.

As sensors picked up severe vibrations from the Deliverance ships cutting through McDivitt's shell, she stood on the balcony outside the food hall and ran a final suit check. She wasn't taking any chances. The suit had four inner layers, starting with thermal regulation, then a self-sealing pressure membrane, then a thermal resistance layer, which Connexion's armourers had greatly enhanced to prevent any external heat getting through to cook her. The last inner layer was a lacework of electromorphic muscle bands, allowing her to move fast and jump high. She reckoned she was going to need it. Over everything else went a hard carapace in articulated segments made of reactive-molecule armour plating with an integral energy dissipator mesh. Then Jessika had added an external stratum of the übercarbon produced in her lab's initiators, promising it would protect the suit from the web weapons that had been used in King's Cross – adding even more to the suit's weight. So much so that without the electromorphic muscle taking the strain, she wouldn't have been able to stand up, let alone walk.

Her backpack fed power and munitions to the guns on her forearms. Not that she expected to use them – apart from one. She brought up her left forearm to inspect an additional barrel that had been affixed. It was twenty centimetres long and contained one thing: the blue cylinder that Jessika had given her, which – in theory – would jam a quint's entanglement to its other four bodies.

The suppressor had to be fired at the right time for the whole snatch scheme to work. They needed a quint, out of its vehicle and alone, at the same time as the rest of the habitat was being obliterated. That way its other bodies would assume it had been lost when all the quints inside were killed. Kandara would spirit it away it directly to Jessika and Soćko via a portal, and they would use their neurovirus on it. And the fightback would begin.

It was a bold plan. *If your definition of bold is plain batshit crazy.*

Even now she got the cold shivers thinking about how audacious they were being. As soon as the spheres emerged and the axis light failed, bioborgs three and four would use torches out on the plaza. The Olyix flying scouts would see it, and direct the nearest spheres to head straight for them. Bioborgs one and two, distraught parents that they were, would appear, and the whole family would run for cover – right up the stairs and into the food hall, vanishing into a corridor at the back. Kandara had chosen that specific corridor because it was too narrow for the sphere to follow. The quint driving it would have to get out and chase the fugitives itself. If there was more than one sphere coming after them, then the four bioborgs would split up and each run down a separate corridor. Armed drones under Zapata's control would take out the little flying scouts and any other airborne systems accompanying the pursuing quint, while strategically placed charges would seal off the ambush corridor behind them. Then finally, just before the quint reached the portal to the ultra-secure security reception cell waiting in Connexion's Arizona facility, Kandara would fire the entanglement suppressor, along with a nerve-block pulse which Jessika claimed would work on a quint nervous system. And if not, if it came to using firepower to subdue it, Kandara had a lot of confidence in her own weapons. Which included heavy-duty tangle rounds that would smother the quint in foam and lasso cords. The idea of rolling a quint through the portal, cemented inside a giant beachball, was one that had a dark appeal.

There were plenty of maybes in there, but they'd worked out a fallback for each one, and the overall idea was sound. If they could just get one alone . . .

'Here they come,' Yuri said.

Kandara's splash showed her three mini-volcanoes rising up out of the cylinder landscape amid a maelstrom of stone fragments. The rubble was still falling when the little ovoid scout gadgets came flooding out of the gaping holes. Even though they were fifteen kilometres away, Kandara felt her adrenalin ramp up. She quickly checked her gland, making sure its output hadn't fallen too much now that she'd dialled it down. If there was ever a time to lose all restrictions, this was it. Splash icons showed that her neurochemistry was under control, but its grip on her deep daemons was loosening. Her anger with the Olyix was intensifying, paired with the excitement at the prospect of physical confrontation. After days of endless meetings and planning, things were finally heading towards a resolution.

'I'm going to take up position,' she said. 'Don't want to be seen here.'

'Roger that. Good luck.'

'Yeah,' Alik said. 'Break a leg.'

'That's for actors going on stage, asshole.'

'Okay, so break one of their legs.' He laughed.

'Consider that favour in the bag.'

'We're still playing the long con,' Yuri reported. 'As far as the Olyix know, there's a lot of panicky humans in McDivitt terrified they're about to be captured.'

'As long as you've still got control of the solarwells this'll work just fine,' she said as she turned and headed back into the food hall.

'They're all entangled channels. All I have to do is press this big red button.'

'Thanks, Yuri. Let's do this.'

'Here come the big boys,' Alik said.

The dark spheres were now surging up out of the holes which the Deliverance ships had rammed through the habitat shell. An hour earlier, Connexion Security had released a swarm of bees into McDivitt's interior. The insects had synthetic eight-letter DNA to give them bioneural circuitry instead of a natural brain, as well as enhanced visual reception. Individually each bee had a limited view, but linced they were a multifaceted eye with prodigious focus.

Kandara paused mid-step as a high-resolution image splashed across her tarsus lens. 'I can't see a track around those spheres they're using. But they're moving fast.'

'They're not rolling along, either,' Yuri said.

'Then how's—?' She ordered Zapata to zoom in, concentrating on the bottom of the sphere. There was a small gap between it and the ground. 'Mother Mary! Is that thing flying?'

The image pulled back, revealing that a group of spheres had risen far above the holes in the shell to skim across the treetops.

'Shit,' Alik spat. 'Okay, so they fly. It doesn't change the basics of the operation. Everything's just going to be quicker is all.'

'You think?'

'Kandara,' Jessika said, 'the Olyix may be using a miniature variant of their gravatonic drive in those vehicles.'

'If they have miniaturized the drive, then our information is out of date,' Soćko countered.

'Hey, you two!' Kandara snapped. 'Less nerdism, more practicality.'

'Okay. Sorry,' Jessika said. 'But it means Alik is right. They'll be able to move fast.'

'What else is out of date?' Alik demanded.

'Unknown,' Soćko replied meekly.

'Dammit.' Kandara grunted and turned back.

'What are you doing?' Yuri demanded.

'Repositioning the bioborgs. If those spheres can fly, we need to rethink the distance the children have to run.'

'All right. But be careful.'

'Middle name.'

'Ha. I've seen your file.'

Kandara arrived back at the balcony and jogged along it towards the giant crystalline canopy that fronted the public hall. The bee swarm visualization was showing her a continuing procession of quint spheres pouring out of the holes. The majority were heading straight for the endcaps. During previous habitat invasions they'd spread out in formation to scour the cylindrical landscape before swirling around the habitation sections.

'Mother Mary,' she muttered. 'They are fast.' Zapata gave her an estimate of four minutes before the first ones reached the plaza. She brought her gaze back to the plaza where two small figures in sweet dresses stood motionless beside a big bronze statue fountain. 'Crap.' A less childlike pose she couldn't imagine. 'Three and four,' she ordered. 'Start moving back to the public hall now. One and two, go grab them, make it frantic.'

The two small bioborgs began a reasonably realistic run across the plaza, holding hands and calling for their parents.

'Kandara!' Yuri warned.

She saw it in the splash from the bees. The leading spheres started to speed up, their wake rippling the tallest tree fronds as they soared over them.

'Abort! Get the fuck out of there!'

She turned and began hurrying back to the food hall. 'This might still work.'

'There are fifteen of those fuckers heading for you. Just get out.'

'I'm going for the portal. But at least see what happens to the bioborgs before we cancel.'

'Crap! All right, we're reviewing.'

By the time she reached the food hall her heart was palpitating as if it'd been hit by a defibrillator charge. Back on the plaza, the four bioborgs had all met up underneath the colonnade in a hectic family reunion. Arms pointed in shock at the approaching Olyix spheres above the jungle, then parents grasped their children firmly, hauling them along. Even Kandara was impressed by the authenticity of the performance.

'They might just make—'

Violet energy beams ripped out of the two lead spheres. Flame engulfed the bioborgs as clothes ignited, their bodies dissolving into carbonized slag. Abdominal power cells ruptured, ripping open what was left of their torsos.

'Busted,' Alik declared.

'Get out!' Yuri cried. 'I'm triggering the kamikaze. You can survive it, but it'll make them withdraw.'

Kandara didn't hesitate. She charged for the door at the back of the food hall, the armour suit smashing through. Four kilometres above her, the six small MHD chambers which technicians had taken out of McDivitt's industrial stations and installed around the axis spindle opened. Plasma direct from the sun's photosphere seared into the habitat. The MHD chambers had been reprogrammed to defocus the streams from narrow spears that would have punctured clean through the opposite endcap into wider torrents that merged to slam down the cylinder as an incandescent wave. It hit the opposite endcap and ricocheted back. Within seconds, the habitat's entire carpet of vegetation burst into flame, and the atmospheric pressure began to rise drastically, sending tornados of superheated air roaring down the holes through the shell and into the Deliverance craft that had cut them. The plasma wasn't just hot, it carried a phenomenal electrical charge. Massive lightning bolts erupted within the cylinder, lashing around in all directions as the devastated atmosphere sought to establish equilibrium. Spheres out in the open were flung around helplessly as their fuselages instantly turned silver in an attempt to reflect the energy deluge. Dozens were caught by savage lightning forks, exploding in a hail of actinic debris. The million windows of the habitation section shattered, turning to molten droplets as they pounded into the big ornate rooms behind, igniting every piece of furniture and fabric. Lightning stabbed in though the gaps, clawing at the burning walls to ground out through structural girders.

Around the root of the axis spindle, the energy rampage battered the MHD chambers, and the plasma streams failed as the small portals feeding them disintegrated. Total elapsed time since they were switched on: nine seconds. But it was enough to annihilate the habitat's interior.

Kandara's universe turned from a gloomy cavern of shadows to a reality constructed entirely of pure white light as her suit sensors struggled to interpret the photonic overload. Scarlet warning icons splashed across half of her tarsus lens display as the ionized atmosphere buffeted her. But her suit could resist the appalling barrage for at least a minute, or so they had calculated during the worst-case scenario stage of planning.

Zapata framed the corridor in a grid of navigation graphics, showing her the way. Sparks and smoke turned the air to a gale of dragon's breath, while rivulets of molten metal slithered down the walls and across the floor. Geysers of hypercharged atmosphere whorled around her suit as the deadly electrical storm raged.

'Keep going,' Yuri demanded. 'You're doing fine. We're ready for you.'

In the vast public hall, three of the drones had survived being pounded into walls, their fan blades sagging and melting as they dropped to the floor. But some of their combat-hardened systems remained functional. Sensors saw the massive crystalline canopy shatter as a quint sphere crashed through it. The sphere came to a halt twenty metres above the smouldering floor as balconies and staircases crumbled, flinging clouds of embers into the hazed air. Every particle danced with static that spun out slim strands of lightning, filling the hall with a cascade of furious electrons. The silver sphere hung resolute at the centre of the cataclysm, reflecting the terrible light like the devil's own Christmas ornament.

'Mary! You've gotta be fucking kidding me,' Kandara said numbly. The door ahead of her was already buckled and melting as she knocked it aside. She swore she could hear the lightning savaging her suit – the same sound a T-rex's claws would make scouring the carapace segments.

'Run!' Alik implored.

The sphere shifted position in a smooth curving motion, coming down level with the floor of the collapsing food hall. It powered forwards, trailing a massive vortex of lightning through the livid air.

Kandara used a forearm gaussrifle to blow apart the door ahead of her. Elecromorphic muscles punched the fiery wreckage aside as they accelerated up to a sprint speed she could never have achieved with her own flesh and blood. She took one corner so fast that her suit grazed the sagging wall, fracturing it to igneous chunks.

The quint sphere hit the back of the food hall where the door to the corridor was now a charred puddle on the floor. It started to plough through the narrow corridor like a bloated chainsaw, ripping the walls, floor and ceiling apart in violent fantails of sizzling rubble as it forced its way through the structure.

The measured discharges of Kandara's gland did absolutely nothing to stop the animal panic that threatened to overwhelm every rational thought. Her gaussrifle shots pummelled any and every remaining solid surface ahead, saving precious milliseconds she would otherwise have spent breaking through them. Behind her the sphere was a cyclone of destruction smashing its way relentlessly onwards through rooms and corridors. She just knew it had weapons powerful enough to take her down, but that wasn't its purpose. Oh, no. The Olyix wanted *her*, alive and entombed in her own mutated flesh, preserved for the rest of eternity until their diabolical god emerged to subsume her soul.

The floor was shaking furiously as she reached the last room. Cracks multiplied in the surfaces around her as the sphere hurtled across the last few metres, the roar of its destruction trail making her armour vibrate. The portal was dead ahead, a dark circle amid the inflamed atmosphere. She powerdived for it. Yelling in relief as she shot through the gap, pulling a writhing glob of ruined air with her. A yell that turned to a scream as she came to a bone-snapping halt in mid-air. Something had wrapped itself around her lower legs, suspending her –

Gravity abruptly took over and she crashed to the ground, thick fronds of static drilling into the concrete while the suit discharged its colossal load. She was scrabbling around manically on the floor of the high-security cell as the light levels changed and her sensors pulled everything into focus. A slim, glowing tentacle was coiled around her ankles, attached to nothing. Behind her, the portal had become an inert circle of solid-state circuitry. Six heavy-duty military drones were poised overhead, each with several ominous muzzles extended towards her. Thin spurts of smoke were rising from the blackened points where her armour was touching the floor. A fast wind of cold air jetted over her from vents in the ceiling. She reached down gingerly and gripped the tentacle. It didn't put up any resistance as she unwrapped it and flung it across the room, now nothing more than a length of exotic rope. She didn't trust it for an instant.

'You okay?' Yuri asked quietly.

'Mother Mary, just get me the fuck out of here!'

'Your suit's cooling nicely. We'll open the door in a minute.'

She sat back, feeling the tension slackening – slightly. Glad she was wearing a helmet, that there was no way the others could see her face right now. The post-combat shakes would hit her any minute; they always did. They'd fade soon enough, but not the paranoia, not even with the gland turned up to maximum. That terrible sphere was an irresistible force that would hunt her for the rest of her life. 'We don't stand a chance, do we? Not against that. I was kind of bulling it out before, but . . .'

'Jessika and Soćko may have a point about building those exodus habitats,' Alik said.

'How long before the Deliverance ships reach Earth?'

'Couple of days.'

Kandara clasped her heat-tarnished gauntlets together. 'Sweet Lord save us when those things get loose down here.'

Vayan

Year 56 AB

I am composed of many advanced technologies, but not even my drive units can defy the lightspeed barrier. If I were to accelerate up to my cruising speed of point nine C, it would take me nearly forty days to reach the incoming Olyix ship. That would make me very late for the party.

I'm going to have to hitch a lift.

I accelerate at two hundred gees, reaching Sasras in seventy-two minutes. The gas giant is beribboned in saffron cloudbands, interspaced with moon-sized rivers of white ammonia cyclones, the two locked together by ever-shifting curlicues. Comparative association brings up memories of Saturn; I remember having a banqueting suite on Titan, whose windows looked out on a ginger sky with the pale gas giant looming above the horizon. Jupiter was impressive simply because of its size, but Saturn's rings were an incomparable beauty.

My perception fronds are a gentle rain upon Sasras's upper atmosphere. They provide accurate coordinates to the two hundred variable portals the *Morgan* has seeded across the upper atmosphere. Flood mines are dropping out of them, thousands of them freefalling for hundreds of kilometres through the thermosphere then stratosphere, and further still, down to the incredible pressure at the bottom of the troposphere where they finally achieve neutral buoyancy and float above the boundary layer.

I hang high above one of the variable portals, shielded from its sensors, until the last mine has come through.

Three hours later, the expansion portals in every flood mine open a kilometre wide, and Sasra's super-pressurized atmosphere screams through the multitude of holes into the hard vacuum on the other side. The torrent lasts for twelve minutes.

When it is over I descend. The base routines of the genten which controls the variable portal are completely familiar to me. There have been many layers of additional procedures built on top by all the generations of humans that have fled deep into the galaxy, adding sophistication but not expanding its primary rationality. Nor do they prevent me from taking full control of the operating system.

I command the portal to expand, and slip through.

*

Dellian was already in his armour when the *Morgan* went through the portal to interstellar space. They'd emerged thousands of kilometres away from the Olyix arkship, but Captain Kenelm insisted they were prepared and ready for immediate combat.

It was bull, Dellian knew. If the Olyix were capable of detecting and engaging the *Morgan* right after it emerged, then it wouldn't be any kind of fight which squads wearing armour suits were going to be taking part in. Nor were they likely to survive such an encounter. But he complied without protest and made sure the rest of the squad were sealed up tight and snug. The longest they'd ever remained in their armour was five days straight; it had been a bitch of a training simulation. But apart from seriously needing a shower afterwards, it wasn't that uncomfortable. Besides, being inside the tough suits right from the start was as reassuring as any neuro-chemical squirted out by his gland. He just hoped Fintox could cope with the physical isolation.

Dellian's databud played the tactical display from the *Morgan*'s command network across his optik. The Strike fleet's emergence deployment was good, with everything well inside the positioning error margin. Three thousand flood mines were strung out twenty kilometres apart in a line that stretched ahead of the arkship's course, while the *Morgan*'s attack cruisers were poised, waiting in a circular formation five thousand kilometres out from the arkship. But the delivery portals they'd come through had spent days manoeuvring to match the alien's course and speed, delivering the cruisers on a parallel vector. The *Morgan* itself was another thousand kilometres further out.

When the arkship was one lightminute from the first flood mine, Sasra's atmosphere began to vent out into interstellar space from the entire formation. As it emerged, each colossal jet was semisolid matter, held in its uneasy state by the gas giant's crushing pressure. Once through the portal into the freedom of the vacuum, it expanded at an incredible rate. A cloud of molecular hydrogen billowed out where seconds before was only clear space. It dispersed rapidly, but thanks to the continuing jets at its core, retained the same high density.

Travelling at point one three C, the arkship would now take less than ten minutes to reach the flood cloud. If its sensors did manage to detect the dense blot of hydrogen swelling across the stars directly ahead, it probably had no way of determining that it was actually end-on to a mass of vapour sixty thousand kilometres long. As the seconds wound down, Dellian could see it was making no attempt to change course. The gravitational distortion it was generating was sufficient to deflect any natural nebula of dust and gas adrift between the stars, allowing it to fly straight through the tenuous wisps of atoms unscathed. Then, with a minute to go, the arkship began to change its vector. Even with a gravatonic drive, shifting a multibillion-tonne mass took a long time.

'It's going to hit,' Dellian declared, grinning inside his helmet. A cheer went around the squad. The induction sheaths entwined with his muscles trembled in patterns he could instinctively read; his combat core cohort was sharing his excitement and satisfaction.

'Wait,' Ellici said. 'They might switch on the antimatter drive. If that exhaust hits the flood cloud, it will weaken the impact.'

Dellian let out a silent sigh. *She always assumes the worst.*

'It'll take too long to activate the antimatter rocket,' Tilliana said. 'It's not something the onemind will just flick a switch for. Not with forty seconds to go.'

Dellian watched the feed with anxiety and exhilaration. The arkship continued its slow deviation away from its original course. Less than two million kilometres ahead of it, the flood cloud continued its wild inflation as the mines fed it with billions of tonnes of hydrogen every second. It was now too broad for the arkship to avoid.

Space was besieged by a micronova flash of ultra-hard radiation as the arkship tore through the entire length of the flood cloud in little more than a second. Its protective distortion effect was completely overwhelmed by the sheer quantity of mass impacting its boundary. For all that the hydrogen was nothing more than a nebulous fog, at that velocity the outcome was the same as if the arkship had struck a solid wall. The radiation from molecular hydrogen converting to pure energy from the collision stabbed into the arkship, penetrating the rock to a depth of over a hundred metres. It annihilated any machinery or biological components it struck, while the corresponding electromagnetic pulse sent vast electrical currents surging through metal structures, melting the larger mechanisms and burning smaller items to slag.

Milliseconds after the energy cascade, the physical shockwave manifested down the arkship. Along with everyone else, Dellian held his breath. If the flood cloud was too thick, or too long, the resulting quake would be violent enough to pulverize the huge ship, and everything they'd done since leaving Juloss would've been for nothing.

The arkship emerged from the irradiated miasma of the flood cloud with its own coma of ionized gas elongating behind it. As the distortion generators were now so much cooling lava, there was nothing to protect the arkship's surface from genuine interstellar gas and dust crashing into it at point one three lightspeed. The blunt forward section of the massive cylinder crawled with dazzling collision sparks that began to chew their way through the dark nickel-iron rock.

'Drive systems are off,' Captain Kenelm announced. 'As is the gravitational deflector. Overall physical integrity is holding. And we're picking up a negative energy signature, so the wormhole is still intact. The interstellar medium here is giving it a good kicking, so let's get this over with before the damn thing starts to fragment.'

The squad cheered so enthusiastically Dellian thought he was hearing it through the suit insulation rather than their secure channel. His optik's tactical feed showed him the assault cruisers accelerating hard, closing in on the crippled alien craft. Then the *Morgan* was moving, following the assault cruisers inside its own protective formation of eight heavily armoured escort vessels.

Dust abrasion created a glowing violet halo around the front of the arkship, providing an easy visual target as the Strike fleet closed in. When they were a thousand kilometres away, the first of the Olyix ships launched to fight back. The flood cloud impact was calculated to destroy between twenty to thirty per cent of the arkship's systems, leaving enough mechanisms intact to make the boarding operation worthwhile. Any more damage and they wouldn't be able to extract the vital gateway information. Any less, and they'd have a serious fight on their hands. And of course without the gravitational distortion, dust impacts at point one three lightspeed would eventually reach a crescendo resulting in the whole rock shattering, which put them under the clock.

'Stand by,' Wim announced over the general channel. 'We're seeing activity around the forward end.'

The craft that came sliding out of the openings around the arkship's forward rim were a kind Dellian knew well, they were so familiar from the ancient files of Sol's invasion. Deliverance ships: their sleek rounded delta-shape fuselage so dark out here between the stars it was barely visible in the erratic aurora engulfing the flailing arkship. Seeing a whole squadron of them manoeuvring with easy grace as they accelerated towards the incoming assault cruisers made Dellian smile in welcome. It was an odd feeling, as if they were back in history, fighting for Sol all over again.

'The *Salvation of Life* never had hangars full of Deliverance ships,' Ellici said. 'They've changed the design. They've definitely been lured before.'

'How bad is it?' Dellian asked as the sensor images played across his optik.

'We know the Deliverance ships,' she replied in a soothing tone. 'Our assault cruisers outclass them.'

Dellian wondered what had happened at all the other lures. The Olyix were still sending out arkships, so they hadn't been defeated yet. *But they've never had a Neána board them and snatch the gateway coordinate from the onemind. We can do this. We can be the turning point in the whole war!*

Both sides might have been hurtling towards Vayan's sun at thirteen per cent of lightspeed, but their relative velocities were matched. And there were over five hundred assault cruisers against a hundred and fifteen Deliverance ships. They closed on each other at heavy acceleration. Coherent radiation beams pulsed, cross-hatching the void like short-lived rapier stabs. Deliverance ships launched a barrage of missiles armed with antimatter, some of which detonated hundreds of kilometres from their targets. The explosions had two functions – first to channel and focus the energy release from mutual mass eradication into a single coherent beam of gamma rays, and secondly to create a lethal shrapnel cloud expanding so fast the *Morgan*'s assault cruisers couldn't possibly change course in time.

The active baffle hulls of the assault cruisers deflected the energy beams with ease, while their own gravitation distortion batted away the majority of the shrapnel. X-ray lasers targeted the remaining antimatter missiles before they got anywhere near the attack cruisers. For all their power, Deliverance ships were not so capable. The assault cruisers launched Callumites: slender plasma rocket missiles encased in a teardrop-shaped portal. As they approached their targets, the Olyix retaliated with a prodigious amount of energy weapons, missiles and all-out kinetic barrages. None of it was any use. The attack – whether material or energy – simply passed through the hole in space which was the Callumite missile and flashed harmlessly out of its portal twin, orbiting low above Vayan's star.

In the last second before a Callumite struck a Deliverance ship, its portal fuselage expanded out to fifty metres, allowing it to slice a huge chunk out of the hapless ship, or even bore a hole clean through it.

The battle was over in less than a minute, its conclusion a swathe of highly radioactive debris flashing through space, each piece spewing its own scintillating ion tail from the unrelenting interstellar gas impacts. Assault cruisers closed on the arkship. A second wave of Deliverance ships shot out to meet them.

Dellian watched the subsequent clash with trepidation. Any of the weapons the two sides were firing at each other now had the potential to wreck the arkship. All it took was one misaligned trajectory.

Extreme radiation saturated the arkship's surface, assailing the already-damaged rock. It began to slough off rivers of rock fragments amid spurts of lava that twirled away into the abyss.

'Saints, it's like watching the *Titanic* hit the iceberg,' Dellian complained. 'You know it's going to sink, it's just a question of when.'

'After we get off,' Xante said.

'Got to get on, first,' Janc chimed in.

'We're modelling the arkship's overall integrity as fair,' Tilliana told them. 'It should retain cohesion for another three hours.'

'Unless the interstellar gas density increases,' Ellici said. 'Increased impact ablation could accelerate its structural breakdown.'

Dellian gave up. 'Good to know.'

'Don't worry,' Tilliana said. 'Now we've gone overt we've launched a batch of Mark Twelve sensor webs. They're sampling space ahead of you. If there's anything untoward out there we'll be able to warn you in time.'

'Better to know,' Uret said smugly.

'Squads stand by,' Kenelm ordered. 'We're going to launch the first interception group.'

Dellian felt only the smallest bout of envy, which he suspected would have been larger if it wasn't for the gland keeping him calm. *Like Saint Kandara.* But he'd been the one who asked for the Fintox mission, so had no right to complain about not being in the lead boarding party. For the life of him he couldn't remember his reason at the time.

The *Morgan* closed to within five hundred kilometres of the arkship and released its troop carriers. The flight consisted of bursts of acceleration and long stretches of freefall, tension interspaced with tedium. Dellian accessed his ship's sensors to watch the approach. The arkship in its nebulous cloak of ablation impacts grew larger, providing a more detailed image of the melted, broken surface. It looked almost identical to the *Salvation of Life* – a solid-rock asteroid that the Olyix had carved into a relatively smooth cylinder forty-two kilometres long and eleven in diameter. The *Morgan*'s Mark Twelve web sensors sashayed around it, confirming there were four major internal cavities – three large ones, eight kilometres across, which would contain the biospheres full of life from the Olyix 'homeworld', proving the lie it was slowly travelling between the stars. The fourth cavity was only four kilometres in diameter, and housed the wormhole which connected the arkship to the Olyix enclave gateway. Smaller cavities, like bubbles in the rock, were grouped between the large biospheres: hangars and chambers full of life-support machinery, some that were nothing more than giant reservoir tanks.

Escorted by attack cruisers, the lead troop carriers slipped into the cave-like holes at the arkship's forward rim. The whole of Dellian's squad watched keenly as their colleagues disembarked and began to advance down the endless maze of tunnels that linked the chambers. They were due to reach the wormhole generator in an hour and a half. Twenty minutes later Ovan reported the docking area was secure.

'Let's go,' Dellian told the troop carrier's genten.

They flew in alongside five other vehicles, each containing squads with specific extraction missions. There was a big semicircular cavern beyond the entrance, with five airlock doors wide enough for two Deliverance ships to pass through at the same time. Three of the doors were missing altogether, with the remaining two bent out of place. The inner doors at the far end had also been wrenched aside. Dellian wondered if it'd happened from the flood cloud impact or if the Deliverance ships had broken through in a rush to defend the arkship.

The hangar beyond the broken airlocks was so big its floor followed the curve of the arkship. It looked arboreal, with the walls and ceiling covered in a web of organic tubes that reminded Dellian of ancient tree trunks, with black bark deeply fissured. They must have taken decades to grow to that stature.

The majority of the woody tubes had split open to spray oily fluids across the marble-like floor, where the puddles were still bubbling away merrily in the vacuum, creating wispy layers of vapour that gusted gently out through the gaping airlocks. He counted seventeen smashed-up Deliverance ships jammed against the walls. All of them had burn holes corresponding to assault cruiser X-ray laser shots, finishing the job. Three assault cruisers patrolled the hangar cautiously, backed up by hundreds of armoured drones. It was their broad spotlight beams which provided the only illumination.

'Are you ready for this?' Dellian asked Fintox through a private channel.

'I am.'

He wished he had some way of judging the metavayan's state of mind the way he could from just reviewing his squad's medical data in his optik. But then not even Yirella had anticipated a real Vayan body coming into existence, so he had to rely on Fintox simply being honest. That was hard.

The troop carrier landed near a working internal airlock. The rear doors opened and the squad's combat cores lifted off their cradles and coasted out. Amid the devastation of the hangar the cores were bluntly impressive, the central cylinder with its wasp-waist constriction now encrusted with an aggressive array of auxiliary weapon pods and drive units. Despite the added bulk they retained their agility as they slipped over and around the carrier in a frisky fashion. That playfulness told him the munc brains hadn't entirely lost their glee along with their bodies.

Dellian hurried down the side ramp. His boots clumped onto the hangar floor, kicking up embers and sticky fluid.

'Ellici, what have you got for me?'

'Motaxan has been reviewing sensor data. The front end of the arkship has taken heavy damage. We need you to head back towards the second chamber. There are some caverns between the two that are full of life-support systems; they should have a major nexus in them.'

'Roger that.'

He led the squad towards the working airlock, whose door was four metres high. Ovan's squad was in charge of securing the hangar and the area immediately beyond. Suited figures, with their combat core cohorts hovering overhead, were examining larger chunks of wreckage.

'We haven't seen a living quint so far,' Ovan told them as they waited for the oval door to open. 'Some bodies, though. Bagged up a couple ready for transport back to the *Morgan.*'

'So where are they hiding?' Dellian asked.

'Inside. Drones and lead squads are heading for the first chamber. They'll find 'em soon enough.' He gave Dellian a thumbs-up, a gesture that didn't work well in armoured gauntlets.

Three of Dellian's cohort hovered in front of the airlock door, shining their powerful lights on it. Ovan's people had patched some kind of override control into the circuitry, which puzzled Dellian. The hinges looked like bands of raw muscle, oozing fluid from cracked capillaries. But the override was working, even though the door's movement was ponderously slow.

That made him cautious. 'Janc, Uret, Falar: you're point, each take half your cohort with you. Check the passage on the other side is clear.'

'It is,' Ovan protested.

'Sure.' He trusted Ovan, as he did all the squads, but these were his people. And the alien arkship was one creepy shambles with the Saints knew how many hostiles lurking in the shadows.

He sent a couple of his own cohort through with Falar. When the inner door opened they showed him a honeycomb of passages and small chambers, whose weave of branches and fronds and conduits were jumbled and fractured. Drones and combat cores fanned out, verifying the area was clear.

The rest of the squad escorted Fintox through. The drones were advancing through the maze, seeking out the broad passages that led down the length of the arkship.

'SR 3 is the one we think you should take,' Tilliana told them. 'It seems to be one of the major transport routes that runs the whole length of the arkship – at least, they did in the *Salvation of Life*. If we're right, that'll take you to a life-support compartment between the first and second biochambers. Motaxan thinks there'll be a nexus in there.'

'Roger that,' Dellian said, studying the tactical chart which was growing rapidly as the drones and squads penetrated deeper into the arkship. 'Okay, people, this way.'

SR 3 was triggering another déjà vu moment. It was the same layout as the tunnel system Feriton Kayne had walked down on his fatal mission in the *Salvation of Life*. 'Do you think Feriton was telling the truth about where the tunnels led?' Dellian asked Ellici.

'His debriefing couldn't go far off-truth,' Ellici replied. 'The Olyix probably caught him sneaking around in the tunnels, because we know the obelisks and fourth biochamber he said he saw were a lie. But the early recon teams established the general layout before his mission.'

Dellian focused on the woody pipes that ran high along the tunnel walls in long twisting knots. 'Great. So he got ambushed in something like this?'

'Come on,' Janc said. 'He was a spy creeping around in the dark. We're a squad in armour suits with cohorts of combat cores, backed up by a fleet of assault cruisers with enough firepow—'

'Don't say it!' Xante called out.

'Say what?'

Dellian chuckled at the mock innocence in Janc's voice.

'Saints, don't make me say it!' Xante exclaimed.

'Need to know,' Uret taunted.

'I don't understand,' Fintox said. 'What do some of you not wish to be said?'

'They are joking to relieve tension,' Ellici said. 'Traditionally in a situation like this, nobody should ever say –'

'No!'

'– What can possibly go wrong?'

The comms were flooded with a deluge of jeering.

'It doesn't count if I say it,' Ellici protested. 'I'm not there.'

'That is humorous?' Fintox asked.

'It used to be called tempting fate,' Dellian said. 'And that was a serious thing. Then it got badly overused by Earth's drama industry, so it became funny. But some people still think it *is* serious.'

There was a long pause. 'I do not think I fully comprehend human psychology,' Fintox announced.

'You and me both,' Dellian muttered.

The tunnel was reasonably wide, but not enough to accommodate clumps of combat cores, so they had to glide through it in single file, the squad all spaced out. Dellian had kept Janc on point duty, with drones and half a dozen combat cores flying on ahead of him. Then the rest of the squad followed in a line, with combat cores between them. Dellian was in the middle of the line with Fintox by his side. As they went on, they found sections of the tunnel illuminated by a pale pink light shining out of long leaves that sprouted from the tubes.

'Squads are engaging with armed quints,' Tilliana informed them.

'Where?' Dellian asked.

'The entrance to the first biosphere. The quints are in huntspheres, and using high-powered weapons. Combat cores are taking them out, but it's difficult. They're bedded in good and putting up a hell of a fight. Anyone would think they didn't want us in there.'

'Del,' Janc called, 'there's a big room up ahead.'

'Wait for the rest of us,' Dellian told him. 'We'll check it out together.'

The tunnel opened into a high circular junction, with three more tunnels leading away into the gloom and a five-metre archway filled with mist that flowed out along the floor, dissipating quickly. It left the walls slick with condensation and slim lines of frost.

Dellian's suit sensors reported the mist was nitrogen at minus twenty-five degrees Celsius. 'Cryogenic leak?'

'Looks like it,' Ellici said. 'That ties in with the chamber being part of life support. They'd need a decent reserve of atmosphere gases.'

'Okay.' Dellian activated several weapons. His cohort did the same. 'Janc, Uret, you're on. The rest of us are behind them, hexagon formation. Xante, cover Fintox and watch the rear. Janc, scout it.'

A dozen drones and two combat cores nudged forwards into the mist. Visually there was nothing; the entire chamber was full of the subzero fog. Active sensors sliced through it, building up a map.

Dellian followed Uret's combat cores through the archway, his optik providing an overlay outline. The chamber was stadium sized, with huge cylindrical tanks lined up along one wall. Pipes and heat exchangers took up plenty of floorspace.

The flood cloud impact had punished the tanks severely, dislodging them from their fixings. They'd knocked against each other, opening up various splits from which liquid nitrogen was still spraying. The air was thick with mist as a result, its temperature still dropping. Dellian's cohort slowly pushed their way through it, picking up on his tension to swing their noses about as if they were sniffing for scent.

'What's this cold going to do to the arkship's neural seams?' Dellian asked.

'The temperature will be an inhibitor,' Fintox said. 'Many of the seam's cells will be damaged and dying. It will be difficult to make a flawless interface to the nexus here. I suggest we find another location, one with an unharmed nexus.'

'Okay. Tilliana, where do we go?'

'Wait one,' Tilliana said. 'Del, I want you to check the—'

'Power source emerging,' Janc called.

The sensor sweep splashed the errant appearance across Dellian's tactical display. Three more materialized, growing out of nowhere, magnetic and electromagnetic emissions expanding, temperature points erupting as if someone had pulled a veil back.

'Saints, where did . . .'

Several cryogenic tanks burst apart, sending a vast wave of

liquid nitrogen sloshing across the chamber. Combat cores floated serenely above it, but the squad in their suits were buffeted by the vigour of the surge. Foaming liquid came up to Dellian's waist, pushing hard. His suit's strength resisted it, though the floor had become treacherously slippery. He was shoved back several metres before his shoulder thudded into a column of bent piping, steadying him. His cohort followed the motion instinctively, tightening up protectively above him.

Sensors showed five huntspheres rising out of the wrecked tanks. Dellian's databud picked up an all-frequency radio broadcast.

'Dear humans, you are welcome even though your intent is misguided. Please join us of your own volition. We love you, and wish only to elevate you to the final revelation of the God at the End of Time. Do not believe the lies your predecessors have cursed you with. Our voyage is the destiny and reward for all sentient species. We are happy to address any fears you may—'

Dellian smiled brightly inside his helmet as a feeling of complete satisfaction buoyed him up. 'Hi, guys,' he said. 'Go fuck yourselves.'

One of the huntspheres fired an incredibly powerful violet energy beam at him. His suit surface turned silver, reflecting the beam to score a burning line across the chamber wall. Lava squirted down, adding to the vehemence of the boiling liquid nitrogen.

'Guess where we learned that tech trick from?' Dellian taunted. 'Your cold dead corpses that litter Earth even today. Now you surrender calmly to us and we'll let you live.'

'Dear human, have you not yet understood? We live forever. With or without you.'

'Okay, then, Saint Kandara says hello.' He opened fire. His combat cohort joined in. The chamber was instantly filled with the kinetic blitz of gaussrifles pumping hypervelocity metallic hydrogen bullets into the huntspheres at a ferocious rate. The spheres burst apart, their shattered, dying components throwing out a hellish blastwave that succeeded in knocking the squad off their feet. Glowing wreckage plunged down into the retreating tide of liquid nitrogen, along with burning quint flesh that immediately flash-froze into raggedy glistening lumps as it hit the listless liquid.

Dellian laughed victoriously as he went with the force of the blast, rolling smoothly to his feet after it passed. Quick check on the tactical display and all the squad were intact, medical telemetry good.

'Well done, people. Final scan, please. I don't want any more surprises.'

For the next couple of seconds the life-support chamber once again filled with the shrieks of more metallic hydrogen bullets being fired into the largest surviving sections of tanks. There were no more huntspheres camouflaging themselves within.

'Move out,' he said. 'Tilliana, I need a new nexus location.'

'If Motaxan is right, there'll be another life-support chamber about a kilometre spinward. Take SR b5 from the junction outside.'

'Got it.'

'Oh, and Del –'

'Yeah?'

'Great supervillan laugh.'

*

Yirella had nowhere to go, no one to be with and talk to, to share the worry. So she sat cross-legged on the grass of the habitat torus and watched the Strike play out across her optik. She had never realized it would be so hard. Those first hours were an endless empty wait as ships and flood mines assumed their positions in the cold emptiness out beyond Vayan's cometary belt with the unsuspecting arkship heading straight for them. Time stretched to torment.

Then when it came, the Strike was sudden and brutal. So much so she felt her databud was accessing some kind of weird time-lapse feed. The arkship was devastated by the flood cloud, Deliverance ships bursting out like furious wasps from a broken nest. Assault cruisers charging in, confident in their superiority.

Then came the troop carriers, nosing carefully into the arkship's entrance caverns. Her breath came hard as she drank down Del's suit data, revelling in her role as his invisible guardian angel. Yet her wings were clipped; she could say nothing to him. She had sworn that above all things. Tilliana and Ellici were the true tacticians now, rich with data from multiple sources, all perfectly analysed by the remnant thoughts of their muncs, their years of training and experience guiding the squad with care and skill. They would make sure no harm came to them.

Trust them.

'The tanks,' she said in exasperation as the squad crept into the vast life-support chamber. Her voice rose in anger. 'Come on, check the cryotanks, idiot!' She focused on the emergency comms icon which would give her direct contact to Ellici and Tilliana – which was the last thing they needed. *They'll see the tanks are the only possible hiding place. They will!*

Her gasp of relief was almost a sob when Tilliana began her warning. Seconds later Dellian went tumbling through waves of liquid nitrogen. Suit schematics splashed across her optik, checking the temperature-resistance levels. Okay, they can handle liquid nitrogen immersion for three hours before degradation creep.

Then Del was fronting it out with the huntspheres, all stupid fearless bravado.

'For the love of the Saints, just shoot!' she implored.

But then her wish came true, and she squealed and whimpered as the firefight raged, hating herself for every pathetic sound coming from her throat.

Get a grip.

The last huntsphere was blown apart by the squad.

Thank the Saints.

She clambered to her feet and stretched as the squad began to make their way to the next potential nexus. Her body was convinced she'd been in the arkship right alongside her friends, enduring all the physical stress of the firefight. There was way too much nervous energy churning through her; fingertips tingling, random tremors in her legs and arms.

The torus parkland was almost black, with only a few safety lights glowing along the edges of the paths. So she did some fast running on the spot, then shadow boxing – which made her feel silly, especially with her long spindly arms, which was a good climbdown.

Better.

She exhaled, forcing herself to return to that calm analytical state that might actually be some use. Squaring her shoulders resolutely, ready to sit back down and return her full attention to the squad.

A wan cobalt-blue light shone through the curving roof of the torus so far above her. She knew that shade of blue: the expansion rim of a portal.

Out there in the unsettling blackness of their cryoplanet's central cavity, a portal was enlarging. Yirella knew the Strike plan by heart, and none of Bennu's portals was supposed to be opening right now.

Her optik tactical display confirmed she was correct, no portals were active during this phase of the Strike.

'Huh?'

She gazed dumbly at the radiant blue circle, her optik zooming in. Something was coming through. Something huge, and bizarrely elegant. A tower of cubes and pyramids encased in a cage of glittering white helixes – with wings.

'Oh Saints, we have a problem.'

New York

1st July 2204

As soon as Callum walked out of the door, the wind ruffled up his thick hair. He zipped up his jacket against the pre-dawn chill. 'I didn't think there'd be any wind left here,' he muttered.

'Thermals probably,' Eldlund said. 'The shield does let some sunlight through in the day.'

Callum glanced up at the shield covering Manhattan Island. Its haze boundary seemed to be reflecting the grid of streets, where block-long laser and neon adverts blazed as if there was no power supply issue and every solarwell was still pumping electricity into Earth's grid at full capacity. Looking down was an altogether more cautious act. They were on the roof of Connexion's headquarters, a full hundred and twenty floors above the ground. He never suffered from vertigo, but still . . .

The rest of the assessment team were waiting for him on the West Fifty-Ninth Street side. Huddled together in a gloomy group, their faces pale in the city's multicoloured nightlight. Callum knew his treatment-heavy skin would suppress most of the surprise he felt at seeing Jessika with them. Loi walked over, nodding respectfully at Callum. 'Come on,' he said to Eldlund. 'Let's go grab a coffee.'

'But—' Eldlund started to protest.

'See you later,' Callum told his aide.

Eldlund's face was unreadable as sie left. Callum went over and joined the others as they looked down on Central Park. Some kind of vigil was being kept on the Bethesda Terrace, with hundreds of candles held aloft.

'What are that lot protesting about?' Callum asked.

'They're not. It's a multifaith gathering,' Alik said. 'Praying away the aliens.'

'Which is about as much use as anything we've tried so far,' Yuri said.

Callum gave the security chief a wry grin, then turned to Kandara. 'You okay?'

She shrugged. 'Still alive.'

'Good. Why are we meeting up here?'

Yuri indicated the crowd on the terrace far below. 'They make a good metaphor. We, the five of us, have to put everything aside – every quarrel, every moral – and work together to defeat the Olyix.'

'I already know how to defeat them,' Callum told him.

'Yeah,' Yuri said. 'We know. It's a neat idea, I'll give you that. Fire one of our starships into the *Salvation of Life*. There are no weapons they can attack it with, because it's essentially a giant hole in space. And when it hits, it'll punch straight through. If you aim it right – along the axis – it can take out the biosphere caverns and the wormhole in less than a second; hit it with three or four star-ships, slicing strategically along the length, and the bastard will probably break up from the spin stress.'

'Well . . . yes.' Callum really didn't like Yuri's flat voice. Too many memories about that unforgiving determination the old Russian possessed. 'You got a problem with that?'

'Several,' Jessika said. 'Starting with, it won't defeat them.'

'All right, it won't destroy their enclave. But you said yourself it'll buy us years before they return. We can begin the whole exodus habitat project.'

'So our descendants can be hunted across the galaxy,' Yuri said harshly.

'Well, fuck you all. Sorry for bringing good news.'

'It's great news, Callum,' Kandara said. 'But we have to be smart how we apply it.'

'We apply it fast and hard. Our window to destroy the *Salvation of Life* is closing fast. They'll already have everyone from the Lobby cocooned and on board. The people they caught in the habitats are on their way back there. If we turn this into a crash priority project I think we can launch it in fifteen hours, twenty max. Get the council or Ainsley or whoever to give me the go-ahead.'

'Yet even if it works perfectly, all we do is buy some of us some time,' Alik said ruefully. 'We have to do better.'

'You as well?' Callum asked in dismay. 'Bloody hell. Are all of you Neána, or something?'

'Fuck you,' Alik sneered.

'The Neána are here to advise and to help you,' Jessika said. 'It's why we exist.'

Callum always considered that out of all the assessment team, he was the one who had the most trouble accepting Jessika was an alien. And with good reason. They'd worked together several times over the decades he'd been Emilja's troubleshooter. She was the essence of human, with her sense of humour and her insights and a decency that practically shamed him. *The idealized human – like something a machine would make if you gave it the right parameters. Hindsight is such a bitch.* 'So you're advising us not to kill the *Salvation of Life*?'

'Yes. The four of us have come up with a different strategy. One with a greater chance of success.'

'*What?*'

'We have an opportunity here, Callum,' Yuri said. 'POTUS and the General Secretary have asked Ainsley and Emilja to produce a plan for our species to survive. All of us.'

'Typical asshole politicians,' Alik groused. 'They want someone else to do the dirty work so they keep their hands clean, especially if it's successful. Because to work – really work – it's going to have to be dirty on a scale the devil would turn his back on.'

'Oh, shit,' Callum muttered under his breath.

'Yeah,' Kandara said. 'And Ainsley and Emilja's fancy committee take advice from us, because – like it or not – we're the experts. We also have Jessika and Soćko.'

'What?'

'The neurovirus,' Jessika said. 'I can take over an Olyix ship's onemind.'

Callum wiped a hand across his forehead. 'I hate that I'm even asking this, but . . . If we're not going to destroy the *Salvation of Life*, why do we still need to hijack an Olyix ship?'

'To get to the enclave, of course,' Yuri said.

'But . . . I thought you said the enclave was too big for us to defeat.'

'It is.'

'Then what's the point?' Callum's anger was rising to match his bewilderment. He resented missing out on everything the team had been discussing while he was away. *Trying to save our arses.* 'I thought finding the gateway and spying on the enclave was what's going to happen in the future.'

'It was,' Alik said.

'But the Olyix know that anyone who survives their invasion wants to fight back,' Jessika said. 'And the only way to do that is by finding the gateway. The fact that the Olyix are here in Sol shows the Neána still haven't located it yet. *But –*'

Callum winced. 'Yeah?'

She smiled at him. 'Right now we have a perfect opportunity to obtain the gateway's location.'

'How the fuck do we do that?'

'The *Salvation of Life* has a wormhole which leads directly back to it.'

'So?'

'So we take our hijacked ship and fly it down the wormhole to the gateway.'

'You've got to be kidding me!'

'No. As soon as we have the gateway's coordinate, we broadcast it loud and strong. A signal that can be picked up clean across the galaxy.'

'Won't the Olyix just move the gateway if you do that?'

'By its nature, the gateway has to occupy the physical space of the enclave. It's like a dimensional trapdoor. Open it up and you're inside. Find the gateway, and you find the enclave.'

'Christ.' Callum said. 'Then what?'

'What do you mean?'

'What happens to the hijacked ship after it sends the signal? Do you fly back here? To Sol?'

'Certainly not,' Yuri said. 'We stick to the plan, we carry on through the gateway and into the enclave. We become the greatest motherfucking Trojans in the galaxy, gathering intelligence.'

'What intelligence?'

'On the conditions inside,' Alik said. 'Because even Jessika and Soćko don't know squat about that. We also keep track of the *Salvation of Life* when the Olyix bring it back to the enclave. Ready.'

Callum closed his eyes. 'Ready for what?'

'Everyone who comes in after us.'

'Everyone who?'

'The exodus habitats. Generations of them, who will spend the next thousand years developing doomsday weapons that'll make the Olyix shit themselves. Who will grow and build armies of super-soldiers who are going to invade the enclave and rescue our whole species.'

'Oh my God.'

'It's actually quite elegant from an emotionless technocrat point of view,' Alik said. 'We find the gateway. The future human armada invades the enclave, wipes out the Olyix and flies the *Salvation of Life* back here. Endgame!'

'I warned you,' Yuri said. 'This is going to get dirty.'

'We're going to lose the Sol system,' Alik said bluntly. 'Even if we use your starship missile idea in fifteen hours and take out the *Salvation of Life* before they start stacking up cocoons inside, they'll just send another, backed up with a big fleet of warships.'

'Resolution ships,' Jessika said. 'And you don't want to be facing those.'

'There is no war for the Sol system we can win,' Yuri said. 'Not now, not in a year or two when our plan will be ready. We cannot save all twelve billion people on Earth from this. So we don't try. We go tactical, and play our endgame right from the start.'

'Oh no,' Callum said bluntly. 'No, no, no, no.'

'If we convert all the existing habitats, then combine the manufacturing capacity of every terraformed system for the next ten years, we can possibly produce enough interstellar-capable habitats to carry half a billion of us if we really cram them in,' Kandara said. 'That gives us a good base to build that future armada.'

'And we leave the rest for the Olyix,' Alik said.

'No! We have to fight!'

'This *is* the fight,' Yuri growled back.

'The humans they cocoon are still alive, Callum,' Kandara said. 'And they stay alive for . . . ever, if you believe the Olyix. That's the point of all this madness. And anything Olyix biotechnology can do to them, we'll ultimately be able to undo. That's why we have to keep track of the *Salvation of Life*.'

Callum gave Jessika a stricken look. 'Is that right?'

'Neána biologics can probably reverse a cocoon already. With a few years of research, I can practically guarantee it. In a thousand years, it'll be a walk in the park. Soćko has already started examining the process.'

'Jesus fucking wept!' He hated it, hated how they blocked every protest with logic.

'Right now, we're too small,' Alik said. 'Too unprepared. Too primitive. We gotta to play the long game here, man. It's the only way.'

Callum didn't trust himself to say anything. He nodded. *Yuri's beaten me again.*

'Of course, this might all become irrelevant in a couple of days anyway,' Kandara said cheerfully.

'Why?'

'If the city shields don't hold, we're going to be seriously screwed,' Alik said. 'We need governments to hold society together, at least in the short term, so we can organize the hijack and the exodus habitats project. If Earth falls this week, then the odds of getting a decent fraction of settled worlds' residents launched into the galaxy shrinks like a naked dick at the North Pole.'

'And we're back to that initial problem of hijacking an Olyix ship for ourselves,' Jessika said. 'Which is going to be tough.'

'But it's going to have to be done,' Kandara said grimly. 'Without that Olyix ship, there is no plan. And step one is securing us a quint body so we can take it over with the neurovirus. And yours truly fucked that up big time in McDivitt.'

'Nobody could have done better,' Alik said quickly.

'Thanks. But if you're right about that, then we are seriously up shit creek. I had a good armour suit, a good plan and good backup. I still lost. Those fucking hunting spheres the quint fly around in are bad news.'

'She's being very self-deprecating,' Alik grinned. 'She's already come up with a solution.'

'What?' Callum asked.

'Simple. We need to find us a quint that isn't riding around in a hunting sphere. One like Feriton Kayne. There's God knows how many of those shits walking around Earth overseeing their sabotage attacks.'

'It'll be different next time,' Kandara said. 'I swear on Mother Mary's grave. Just point me at one.'

'Yeah,' Yuri said. 'Working on that.'

Richmond, London

2nd July 2204

Times like this, Ollie wished he had an off switch. He'd slept through most of the come down, but even now, sitting up on the cushions littering the lounge floor, he felt nauseous, cold, hot, sweaty, grossly tired and not entirely sure where he was. Claudette's house in Richmond, sure. But where, in this uncertain reality that was twisting so badly out of alignment, did that leave him? Taking zero-nark continually hadn't given him what he wanted; instead of mellowing everything out nicely, it had started soaking him in fear until he felt he was drowning in it. *You're not paranoid if everyone really is out to get you.* And in this universe, on this planet, at this moment, it seemed everyone was. He just couldn't quite remember all the details. The nark's legacy was a jumble of confused thoughts hosting whispering voices in the distance which might have been daemons nesting in his skull or the vanishing memories of a dream.

Is this how Lars sees the world: forever dim and bewildering?

He put his head in his hands, closing his eyes tight. All this chaos was leaking from the dregs of zero-nark still in his blood, he knew that. Until sometime yesterday he and Adnan had managed it okay. The cut-down doses had worked, taking the edge off the torment of a world where the government was hunting him down in the brief time before they all got invaded by aliens. They'd coped well with the solnet and lownet feeds, using seriously bad-taste jokes to ride over the horror of it all. Then they got bored. The Deliverance ships had all but abandoned the habitats to fly off to the outer edge of the solar system and blow up the MHD asteroids. The crumbling lownet became as dull as watching shit dry. That was when it started to go wrong. Instead of harmony, the zero-nark had summoned up terrible nightmares from his subconscious – sick perverted things that left him ashamed for having a brain that could think them up. He kept seeing people being mummified in their own flesh. Held in silent torment by their teratoid organs. Hacked apart or burned by angry villagers with pitchforks and flaming torches that marched straight out of a Hong Kong Frankenstein virtual. Whole city populations consumed by hatred, screaming in anger and fright. He couldn't tell if it was his throat or theirs that the yells had burst out of, just that he wanted the awful delusions to fuck the hell off.

Looking around the squalor of the lounge, he saw the stage was filled with the numbing blue-green haze of a dead feed, its speakers hissing with static. 'Switch it off,' he told Tye.

The worthless haze blinked out of existence, and the unnerving silence of the slumbering house grew deeper. He was mildly surprised Tye could still do that. Seemingly every other chunk of technology had either shut down or glitched. At the end, they'd been struggling to find any kind of solnet access, let alone the lownet. Or was that more paranoia courtesy of the zero-nark?

Without even the stage to watch, the rest of the room seemed to jump back at him, crying for attention. They really had made a complete mess; it looked like a stockpile of crap ready to be shoved through a rubbish portal to Haumea. Uneaten sandwich crusts lying between the cushions were mouldy. Beer and wine bottles were scattered about, some only half empty. And the smell . . .

'Oh, shit,' he groaned miserably.

Adnan was nowhere to be seen.

Has he left me?

A lurch of panic set his heart racing. Skin already cool, dropped towards freezing.

'Adnan?'

No answer.

Louder: 'Adnan? Where are you, mate?'

Nothing.

'Crap! Tye, get me a location on Adnan.'

'Upstairs in the second bedroom's en suite bathroom. House management network shows the shower is drawing power. The domestic water tank is down to thirty per cent; the water utility supply failed thirty-nine hours ago.'

'He's upstairs?'

'Yes.'

Ollie flopped back down on the cushions and let out a pitiful sob as he kicked at the small pile of empty pads. *I've got to stop taking this shit.*

It took a minute to get his breathing back to normal. His heart calmed. He wished that returned the rest of his body to normal, but he still felt awful. Didn't know when he'd eaten last, nor what it was. And there was a big patch of skinaid on his hand. When he prodded it tentatively, it felt sore.

He slowly got to his feet, sniffing suspiciously at his armpit. 'Is there enough water in the tank for another shower?'

'Assuming Adnan finishes in the next eight minutes, enough water will remain for you to shower,' Tye said.

'Great.'

Ollie started walking, expecting a hangover-style headache and mildly relieved to find none. At least that was one advantage of zero-nark. 'Lars? Hey Lars, you awake? You want something to drink?' Not that he knew when either of them had last taken food and drink to the big oaf.

He was very aware of the calendar icon in the corner of his tarsus lens display. They'd been here too long. So that meant he needed a serious sober discussion with Adnan, because just waiting around for things to get better clearly wasn't an option any more. They needed Tronde to make Claudette hand over her trust fund money. Honestly, he didn't see any problem. She'd transformed into an even bigger narkhead than Tronde, which was saying something. Ollie was still perturbed by the way his friend had turned out.

The conservatory door was wide open. He went through. It took a few seconds for the grotesque scene to register. Next thing he knew he was on all fours, puking his guts up between incoherent screams as the memory clot broke and yesterday came roaring back into his neurons with a terrible hammer blow.

It hadn't been a deranged zero-nark-fuelled fantasy he'd lived through. After the house lost its lownet feed, they'd watched the ordinary news feeds as the story exploded across the world. People were melting, their muscles dissolving to bloat weird growths in the torso. Limbs shrank while ribs expanded and merged to form a hard protective carapace around mutating organs. Then in the more advanced cases, eyes and ears were being sucked down into the skull, no longer required by whatever monster they were transforming into. It was happening everywhere, in every shielded city.

Cocooning, the frightened news anchors called it. The victims' bodies self-modifying in preparation for aeons in suspension on board the *Salvation of Life* as it flew off to the end of time. Tarsus lenses captured the images of people who had undergone dramatic changes overnight, now lying helpless in their beds as their legs and arms withered, unable to move as their consciousness slipped away. Distraught families gathered around, not knowing what to do other than cry. Rich people attended by top-grade paramedic teams, all with perplexed fearful faces; the middle class with agency nurses administering sedatives and trying to arrange hospital admission; the truly poor with priests and prayers and garlands of flowers, some having acupuncture needles piercing the freakish tumours. They were the lucky ones.

Fear had begun to rule the streets, inciting hundreds of riots. Ollie and Adnan had watched in sick dismay as the feed from Caracas showed paramilitaries standing by uneasily while newly formed anti-Olyix activists surrounded a clinic. Cocoons were dragged into the public square outside, some of them still conscious and shouting. A broad pyre had been set alight, with flames pumping out greasy smoke as the living cocoons were flung on by men who had to wear cloth over their faces to ward off the stench. Some cocoons had their relatives clustered around protectively, engaged in bloody tug of war fights with the fearful crowd. They were always destined to lose.

What happened in Caracas started to spread across the globe. People were afraid the cocoons were contagious, and government reassurances did nothing to damp down the primal panic. The smaller cities were hit worst. Too many refugees had poured in from the countryside, stretching resources. Initial resentment at the outsiders together with the fear of cocooning was an incendiary combination. The pyres rose relentlessly.

Consensus on allcomments was that cocooning only happened to anyone who'd had a Kcell implant, which saw hospitals and clinics besieged with people desperate to have theirs removed. Paramilitaries and riot police had to be called in to public emergency centres as the frantic and fearful demanded the alien cells be extracted, no matter what consequence it would have on their health. Reports and images started to come in of grim attempts at DIY operations.

Ollie closed his eyes in dismay, but the memories didn't stop burning his brain. Then the real horror surfaced. Bik and his Gran both had Kcells. *It's gonna happen to them!* Unless . . . those operations. People were having their Kcells extracted before the cocooning began in earnest. But you'd need a serious amount of wattdollars for that.

Claudette's got that kind of money.

He opened his eyes, knowing what he had to do. Screw his friends, and screw Jade. The aliens had come for his family. Nothing else mattered now. With his stomach completely empty, Ollie stared at the settee where Lars was lying. That is, what had been Lars once upon a time.

The swelling that had begun around the man's upper torso had now expanded so much it'd split his T-shirt open, exposing pale skin that bulged with blue veins. His neck had been engulfed by the new growth, leaving his head as the apex of a body that was little more than a wedge of curving bone that had four sticks protruding. Ollie realized they were all that remained of Lars's limbs, the humerus and femur bones jutting out of him like some obscene nonhuman genitalia, shrink-wrapped in pasty skin, veins throbbing. And his dumb semi-Neanderthal face . . . Ollie started sobbing. The eye sockets were empty craters of blank skin above a nose which had now compressed more than any fist had ever flattened it, sealing over the nostrils as it withdrew, while his mouth had frozen open in a wide O of what must have been a last conscious gasp of surprise. But then anyone would have been shocked when their groin started sprouting thin tendrils that wormed over the settee and sank down to penetrate the carpet.

Ollie turned and staggered out, wailing brokenly. In his mind he could see Bik and Gran, bodies distorted, roots anchoring them to the floor at home. *But not yet. They didn't have a lot of Kcells. There's still time. Lots of time.*

Adnan was standing there at the foot of the stairs, still wet from the shower, towel wrapped around his hips, and holding one of Claudette's fancy leather handbags.

'Lars!' Ollie snivelled.

'I know, mate, I know.'

'He's . . . he's . . .'

'Yeah. I get it, all right. I've already seen him. Face it, the daft old sod had so many Kcell implants, especially muscle ones, the stuff made up half his bodyweight. It was bound to happen.'

'Fuck!'

'Nothing we can do, yeah? He's gone. He belongs to the Olyix now. Understand?'

'I can't do this. I've got to go.'

'Ollie!' Adnan gave him a shake. 'Get a grip. We've got to sort this out. We've got to think of ourselves now. New identities, right?' He dangled the handbag in front of Ollie's face. 'Or maybe better.'

'What?'

'Claudette's got cryptokens. I can break them. I'm not Gareth, but I'm good enough. You know that, right? So I'm going to get on with that right now. And you, my friend, need a shower. Get cleaned up, find yourself something to wear. Get normal; it'll help. Then you and I will decide what we're going to do.'

Ollie stared at the cryptokens as if Adnan had just produced a miracle. *Which he has.* 'Okay. Yeah, right.'

'Good lad. I'll stick something in the microwave, too. There's still a bit of food left. I don't know when we ate anything last.'

'Me, neither.'

'Ollie?'

'Yeah.'

'You're all right.'

'Thanks, Adnan.'

Adnan lowered his voice. 'We're going to have to think if we ask Tronde to come with us.'

Ollie gave his friend a solemn nod. 'I know.' *That's never going to happen. I've got something much more important now.*

'Last of the Legion,' Adnan produced a bleak smile, and clapped Ollie on the shoulder. 'We're going to make it, us. We're never going to stop.'

'Fuck, yeah!'

*

The shower was a good idea. Ollie knew he'd washed the night they arrived at the Lichfield Road house, but wasn't entirely sure if he'd cleaned up since. He stayed under the jets for maybe longer than he should, but figured if they were leaving in a couple of hours then it didn't matter. It was one of those variclenz models that posh people had, with modes to inject soap and shampoo and dermal conditioner into the water. So he ran it for a couple of cycles before stepping out.

With the last clean towel in the house shrouding his shoulders, Ollie went through the drawers and wardrobes in the guest bedroom. He guessed that Claudette hadn't scissored her ex's clothes in a psycho rage – odd, because that's exactly what he would have expected her to do. But there was a tonne of expensive men's clothing, all neatly laundered. Varying sizes, too. So perhaps she was like that female spider that ate her male after they'd screwed, and these were the trophies. Smirking at that thought, he chose himself black silk underwear and socks. On top of that went dark-green leather trousers and a burgundy-toned Cruftan shirt with its small scarlet logo on the breast pocket, unbuttoned and knotted at the front to display his midriff. Midnight-black brogues, hand made by a Jermyn Street cordwainer – a bit tight, but he didn't care because he knew how fabulously expensive they were. A dusting of make-up on the cheeks to deepen them, and a slick cherry-red lipstick. Decided against mascara.

Ollie studied himself in the mirror. The ensemble worked. Anyone who saw him would know he was a playa at the top of the world. *I can do this. I can save them.*

Being dressed properly again didn't bring the buzz back, but he strutted into the house's master bedroom with the soundtrack from Sumiko's latest virtual playing in his head. Funny smell in the air, and the curtains were open, not that the weak ochre twilight refracted by the London shield provided much illumination. The way it had been decorated wasn't what he'd have chosen if he'd had Claudette's money, but he could appreciate the 1930s Parisian decadence ideal she was aiming for.

Tronde and Claudette were in bed together, her on top of him, arms around each other, nestled together as if they were one creature, her stroking his face and pecs adoringly. An imperial purple silk sheet was drawn up over his groin, though Ollie had to concentrate hard on the memory of news feeds about cocooning so he didn't smirk at Tronde's perma-erection tenting the fabric.

'You okay, fella?' Tronde asked.

'Sure. Just wanted to tell you, Adnan and I are thinking about splitting soon. There's some bad shit going on out there and we need to get to a terraformed system somehow.' Ollie gave Claudette a significant look. 'Gonna need us some serious cash for that.'

'Yeah,' Tronde sounded so uninterested Ollie knew he was tripping higher than clouds. 'I see that.'

'My baby's not going anywhere,' Claudette said. She never even looked up at Ollie, just stared lovingly into Tronde's dazed eyes. 'He's going to fuck me to the end, because he's a bad boy.'

'The baddest,' Tronde said.

'Sorry, love,' Ollie said, 'but that's not up to you. Tronde, pal, we can't stay here any longer.'

'No!' Claudette yelled. 'No, no, no. He's mine! My bad boy! You just want him to fuck you, too. But he's not going to, are you babe?'

'Oh, shit,' Ollie grumbled under his breath. Her brain had finally broken under the weight of neuroses from that weird hifli mix Jade had given them. 'Not up to you,' he told her sternly, trying to channel that cold power Tronde had shown.

Claudette sat up in a surprisingly fast motion, started pummelling the bed with her fists, dishevelled hair flying. 'Fuck you, fuck you. Fuck off. Go on, fuck off out of my house! You're not real bad boys, not like my Tronde. Leave us alone. Go away. Away. Forever. I will not let him go. Not now. He's perfect now. And he's mine and I'm his. You'll never have that. You're already dead because you have no soul. All that's left of you is money and dirt.'

'Shut it,' Ollie sneered. 'Tronde, mate, you need to come downstairs. We'll be there.'

But all Tronde did was smile dreamily at the ceiling. 'You go. You have my blessing. I'm going to stay here. The end is coming, Ollie, and it's going to be glorious for anyone who welcomes it properly.'

Claudette started a demented laugh that made Ollie think of a witch's cackle. That was when he knew he'd lost. *Who'd have thought it? Tronde fallen into the hole he'd dug himself.* 'Your choice, mate,' he said and left – one backward glance because, well . . . even in this state, she did have a great-looking arse.

*

Adnan was waiting in the kitchen. All the empty food packets had been pushed to the end of the polished granite work surface. Real coffee was brewing in the cafetiere, and the microwave was heating two packs of pappardelle with lamb ragu. Just smelling the food lifted Ollie up another level of sobriety, allowing him to think clearly.

'Is Tronde coming down?' Adnan asked.

'No. And we're not going to get Claudette's trust fund, either. The stupid bastard's too narked-out to— Oh, *shit!*'

'What?'

Clarity was a real bitch, it allowed Ollie to work out what was actually happening. 'His dick.'

'You talking about Tronde?'

'Yes. Bollocks. When he went for his treatment, did he have printed stem cells or a Kcell implant?'

Adnan's humour vanished fast. Both of them shifted their gaze up to the ceiling.

'Kcells,' Adnan said quietly. 'That kind of printed stem is expensive.'

'Jesus wept, it's just not fair. How bad can our luck get?' *And what the hell was underneath that sheet?* Just thinking about that was making his hands shake.

Adnan poured the coffee into two mugs and slid one carefully over the work surface. There was no expression on his face. 'Just you and me, then.'

'Yes.' And Ollie knew he wasn't hiding the fear in his voice. *If this was one of Sumiko's virtuals, now would be the time one of us betrays the other.*

A cryptoken followed the coffee mug. 'I cracked them.'

'Hell, Adnan. That's amazing! How much?'

'Enough to live like a Zangari for a month. Or in our case, buy ourselves *one step* to the billionaire belt.'

Ollie picked the cryptoken up. Tye told him it was open, waiting to be re-coded to him. And there was a shitload of wattdollars loaded in. *Enough for Gran and Bik? Maybe if I had both . . .* He stared over at Adnan, who flipped another of the cryptokens like a bank-buster casino win. 'Thanks, mate.' In his head, he was trying to do his thing, plotting out the moves ten steps ahead. It wasn't easy.

'No problem. Billionaire belt, here we come.'

'Adnan. About that . . .'

'Yeah?'

'I've got to check on Bik and Gran first. They both had Kcell treatments a while back.'

'Shit. I'm sorry, mate.'

Ollie held up the cryptoken. 'The news feeds: some of them said hospitals were cutting out the Kcell tumours. Do you think this is enough money for the op?'

'Two ops, Ollie. Then what?'

'What do you mean? They're my family!'

'And if you save them from cocooning, where are you going to go? Even if you manage to buy them into a hospital tonight, you're talking about major surgery. It ain't quick. The first Deliverance ships are going to be here within twenty-four hours.'

'There'll be enough time,' he said desperately. 'There has to be. The bloody universe owes me that.'

'The universe doesn't care.'

Ollie was too scared to ask those four simple words. *Will you help me?* If the answer was no, he didn't know what would happen. *Did Adnan tool up while I was in the shower?*

Then Adnan gave a start, which made Ollie flinch and spill his coffee. It was painfully hot. 'Ow!' He looked around to see what had unsettled Adnan.

'Hello, boys,' Jade said.

*

The universe had slowly and peacefully shrunk around Tronde until all that was left was Claudette's bedroom. He didn't even mind that any more. The murky light from outside gave it a soft-focus neutrality that helped keep his mood level. Even so, he seemed to be losing chunks of time.

Ollie had been in, he was sure about that; his friend had said he was leaving. Sometimes Claudette would be absent when he woke. If that happened he didn't let it bother him, just closed his eyes and dozed again until she returned. He always knew when that was. The hifli would lift him out of the calm and into the right place, where he could see and feel and hear properly, the recipient of pure pleasure. There didn't even have to be sex any more to experience it. He couldn't now anyway. All feeling below his shoulders had gone. Claudette still relished the carnal excess accomplished by the hifli state, impaling herself on the strange protrusion of flesh that had hardened between his legs. Though even that was diminishing now.

He blinked slowly and looked around. Claudette wasn't there.

Though he felt, or imagined, the warmth of her lingering on his bare chest. No matter, she'd be back soon. She always was.

There were voices downstairs, soft murmurs that slipped through the house, mostly absorbed by the cushions and carpets and curtains. He couldn't hear what was being said, and anyway it didn't matter. The room sank into pleasant darkness.

Claudette was climbing onto the bed with him, naked, with wild hair making her alluringly erotic. The parts of his body that still functioned tingled in anticipation, banishing the cosy lethargy.

'I was worried about you,' she cooed. 'She's back. I hate her.'

'Who?'

'That woman. The corporate cow that was here before. She said you were ill, but you're not. She's taking your friends away with her. I heard them talking about it. They're going to blow stuff up again for money.'

'They shouldn't go with her.' Some thoughts from the time before the bedroom and the hifli sneaked into his mind, something about trust. He'd spent several hours worrying about Jade and the Croydon raid she'd sent them on, the one which had ruined the Legion. With everything else that was happening right now, another risk just didn't seem right.

'That's right!' Claudette exclaimed. She started kissing him urgently. 'I know that. So I called the police.'

'What?' Tronde wondered if he was still dosing on the last of Ollie's zero-nark, so tranquil were his thoughts.

'The police, babe.' Kisses moved down his neck, and around to below his ear where the skin was most sensitive. 'They'll take them all away. Then there'll just be you and me.' She grinned triumphantly as she pulled the sheet away from his body. 'And you can't go anywhere now, so I'll have you all to myself. That's so sexy. So perfect – like you.'

Tronde looked down at the misshapen bulges of flesh and bone which his legs and abdomen had warped into, and grinned. 'You got me.' Nyin splashed Ollie's icon, and it went active. Some part of the house network was still working. **You need to leave**, he sent to his friend. **The police are coming.** It made him feel good. The

Legion looked after their own, even now when there was nothing left in the world.

Claudette straddled him, then slowly bent forwards. More kisses. Her riotous hair curtained the room and the bed. He breathed it all in, the intoxicating moment allowing it to stretch out . . . Then she was straightening up again, a hand holding out two white hemispheres.

'Together,' he told her with the old firmness.

'Together,' she echoed worshipfully.

The hifli was as good as ever, attuning his nerves and neurons to the real universe to be found amid the secret folds of the one that imprisoned him so cruelly. Better even, as he knew he would never return to the misery of the life he'd lived. The nark flowed into his blood with the ease of a fine wine, teasing out the delicate harmonies of his body, allowing him to hear his strange modified organs sing with purpose. Up ahead of him the end of the universe was opening like a black flower whorl, sending out tendrils of darkness to embrace him. The sight of the apotheosis was raw pleasure.

'This is it,' he declared lovingly, raising his hands in salutation.

The ceiling disintegrated in a breath-taking multicoloured fractal pattern that ruptured his skin in gratifying tatters. An angel clad in shining black armour descended from the glowing sky amid a cacophony of exquisite sound. Fabulous celestial supernovas erupted all around, shattering the glorious remnants of the bedroom to liberate Tronde from gravity.

He fell through air saturated with lethal blast fragments that manifested as an aurora of sensual delight as they sliced open his body. Overloaded nerves penetrated his cerebellum with a climatic orgasm of fire, extinguishing his mind in a rapturous blaze.

*

'We're going to hit the East Bedfont relay station,' Jade said as her altme sent files to Ollie and Adnan. 'It supplies electricity to the Ollaka biogenetics manufacturing facility a couple of kilometres away. And that is one big facility. It'll have backup power, but not enough. We have other teams in place who can utilize the brownout.'

'For what?' Adnan asked.

Ollie couldn't quite believe how his friend could stay so calm. Jade had strolled into the kitchen and poured herself a mug from the cafetiere as if *nothing* was wrong; that this was just another opportunity she was generously handing to the Legion. But that composure didn't fool him for a second.

She was wearing a stone-grey one-piece that first glance made you think was from some Sloane Street fashion house, because of the intricate patterns of gold embroidery. But not him. Best guess, it was a stealth suit similar to the kind the Legion had worn for the Croydon raid, but itself camouflaged. And the stylish cut took the emphasis away from how big she'd become. But sure as Sumiko was hot, Ollie knew Jade was not the kind of person who put on weight, never mind in just a couple of days. Something else she was wearing under the fabric was bulking her up. *Crap, how much weaponry does one person need?*

So fear kept him in the kitchen, kept his anger buried below visibility, kept his hatred from being shouted out. And if he knew her, she most likely knew him . . .

'I told you,' she said levelly. 'Medicines are fetching a high premium now. Actually, a lot higher than we anticipated, given the cocooning issue.'

'Issue?' Ollie challenged. It was getting harder by the second to restrain himself. 'You call that an issue?'

'Yes. Ollaka make anti-cancer nanoparticles that golden bullet tumour cells. Which makes their production facility the most valuable piece of real estate in all of London right now. The profit we will make tonight can buy you a habitat.'

'These nanoparticles,' Adnan asked. 'Can they cure Lars and Tronde?'

'I don't know. How far has the cocooning progressed?'

'I reckon it's run its course with Lars. He ain't a person any more.'

'I see. Well, I'm hardly an expert, but I can ask around for you.'

'Cheers,' Adnan said in a voice dripping with irony.

Claudette walked into the kitchen. It was all Ollie could do not to groan out loud, but that would mark him out as being bothered by her. Showing weakness right now simply wasn't an option.

Jade looked down on the naked, frowzy woman from the heights of amused contempt. 'Grown-ups talking in here, sweetie. Go away.'

'This is my house,' Claudette bellowed. 'You go away. Now!'

'We are going,' Jade mocked. She flicked her fingers in aristocratic dismissal. 'Out.'

'Fuck you, bitch! My Tronde doesn't need curing. He's perfect.'

'Good news for you, then.'

Ollie watched Claudette's hands slowly clench into a fist. 'Tell Tronde I'll come upstairs and see him in a minute,' he asked. He really didn't need to be standing here when whatever abominable peripherals Jade had blew the crazy woman to bits. 'I'll say goodbye.'

Claudette spun to face him. 'You don't go anywhere near my bad boy!'

Hands up in surrender, a half-step back. 'All right. Okay.'

She flicked a V sign at him and stormed out.

'Nice,' Jade said.

'Look,' Adnan said, 'I appreciate you coming to us with this, but the fact is there's only the two of us left now. We can't guarantee we'll be able to take out the relay station. Hell, we didn't really manage it last time in Croydon when *all* of us went.'

'I understand. This raid will be using more bird drones than last time. We just have to get close enough once the darkware hits their network.'

The fine hairs along the top of Ollie's spine stood up at the chill of those words. 'We?'

'Yes. Adnan's right, two people isn't enough. I'll be coming with you.'

Ollie couldn't believe he had the self-control necessary to stand still. All he wanted to do was turn tail and run – maybe even all the way to the police. 'And the bird drones?' he asked weakly.

'They're in my bagez. You can carry them on a modified harness.'

'Right.' It would be like wearing old-style suicide vests if security shot at them. The map data Tye was splashing showed the East Bedfont station had two large fusion systems that supplied backup power for one of London's shield generators in its adjoining compound. *Holy fuck, she really is working for the Olyix!*

'If you want me to carry flying bombs, I'm going to need to check my stealth suit over again with some serious diagnostics,' Ollie said. 'It got hit with some bad glitches when we were on the Croydon raid.' Spoken all calm and level, as if it was a perfectly standard part of the operation. No need to panic and run screaming from an alien secret agent. Not at all. He even gave Adnan a rueful smile. 'You need to do that as well.'

'Sure,' Adnan said, 'but I want to see the bird drones first. What have you got?'

'Some kestrels, doves, plenty of parakeets,' Jade said reassuringly. 'They'll blend in just fine.'

'So why do you need us?' Adnan asked. 'Just release them a couple of kilometres away.'

Ollie's half-smile froze in dread. *Why are you questioning her? Don't you get how dangerous that is?*

'I need the darkware loaded from the closest solnet nodes, to avoid G8Turing analysis and protection. You will have to physically attach the modules onto the defence-grade cables leading into the East Bedfont station; that way it can be routed into the compound network with only one level of protection to get through. You'll also be sniping the boundary sensors.'

'Weapon?' Adnan asked keenly.

'Micromaser. Three-hundred-metre range.'

'That's close.'

'Too much for you?' she challenged.

'No, but we'll be in harm's way. That's expensive for you.'

'Trying to leverage me at this point is a bad idea.'

Tronde's icon splashed across Ollie's tarsus lens. **You need to leave**, the message said. **The police are coming.**

Ollie was sure he whimpered. The other two either didn't hear, or ignored him.

'No, it's not,' Adnan said. 'Because you just told us there's even more profit to be made from this now. You're not going to deny us a fair share, are you? Given how critical we are to it, and everything.'

Jade's index finger traced a full circle around the rim of her coffee mug, as if she was giving the demand serious thought. 'I could increase your bonus by seven per cent. Final offer.'

'As you and Piotr agreed before: nine.'

'Very well, nine it is.'

Adnan stuck his hand out. Jade shook. Then she turned to give Ollie a questioning look.

'Now I'm definitely going to check my stealth suit,' he said. Turned his back on her. *Oh shit, will it hurt? She'll go for a kill shot, right? To the head? Maybe not. Maybe it'll be a flesh wound. A warning. Will she shove Kcells down my throat, or up my—? Not that, please! Shit, shit, shit!* He didn't – couldn't – breathe. Just kept walking. Every facial muscle was rigid, locking his expression to a grimace. If anyone saw that, they'd know . . .

The shot never came. As he left the kitchen, Adnan was saying: 'How much do the bird drones weigh?'

The blessed sanctuary of the lounge. Ollie never hesitated, never fumbled. The stealth suit went on fast, its heavily screened systems coming on line glitch free. He put his purloined cryptoken in an internal pouch along with the one Jade had brought before and the one intended for Lars which he'd never quite got around to handing over. A shaking hand sealed up the front of the suit. Hood on, mask down. Theoretically, he was invisible to most active scan sensors, but visually he remained a blatant fuzzy grey human-shaped lump. He switched the lounge lights off. Now he had as much optical substance as a shadow.

The window opened and he went through with the ease of a pro gymnast. Tonight the civic power grid was so patchy London's streets were as dark as they had been back in the nineteenth century when they were lit by gas lamps. The shield refracted that sparse luminosity as a wispy nebula curving overhead. Without his suit's optical amp he wouldn't have been able to see a thing in the garden, which finally gave his confidence a boost. This was the perfect milieu for the suit. Without background illumination to silhouette him, he was effectively invisible in every spectrum.

He hurried away from the house, reasonably sure that none of Jade's peripherals were locking on. *I did it. I'm out.*

There was some small tinge of guilt. About Adnan. Tronde, maybe. Lars, not much.

Tye splashed up locations and status for the sensors embedded in the boundary wall as he slipped through the rhododendron bushes and Japanese maple trees that surrounded the lawn. Like all the houses on Lichfield Road, Claudette's boundary incorporated all the requisite safeguards to assuage the middle-class fear of interlopers and their street violence. His suit would negate most of the gadgets. But when he got over the wall, there would be more alarms in the neighbour's garden to contend with.

Without drones, he couldn't scout whatever lay beyond. As he was studying the moss-covered brick, he saw something flicker against the shield's meagre glimmer above. For a second he allowed himself to believe it was a bat or bird, but then his suit was warning him the garden was being scanned with micro-power ultrasonics. The sweep was close to a bat sonar but too regular, too persistent.

Police drones!

Ollie froze. His suit fabric was quite capable of absorbing and cancelling a sonic pulse, and he was already under the boughs of a beech tree, which would distort the sweep even further. Tye switched his view feed to upright, using the passive sensors on the top of his hood. It wasn't the clearest image, the beech leaves cluttered his observation as much as they would for the drones. But larger shapes were flitting through the sky now, big enough for Tye to illustrate the silent downwash from their fans in bright false-colour green plumes. He held his breath. There were over thirty of them, including some big urban counter-insurgency drones. Which was a ridiculous overkill deployment. Special Branch must *really* want the Legion.

Originally he'd intended to scramble over the wall into next-door's garden, then maybe move along a couple more properties before creeping out into Lichfield Road and sneaking away. But now he was worrying about what else the Specials had brought to the game. It didn't matter, he knew; he had to make a move. Staying this close to the house was definitely going to get him caught, while distance at least gave him a chance, however pitiful. Though he was scared the police teams would already be sneaking towards him in the neighbouring gardens . . . *which means the houses on either side have had their alarms deactivated.*

Ollie made his decision and sprinted for the wall, jumping with his arms outstretched to get a hold on the top. The moss was spongy but his fingers managed to grip and he began to lever himself up.

Tye splashed a dozen alert icons. Claudette's house was hit with a monster EMP. Simultaneously, the drones which had now encircled it fired a barrage of nerve-block pulses. His suit protected him from the worst of the effect, but his flesh burned hot, as if an entire army of soldier ants had crawled inside the tight fabric to bite his skin. He strained hard to pull himself over the wall.

Behind him, the roof exploded. Fierce orange light flared as the fireball erupted, hurling slate fragments and splintered timbers across the garden. Every window shattered. Ollie knew this was his only chance, that he should be racing frantically across the neighbour's garden. But he paused for a moment, dumb animal instinct making him watch the crazy scene play out.

A dark armoured figure hurtled down out of the dull sky at a terrific velocity. Jetpack exhaust nozzles roared like a continuous thunderbolt as they fought to slow the descent. Even so, the suit crashed through the centre of the broken roof, plunging into the house. A second later, multiple explosions inside smashed the upper floor apart, and the remnants of the roof beams shuddered before folding down in pained slow motion. Brickwork cracked and shivered as upper sections toppled inwards to follow the roof down.

The blastwave shunted Ollie off the top of the wall to thud down hard into the rose bushes below. Bad landing.

More explosions produced a flickering phoney dawn behind him. Some kind of combat was going on inside the wreckage. *How can anybody still be alive in there?* Drones skidded chaotically through the air. Intense electronic warfare was hammering against the suit's processors, and his lens splash wobbled dangerously as icons dissolved into static. The animal fear which had betrayed him on top of the wall kicked in again and sent him running across the garden. He vaulted another wall somehow. Then a fence. Sirens were rushing along Lichfield Road, blue and red strobe auras clotting the air above the line of elegant homes. Claudette's house was an inferno, casting uncanny shadows over patios and grass. He did his best to outrun them. Every alarm on the street that had survived the outbreak of electronic warfare was shrieking for attention now. Nobody was going to notice any additional sensors he tripped.

Finally he reached a short alley and shambled along it to Lichfield Road itself. He turned his back on the flames, police and drone swarm at the other end and walked on towards the junction with Kew Road ahead. Three police vehicles raced past him; each time he pressed up behind a thick old horse chestnut trunk, dodging their camera sensors.

The other side of Kew Road was lined with a brick wall at least four metres high that guarded the botanical gardens. But directly opposite the junction was a set of wrought-iron gates. He slipped across the road to them. A small activeblade cut through the crude locked bolts in a fanspray of sparks. It was only while they bounced off his suit mask that he realized he couldn't hear a thing, not even the unrelenting sobs inside his hood. The explosion had wrecked his eardrums or an EM pulse had burned out audio circuitry, he didn't know. And as he stood motionless, he realized his left ankle was agony.

Finally the stubborn bolts gave way, and he pushed the big gate open. The sprawling parklands of Kew Gardens were spread out before him, as lightless and empty as a midnight desert. He limped off into the darkness.

Vayan

The chamber at the end of passage SR b5 was as big as the first one Dellian's squad had ventured into. Instead of cryogenic tanks, this one had three rows of big hemispherical vats. They were full of what everyone took to be proto-swamp muck that was bubbling away softly. Suit sensors reported heavy traces of sulphur in the air, along with other complex organic particulates.

Living pipes formed a buttress cradle holding each vat aloft. Underneath, glass spheres formed a nest around the base, with thick mustard-yellow fluid circulating inside. From there the pipes wound around each other in a three-dimensional grid along the centre of the chamber before rearing up like serpents to feed into five big cylinders.

'Cellular conveners,' Fintox said. 'This is one of their organism assembly centres.'

In the air above Dellian, his combat cores silently swung around so that their primary weapons were aligned on the cylinders. 'You mean this is where the quint bodies are manufactured?'

'Among other things, yes.'

'Del,' Tilliana said. 'Drop a drone into each of those vats and check they're not hiding any huntspheres.'

'Roger that. Falar, Uret, take a look.'

Drones glided along the chamber, deep scanning the aerated vats. Combat cores hovered above, ready for any sign of hostility.

'So what does a nexus look like?' Dellian asked.

'There will be one for each convener,' Fintox said. 'I will locate one.' The metavayan walked over to the closest cylinder and balanced on top of a glass sphere to examine the various pipes and struts that supported it.

Dellian reviewed the chamber. So far it was clear of any Olyix presence, but that didn't mean they were unobserved. He ordered the drones to spray out the aerosol which would close down the layer of external receptor cells that all Olyix biological systems incorporated. The chemical mist was a more sophisticated version of the one Connexion had developed for its spy missions on board the *Salvation of Life*. Using it made him feel nervous. *Look what happened to Feriton Kayne when he used it.*

More drones were spread out along passage SR b5, making sure nothing was creeping up on them. Xante had sent a whole batch of drones whirring off down the other corridors that led away from the chamber, checking for any activity.

'Two-hundred-metre perimeter is clean of Olyix activity,' Xante reported.

'Yeah. I wonder where they are?'

'Dunno. But not complaining. I'm expanding the scout drone perimeter.'

Dellian checked the tactical feed again. The squads were close to getting inside the first biosphere now. It wasn't easy; the corridors were narrow and strongly defended. Olyix huntspheres would burst out of cavities at random, attacking drones and combat cores, but never the armour-suited squad members.

Between the first and second biospheres, the squads heading for the wormhole generator moved cautiously forwards through the maze of tunnels. Four of them had already reached the main passages below the second biosphere. Dellian watched keenly as their icons progressed deeper into the tactical map graphic. The huntspheres were no match for the squads. Human weapons and tactics were proving superior every time.

'Shouldn't there be more of them?' he asked.

'We conclude the onemind may be regrouping quint units in the second and third chambers,' Ellici said. 'The flood cloud impact was a highly disruptive calamity for them. So far you've only encountered wrong-place wrong-time survivors. This would account for the sporadic resistance.'

'So we stay alert.'

'Yes. We're watching every sensor input for you, don't worry.'

'I wasn't.'

'Chamber's clear,' Falar said.

'Thanks.' Dellian watched the drones and combat cores revert to a defensive formation, a constantly moving shoal circling the big chamber. 'Fintox, how are you doing?'

'I have it.'

Dellian stepped over to where the metavayan was standing below a convener cylinder. One of the support struts resembled a pillar carved from pale green polyp, with innumerable living pipes spiralling up it like ivy besieging a tree trunk. Fintox was standing next to it, upper limbs holding a gadget to the rough surface. A metre-wide circle of the polyp flowed apart, as if it had turned to liquid, revealing a mass of hair-thin cyan fibres underneath.

'Is that it?' Dellian asked. 'The nexus?'

'A portion of the neuralstratum that leads to it, yes.'

'What now?'

'I will attempt to insert myself into the arkship neural network.'

Dellian had no idea what to say. *Good luck* seemed wholly inadequate given the circumstances, not to mention a little too human. 'Okay. Just . . . be careful.'

'Yes. I will proceed with care.'

'Tilliana, Ellici, you getting this?'

'We're monitoring,' Tilliana said.

Fintox adjusted his lower limbs and bent forwards until the top of his suit helmet that carried the interface unit was resting against the fibres. He became perfectly still.

'Uh, are you . . . in?' Dellian asked.

'I can identify the impulse flow,' the metavayan replied. 'It is extremely complex. Pattern interpretation is beginning.'

'Right.' Dellian scanned around the chamber again, checked the tactical display, reviewed one of the attack cruisers' images of the arkship to see the glowing haze of particle impacts on the forward end.

'Saints, this is dumb,' Janc declared. 'We could be fighting the huntspheres.'

'We *have* fought the huntspheres,' Dellian replied, irritated. 'What we're doing here and now is tactical, and the most important part of the whole Strike mission.'

'Yeah, right.'

Trouble was, Dellian knew exactly how Janc was feeling. He had that same itchy frustration. Years – their whole life – training for this, and all they were doing was guarding a non-real alien biologic while he tried to perform a data heist which could have come from an old Hong Kong virtual game. Right now, Dellian would have welcomed a whole flotilla of huntspheres charging towards them. That way, he could blow shit up.

'I have discharged the neurovirus,' Fintox said. 'It is spreading within the ship's neuralstratum.'

Another scan around. The least Dellian expected was the cavern lights to flicker – *something*. Maybe the onemind would know its thoughts were being distorted. It would send huntspheres . . .

'Okay, Fintox is in,' he announced. 'Let's stay alert, people.' Now he wanted some updates from Fintox. How was it going? How long would it take? But he didn't want to distract the metavayan.

'Falar, get some drones all the way back down the passages we travelled through,' he said. 'Keep them scanning for any Olyix activity. I want a smooth withdrawal when we have what we came for.'

'Got it.'

'I am aware of the wormhole mechanism now,' Fintox said. 'The knowledge the onemind contains is deep. Filtering through it for the gateway coordinate will be difficult while we remain in here. I think it would be best if we simply copied what I perceive. My colleagues and I will analyse it when we are back on board the *Morgan*.'

'Ellici?' Dellian asked automatically. 'Do we go with that?'

'We know the wormhole generator will require a massive operating system, so if the neurovirus can extract it, then yes, tell Fintox to go ahead. We can transfer yottabytes of data to the *Morgan* if necessary.'

'Right. Uh, do we have that kind of bandwidth?'

'How long it takes depends on how much data there is. But Yirella built a high bandwidth entanglement into Fintox's suit for just this kind of event.'

'Of course she did,' he said, smiling inside his helmet. *Saints, she really should be in the* Morgan's *tactical centre with Yirella and Ellici.*

His tactical display showed three squads enter the arkship's first biosphere. Confused chatter filled the channels.

'Tilliana?' Dellian asked. 'What's happening?'

'The biosphere isn't what we were expecting,' she replied in a strained voice.

'What do you mean?'

'Its not a single empty space like the *Salvation of Life*. This is . . . The drones are exploring.'

Dellian checked around the chamber they were in, then risked expanding drone images across his optik. The visuals from biosphere one were difficult to understand. He was looking directly out at a cliff face of silver and black hexagons, bound together by the woody pipes of Olyix biotechnology. The drone began to rotate. No – it was two cliff faces; the drone was hovering in a gigantic canyon with the squad members standing at the bottom, not even ant size on this scale. There was a base, but above the drone the cliffs extended upwards forever, the stacked rows of hexagons blurring into radial lines then a sold haze.

'What the Saints . . .?'

'It's like a hive structure,' Ellici said. 'Tilliana, do we have—?'

'Wait,' Tilliana snapped. 'Yirella is calling, she— *What?*'

'What's happening?' Dellian demanded. The tactical display was reformatting as the *Morgan*'s gentens analysed and mapped the surge of data from the drones in the first biosphere.

'One of our attack cruisers has just come under fire from a pair of weapons mounted on the arkship's hull,' Ellici said. 'They were camouflaged.'

'The transfer is beginning,' Fintox said. 'I will show you.'

'Thanks,' Dellian said. 'Ellici, what's happening?' Fintox's icons appeared in his optik, larger than usual. They didn't make a lot of sense, and they were brighter than he was expecting. So much so he wanted to blink.

'Yirella says there's a ship,' Tilliana said. 'Inside Bennu!'

'What do you mean, a ship?' Dellian's tactical icons flared scarlet, though they were just dim moons relative to Fintox's strangely beautiful giant star.

'Bennu's breached. Repeat, Bennu's been breached!'

'Fucking Saints, how did they get inside Bennu?'

Fintox's icon was now showing a complex flow of patterns that Dellian intuitively knew, but couldn't quite focus on. He resented how elusive they were and expanded the icon to see if that would make them clearer.

'That doesn't look Olyix to me,' Janc said in an uneasy voice.

'Deploying Bennu defence cruisers,' Tilliana said. 'Yirella has command.'

'Oh my Saints!' Ellici cried. 'They're hibernation chambers. All of them.'

'What are?' Dellian grunted.

'The first biosphere. It's just a giant honeycomb of hibernation chambers.' She let out a sob. 'Oh Saints, no. No. They've got people in them.'

'People?' Dellian asked. He couldn't quite make sense of this. It was important, he knew, but there was sound twittering into his brain now to accompany the bewitching flow of fluctuating shapes that were still expanding to fill his optik. A slow gentle melody that brought back memories of the peaceful times back on Juloss, when he and his yearmates ran free through the estate's parkland playing their games. The fun and laughter they'd shared.

'Cocoons,' Ellici said. 'The drones have found some hibernation chambers with human cocoons inside. They're alive.'

'This is Captain Kenelm. All squads, hold your current position. Do not engage the enemy, repeat, do not engage. Use your weapons only if under attack. We cannot risk further damage to this arkship. It is carrying humans.'

'Dellian?'

He thought that was Tilliana calling, but couldn't be sure. It was a loud voice, but somehow coming for a great distance.

'Dellian, are you all right? What's happening?'

'Dellian!' Xante pleaded. 'What are you doing with your cohort? Stop –'

The images and music were rushing past him now, swirling into a tunnel of memories which he began to fall through, faster and faster. Every memory he had, detonating into sharp focus. Forcing him to relive each moment of his life.

'Great Saints, what's Fintox downloading to him? The data density in his optik has maxed. The genten can't get a pattern lock.'

'What is it?'

'Fintox? Fintox, can you hear me? Withdraw from the neural-stratum. Now.'

Some of Dellian's memories started to hurt. Every childhood tumble and fall. Every bruise and graze received. Every collision in a game. They jumped out at him, the pain from each one flashing down his nerves as before. Harder this time, more intense. They made him yell out in panic and fright. Alexandre wasn't there to comfort him. No one was. He was on his own. Nobody loved him.

'Saints. Dellian, your med telemetry is hitting redlines. Del, what's wrong?'

'Del, pull your cohort back. Power the weapons down. Shit! Tilliana, help!'

'I can't do anything. Yirella! *Yirella!*'

But there was love. Love so strong. For him. For all of them. He raised his hands up in worshipful greeting. 'They love us,' he declared. And there it was. The Message. Divine in nature. Coming from the future – a tachyon cascade pouring back through the aeons where whole galaxies dwindled to embers and died. Pure as sunlight, clear as air. Calling him.

He welcomed it, opening himself to the angelic wonder. Letting it in. The Message from the God at the End of Time. Nothing else mattered. He let his thoughts dissolve in the glorious light that spoke directly to him.

'Del? Del, darling. It's me. It's Yirella. Del, power down the cohort. Let the dears rest so I can be with you. You and me. I love you. I want us to be together. Power them down, darling. Please.'

'Yirella?' He could hear her, but her image was somehow lost to him. She was draining into the light, slipping away into the future where they all belonged.

'Fuck, fuck, FUCK! What's happening?'

'Del, for Saints' sake stop fucking shooting at us!'

–

'Are you okay? Answer! Anyone in the squad, are you receiving this?'

'We're okay, Ellici. Big earthquake in here.'

'Fuck the Saints, they've blown whole sections of the arkship into space with nukes. Fucking nukes!'

'We won't die,' Dellian told the crazy voices. 'We're going to the End of Time. The God awaits us there.'

'Oh, crap! What is happening to Del?'

'Our attack cruiser sensors are showing up big caverns below those explosions. They've exposed them to space.'

'Decompression! Here it comes. Hang on to something! Uret, for Saints' sake, grab Del!'

'He'll kill me.'

'Grab him! Yirella will stop him.'

Dellian seemed to be flying, twirling uncontrollably down the great storm of light and sensation that had engulfed him. It was growing chaotic now. And the noise in the background was building. A physical force came to rest on the surface of his brain. Shoving inwards in a rhythm that matched his racing heartbeat. It began to hurt, and the light and sound was amplified with each blow.

'Del, it's me, it's Yirella. I love you, Del. I want to be with you.'

'I love you, Yirella,' he whispered.

'Del, power down your cohort. For me, my love. Let them rest.'

'Yes.'

'Thank fuck!'

Something was shaking his body. Not the power of the message that was expanding to fill him. This was physical. It inflicted yet more pain.

'Fintox!'

'He's gone, Tilliana. Decompression's hitting us like a gas giant's hurricane in here. Why didn't he hold on to something?'

'He's dead. Suit telemetry flatlined.'

'Is this neurothing going to kill Del, too?'

'Listen to me all of you, you need to linc your armour to your combat cores. They can hold you steady inside the decompression torrent. There are doors closing all along the passages that've been breached, but the vent is going to last for hours.'

'Gone! They've all gone! All the forward squads, they were too close to the explosions.'

'Did Fintox use the neurovirus to make the onemind do this? Did the metavayans betray us?'

It was becoming difficult for Dellian to concentrate through the pain in his head. His mind was being crushed. Drowned. His thoughts were wrong, no longer all his own. The Message was too powerful, and there wasn't enough left of him to fight it. He couldn't see Yirella at all. And somewhere close by his friends were bellowing in fright. 'It's all right,' he assured them. 'The God will be there for us. I can feel its message coming.'

'Del, stay with us. Can you understand me?'

'No, no. Are you getting this? The three chambers they blew open, there are ships inside them. Launching. Oh Saints, Resolution ships!'

'Fuck! We're dead. We're all dead.'

'No,' Dellian wasn't sure if he managed to get the word out, to reassure everyone. He knew what was coming. The humans had tried this scheme so many times: the false species rising, the ambush, the fight, the invasion of the arkship, desperate to discover the location of the gateway. Their spirit was so bold, so exquisite. No wonder the God at the End of Time yearned for them.

The Message had arrived in full now, permeating his head in bright flame. Nothing could withstand such grace and love. It consumed him, became him. **Bring me all your life, bring me all your light. Together we will see the universe reborn out of us.**

There was nothing else. Dellian opened his mouth, and screamed and screamed –

*

Fright rooted Yirella to the spot for a long moment. Then the old training, the kind she'd rejected, kicked in. Analyse. React. Don't waste time to rationalize. Instinct is always true.

Focus on the emergency comms icon. Captain Kenelm, hirself. Go.

'This is Yirella, Bennu has been breached. I repeat, we have an alien spaceship coming through one of our portals.' Sending her live optik feed, focused on that oh-so imposing shape gleaming in the cobalt light of the expansion portal's rim. A rim that was now shrinking and dimming as the ship cleared it. 'Type unknown. Size –' Breath snagged in her throat as her databud calculated the parameters – 'Approximately two kilometres long, extremity width one point two kilometres.' Because she wasn't sure those relatively flimsy wing-structures counted as fuselage.

'Saints,' Kenelm said. 'Yirella, we have three assault cruisers stationed in Bennu as reserves. Will you assume tactical command?'

'Yes.' Stomped her foot down in anger. Saintsdamned training. React indeed! She had spent years priding herself on her rationality. Now one problem, and she was acting like Del in a partynight brawl. Except *problem* didn't even begin to cover this. So maybe she was the best person to tackle it.

'Assigning command authorization,' Kenelm said. 'They're all yours, Yirella.'

Senses expanded through her databud as the assault cruisers' gentens established secure comms. The ships' powerful scanners swept across the interloper, refining her hazy visual image and

building a more comprehensive picture. Confirming size, and . . .
'Saints!' The thing had the mass of a small moon. 'It must contain some kind of neutronium structure, or a micro black hole. This is completely outside our knowledge base.' There was something wrong with spacetime around the fuselage; quantum signatures were fluctuating erratically. Powerful gravity waves emanated from its rear section, propelling it forwards effortlessly. She imagined tidal forces washing through her, making the toroid parkland's lakes and streams spill over their banks.

Then Ellici was yelling that there were cocooned humans inside the arkship. For a moment, shock made it impossible for Yirella to draw a breath.

Calm down. Morgan *will handle the arkship. Analyse this. Everyone is depending on you.*

But . . . *Cocooned humans! Where have they come from?*

Stop it. Focus!

She ordered the cruisers to approach the strange intruder, but not to go closer than a hundred kilometres. The ship wasn't doing anything hostile. *Anything else hostile,* she corrected herself. Sneaking into Bennu wasn't part of any friendly first-contact contingency file she'd ever accessed, but some deep instinct was telling her it wasn't Olyix. *Instinct, pah!* But if the Olyix had this level of technology, they wouldn't be riding around in arkships any more. Something close to fear goaded her.

She expanded her tactical display to take in the whole of the Strike arena. Seeing the treacherous arkship and the vulturous assault cruisers circling, the progress of the squads. The *Morgan* standing off, imperiously observing the mission's progress. Dellian in the convener chamber, where Fintox was attempting to interface with the neuralstratum. That was where the action was.

Her attention flicked back to the intruder. *So why are you here, not out there?* The portal it had come through was twinned to a portal in Sasra's atmosphere, one they'd used to drop flood mines through. Therefore . . . 'Ah!' She used her command authority to take control of every portal inside Bennu's vast cavity.

The lead attack cruiser aimed a communication maser at the

ship. 'This is Yirella, acting commander of Bennu forces. As you know how to subvert our portal management network, you understand our language. Please tell me who you are and why you are here. Your presence at this particular time is making us very nervous.'

'Don't be alarmed, kiddo. Like you, I got terrestrial humanity in my origin. I don't have any hostile intent towards you. So, chill.'

One of Yirella's eyebrows rose in bemusement at the somewhat archaic speech pattern. 'Good to know. Your arrival here and now is not a coincidence, though.'

'No. Like you, I've been sitting around waiting for the arrival of an Olyix ship.'

I knew it. She began to send instructions into the portal power network. 'To what ends?'

'The same as yours, of course. I want the location of the enclave's gateway. And when I have it, I'm going to blow those motherfuckers out of existence.'

'Who am I talking to? Are you the captain?'

'I have no crew. I am the ship.'

'You are a genten, then?'

'Sorry, honey, but I left that level of thought behind a long time ago.'

'I see. If your origin is terrestrial, then we would certainly consider sharing the information we extract from the Olyix ship.'

'Yeah. About that. You need to be real careful with that arkship.'

'We know. It appears that there are cocooned humans on board.'

'Yeah, I wasn't expecting that, either. Should have been, though. The Olyix are sneaky fucks, and they've got even sneakier since we fled Earth. I'm not sure your new Neána friends appreciate that. Their abode clusters are all independent. They don't follow the evening news like some of us do.'

'Thank you for the warning. But do you have any proof that you are not Olyix? Look at this from my point of view; you could easily be here to attack us.'

'You'll see for sure in a minute when I take down their goddamn arkship.'

'You cannot destroy the arkship.'

'Shit, girl, I'm not going to blow it up. I'm going to burn the onemind to death. After that, we can start thinking about what to do with its cargo.'

'If you have been stealthed in Sasra's atmosphere, then you're here in Bennu as a stepping stone to the arkship. My sensors show me you're currently travelling to a portal with a twin that will take you there. I assume our attack cruisers would be unable to prevent you from using it?'

'You assume right, honey.'

'Not quite. I can cut power to the portal and end the entanglement. In fact, I can cut the power to every portal. You'll be trapped in here with me. And given you need a portal to reach the combat zone, you will not prevail, whatever your task is.'

'Don't do it, sweetheart. That would just be an inconvenience. And trust me, I'm not someone you want to inconvenience.'

'If your thoughts are superior to a genten's routines, then you will understand that I require evidence you are truly allied to us. Something considerably more substantial than talking like a refugee from pre-Olyix-era Earth.'

'Actually, the one thing I wasn't prepared for is you. Can't you just take it on faith?'

'Faith is not something those of us who flee for our lives have any more. Try again. Try facts.'

'I can blow you straight to hell if you interfere with that portal.'

'Do that and all the power goes off. I'm not stupid.'

'Yeah, beginning to see that. Okay, Commander Yirella, what would you consider proof?'

'Please. You are ninety seconds out from the portal. I have to make that decision. Don't—' Bright scarlet icons came on across her optik's tactical display, demanding her attention. 'Oh no.'

'Yirella,' Tilliana called, 'we've got trouble here. Something's wrong with the neurovirus. Del's been caught in some kind of overspill, his medical readouts are going hot. The gentens don't understand what it is.'

Yirella expanded the feeds from Dellian's squad. The convener chamber was lit by macabre green-tinged light emitted by leaves that sprouted from all the wooden pipes and creepers, a scene she could only associate with the shrine of some historical gothic death-cult. Dellian was staggering about as if drunk, his gauntlets pressed against his helmet in a classic final breakdown pose. Overhead, his cohort of combat cores were flashing about like berserk hornets, constantly changing course, coming perilously close to crashing into walls and vats before darting away again. Fintox was motion-less underneath a vat, his top-hat helmet stuck to a pillar, every limb extended and rigid as if he was being electrocuted. Squad members were running and ducking, trying to avoid being swatted by Dellian's frenzied combat cores. In turn that was agitating their own cohorts.

'They love us,' Dellian said.

Yirella trembled from shock and rising outrage. The tenderness in his voice was one she thought was only ever directed at her.

'You've scanned me,' the ship said. 'You know how powerful I am. If I wanted to harm you, then you'd already be dead.'

'That's not the purpose of the Olyix,' Yirella told it flatly. 'They never kill humans. They take us alive.'

'Okay, the paranoia is healthy. But seriously, this time you've got to take me on trust.'

'The one thing I can't do.' She winced as Dellian began firing his suit gaussrifle. Metallic hydrogen bullets shredded the vats and pipes. Then his cohort opened fire, annihilating the same targets. The rest of the squad dived for cover.

'Yirella,' Tilliana implored. 'Calm him down! You can reach him.'

'Del? Del, darling. It's me. It's Yirella. Del, power down the cohort. Let the dears rest so I can be with you. You and me. I love you. I want us to be together. Power them down, darling. Please.'

She heard him call her name, sounding so confused.

Three nuclear explosions blossomed on the arkship's surface.

It was on the edge of Yirella's optik display, a visual feed from the *Morgan*. The tactical administration genten shrank the rest of the display until that was all she saw. A trio of solar-bright bubbles were emerging from midway down the massive cylinder. For an instant she thought the neurovirus had triggered the bombs, but couldn't see what that would achieve. Three massive plumes of vaporized rock streaked out into space, irradiated to an intensity only just short of the fusion blasts that created them. In their wake, the surface of the arkship now had a trio of craters with glowing edges.

She heard a babble of frantic voices swamping the comms as the survivors called to each other, and the tactical supervisors tried to re-establish order. Her optik display snapped back to full overview. Yirella cried out when she saw nearly a quarter of the squads were missing. They'd all been on their way to the wormhole, in the passages winding underneath the second biosphere – where the fusion bombs had detonated.

The blasts seemed to have goaded Dellian to a frenzy. He was shooting continually, completely at random. Around him, the convener chamber's atmosphere was howling out through the entranceways. Drones were being sucked along, to crash their way down the passage outside; only the combat cores were holding steady, their miniature gravatonic drives straining against the erratic gravity and punishing wind. Several of Dellian's shots struck his friends as they clung to pipes. The armour held, but she knew it wouldn't withstand repeated hits.

'Del, it's me, it's Yirella. I love you, Del. I want to be with you.'

'I love you, Yirella.'

'Del, power down your cohort. For me, my love. Let them rest.'

'Yes.'

A moan of relief escaped her mouth as he stopped shooting.

'Commander Yirella, you need to let me through,' the intruder ship said.

The tactical display showed her it was poised in front of the expansion portal that would take it out to the arkship – and the *Morgan*. Her control of the power feed was solid, though the genten reported the processors were being subjected to a dangerously effective darkware attack. The rate her code locks were failing gave her about another minute before she lost control of the power supplies altogether.

'I can't,' she said.

'My perception fronds are showing me your colleagues attacking the arkship are in deep shit. I can help. Can you?'

'It's all right,' Dellian said. 'The God will be there for us. I can feel its message coming.'

'Great Saints,' Yirella said. 'What have they done to him?'

The new craters in the arkship possessed dark centres, a light-less depth defying the gaudy radiance shining out of the molten rims. A multitude of vapour jets came squirting up out of the gloom, as if the arkship was a creature losing its arterial lifeblood.

The *Morgan* was directing a squadron of its attack cruisers inwards, scanning the dark caverns that had been exposed. Each one had a large shape moving outward, lifting away from the curving surface.

Yirella groaned. 'Resolution ships.'

'New type,' the intruder said. 'Bigger and more powerful than the ones in my records. Let me through. They will systematically break the *Morgan* up into chunks and capture the crew before they round up the surviving squads. Then they'll come for you in here. Is that what you want?'

'No,' Dellian said. 'We will live forever with the Olyix guiding us.'

Tears threatened to blur Yirella's vision. *I've lost him. We've lost.* And with that understanding came absolute clarity. The tactical display showed her some kind of negative energy beam stab out of the first of the giant Resolution ships. Two assault cruisers crumpled, shrinking to perfect black spheres ten centimetres in diameter. The collapsed matter hung there inert for an instant, then began to glow purple as the spheres suddenly inflated out again. Their growth rate accelerated into a colossal explosion that saturated local space with hard radiation as particles broke into pure energy.

Yirella issued her order through the Bennu command network. 'Go through,' she told the ship. 'Help us.'

The expansion portal rim shone with sapphire light as unrestricted power flowed into it.

'Yirella, what have you done?' Ellici yelled.

'The only thing that's left,' she replied calmly. 'We have nothing to lose any more.'

*

Finally! That Yirella kid was a pain, but she came to her senses in the end. Aaaand I'm through, relative emergence velocity thirteen per cent lightspeed. Interstellar crap glows green and violet as it smacks into my quantum discontinuity boundary. Up ahead the Judas arkship is crowned in a violet glow as it ploughs through the scattered hydrogen atoms that inhabit space out here. Ambushing the ambushers. Smart tactic.

But humans on the exodus flight have been running the same lure/ambush strategy for too long now – by about six thousand years. What the fuck did the dumbasses expect?

The three upgrade-Resolution bastards are soaring out of their lair. Attack cruisers closing on them. Jesus! Gravaton beams. That's trouble. My discontinuity boundary should be resistant. But let's not put that to the test today.

So now the *Morgan*'s throwing all its attack cruisers at them. Crazy humans. They've just seen what the Resolution ships can do. It might make sense as a holding action if the *Morgan* was turning to run. There were portals back in Bennu that reached tens of lightyears away. It could have got out free. But no. The Captain is obviously a stickler for noble tradition. One for all and all for one – and all that crap. Nice sentiment, but it will get them killed one of these days.

Yirella, now she was a pragmatist.

Oh for fuck's sake, now the *Morgan* is accelerating to meet the Resolution ships – three gees. It's got some mighty fine weapons, but it's no match for these new-style ships. I'm nearly five thousand kilometres away from the action, and the bad guys have spotted me.

Shit. Two of them are coming at me. I don't care about that. But the third is vectoring out to tackle the *Morgan*.

Comm maser: 'Captain Kenelm, stand down. Leave this to me.'

'Who are you?'

Ah, I don't have time for this crap. The *Morgan* and the Resolution ship are accelerating hard, like they're both going to ram each other. Twenty-three seconds until they reach intersection point. They'll be a hundred kilometres distant when they pass, but that won't save the *Morgan* from those negative graviton shots.

Accelerating. Two hundred and fifty gees. Christ, that's fast. My discontinuity boundary is lighting up like a dinosaur-killer asteroid hitting the atmosphere. Cool.

My course will carry me equidistant past the three Olyix warships. Three of my q-v missiles go active, loaded with target data, and anticipating any microsecond evasive manoeuvres in the unlikely event they detect the incoming threat and fire. Missiles gone, five hundred gee acceleration. Given our separation distances, they have barely a second of flight time.

I predicted that right. None of the Resolution ships have time to react. That's cellular processing versus photonic for you.

The missiles trigger their quantum-variant warheads, warping the field stability of spacetime within a hundred-kilometre radius. My processing is fast enough to catch it, but the oneminds will never know what hit them. Just call me merciful.

The atoms from which the Resolution ships are made perform weird alchemy transformations. Sections of mass shift at random between solid, fluid and gaseous states. The abrupt loss of nuclear cohesion breaks the ships apart in plumes of distorted molecules tormented with rudimentary energies.

And I'm already flashing past the trio of destruction blooms. Switching acceleration direction to slow and curve around back to the arkship.

Three minutes – a long time in space warfare terms. But I'm sliding into rendezvous with the big bastard. Scanning to see if there are any more Resolution ships waiting inside.

Clean.

Their wormhole generator is powered down. All the debris spilling out of the craters is clotted with scraps of organic matter, some vegetation, some Olyix cell segments, even a few explosively decompressed quint bodies scattered across the uncaring stars.

I have five hundred autotroops, like human combat drones, but with vastly superior weapons technology. They'll chase down and slaughter all the arkship's surviving quint, leaving us with the major headache of what to do with the cocoons. But first I dispatch five mentalic subsections into the arkship. Ironically – or pleasingly, depending on your sense of humour – human-sized oblates. They zip into the passageways and scurry into the big chamber containing the wormhole generator. Four attach themselves to the control network and begin retrieval. The onemind initiated a total wipe procedure, of course, but my subsections execute a detailed quantum analysis scan, extracting the past electron states of every molecular junction. The data is as easy for me to read as a kindergarten text.

My remaining subsection inserts a needle into a nexus. The arkship neuralstratum is massive. So many thoughts, and not nearly as ordered as I was expecting. The Olyix haven't lifted themselves quite so far from their messy evolution as they claim, then.

'Well, hello there,' I say.

'What are you?' it asks.

'You don't know. That's good. And, please, you can stop trying to slip a neurovirus to me. I'm not an out-of-date Neána.'

'Your mind is so hard and bright. How beautiful you are. Join us. Come with us to meet the God at the End of Time.'

'Oh, pal, that hook-up just ain't going to happen. It never was. But now I'm going to make fucking sure of it.'

'Human, then. More advanced than any of the exodus wave we have encountered.'

'No clues. No masterplan monologue. You're sneaky bastards. And I can read in your memory that you sent a message about me down the wormhole before you shut it down.'

'The enclave will rejoice in the knowledge that an entity of your stature exists.'

'You are just so full of bullshit. And FYI, there is no end of time. The cyclic universe theory is a crock of shit.'

'Such a human view.'

'Yeah well, it's been a blast. But I've just downloaded the gateway coordinates for your enclave. I'm off to pay your kind a visit now.'

'I have a message for you.'

'I know. I've already pulled it out of you, right from your sacred soul. Bring me all your life, bring me all your batshit crazy followers, yada, yada, yada.'

'It comes from the future. It was sent to us, because the God knows we will travel successfully to reach it. Neither you nor I can escape divine destiny. The loop is closed and eternal.'

'Good talk. Now die.'

London

For two days the people living under Earth's city shields vented their panic in protest marches, riots and violence. Always, their targets were the cocoons – most of which were burned, with many more hacked apart, while some were simply thrown from high buildings to the cheers of spectators on the ground. Curfews were ordered, then martial law in the most aggressive cities, prohibiting anyone from venturing outside.

Gwendoline watched it all sporadically, mostly accessing public news and the more frank feeds from her globalPAC, but sometimes staring at the columns of smoke rising into the listless air above London. When she wasn't doing that she helped Horatio nurse Crina. It was pointless, of course; there was nothing they could physically do to stop the woman from cocooning. Her flesh had been completely annexed by the Kcells, remodelling her body to chillingly nonhuman specifications. But they could provide some comfort as she drifted in and out of consciousness over those excruciating forty-eight hours. Talking calmly, offering reassurances that they'd contact her family, promising no one would disturb her cocoon when the process was complete.

Those conversations were bad enough, and Gwendoline had to

415

summon up her deepest reserves of patience and determination to keep going, providing the kind of companionship and sympathy reserved for the most precious of dying relatives. And this for a woman she'd known for less than a week. That Crina was suffering no pain at all made it even worse. The few times Gwendoline had managed to call Loi, he confirmed one of the earliest cocoon malformations was a gland that secreted an antidepressant, keeping the victim unnaturally relaxed throughout the ordeal.

Attempting to soothe Crina got so bad that Gwendoline simply couldn't face those last few hours, leaving Horatio to provide what consolation he could. Instead she sat in the semi-darkness of the lounge, drinking coffee brandy (with too much brandy) and despising herself for being so weak. She couldn't bring herself to access any feeds, instead playing old music tracks and trying not to think about anything, let alone the choices she was about to face.

London had finally quietened down, with only a scattering of buildings on fire visible from her elevated windows. The authorities were gradually recovering control of the streets. There was talk now of assigning safe zones for the cocoons, where they could be brought by their relatives to be guarded against any further mayhem. She couldn't quite see that working, but applauded the initiative.

It was sometime before dawn when Loi's icon appeared. 'Hello, Mum, how are you?'

'Drunk. Miserable. Frightened. Tell me again cocooning isn't contagious?'

'It's not contagious. You have to have a medical Kcell implant. Though we've seen cases on Earth where Olyix agents have used nerve-block shots on people, then inserted the Kcells into—'

'Stop! Not today, darling. Just . . . I can't handle much more bad news, okay.'

'That's good. I've got some better news for you.'

'Thank fuck.'

'Mum!'

'Yeah. Sorry. What is it, darling?'

'You'll get a visitor in the next ten minutes. I swung the family name around hard and pulled in some favours. He's bringing you a twenty-centimetre portal.'

'What do I want with a twenty-centimetre portal?'

'It's from Connexion's Civic Emergency Support division. It will thread up to a two-metre rectangle portal and take you direct to the Greenwich tower. That's just one step from Nashua, Mum. You and Dad can be safe in the Puppis system in less than a minute.'

'That's . . . that's fabulous. Thank you, darling.'

'You need to pack light, okay?'

'Loi . . . darling. I'm not sure we'll use it.'

'What?'

'Listen to me, darling. There are so many people here. What are *they* going to do?'

'There's a contingency plan for everyone, Mum. And you know better than to ask.'

'She was frightened you know, even with whatever sedatives those bastards were filling her with. How horrible is that? Lying there watching alien cells eating your body away, knowing the cotton wool wrapping your thoughts is made out of chemicals raped from your own blood. But she didn't let it win, she was too strong for that.'

'Oh Christ, Mum. Just use the portal, okay?'

'I will. But what about everyone else? We can't just desert them . . .'

'We're not going to desert them. But you can't help them, not by staying in London.'

'Your father thinks we can. He wants to stay, even though he hasn't said it. I know him. People from his agency have been calling him for days, asking for advice. It's bad. There are whole communities out there that have been abandoned.'

'Mum. Please! Come on, you've got a cocoon in your home – inside the security boundary. You and Dad have to leave.'

'I should stay with him.'

'No, Mum, he should stay with you. We are going to need every capable large-project manager we can find to help build the exodus habitats. And that's you, Mum. Those habitats are what's going to save the human race, and nothing is more important than that. Ask Dad if you don't believe me.'

'Hell, you really do take after him, don't you? My genes never got a look in.'

'We both know that's not true. Look, the Deliverance ships will be here by the end of the day. I wasn't kidding: we don't know what is going to happen. They have the power to kill Earth and everybody on it, and there is nothing Alpha Defence can do to stop them. You have to leave. Now, while there's still time.'

'If I leave now and the London shield falls, I'll never forgive myself.'

'All right. How about this: you both wait where you are until the first Deliverance ships reach Earth. If they can break the shields, then the pair of you leave right away. If the shields hold . . . then Dad has to make the decision. Not you. Understand?'

'All right. I can't argue with the logic.'

'Good. So when the portal arrives, thread it up.'

'Yes, yes.'

'I mean it, Mum. If you think I won't send someone through to carry you out of there by force, think again.'

She couldn't help the smile creeping onto her lips. 'Why did you have to grow up?'

'So I can look after you.'

'My son.'

'Mum, be careful, please.'

'Of course.'

'I'll get you a live feed from Alpha Defence. You can see what happens to the city shields in real time.'

'Thank you, Loi. I love you.'

'You're the best, Mum. Stay safe.'

Gwendoline tipped her head back until it was resting on the settee's deep cushions. Exhaled a long, long breath.

'You still amaze me,' Horatio said from the doorway.

She pressed her lips together. 'How much of that did you hear?'

'What I didn't hear I could guess at. He's right, of course; you have to go to Nashua. At least someone has a working plan how to save people.'

'Some people.' She gestured at the window. 'Not those out there, which is where you want to go.'

'I do, because if the shield stands up to the Deliverance ships, then the people living underneath will need a lot of help to get through the next few years. Don't they deserve that?'

'Why you?'

'Same reason they need you to help the exodus project. It's what we do. No – it's what we're good at.'

She took his hand and pulled him down onto the settee. 'It's not fair, though.'

'Life generally isn't.'

'I can't stand the thought we'll be separated. For ever.'

'We have hope. That will be shared, like our own private entanglement. The Olyix can never take that from us.' He smiled.

'Right.' As always, that smile did wicked things to her soul. She never could resist the Horatio smile. Because of it, traitorous liquid was building up behind her eyes – tears she could never shed, because that was unfair to him.

'Okay,' he said. 'So now what?'

'Is it over?'

'Crina? Yes. She's been unconscious for the last two hours. I was only in there to make absolutely sure.'

'Christ, that's a horrible way to go. And how's that cocoon going to keep her alive? We're on the top floor. It can't send out roots from here.'

'I left some of the packets of protocarb pellets next to her. And there's the ensuite bathroom; it can get water from there, I guess. That'll sustain her for a while.'

'At least none of the anti-Olyix crazies can get at her in here.'

Theano told her that Loi's messenger was outside the penthouse and splashed a camera image of a self-conscious intern-type standing there holding a small case. 'Close the vestibule security door,' she told the altme. 'Open the entrance. Tell him to place the case inside, then leave.'

Horatio raised an eyebrow. 'Crina has rubbed off on you.'

'She taught me not to be complacent, yes.'

A minute later she stood beside the vestibule security door as it slid back. The case was standing in the middle of the marble-tiled floor. She picked it up and Theano gave it her executive code. The top hinged up silently, and she stared at the portal inside.

If I go, I'll be safe. I'll never have to worry again. I'll be taken care of.

I'll have no say in my life. Protected, a beautiful rare animal in a breeding zoo flying off blindly into the galaxy.

The case closed, and she walked back into the lounge.

'What now?' Horatio asked.

'Now we see if the city shields can withstand whatever the Deliverance ships are going to throw at them.'

'Right.' He shifted uncomfortably. 'And if they can't?'

'We run away. And I do mean *we*.'

'Above all else, I love your practicality. When do the Deliverance ships arrive?'

'The first ones will reach the atmosphere in eight hours. Then the next *twenty-five thousand* follow them down over a week or so.'

'Holy shit!'

'It's an interesting number. There are approximately five thousand city shields, so that works out at about five Deliverance ships per city. Of course, some cities are a lot bigger than others. Who knows what the actual distribution will be?'

'Do they know which city the first ships will go to?'

'No. But if they keep their deceleration constant, they'll be coming down somewhere over the Indian Ocean.'

*

They spent the rest of the day preparing for three outcomes. The first option was easy enough. Set the portal up in the middle of the lounge, with a couple of bagez standing ready beside it like a pair of bulbous sentry drones. If the Deliverance ships broke through every city shield they attacked, thread up fast and go.

Second option: If some shields held and some fell, wait to see what happened to the London shield. If it fell, run like hell through the portal.

Option three, the one she dreaded: The shields all held, London held. She went to Nashua. Horatio stayed.

'I want the shields to fall,' she confessed miserably. 'Does that make me a bad person?'

He scrunched his face up as if in deep thought. 'Slightly on the selfish side, there, I feel.'

'Where will you go? I mean, you're welcome to stay here, but . . . Crina. The Kcells transformed her once. Maybe they'll do it again.'

'I'll just go back to my flat.'

'In Bermondsey?' she exclaimed; she hoped the dismay wasn't too obvious.

'It's not a leper colony, you know. I like it there. The Benjamin agency has a couple of centres in the borough, and they do good work with the local kids.'

'It's next door to Southwark,' she pointed out.

'Ah, the wilderness. 'Tis said there be dragons there.'

'You know what I mean. There are a lot of gangs.'

'There's a lot of lost, impoverished, disenfranchised kids who need help, if that's what you mean. The news and allcomments demonize them.'

'How come you never stood for office?' she asked abruptly.

'I don't want to be a politician. I want to accomplish something in my life. The agencies I work with make a genuine difference to a lot of lives.'

'And you might have lost the vote, or had to compromise if you won.'

'True.'

'All right. Worst-case scenario, I go through alone—'

'People living in London might disagree with your ratings system, there.'

'Shut up! I go through. You're left here. As soon as I'm on the other side, we rethread. You take the twenty-centimetre portal with you; I make damn sure it stays powered up and the entanglement is maintained.'

'Can you do that?'

'I'm Ainsley fucking Zangari's granddaughter. I am a Connexion executive board member, and I'm going to be running part of the exodus habitat project. I can do it, or people will be wishing they were cocooned.'

He swayed back, only half joshing. 'Damn, I always fall for the so-pretty-so-she's-gotta-be-sweet delusion.'

'And don't you forget it, mister. Because when I've built those exodus habitats, you're going to be in a first-class cabin to the stars.'

'Yes, ma'am.'

*

Gwendoline spent the afternoon reviewing routes from her penthouse to the Bermondsey Spa Gardens where Horatio had his flat. Skycabez were out, because the police had shut down all airborne traffic except for their own drones. That left taxez and cabez, which a lot of companies weren't letting out of the garage because of the damage inflicted by the anti-cocoon mobs during the last two days. Cycling, which Horatio laughed at when she suggested trying to order one for delivery. And walking.

'Eight kilometres,' he said. 'Two hours max. Easy.'

'Not easy. Half the streets have no-gathering notices imposed, and there's plenty of looting. I need to find you a safe route. And I think I've got it.'

'Where?'

'You walk down the river.'

'You're kidding!'

'No. There's no water in it any more, not at this end, anyway. It'll be like one of those old motorways they used to have.'

Theano had been splashing real-time situation maps from Connexion Security. One of the first things she noticed was where all the water from the Thames outside the penthouse had gone. The eastward flow had pooled against the shield at Tilbury, rising to the top of its banks. It still looked full from there all the way back to Thamesmead, where it had spilled over to flood the Rainham marshes.

That made her check the satellite imagery. Outside the shield, seven days' worth of river water had quickly filled the Wraysbury reservoirs. The overspill had probed its way along the edge of the shield, finding the easiest route and flooding down it. Now the entire river was pouring through the fields and woods that ringed the south-western quarter of London, cutting deep channels through the soil as it sought a way around the implacable boundary. A vast new lake was expanding southwards across the land, drowning forests and the elaborate manor houses that sat inside their tasteful clearings. Foxes, badgers, squirrels, rabbits and a dozen other kinds of confused forest creatures were scampering ahead of the scummy leading edge as it advanced ominously.

'I wonder if they'll find a new home,' she mused as they watched the feed together.

'Easier than humans will,' Horatio said. 'I'm not the greatest mathematician, but even I know we can't all escape on these exodus habitats Loi's talking about. The numbers are impossible. There's billions of us.'

'There must be a way. Loi sounded very confident of whatever plan the committee has drawn up.'

'I hope so, but self-preservation changes people's behaviour. There's very little humans won't stoop to if they are threatened.'

'I won't let them,' she said fiercely. 'We will not abandon you. I promise.'

'No. Don't make promises you can't keep. The populations of the settled systems might make it, but Earth . . . We need to come to terms with what's going to happen to us.'

She clamped her hands over his ears, forcing him to look at her fierce stare. 'Not you. There will be a way. And I will find it. I promise you that.'

*

Alpha Defence tracked the armada of Deliverance ships approaching Earth in a line that stretched for nearly two hundred thousand kilometres, all of them decelerating so they would match the planet's orbital velocity as they closed to within a thousand kilometres of the surface. Earth's weapons platforms were manoeuvred so six of the nine would be over the Indian Ocean when the first of the invaders arrived. Supreme Commander Johnston was under no illusion they'd survive, but an early blow against the Deliverance ships would be good for morale. Defence analysts were more interested in the data the brief conflict would provide, revealing more about the Olyix capabilities.

With less than an hour to go, the first two Deliverance ships began to change course.

'What are they doing?' Horatio asked.

Gwendoline shrugged. 'Don't ask me.'

Like the rest of the planet, they watched the two sleek shapes accelerate towards the moon. G8Turings projected their course, showing them streak over the surface in a shallow parabola, coming down to ten kilometres directly over Theophilus crater.

'Oh crap!' Gwendoline exclaimed.

'What's wrong?'

'That's where Alpha Defence put its primary Command Centre.'

'How the hell do you know that? Surely it's secret!'

'Sol Senate category-one clearance only, yes. Connexion has contracts with Alpha Defence for several ultra-grade projects.'

'You never told me.'

She rolled her eyes. 'Category one. Clue's in the name.'

'Oh. Right. Sorry. But the Olyix clearly know about it.'

'Yeah, and that's got to hurt.'

When the two Deliverance ships were a thousand kilometres out, they began firing missiles. After they'd launched twelve each, the ships changed course again, taking them away from a Theophilus crater overflight.

The first missile struck five kilometres to the north of the central mountain. A nuclear plasmaball erupted, swiftly expanding over the triple-peaked mountain. Theano splashed the sensor data accrued from high-orbit satellites.

'That cannot be right,' Gwendoline muttered. 'Five hundred megatons? *Five hundred?*'

The second missile pierced the hazy plume of super-energized vapour and slammed into the base of the mountain. Another plasmaball soared out, carrying with it an immense storm of rock fragments. By the time the seventh detonated, the terraced rim of the crater was shaking violently, setting off vast avalanches of regolith that cascaded down the irregular ledges to smack onto the floor as a dusty spume.

The missile impacts continued relentlessly. Their explosions inflated a massive cloud of regolith and molten basalt chunks over the crater. Every few seconds it was tormented by a new energy flare as another warhead struck.

'Five hundred looks right to me,' Horatio said. 'Christ, what'll happen if they attack the shields with those?'

That particular ultra-classified data was already being splashed across Gwendoline's tarsus lens from an obscure Alpha Defence nuclear analysis group. 'They'll punch straight through,' she said. 'And take out the entire city along with any buildings, forests and people for a hundred and fifty kilometres in every direction.'

'Time to thread up, then.'

'They won't use them on cities,' she said, wishing it was fact, not dubious speculation.

The last missile hit Theophilus crater; its hundred-kilometre diameter was now obscured by the assault's toxic cloud of rubble, dust and hypercharged vapour, bulging over thirty kilometres high. The debris was lit from within by tremendous lightning discharges that looked like a continuing chain of explosions.

Theano splashed a status update from Alpha Defence. 'They took out the Command Centre,' she said wearily.

'But Alpha Defence has other centres, right?'

'Of course.'

'So it was overkill for no purpose.'

'No, it was propaganda. The Olyix are showing their strength.'

The remainder of the Deliverance armada continued their descent towards Earth. Waiting for them were the six weapons platforms in their ten-thousand-kilometre orbit, three of them traversing the African coast as they followed their orbital track eastwards, one coming around from Antarctica, with the remaining two heading over from Iran and India.

With the Deliverance ships crossing over geostationary orbit, the platforms powered up their shields, enveloping themselves in a six-hundred-metre sphere of sparkling gold haze. The lead Deliverance ship launched twenty-four missiles down at them. In response, the platforms activated their railguns. Each gun fired two hundred rounds per second along their hundred-and-fifty-metre length, accelerating every bullet to a final velocity of fifty kilometres per second. The platforms didn't carry any bullets on board; they came into the railgun's feed mechanism via portal from huge reserve bunkers distributed across defence bases all over Earth – which gave them effectively unlimited munitions. With each platform sporting eight railguns, forty-eight dense swarms of hypervelocity projectiles hurtled up towards the attackers in unending torrents. The missiles' acceleration fluctuated wildly as they tried to evade the near-solid rivers of metal stabbing up at them.

The railguns didn't have to be accurate; the sheer quantity of bullets flung out constituted a barrier that guaranteed a strike no matter how widely the Olyix missiles tracked away from their original flightpath. As the first bullets closed on the missiles, it was obvious that they had some kind of short-range defence mechanism; the bullets twisted out of alignment with only a few metres to go before impact. But while the deflector systems could cope with an occasional potential strike, they were soon overwhelmed. At their phenomenal closing velocity, it only took the slightest graze for a bullet to obliterate a missile. Within thirty seconds, all twenty-four were destroyed.

'So we *can* damage them,' Horatio said. 'They're not invincible.'

'That was nothing,' Gwendoline contradicted. 'Our worthless counter-propaganda.'

They watched the twelve lead Deliverance ships accelerate smoothly, changing course to take them around the confluence of weapons platforms. They split into pairs, which matched each platform's orbital track, then closed in to within five hundred kilometres. The platforms did nothing as they slid inexorably eastwards, their orbits carrying them towards Australia. The Deliverance ships fired X-ray lasers, the same kind they'd deployed against habitat shields and then MHD asteroids. All six platform shields soaked up the energy pumped into them, blooming into golden mini-suns, bathing the Indian Ocean in a primeval dawn. The Deliverance ships slid in closer, like cautious predator beasts, and the six platforms fired their gamma-ray lasers simultaneously. The beam focus chambers were one-shot, decaying instantly from the radiation backwash. But before they died, they converted fifty thousand megawatts into an ultra-hard gamma beam, each directed at the heart of a Deliverance ship. Designed to target objects moving with a colossal velocity relative to Earth, the Deliverance ships – in their matching orbital paths – enabled the platforms to hold the gamma beam on them for the full quarter of a second of their existence. The results were spectacular. Four Deliverance ships exploded, and five had giant holes torn into their fuselage, spilling out molten debris and ionized atmosphere. The remaining three simply died, carrying on along their orbit, but beginning a slow tumble that would last for decades until they finally succumbed to atmospheric resistance and disintegrated in the mesosphere.

Above the carnage, a batch of ten Deliverance ships accelerated hard, their dark fuselages turning a perfect silver as they raced towards the platforms. This time they went in low, curving under the thousand-kilometre altitude mark before closing in. The platforms only had short-defence weapons capable of pointing downwards. Twenty missiles leapt towards them. The megaton warheads detonated in a harmonized blast, creating a ferocious rosette of interlocking plasmaspheres around the platforms. The thermosphere flared in response, and dazzling auroral ripples over a hundred kilometres in diameter burned their way through the tenuous gas. Beneath that, the ocean reflected the actinic light, turning the air to a pale solar photosphere.

Deliverance ship energy beams slammed out, puncturing the radiation vortex with superb accuracy. A second wave of nuclear-tipped missiles streaked in to within thirty kilometres of the platforms before exploding. Platform shields failed within seconds, unable to withstand the intense assault. Above the ocean, the atmosphere shimmered in torment as it was broiled by the radiation.

Plumes of super-heated air began their deadly amalgamation into storm-swirls, spinning faster than anything the planet had known before.

Through the emerging maelstrom, the long line of Deliverance ships descended.

Perth was the first city. A clean urban jewel sitting on Australia's coast, it was protected by eight interlocking oval shields that stretched for seventy kilometres end to end, and forty deep. High waves were already slapping at the waterside edge of the shields when seven Deliverance ships came sliding out of the wounded sky at hypersonic velocity, curving around as they lost speed, to deliver a salvo of sonic booms that went unheard by the residents below. The big streamlined craft spread out to encircle the city, then landed a kilometre from the shield boundary, with one coming down on Rottnest Island. One by one they fired energy beams at the shield domes.

Every human on Earth accessing the feed held their breath. The air above the shield began to glow as static webs danced around the strike points, shivering down the dome to ground out in a continuous roar. Columns of searing air fountained up high into the atmosphere, mushrooming out at gale force to repel the clouds rushing in from the sea. The domes themselves began to glow with crimson stress as their enhanced atomic bonds were abused by the severe energy input. But they held.

*

'For how long?' Horatio asked.

'Don't know. The shield generators weren't exactly designed with continual use in mind. But it looks like Ainsley's people were right. Those energy beams are being fired at an upward angle. If the shield fails, they won't hit the ground. The Olyix want us alive.'

'There's a shitload of energy saturating the air outside, not to mention heat. If the shields go, it'll all come hammering down on Perth.'

'Yes. Which is why they've not cranked the power level up even further; those beams aren't operating at anything like the power they used to attack the MHD asteroids. It's a balancing act. And they can keep it up indefinitely. Something will have to give in the end. It's going to be a race between generator failure and us building something that can strike back at them.'

'That won't be us,' he said. 'Not in the Sol system. If there's any resistance, it'll have to come from the terraformed worlds.'

'Yeah.'

'That's what you're going to be working on. I'm depending on you, Gwendoline. Come save us.'

The time for smart, funny, teasing answers was long over. She sat on the sofa next to him; they held hands as they watched the never-ending stream of Deliverance ships drop out of the sky.

In the first hour, three of them shot west over the Indian Ocean to Madagascar, circling Antananarivo. The city's shield generators had been sabotaged back on 26th July, within hours of the assessment team returning from Nkya. Armed teams had blown up three of the buildings housing the generators, reducing them to rubble. The authorities had been struggling to install replacements ever since.

Gwendoline watched in dismay as hatches opened across the underbelly of each Deliverance ship. Small spheres dropped out. At first she assumed they were some kind of bombs, then they changed direction and began to form up in a loose circle around the city. There were over a thousand of them in the air when they dropped down to a few metres altitude and began to fly nimbly along the streets.

People ran, but it was no use. The spheres were a lot faster, soaring along the roads and wider avenues. Cybernetic serpents like slim lengths of dark rope came whirling down like bolos. When they landed on someone, they wrapped around tight. Gwendoline winced as she watched one man struggle and yell in terror against one that had coiled around his arms, pinning them to his sides. A couple of friends raced over to help, trying to prise the thing free. The tapered ends stabbed into his flesh, one into his abdomen, the other into his bicep. Blood bloomed against his clothes, and the friends backed away, staring in horror as the tips wormed their way deeper into his body. He sank to his knees, grimacing. The serpent stopped, and the tips slowly withdrew.

Another of the agile machines slithered fast along the ground, rearing up to coil around one of the friends' legs. He screamed as it stabbed into his hips.

'What the fuck!' Horatio exclaimed. 'Are those things killing them?'

'I don't think so. Loi told me . . .' She took a breath, forcing the words out. 'There were cases where Olyix agents injected Kcells into human bodies.'

'Oh, sweet Christ.'

The Olyix serpents spared no one, and children were easy targets. They watched in helpless fury as parents struggled desperately to free their pinioned kids only for the serpents to coil around them as well. The strategy was well thought out, and effective. Citizens armed with ancient weapons and modern peripherals fought a losing battle against the tide of slender monsters wriggling along the city streets. Sections of Antananarivo's already heavily glitched solnet began to drop out. By then it didn't really matter. Perth and Antananarivo were being repeated every minute as the Deliverance ships continued to come. Most cities with shields held firm against their energy beams. Some collapsed in the first minute, wreaking havoc on the buildings abruptly exposed to the overheated atmosphere that thumped down. Olyix spheres flowed down into the ruins, hunting humans struggling to flee –

'Off,' Gwendoline ordered Theano.

'How long till they get here?' a dazed Horatio asked as the images vanished.

'Twenty minutes. Come with me. Please.'

'Everyone has seen what's happening. The Olyix really do want to take us with them on their insane crusade to the end of time. People are scared, and alone. Not just the screwed-up kids I normally help – everyone on this planet. Someone has to help them.'

'We will.'

'I know. But you won't be able to tell them, will you? You can't give details of how we're going to fight back. On top of everything else they'll be in the dark, accessing nothing but propaganda and rumours. There will be nothing to do but fight each other for resources while we wait for the shield to fall.'

'Then come with me.'

'People deserve better than everyone who counts deserting them.'

'I'm not going to desert them. I can help.'

'Yes, *you* can. But *I* would be deserting them. I have to be true to what I am, to what I've given my life to. You know that, don't you?'

Gwendoline couldn't speak, just nodded as the tears flowed.

They didn't use a visual feed after that, just the tactical display, showing them the relentless progress of the Deliverance ships' advance across Europe. Cities fell shockingly, unexpectedly: Ankara, Bucharest, Valencia, Venice, Turin, Lublin, Stuttgart, Enghien, Lyons. Old, dependable names they'd felt sure in their hearts would have withstood the assaults, cities with thousands of years of history and culture that should have carried on through time. Gone. Erased beneath the blast of alien death rays.

Then they came for London. Gwendoline and Horatio went out onto the balcony to watch. The thick barrier of air bound by the shield generators was an opaque copper-gold roof that blotted out the true sky. All they saw were giant ellipsoid shadows manoeuvring overhead. They held hands, waiting –

It happened in seconds. Bright purple blotches appeared overhead – stains which spread rapidly, wiping away the cosy hues they'd become used to over the last few days. Inside a minute the shield was a disturbed violet glow on the edge of eyeburn. With it came a pervasive thrumming sound, a bass organ note played by some demented godling.

'It's holding,' she whispered.

'What?'

'It's holding!'

'Yes.' He gave her forehead a kiss. 'And now it's time for you to go.'

'No. Come with me.'

'I would be nothing, I could contribute nothing.'

'That's not true.'

'We've talked. We've argued. We've drowned ourselves in angst. Now it's over. You go help us the way only you can. And I will help maintain what order I can so the city is still here when you liberate us.'

'I hate them!'

'Good. Now use that.'

They'd already threaded up the twenty-centimetre portal Loi had sent. A two-metre door now waited for her in the middle of the lounge, open to a typically corporate room, windowless and bland.

'We will talk every day,' she told him. 'More than once.'

'We will.'

Her hand refused to let go of him, so he pushed her gently towards the portal. One step beyond that was safety, a habitat forty lightyears away.

'Go.'

She nodded quickly, then turned away so he wouldn't see the new tears. Stepped through.

Horatio watched her bagez trundle loyally through behind her. There was the start of a turn, an arm coming up to wave . . . then the big portal reverted to standby, becoming a blank rectangle with a hint of mauve scintillations within its non-surface.

Thirty seconds later, the threader mechanism activated, aluminium struts and electromorphic muscle activators rotating and sliding with piston smoothness. Big door feeding into slimmer rectangle; that retreating into a square, which in turn vanished into the original twenty-centimetre portal.

Loi's icon splashed across his tarsus lens. 'You still with us, Dad?'

'Sure. Is she safe?'

'Already on Nashua.'

'You look after her, understand? She's not half as tough as she makes out.'

'No, Dad, she's twice as tough.'

'I'll see you soon, son.'

'You can come through any time you want, you know that. Right?'

'I know. Thank you.'

He put the twenty-centimetre portal back into its case and left the penthouse. For once, this part of London seemed deserted as people huddled in their homes, accessing feeds of their planet under siege. So he put his sunglasses on to ward off the shield's dreadful mauve glow and walked east along the Chelsea Embankment until he reached the lovely old Albert Bridge. Halfway across he leant over the rail. Without any water in the river, he was a lot higher up than he was used to. Below him the expanse of chocolate brown mud gave off the fetid smell of sewage and rotting fish. Over by the banks, it was already drying, while directly underneath him a broad trail of liquid sludge occupied the middle of the empty riverbed.

There was someone walking along the semi-solid mud, a kid in a green parka; his footsteps visible in the mud behind him stretching back to Battersea Bridge and beyond. Horatio wondered how far he'd walked along the river – and why.

The kid stood still and looked up. His mirrorshades prevented Horatio from seeing his face. They stared at each other for a few seconds, then Horatio gave a brief nod, sharing the strangeness of the day, and carried on towards Bermondsey.

Kruse Station

4th July 2204

Jade Urchall's body lay on an operating table in Kruse Station's stark medical department. From behind the curving glass wall, Alik regarded it with some distaste. There was plenty of damage: gashes, blood, burns – looking bad. But as a frequent late-night visitor to ER rooms, he knew it was mostly superficial.

Jessika and Soćko, dressed in canary-yellow biohazard suits, were bending over the woman's head. The surgical arms hanging down from the ceiling moved in small increments, like agitated spider legs. Soćko shifted aside, and Alik got a better look. Even he had to clamp his jaw together hard. The scalp had been removed, to be held half a metre above the table by a robot arm.

'Bloody hell,' Callum murmured, 'it's like humans are just built out of modules you can take apart and replace, like fixing a drone.'

'Not a bad analogy,' Yuri said. 'Both of us have had enough replacement parts bolted in, eh?' He clapped his hand on Callum's shoulder.

The way the old Scotsman tried not to flinch was a welcome distraction for Alik.

'Maybe a helpful extension?' Yuri went on.

'How's it going?' Callum asked, ignoring his persecutor.

'Nearly there,' Jessika told them.

Alik glanced over at Kandara. Unlike poor Callum, she didn't seem the slightest bit squeamish at what was being done to the Olyix agent's body. In fact, given how keenly she was watching the bizarre procedure, he got the impression that she'd probably like to finish the fight they'd had in London, preferably with her bare hands.

One of the surgical arms lowered a hemispherical mesh, slipping it onto the exposed quint brain like a particularly tight cap. The two Neána had produced the thing in Jessika's initiator while they were all waiting for news of an Olyix agent. The tip-off about Jade was the first break they'd had since returning from Nkya. But Jessika had promised they would be ready, they just needed a body, alive . . .

'Contact,' Jessika said.

The arm retracted, leaving the mesh in place.

'Stable,' Soćko said. 'Microfibres interfacing.'

The surgical arms moved along Jade's body and began connecting tubes into the ports that had been inserted into Jade's limbs and neck. Clear syrupy fluids started to flow into her.

'What's that for?' Alik asked.

'Intravenous feeds,' Jessika said. 'We need to keep the body alive. For the moment anyway.'

Callum leant forwards, frowning. 'For the moment? I thought this was a long-term strategy?'

'It is,' Jessika said. 'Once we've confirmed the brain is still entangled with the other quint bodies, we'll start fabricating a more reliable life support.'

'Such as?' Alik said.

'Basically, my initiators will grow Olyix organs, which will supply the brain with all the nutrients and oxygen it needs.'

'You mean, we'll cocoon it?'

'Yes.'

'I like it.'

'And Jade Urchall's body?' Callum asked. 'What about that?'

Alik could just make out Jessika's head moving behind her

helmet's tinted visor, looking at each of them. 'That is your decision, of course. Our biologics can sustain the original body for a considerable time. However, the prospects of recovering her brain from the enclave in that timeframe are slim. When we do have her brain back, I'd suggest it would be kinder to grow her a new body.'

'When you say slim . . .?' Yuri enquired.

'She means zero,' Soćko announced. 'The Urchall body will age and die centuries before humans even get close to entering the enclave.'

'Glad you're the Neána diplomatic mission,' Kandara said. 'Wouldn't want to meet your abode cluster's tell-it-how-it-is department.'

The two Neána faced each other for a moment, then turned back to the brain mesh. 'The nodule is intact and functional,' Soćko said. 'We'll be able to scrutinize the cortex impulses.'

'We don't have a Rosetta stone for Neánish,' Alik said. 'So let's have that in English, please.'

Jessika went into the airlock. 'No such thing as Neánish,' she said, as the decontamination cycle filled the glass cylinder with mist and ultraviolet light. 'That I know, anyway.'

'Waiting . . .'

'It goes like this: The five quint brains are all entangled, like a distributed network of processors. Essentially, as this one is unconscious, we've taken it off line. It's not saying anything to the others. Now Soćko is about to insert the neurovirus. We can pacify it, so it will never share that joint consciousness with the others. However, although it won't "transmit" thoughts and senses, it can still receive them. We'll know exactly what the other quint bodies are seeing and doing.'

'Doing and seeing,' Callum said.

Alik frowned at him. 'What?'

Callum shrugged. 'Better grammar.'

'Jezus, man; keep it relevant, here.'

Jessika stepped out of the airlock chamber and began to wriggle out of the biohazard suit. Kandara went over to help her.

'Having a quint intruder inside the *Salvation of Life* is useful,'

Jessika said, 'but the invasion of Earth is an operation that is inter-stellar in scope, and deploys tens of thousands of ships, and probably a million quint bodies. Even five sets of eyes can't tell us everything we need. Fortunately, every quint brain contains a tiny nodule of cells that are entangled with the onemind neuralstratum. It's how the onemind communicates with them. It can see what they see and order them accordingly.'

'You can send the neurovirus into the onemind?' Yuri asked in surprise. 'Will you be able to take control of the *Salvation*?'

'I don't think so.'

'She means no,' Soćko called from inside the treatment bay. 'The onemind is vast and extremely smart. If we tried to subvert it with the neurovirus, its primary thought routines would detect the corruption before it could spread through the majority of the struc-ture. But what we can do is sneak around inside its head and listen to the routines.'

'Jezus H Christ,' Alik murmured. 'We'll have a fantastic advan-tage. We'll know all their sabotage mission plans before they even launch them. We can wipe out every Olyix agent on Earth. The city shields will be safe.'

'Not quite,' Yuri said firmly. 'What we have here is the Bletchley problem.'

'Excuse me?'

'Bletchley Park was where the Allied code breakers deciphered German military communications during World War Two.'

'Great, and?'

'They had to be extremely careful how the information was used. If they outmanoeuvred the Germans at every turn, then the Germans would know their codes had been broken. They'd switch their encryption.'

'You're saying we should let Olyix sabotage teams continue? You're fucking crazy!'

'No, I'm saying we have to be careful how we use the intelli-gence.'

'Yuri's right,' Jessika said. 'Once we initiate passive accumulation of onemind communications, we have to consider the endgame.

This is what we discussed. Ultimately, to win, you will have to lose the start. Allowing ten cities to fall to maintain a strategic advantage is part of the policy. If you win, those humans will be liberated in the future.'

'Have you accessed the feeds from cities without shields?' Alik spat back angrily. 'Those spheres are hunting people down like rabid dogs. They spare no one. Kids . . . the motherfuckers even cocoon babies!'

'That's why we've come to Sol,' Jessika replied levelly. 'That's why we have knowledge about weapons and space drives and biologic initiators. To give it to you, so you can fight this.'

'Why don't you Neána use it, if you're so fucking smart?'

'I *am* the use.'

'No, you're using us.'

'For now, and for a few brief remaining years, you'll have free will, a choice. Exercise it. I can't tell you how, because that's the one thing I have never had. I was created for this purpose alone. So maybe Kandara was right all along, maybe I am just a machine with a single program. It doesn't matter. Choose!'

Alik's clenched fists rose in helpless frustration. He knew she was right, that Yuri was right. They couldn't give away their advantage. They had to fight the long game, no matter how painful. 'Fuck!' He was mildly surprised to find Kandara's hand on his shoulder.

'Yeah,' she drawled. 'Real freedom's a bitch, huh?'

He shook himself free, unable to trust himself to answer.

'So we go ahead with the plan,' Callum said. 'Get a trojan ship into the *Salvation of Life* wormhole and from there into the enclave where it can spy on them. The exodus habitats build an army, or navy, or Ainsley's killer robot legions over the next thousand years. They invade the enclave. Exterminate the Olyix. Rescue our species. Five-point plans don't come much simpler.' His chuckle was bitter.

Alik found he was looking to Yuri for a lead, and resented it enormously.

'Yes, very simple,' Yuri replied with a harsh grin.

'But we still need to get ourselves an Olyix ship to get this plan up and running,' Kandara said. 'When the neurovirus takes over this quint, will it be able to steal one for us?'

'Ah,' Jessika said, brightening. 'Soćko and I have been considering that, and we have an idea that won't risk exposing our tame quint to the onemind. Frankly, stealing a ship was always going to be risky. This way we just have to practise a little mental subterfuge instead – much less likely to get caught.'

Alik followed the Neána woman out of the medical division, trying not to show resentment at how passive he was being. It didn't come naturally. When he gave Kandara a sideways glance, he wasn't entirely surprised to find her smirking at him. 'What?'

'Taking orders doesn't come easy to you, does it?'

'I'm in the FBI, for fuck's sake. All I do is take orders.'

Her smirk grew larger. 'Sure. Just another grunt, you. One that visits the Oval Office for one-to-ones with POTUS.'

Loi and Eldlund were waiting outside the medical division. They fell in behind everyone else and trooped along without asking any questions.

Stepping through three portal doors brought them to a large hangar. Alik let out a soft breath of understanding as he looked at the Olyix ship sitting on a row of cradles. It was the one from Nkya.

Jessika walked over to it and gestured up at the dusty fuselage. 'This is a mid-level transport, remember. The Olyix use them a lot. Fleets of them are going to start coming out of the wormhole over the next couple of months. They'll lift the cocoons from Earth and take them up to the *Salvation of Life*. We took another look at it. The damage isn't as bad as we thought. It's mostly the Olyix biological components that are dead, which the initiators can grow replacements for.'

'So you can fix it?' Alik asked.

'Hopefully, yes. If not, we'll revert to Plan B and steal one.'

Alik joined her, giving the ship a close appraisal. 'Now you're talking. Something physical, at last. I hate goddamn abstracts.'

The rest of the group came up to stand beside them.

'So what are we going to call her?' Kandara asked. 'A ship on a mission like this, she needs a name.'

'*Avenging Heretic*,' Alik told them, and forced his stiff face to smile.

'Works for me,' Kandara said.

'She's going to be carrying all of us a long way,' Jessika said. 'Maybe even the other side of the galactic core. Imagine that.'

'Er . . .' Callum said. 'When you say: Carry *all* of us . . .?'

London

Ollie had laid up in Kew Gardens for a day. No staff had come in. There was no functional solnet anywhere inside the grounds. All the gardenez were inert.

The first night, he'd broken into the ancient wrought-iron palm house and curled up on a bench to sleep underneath the huge cycads. At least it was warm.

Dawn woke him, such as it was under the shield – a murky ochre sky not much brighter than a full moon. His stealth suit was covered in dew from the sprinkler-mist that maintained the palm house's overbearing humidity.

He waited for a while, staring through the building's glass walls to see if anyone came. The only things moving were the ducks on the big pond outside.

It was odd walking along the broad pathways by himself. He was wanted by the police, yet here he was out in the open for anyone to see. Yet nobody was looking.

But only in here.

He had to stop every few paces. His ankle could barely take his weight any more. It was badly swollen, which gave him a nasty flashback to the way Lars's flesh had distended to begin the cocoon process. Logically, he knew he was being stupid imagining he was suffering the same fate; he'd never had any kind of treatment involving Kcells. But still, these were strange times.

He hobbled into a big cafe through tall arched doors that someone had already broken open. Whoever had done that had also ransacked the kitchen and storeroom, cleaning out all the food. But when he started to hunt around, he found a few half-full packets and jars in cupboards that the looters obviously couldn't be bothered about.

An hour later, with many rests for his ankle, he was eating a breakfast of French toast and fruit tea (organic raspberry and honey, which looked just like bird droppings to Ollie). Not his ideal choice, but at least the kitchen had backup power so he could heat it.

The rest of the morning was spent exploring the offices and staffroom at the back, which had a couple of mandatory first-aid kits. He applied anti-inflammatories and painkillers to his ankle, then pulled on a fibre-reinforced support sock.

Lunch was French toast and fruit tea.

Afternoon was resting up. He sat outside, trying to see if anything was happening on the other side of the glowing shield. The Deliverance ships were due to arrive soon, he knew that, but without a link to solnet he didn't know exactly when.

Supper was French toast and fruit tea.

There were enough printed egg sheets left for one more meal, for which he was grateful. He gathered a bunch of cushions from the cafe's chairs and piled them up to sleep on.

Breakfast was French toast and fruit tea.

His ankle didn't feel so bad now. When he checked it, the swelling had gone down. So he applied another anti-inflammatory pac and pulled the support sock back on. There were some jackets in the staffroom, which were so basic he never wanted to meet the owners. He chose an olive-green parka because it had a hood. Solnet and all the civic sensors networked to it might be off in Kew Gardens, but he was pretty sure there would be parts of London where everything was still functional. The hood would help, along with a wide mirrorshade band he'd found in the manager's desk. Wearing the stealth suit during the day was pointless, so he rolled it up and stuffed it into the parka's pocket. Then, before he left, he raided the cafe's counter for the remaining biscuit packets.

Ollie had spent most of the evening thinking how to get back to Copeland Road. He had friends there who'd put him up, he was sure they would. He was part of the Legion; people respected that. Once he was there he could work out what to do next.

Tye had been working out possible routes for him. It was an eighteen-kilometre walk if he travelled straight. And that was when he had an idea, planning things out properly like he used to. The Thames was empty; he and Adnan had seen that on the news feeds. If he walked along the riverbed, he'd reduce the risk of a bankside sensor identifying him, especially in the parka. The river couldn't take him all the way, but he could get to Vauxhall Bridge, which was well over halfway. He'd take it steady during the day because of his ankle, then wait up until dark and put the stealth suit back on for the final five kilometres. Not the greatest plan he'd ever come up with, but better than nothing.

He walked to the edge of Kew Gardens where it bordered the river. There was an old brick wall which he managed to scramble over, delivering him onto on a wide lane running along the top of the riverbank. The sight of the empty river was weird for him; somehow it made the shield and what it represented more real. He slid and blundered his way down the slope until he was standing on the muddy stones at the bottom. The smell of the exposed bed was something he hadn't anticipated, but he pulled the hood down tighter, settled the mirrorshades, and started walking.

*

Hours later Ollie was approaching Battersea Railway Bridge, which was now an elevated greenway of trees, when a change in the shield's uniform, mundane light made him look up. By now he couldn't even count the number of times he'd fallen over, his feet slithering around on the precarious slime-slicked stones to send him tumbling. His ankle was throbbing again, those sweet leather trousers were caked in the wretched, stinking stuff, and wearing the brogues had been a big mistake; he should have stuck to the boots he'd used on the Croydon raid and to hell with vanity. *Hindsight!*

When he looked up, a giant shadow was sliding across the shield.

'Oh crap!' It was a Deliverance ship, it had to be. Tye had reported several public solnet nodes were active and in range as he tramped miserably along the filthy riverbed, but he never accessed any of them in case Special Branch's G8Turings were still hunting him.

He'd just passed a clump of glitzy houseboats sitting on their hulls to the west of the bridge, as useless now as beached whales. They were moored to a floating pier which was the easiest way for him to get up to the path along the south embankment. He took a few steps in that direction, then stopped. *What's the point?*

If the shield fell, the Olyix would come, and being on the riverbed or riverbank would make no difference. If the shield held, he was better off down here where the civic sensors weren't focused.

There were times he hated his ability to map out events.

So he resisted the instinct to get to solid ground and waited passively to see what would happen. Then he realized if the shield fell, the water dammed up outside would come roaring back. 'Shit.' He hurried towards the boats, trying to keep his balance on the uneven ground.

Above him, purple blotches burned bright on the shield. They began to spread rapidly, washing away the lacklustre amber of refracted morning sunlight. Then strangely came the noise, like high-pitched thunder. Lifting the mirrorshades and squinting against the violet radiance, he thought he could see lightning outside the shield, writhing against the vast curving surface.

The shield was holding. He paused for a long while, his gaze darting from the horizon up the apex of the solidified air and back again, searching for any signs of collapse, of the lightning stabbing down onto the city's roofline.

'Fuck you, Jade!' he yelled upwards. 'We beat you. Do you hear? You lose. Are they letting you see that down in hell?'

Ollie let the mirrorshades drop again, glad to have them now the shield was emitting an extreme violet light. For the first time in too long he smiled as he started walking onwards again. He'd just cleared Battersea Bridge when he saw someone up ahead, standing in the middle of Albert Bridge, where the suspension cables were at their lowest. There had been so few people visible along the Thames embankment this morning that he was immediately suspicious. His tarsus lens zoomed in, which is when it got creepy, because he knew that face. It was one of the blokes from the social agency who were always trying to get Bik's équipe involved with more mainstream activities. *Fuck! Is he here for me?*

The man gave him a quick nod, and carried on along Albert Bridge.

Ollie let out a nervous breath. Any other day that would have been weird. Today it barely registered. He started forwards again.

*

Eleven o'clock at night saw Ollie standing at the south end of Copeland Road. He was so tired he could barely stay awake. His legs ached from a stiffness that made every step an effort, and he was genuinely worried his ankle injury was much worse than a simple sprain. He'd even started using a pole as a walking stick to take some of the weight off it.

After he'd reached Vauxhall Bridge, he'd clambered wearily up the short St George Wharf Pier and sat down amid the deserted tables of a riverside restaurant. Tye was reporting solnet was active in this area, but with a very low bandwidth. Frankly, he no longer cared.

This section of town had more people on the streets, not that any of them looked like they knew what they were doing there. He took a guess that several of the groups were out hunting for food. The glass doors of the restaurant had already been smashed.

As his overstressed legs recovered, he started munching on his little store of biscuits and told Tye to access solnet once more. A false registration code was the simplest thing in his personal memory cache. Once he was in, he used every trick he knew, as well as everything Gareth had ever taught him, layering up protection proxies to keep security G8Turings questing his identity. Carefully, he teased out information from public sources, staying clear of the old sites he used to employ as second nature – avoid patterns, anything that could give the G8Turings a lock.

Lichfield Road was officially a raid on a suspected nark gang house. No survivors. An hour after the raid, the Metropolitan Police had removed the Southwark Legion from their alert-one bulletin. Given the damage to solnet, he doubted even residual characteristic recognition profiles would be in the civic networks.

I'm free!

Paranoia banished that thought fast enough. Cancelling the alert-one didn't mean anything. Jade had been an Olyix agent, so it wouldn't be the police that were leading any investigation into her associates – a list in which the Legion would be featuring prominently. This was the arena of the security agencies, and they would know who had survived Lichfield Road.

He started to explore the state of solnet around Copeland Road. It was completely dead. Power seemed to be off for the whole area, too. That still didn't mean it was safe; the spooks could have planted all manner of non-network sensors and spy drones in and around his house – the kind he could never track through a restaurant's low-bandwidth public solnet node.

No, if he wanted to know what had happened to Gran and Bik, he'd have to go there in person. He could wait, make more plans, scout cautiously over a week, build a digital emissions profile – if spook sensors emitted anything he could print a detector for. Or he could be bold.

The dangerous light shining down off the dome and its accompanying howl decided for him. This wasn't a time for pussies.

Stupidly, he waited for night, when he could slip into the stealth suit, but there was no night. Not any more. The Deliverance ships continued their remorseless energy bombardment, which generated the light and noise. This was London now: the unnatural frequency of the glow, the gut-felt noise. It was never going to end.

When he finally realized his mistake it was late afternoon and his ankle was numbed from the new painkiller pac he'd applied, so he set off on the final stage of the trek – a meandering route that took advantage of every interlinked backstreet and low solnet capacity. Three breaks to rest, because he really was exhausted, not to mention depressed and obsessively fearful.

Copeland Road didn't look any different – apart from the bizarre colour-wash inflicted by the violet shield light. He stared down it for a long time. Nobody was about, none of the windows showed any light – and he knew the neighbours and which houses were in use. Nothing gave that away now. There was nothing visible in the sky either, no drones or birds.

'Fuck it.' He hobbled along to his house. If armour suits came crashing down out of the sky now, he wasn't going to resist. In fact he'd be happy to tell them everything he knew about Jade and her associates. They were the ones who were responsible for this Armageddon, the end of his life. His anger at Jade and all she'd done burned like a dark star in his head.

The front door was closed but not locked. There was a rough hole where the handle had been. He pushed it open. Knowing what he was likely to find inside didn't help make it any easier.

They were there in the lounge. He could tell which was which: Bik's cocoon still had his brother's wild fuzzy hair around its blank head like a colour-inverted halo. While even in this state, Gran's distorted flesh looked frail somehow.

Ollie sank to his knees between them and sobbed helplessly. Some pitiful part of his mind had clung to the hope that they'd be okay. There they'd be, sitting waiting for him to come back and take them away, holding their hands as he led them along a gilded path to the magical house by the sea.

Someone was coming down the stairs, making no effort to be quiet. Ollie turned around as they came into the lounge.

'It's you!' Lolo squealed.

They clung together in the semi-dark, touching each other tenderly to make sure it was real. Ollie's fingers traced the bruises marring Lolo's beautiful face. 'What happened to you?'

Sie shrugged, but there was fear in hir eyes. 'Nothing. I'm fine.'

'It was the police, wasn't it?'

Lolo nodded miserably. 'I don't want to talk about it. They're animals. I am my own person, therefore I banish them from my mind and refuse to be contaminated by their memory.'

'Why are you here?' Ollie asked.

'Because I knew you'd come back. I can't live without you. Whatever's going to happen next, it will happen to both of us. That makes it bearable.'

'You silly, silly thing. You could have gone, couldn't you? Back to Delta Pavonis.'

'I'm not leaving. I love you, Ollie.'

'And I love you.'

'I'm so sorry; there was nothing I could do for them. I couldn't stop them changing. But they weren't in pain, I promise.'

'I know. I've seen it happen to other people.'

'Other . . . What happened to your Legion friends?'

'They're dead.'

'Oh, Ollie.' Sie hugged him closer. 'I hate this universe. How could it have something so horrible as the Olyix in it? What's going to happen to us?'

'We're going to live,' Ollie said decisively. 'We're going to get through this. And I'm going to rescue Gran and Bik.'

'Rescue them? How?'

'The Olyix did this with their biotechnology. They can undo it.'

'But . . . will they do that?'

'Oh yeah.' He smiled at hir concerned expression. 'They will. Because I won't give her any choice.'

'Who?'

'Nikolaj: Jade's partner. She's part of this. She's a traitor who works for the Olyix, just like Jade did. I'm going to find her. I swear it on the Legion, Lolo. Whatever I have to do, whatever it costs me. I don't care. She will face me. And that's the day she'll know what real vengeance feels like.'

Vayan

Year 56 AB

The sedatives the medic team had pumped into Dellian were the maximum a human body could tolerate before the chemicals started to damage the tissue they were intended to soothe. Even so, they weren't enough. The doctors had him strapped down on the clinic bed. His limbs were flailing about, nails digging into his palms, head shaking from side to side.

Various scanners above the bed moved about in smooth urgency, tracing nerve impulses. His head was almost invisible behind a nest of sensors. Four doctors studied the tabulated results on a hologram projection so wide it covered the whole of one wall. In the centre of the ever-changing graphs and figures was a three-dimensional map of Dellian's brain, turning with the ponderous motion of a planet's rotation. It should have been completely quiescent. Instead, his neurons were a blaze of activity.

Yirella didn't need any of the doctors to tell her how bad that was. She stood outside the glass door, her head resting on Xante, his arm around her – providing no comfort whatsoever. Tilliana was on her other side, face blank as she tried to be optimistic despite the sight they faced. The rest of the squad was hanging around in the annex behind her, saying nothing and holding on to cups of coffee that had gone cold hours ago.

So she remained outside the treatment room, watching numbly. It was easy not to think; if she did she'd start remembering how many squads they'd lost when the arkship blew open the caverns containing the Resolution ships. Over a hundred people gone, snuffed out in an instant. People she knew. Friends she'd grown up with. She couldn't begin to cope with that much grief, let alone start mourning. Everybody on the *Morgan* knew the Strike carried a terrible risk. But to lose that many in one action . . .

Would it all have been different if I'd just let the intruder ship through straight away? Would they be alive now?

It was a stupid question, she knew. The kind of thing survivors always asked themselves. *And for what? So guilt becomes absolution?*

So she ignored the guilt and brought all her attention to rest on Dellian. Because that's who really mattered. The dead would forgive her if they knew.

One of the doctors, Alimyne, came out of the treatment chamber. Sie looked weary, almost embarrassed to face the squad as they gathered around. 'We don't understand exactly what it is,' sie said. 'Something is keeping his grey matter animated despite the chemical inhibiters.'

'The Neána neurovirus?' Janc asked.

'Motaxan says no. Or at least, not *their* neurovirus. But these Olyix obviously have techniques the metavayans weren't aware of. The patterns they fed into Dellian's brain through his optik were unknown to them.'

'So it *is* a kind of virus?' Tilliana said.

'I don't know how else to describe it, so . . . yes. His optik was forced to project approximately seventeen terabytes into his brain. That is an extraordinary amount of information and memory for the human brain to absorb and incorporate. Maybe too much, given the frenzied state of his brain right now.'

'When it happened, it was like an Olyix talking,' Uret said. 'Not Dellian.'

'He was in there,' Yirella said. 'He responded to me. He was fighting it. My Del would never surrender.'

'Too true,' Ellici said. 'So how do we get it out?'

'There are no guarantees,' Alimyne said. 'But we do have some theories. To start, we are considering inducing a deep coma to see if that will reduce his brain's activity level. Frankly, anything that slows the rate of absorption would be a victory right now. We need time to solve this.'

'That's not neuroscience,' Yirella shot back. 'That's witchcraft! You might as well give him herbal tea.'

'I have a genten analysing the patterns. If we can determine the operational mechanism, we'll be closer to a treatment.'

'There are designs in the *Morgan*'s archives,' Yirella said, 'work our ancestors did on brain–processor interfaces. They weren't optical-based like this is, but an interface should allow us to get a counter-virus into him.'

'The human brain is not a processor,' Alimyne warned. 'And Dellian's mind is not a program. You can't load and wipe memories at will. Our worry is that the longer we leave him in his current state, the more the Olyix patterns will merge with his own thoughts and memories.'

'Then put him into the coma,' Xante said hotly. 'Shut his brain down completely; don't let it overwhelm him.'

'There are dangers in that procedure, too,' Alimyne said. 'I wanted you to understand that before we start that action.'

'Wait,' Yirella said. 'You're asking for my permission?'

'If we were back on Juloss, doctors are obliged to consult with family members in such cases. Here, and with you – and particularly with this case, which is entirely experimental – ethical requirements are unclear. Technically Captain Kenelm has the authority to order or refuse treatment; however sie wanted you to be consulted. All of you; this squad is effectively Dellian's family.'

Yirella glanced at her friends, knowing they would all support her. Their companionship made this almost bearable. 'Do it,' she said.

*

The *Morgan* was leading a cluster of ten assault cruisers that were flying a defensive umbrella formation twenty kilometres in front of the Olyix arkship. Their overlapping distortion fields created a pale lavender aurora as they rammed the tenuous interstellar gas aside, making sure the badly battered rock didn't suffer any further abrasion from particle impacts.

Protecting the arkship and its precious cargo was Captain Kenelm's sole priority. Back in Bennu, the industrial platforms were in full emergency activation mode, producing equipment to initiate the Neána option. Dozens of refineries and manufacturing stations were being dispatched through an interstellar portal whose twin was currently fifteen lightyears out from Vayan. Within a week, they would be followed by entire asteroids selected to provide metals and minerals, along with comets that were ninety per cent ice, enough material for the fledgling civilization to build dozens of habitats. While down on Vayan, the fifty-year lure masquerade was over; vast swathes of the mock-farms were harvesting for real now. Big crude tractors were hauling reapers across fields and meadows, gathering up as many seeds as they could from grass and bushes and trees. They would be used to plant the habitat landscapes as soon as they were built. Three fifty-kilometre-long cylinders were planned initially, with the first scheduled to be completed in six months.

No one knew how long they had before a fleet of Resolution ships decelerated hard into Vayan's star system. Estimates from the tactical analysts ranged between a month to five years. Kenelm had no choice but to assume the one-month option, and ordered an immediate transition operation to ensure the cocoons' safety.

A full third of Bennu's initiators were currently producing systems which could support the continuing hibernation of the humans they'd discovered. Working with the initial survey data supplied by remotes exploring all three arkship biospheres, the gentens calculated there were nearly two billion life-support chambers. So far they'd confirmed a quarter of a million cocoons were stored in the first biosphere. It appeared the remaining two biospheres were empty.

Transfer had already begun, bringing the cocoons from the arkship into Bennu's main torus, plugging them in to the new support machinery as soon as it was installed.

So far, no one had demanded or ordered Yirella help with the Neána option. But it was her field; the work she'd done designing the Vayan civilization would make her invaluable in turning the existing low-level contingency plans into reality.

With Dellian now in a deep coma, and his brain's manic activity reduced (but not entirely suppressed), the other implications of the catastrophic Strike had started to add to Yirella's feelings of dread. Despite, or perhaps because of, the hollow victory of finding the cocoons, some of the universe's light seemed to have gone out for good.

She'd been on her way to the main council room, but took just one slight detour. The *Morgan*'s life-support torus didn't have windows, not like the much bigger Bennu habitat wheel with its glass sky. But it did have a wide lounge, with walls whose texture were fixed on Earth's Mesozoic era, placing her on the edge of a cyatheales forest with a plain of lush grasses stretching out to the horizon, where volcanoes idly exhaled smoke pillars. She and Dellian had come here whenever their schedules kept them too busy for more leisurely outings. If anywhere could help her calm her thoughts, it would be here. She remembered Saint Kandara was always scared before combat, and how she would prepare by obsessively checking her weapons and armour. Well, orchestrating industrial station deployment wasn't exactly going into battle, but what happened over the next few days would decide the fate of those quarter of a million people cocooned by the Olyix. She needed to be thinking rationally – even though the Saints had been unanimous in hating the whole hiding-in-the-dark route.

But not even the familiarity of the lounge and its warm memories could comfort her today. She shut her eyes and let her thoughts roam where they would, not really caring if that was a dark place.

The intruder ship.

The greatest enigma in all of this. After the Strike, it had taken up station a hundred kilometres behind the arkship. It refused to talk to anyone – least of all Captain Kenelm, who had spent hours sending it greetings and questions. The only thing it had done was deploy hundreds of soldier drones into the arkship. They'd been chillingly efficient at hunting down and killing the Olyix quint. They were still inside, because the arkship was huge. Finding and eliminating every quint would probably take months. But Kenelm and the squad commanders were satisfied that the first biosphere was now completely clear. There hadn't been a firefight for seven hours now.

Her databud accessed the *Morgan*'s sensors, and her optik showed her the intruder, its white hull illuminated in the gentle violet glow of dying interstellar gas. After studying it for a long minute she looked around the lounge. Above her, and discreetly woven into the texture of the prehistoric savannah, a lens cluster peered down at her. She gave it a sad smile. 'Are you watching me?' she asked out loud.

A small pure white icon appeared in her optik, which she opened.

'Yes.'

'Thought so,' she said. 'Your knowledge of our networks is quite spooky.'

'They were already old when I was built. If I know them, the Olyix certainly do. You need to reformat and refresh. Maybe come up with something original.'

'We've plateaued. There's nothing new in the universe.'

'Yeah? Tell that to the Olyix. The graviton beam they used against your assault cruisers surprised even me.'

'Thank you for helping.'

'I had fun. I've been waiting for this day for a long time.'

'How long?'

'Couple of thousand years.'

'Saints!'

'Not so bad. I wasn't this conscious until a few weeks ago, and most of time previously was eaten up by relativistic dilation. In a linear timeframe I'm only a hundred and fifty years old.'

'Did you get what you wanted?'

'Some of it, yeah. I've got the gateway location. But the onemind made sure it wiped most of its memory of the enclave itself.'

'Did it tell you why it was coming to Vayan with an arkship full of cocooned humans?'

'Not exactly. The cocoons are from a generation ship they captured. Then, after that, the arkship was assigned to the Vayan mission.'

'Saints! They caught a generation ship? How could they possibly do that?'

'We lured ourselves, Yirella. They have caught so many of us now; I saw that in the onemind's memory. I don't even know if there's anyone else left free. These ships they send to collect humans, they call them Welcome ships – because they're creepy old deviants. They're only this shape and size so they can send them to stars like Vayan that are pumping out signals from a 'new civilization'. That way the humans operating the lure think it's an arkship like the old *Salvation of Life*.'

'No!'

'The Olyix know our strategy, Yirella. They know everything. They know we bioform a planet and live on it for a few centuries, then move onwards in multiple ships. There have been thousands of planets, sending ships onwards – never back. But the exponential expansion wavefront has a constant: it expands at point eight five lightspeed. So they know where we are. And their monitor stations are spread out across the galaxy. There are thousands of them, each with a wormhole back to the gateway. I know where they are, too, now. They're not just behind us, back towards Sol, but ahead as well, which means the Olyix can reach every star before we do. They're waiting for us now, Yirella. They're like the skim-feeding whales we used to have in Earth's oceans. We tiny stupid things fly into their huge open jaws without even realizing it until they close around us.'

'No,' she cried. 'No! The Saints themselves came up with this plan. Because of them there are trillions of us. A third of this galaxy's stars have been seeded with terrestrial DNA.'

'That's how it started. But not any more. Not for a long time.'

'It can't be. They can't have caught all of us, they just can't.'

'The galaxy is a tough place, Yirella. Tougher than we ever knew. Think of it as Darwin going turbo.'

'Saints! What do we do?'

'You're doing it: the Neána option. Hide and thrive in the dark between stars where they'll never find you. This time, you can make it work. You've liberated over a quarter of a million humans. They'll live properly now, Yirella. That's a victory on a scale no Strike mission has known for millennia.'

'If we're all that's left, then we've lost, haven't we?'

'Humans are alive and free. Not just here, but in Sanctuary, too.'

'It's real?' she asked in astonishment.

'I think it will be by now. The people who set out to build it were pretty fucking determined. And the Creator mothership had the technology to make it work.'

'What's that? What are Creators?'

'A race called the Katos. Aliens avoiding the Olyix, like all the others in this galaxy who survive an invasion. We just called them Creators because we're lazy and their technology really was indistinguishable from magic. I mean, come on, it made half of me. And even I don't understand how me works.'

'But the Sanctuary, it's real?' she insisted.

'Oh yeah. My own granddaughter took off with them to find a safe place to live, somewhere outside the expansion wave. How's that for loyalty? But, I gotta admit, looks like she got the last laugh.'

'So you don't know where Sanctuary is?'

'No. That would kind of defeat the object, now wouldn't it?'

'Yes.' She pressed her lips together, giving the lens cluster a calculating look. 'So what are you going to do now?'

'I'll stay here and make sure you're okay until you transport everyone out to a safe haven in interstellar space. Then I'm going to go pay a visit to the Olyix enclave.'

'They'll know you have the gateway location. They'll be waiting with those whale jaws open wide and inviting.'

'Maybe. But this is why I exist. And I've been wanting to do this for a very long time.'

456

'There might be another way.'

'Yeah? What?'

'I'm working on it. And before you sneer, I'm *good* at that kind of thing. Really good.'

'I don't doubt it. Vayan was impressive.'

'You know a lot about the Olyix, their technology, don't you?'

'Is that a question?'

She steeled herself to ask. As before, she had nothing to lose. 'There's someone on the *Morgan* who was harmed in the arkship.'

'This the boyfriend? The one who took the optronic viral right smack in the brain?'

'Dellian, yes. Do you have a cure?'

'It's not quite that simple, sweetheart. There are options available, sure, but the human mind is a funny thing. Good old analogue; you can never quite quantify it, no matter how smart you are. Which gives us a possible window. But I've got to warn you, it's a real small window.'

'If there's any chance, I'll take it.'

'Okay, I'll send some files over. Your biomolecular initiators should be able to produce an interface that'll get you into his mind.'

'That's the one thing the Neána said we should never use.'

'Because it leaves you open to an Olyix neurovirus. Sure. Stable door, locks and horses are what I'm thinking here.'

'Yes.'

'You'll have to help him, become part of the cure. It's risky. For both of you.'

'I have no reason to carry on without him.'

'Whoa! Damn, that's dark. What have you all become?'

'I'm just a realist. Like Saint Kandara. I always admired her. She never deluded herself about life.'

'Ha. She'd laugh her ass of if she heard you say that! I guess history has smoothed the facts some.'

Yirella frowned. 'You *knew* her?'

'Sure. I liked her, too. She had balls. More than most.'

'*Who are you?*'

'Long time ago, I used to be Ainsley Zangari. Pleased to meet you, Yirella.'

*

Alimyne and her medical team spent a day reviewing the files which Ainsley gave them. 'The interface should work,' sie said. 'Physically, that is. It can connect to a human brain's neurons. And our initiators will be able to produce it; the gentens have run construction simulations.'

'But?' Yirella asked. She stared through the clinic's glass door. Dellian was still strapped down on the bed, but at least he looked as if he was sleeping. The big hologram projection of his brain wasn't quite as bright and active this time, either.

'This routine Ainsley has provided,' Alimyne said awkwardly. 'The one that will connect your mind to his. That's something we can't check in a simulation.'

'So hook me up. It either works or it doesn't. We don't lose anything, and if it works we get Del back.'

'Yirella,' Xante said in concern. 'It's risky.'

'Of course it's risky. What's your point? I'm willing to use it. We all want him back. So . . .'

'What if that thing the Olyix put inside him gets into your mind through the interface?'

'Then next time you try something different on both of us.'

'Saints, Yirella!'

'He is the reason I keep living,' she yelled at them. 'Without him, I am dead. Do you understand?'

Xante gave her a short nod. 'I love him, too.'

Yirella let him put his arms around her, resting her chin on the top of his head, rather welcoming the embrace. 'Thank you. I'm sorry I'm such a mess.'

'You're not. Without my gland gushing out suppressors I'd be a gibbering wreck right now.'

'I'll get the biologic initiator to make the interface,' Alimyne said. 'It'll take a couple of hours.'

'I'm not going anywhere.'

458

'Actually,' Xante cleared his throat. 'Tilliana asked if you could join her.'

'Uh, she didn't call me.'

'No. Well, she said I was to judge if you were up to it.'

'Up to what?'

'I don't know. Just that it's important and upsetting. The rest of the squad's with her.'

'Oh, for Saint's sake.' She rolled her eyes. 'Come on, let's go see what's so vital.'

*

The interior of the Bennu habitation torus was changing drastically. Remotes were chopping down the parkland's trees and ripping up the grassland. Plants and soil alike were dumped unceremoniously into waste hoppers that ended in portals, ejecting everything into space. The first line of remotes were followed by a second set, dismantling the ecology maintenance infrastructure. That too was evacuated into space. The refineries didn't even bother to reconstitute it. All that remained was the metalloceramic floor, cleaned to a dull sheen.

Conduits and cables were being laid across it in a grid pattern, ready for the cocoon support machinery. Five thousand modules had already been installed, forming long rows. Production was due to ramp up drastically over the next week.

Xante stood beside Yirella as they walked out of the portal and looked along the torus. Without the overgrown tangle of vegetation, the perspective had sharpened. The way the two-kilometre width seemed to shrink as it curved away somehow made it seem smaller.

'I know it's huge,' Xante said, 'but are they really going to fit a quarter of a million cocoons in here?'

'They're going to have to,' Yirella said. 'And when we've got them all, the toroid is going straight through the interstellar portal where we're going to build the habitats.'

'Hiding in the dark,' he said ruefully. 'Del's going to hate that when you wake him up.'

'The Neána option isn't the endgame,' she said softly. 'Not even close.'

Over a thousand cocoons had already been brought over from the Olyix Welcome ship. Their corrupted flesh had mechanical umbilicals plugging them into the toroid's new systems, keeping them alive until the interstellar habitats were built.

'Do you think we can bring them back?' Xante said. 'I mean, turn them back into humans, with bodies again?'

'Saints, yes. We've been able to do that since before we lost Earth. Lim Tianyu perfected the procedure for human biology in her London clinic.' Yirella smiled bleakly. 'One of my ancestors was the first to be reversed.'

'Uh, I didn't think we had ancestors. You know, not actual family.'

'They let me check my genealogy back on Juloss as part of my therapy. It was supposed to help give me a sense of belonging – which it did, a bit, I guess. Some of my DNA comes from Bik's descendants.'

'Bik?'

'Yeah. He was Lim Tianyu's first patient. It was part of a deal with his brother.' She shivered as she recalled the files she'd accessed. 'Some people make incredible sacrifices for their family.'

'Still do.'

'Right. So we can give everyone their bodies back.'

'Yes. Happy ending, I guess.'

Yirella spotted Tilliana along one of the rows, with most of the squad standing beside her. As they walked towards them, she did her best not to stare at the cocoons. She'd accessed so many recordings of them from back during the original Olyix invasion that she was completely familiar with the shape, a bulbous barrel of flesh with a distended head protruding at the top. The file records were nice and clinical, valuable information. In real life, the cocoons were ruined people, too real. She wanted to be sick, and to run.

Xante was wrong, I'm not up to this.

Tilliana had obviously been crying. So had Janc and Falar and Uret, while the rest of the men looked as despondent as they had at Rello's wake.

'What is it?' she asked Tilliana.

Her friend gave Xante a guilty glance. 'I shouldn't have called you here.'

'Well, too late now,' Yirella replied brittlely.

Tilliana ducked her head. That was when Yirella realized no one else was making eye contact. 'What?' she demanded.

'We're running DNA sequences on all the cocoons as they're brought over from the Olyix ship,' Tilliana said. 'The gentens identified a match for hir sequence this morning.'

Yirella didn't breathe as she turned to look at the cocoon they were all gathered around. The bloated face had no ears; skin had sealed over the eye sockets and nostrils, while the mouth had locked open. And yet . . . those tiny features that did remain hit Yirella with brutal force. Features she could never forget. 'Oh Saints, no,' she whispered.

It was Alexandre, their year tutor from the Immerle estate back on Juloss. The only parent any of them had ever really known. The one who had made Yirella's rehabilitation hir personal crusade. Alexandre, who had left on the last generation ship so sie could live out the rest of hir life in quiet retirement on whatever fresh world they settled.

Yirella sank to her knees in front of the cocoon. 'We'll find them,' she promised fiercely. 'We know where the enclave is now, and when we get inside we're going to kill every Olyix in this galaxy.'

The end of SALVATION LOST

**The conclusion of the Salvation Sequence
will be told in**

THE SAINTS OF SALVATION.

Salvation timeline

1901   Guglielmo Marconi transmits a radio message across Atlantic Ocean.

1945   First nuclear explosion (above ground).

1963   Limited Test Ban Treaty signed, prohibiting atmospheric nuclear bomb tests.

2002   Neána cluster near 31 Aquilae detects electromagnetic pulse(s) from atomic bomb explosions on Earth.

2005   Neána launch sublight mission to Earth.

2041   First commercial laser fusion plant opens in Texas.

2045   First commercial food printers introduced.

2047   The US Defense Advanced Research Projects Agency reveals artificial atomic bonding generator – so-called force field.

2049   US Congress passes Act to create Homeland Shield Department, charged with building force fields around every city.

2050   China forms Red Army's City Protection Regiment, begins construction of Beijing shield.

2050   Saudi kingdom installs mass food-print factories. Twenty per cent of the kingdom's remaining crude oil allocated for food printing.

2050	Russia starts National People's Defence Force, its shield generator project starts with Moscow.
2052	European Federation creates UDA (Urban Defence Agency) – builds force fields over major European cities.
2062	**November** Kellan Rindstrom demonstrates quantum spacial entanglement (QSE) at CERN.
2063	**January** Ainsley Baldunio Zangari founds Connexion.
2063	**April** Connexion twins portal doors between Los Angeles and New York, charges $10 to go between cities.
2063	Global stock market crash, car companies lose up to ninety per cent of their share value. Shipping, rail and airline stocks fall. Aerospace stocks rally as space entrepreneur companies announce ambitious asteroid development plans.
2063	**November** Space-X flies a QSE portal into Low Earth Orbit on a Falcon-10, providing open orbit access. Commencement of large-scale commercial space development.
2066	Astro-X Corporation's mission to Vesta. Establishment of Vesta colony.
2066–2073	Thirty-nine national and commercial colony/ development missions to asteroids (the Second California Rush –so called because of the number of American tech company CEOs involved). Large number of World Court injunctions filed by developing nations and left-wing groups against exploitation of exo-resources by for-profit companies.
2066	Connexion Corp merges with emergent European, Japanese and Australian public transit portal companies to form conglomerate. Major cities now portal networked. Non-commercial vehicle use declining rapidly.
2067	Globally, thirty cities now protected by shields, two hundred more under construction. Start of decline of conventional military forces. Phased Air Force and Navy Reduction Treaty signed at UN by majority of governments. Armies reconfigured

as counter-insurgency paramilitary regiments – numbers cut substantially.

2068   Seven corporations established at Vesta. Astro-X completes its Libertyville habitat colony, housing three thousand people.

2069   First solar powerwell portal dropped into sun by China National Sunpower Corporation. Five-kilometre-long magneto-hydrodynamic chambers built at Vesta, positioned on large asteroids, outside Neptune orbit.

2070   Armstrong resort dome assembled on Moon. Similar resorts under construction on Mars, Ganymede and Titan.

2071   All major cities on Earth linked by Connexion stations – except North Korea.

2071   UN treaty forbidding non-equitable exo-resource exploitation. Any asteroid or planetary minerals mined for use by commercial companies must be equally distributed among all nations on Earth. US, China and Russia refuse to sign. European Federation awards treaty Principal Acknowledgement status; starts to draw up its own non-exploitation regulations, where 'excess profits' of asteroid development companies will be channelled into Federation foreign aid agencies. Commercial asteroid development companies re-register in non-signatory countries.

2075   Seventeen self-sustaining habitats built in asteroid belt. Construction of Newholm starts at Vesta (by Libertyville) – fifty kilometres long, fifteen kilometres in diameter. Takes three years to form, two years to complete biosphere.

2075   Fifty-five per cent of Earth's energy now comes from solar powerwells. Decommissioning of nuclear power stations begins, radioactive material flung into trans-Neptune space via portals.

2076   Increasing number of asteroid developments become self-sustaining and Earth-exclusionary. Start of habitat independence movement.

2077 Interstellar-X launches first starship, *Orion*, propelled by QSE portal solar plasma rocket. Destination Alpha Centauri. Achieves point seven-two lightspeed.

2078 **March** Global tax agreement signed by all governments on Earth, abolishing tax havens.

2078 **August** Nine space habitats declare themselves low-tax societies.

2078 **November** First Progressive Conclave gathers at Nuzima habitat; fifteen billionaires sign Utopial pact to bring about post-scarcity civilization to humanity. Each launches asteroid colony expansion, with an economy based on AI-managed self-replication industrial base.

2079 China National Interstellar Administration launches starship *Yang Liwei*. Destination, Trappist 1. Achieves point eight-two lightspeed.

2081 All Earth's energy supplied by solar powerwells. Connexion largest energy customer.

2082 Major national currencies now backed by kilowatt hours. Global de facto currency is wattdollar.

2082 Interstellar-X-led General Starflight Accord signed between all starfaring organizations (capable of building starships) and governments, ensuring open access to new stars, and no duplicated star missions.

2082–2100 Twenty-five portal-rocket starships launched from Sol to nearby stars.

2083 *Orion* arrives at Alpha Centauri. Psychroplanet discovered two point eight AU from star, named: Zagreus. Too expensive/difficult to terraform. Eleven government missions transfer into Centauri system and establish asteroid manufacturing bases, along with eight independent asteroid companies. Construction of multiple portal starships at Centauri system begins.

2084–2085 Twenty-three starships launched from Centauri.

2084 Last car factory on Earth (in China) shuts down. Connexion hub network serves ninety-two per cent of human population, including space habitats.

2085 Utopials launch starship *Elysium*.

2086 Alpha Centauri asteroid manufacturing stations abandoned. Small joint-venture solar rocket plasma monitoring station maintained in orbit around the star, providing drive plasma for the starships.

2096 Chinese starship *Tranage* arrives Tau Ceti, exoplanet discovered.

2099 Chinese begin terraforming of Tau Ceti exoplanet, named Mao.

2107 US starship *Discovery* arrives Eta Cassiopeiae. Exoplanet discovered.

2110 US begins terraforming Eta Cassiopeiae exoplanet, named New Washington.

2111 European Federation agrees to terraform exoplanet at 82 Eridani, named Liberty.

2112 *Elysium* arrives at Delta Pavonis. Terraform-potential planet discovered, named Akitha. Construction of habitat Nebesa and extensive orbital industrial facilities. Terraforming of Akitha begins.

2127 *Yang Liwei* arrives at Trappist 1. China begins terraforming two Trappist exoplanets T-1e and T-1f, Tianjin and Hangzhou.

2134 New Washington terraforming stage two complete, open to American-only settlers.

2144 Olyix arkship, *Salvation of Life*, detected point one lightyear from Earth as its antimatter drive is switched on for deceleration. Communication opened. Four-year deceleration to Earth/Sun Lagrange-3 point opposite side of sun from Earth.

2150 Earth population twenty-three billion. Nearly seven and a half thousand space habitats completed, population one hundred million.

2150 Olyix begin to trade their biotech with humans in exchange for electricity to generate antimatter, allowing them to continue their voyage to the end of the universe.

2153 Mao declared habitable. Farm settlers transfer from China, begin stage two planting – trees, grass, crops. Fish introduced into ocean.

2162 Neána mission reaches Earth.

2200 Eleven exoplanets now in stage two habitation. Large-scale migration from Earth. Twenty-seven further exoplanets undergoing stage one terraforming. No more being developed; fifty-three marked as having terraform potential. Portal starship missions ongoing, but reduced.

2204 Portal starship *Kavli* arrives in Beta Eridani system, eighty-nine lightyears from Earth. Detects beacon signal from alien spaceship.

CENTRAL   13-11-2020